THE NORU: BOOK VII

RAGE OF ANGELS

Lola StVil

This is dedicated to: You.
You cared enough to
Stalk and threaten me,
until I finished this book.

Thank you:)

Lola St.Vil

PROLOGUE (DEATH SPEAKS)

Sixteen years ago…

The human bartender pours the whiskey into my glass for the eleventh time. I wrap my hand around the shot glass, turning it into Coy Dark. I drink, slam it down on the bar, and signal for him to pour me another. He looks at me with a mix of concern and admiration. According to the others in the Portland bar, his name is Matt. Matt is five foot nine, flabby, and has a long scar on his right cheek. He also has a full beard and a low buzz cut.

"I've never seen a gal handle her drink this good, but maybe you should slow down," he suggests.

"Thanks, but I got this," I reply as I signal for him to line up the shots next to each other. He lines up six shot glasses and looks on in wonder. I blow on the shot glasses and they all turn to Coy Dark. Matt is too busy looking at my cleavage to notice that the whiskey has turned a deep red. I down them in seconds and laugh at Matt's reaction.

"It might be easier if you talk about whatever is bothering you, darlin'," he says.

"Is that so?" I ask.

"Well, yeah. Tell me, what's got you in here drinking my place dry at two in the afternoon?"

"Everything, Matt. Every damn thing," I reply as I signal for him to set up the next lineup.

"You're hot, and judging by your clothes, you got money. And you also have a wedding ring. You should have no troubles at all."

I don't reply. I simply laugh ironically and down the latest round of shots.

"I think that's your last round, darlin'. You should go home. I can call you a cab," he offers.

"Can't go home. I'm meeting someone here," I reply.

"Who?" he asks.

"Matt, what's the worst thing you've ever done?"

"Well now, I don't know you. I can't just be spill'n secrets."

I look at him and signal that if he's not talking, he should be pouring. So he inhales deeply and leans in towards me. He whispers in my ear and tells me that he's been doing some "light" meth and that his girl doesn't know. He says he plans to stop taking drugs.

"You plan to stop today, huh?" I ask.

"Maybe not today but sometime soon. You know how it is," he says with a suggestive smile.

"Yeah, Matt, I do."

"So what's the worst thing you've ever done?" he asks.

"I've killed, I've broken rules, and I lied to my husband about where I am today. But the worst thing, the absolute worst thing, is about to happen in about three minutes," I reply, mostly to myself.

"You've killed someone? Okay, sweetheart, no more shots for you." He laughs.

"Sometimes good people have to do bad things. It's just the way of the world. Right?"

"Well, yeah. So how bad are you and I gonna get tonight?" he asks as he places his hand on top of mine.

"I told you I'm waiting for someone," I remind him.

"Yeah, but you ain't told me who yet. So I think it was a lie," he counters.

"No, it's not. I'm waiting for her," I reply as a figure enters the bar.

"Wow…" Matt says when he spots my guest.

I wave my hand casually, and everyone in the bar loses consciousness and falls to the floor except Matt and the guest. Matt is gripped with terror as he takes in the scene. He stammers as he speaks.

"What the—"

"Well, guess my three minutes are up," I tell myself.

"What happened to them? Oh shit! You were serious? You really do kill people? You some kind of terrorist or some shit? Did you spray some kind of bioweapon in my damn bar?" he says as he gets out his rifle and points it at my guest and me.

"DON'T MOVE!" Matt shouts. We do as he says and we stand still.

"Good, now tell me what the hell is going on. Did you kill my customers?" he demands.

"No, they're just sleeping. They will wake up in about two hours or so," I reply.

"No, wake them up now!" he shouts.

"Can't. Remember the 'worst thing' question? Well, there's the answer. I'm about to form a very unholy union, and I'd rather not have an audience. Besides, it's safer for the humans to be asleep," I reply.

"Then why am I not sleeping like all the others?" Matt asks, still shaking.

"Remember the 'light' meth you have been taking?" I ask sadly.

"Yeah," he whispers.

"Well, Matt, there is no such thing as 'light' meth," I tell him as I wave my hand. Like the other humans in the bar, Matt falls down to the ground. But unlike the others, he will never get back up.

I look across the bar to the figure standing by the door. Any angel who had as much to drink as I had would be drunk and senseless. But I'm not any angel. And even if I were, seeing the figure before me would sober me up immediately.

"Hello, Death."

"Hello, Redd."

***

"Well, don't just stand there. After all this time, I'm sure you could use a drink. Omnis knows I can," I call out. The figure saunters over to the bar and stands next to me. Redd looks like Miku, but her expansive wings are black and have red-colored tips. Her eyes are a dark swirling void of hate and rage. Miku's alter ego is as wicked as she is beautiful.

I pour both of us a drink.

"I can feel your friend inside me," she says.

"Is Miku okay?"

"The weakling is fine. But something tells me you didn't ask her permission to have this little chat with me, now did you?" Redd asks.

"No, Redd, I didn't. I am betraying her and most likely ruining our friendship."

"Yes, and you unleashed a pretty terrifying evil, if I do say so myself."

"I know what I did," I assure her.

"You know my instincts were to flee and then gather an army—"

"Then you read my note."

"Yes. The one where you informed me that I only have half an hour before the pill wears off, allowing my alter to take control again."

"Yes."

"Well, you council members have been busy, haven't you? What's to say that I don't kill you?" she asks.

"You could try, Redd, but really, you're hardly a match for me. In fact, I doubt you could take out a human."

"Then why make them sleep?"

"Precaution," I reply.

"Bullshit," she says as she raises her hands high in the air to manipulate the ground beneath us. Nothing happens.

"I mixed up a lovely cocktail, Redd. It not only allows me to control how long you are here, it also allows me to control access to your powers."

"You bitch!" she says, lunging at me. With a mindless wave of my hand, she goes flying backward into the wall.

"If you were going to strip me of my damn powers, what is the point of bringing me back?"

"I need your help."

"I can't help you with shit! I have no powers, remember, sweetie?" she demands.

"You don't need powers for what I want."

"And what the hell is that?"

"Advice. How do I force a member of the council to give me what I want?" I ask.

"Aren't the three of you bowling buddies or something?"

"Fate knows something, and I need him to reveal it to me. You caused a lot of grief to the council members that came before us. I need advice on how I can do the same."

"So little miss goody wants to be bad, huh?" She cackles uncontrollably.

I sigh heavily, close my eyes, and think back to a few weeks ago, back when my family was happy…

***

"I'm here! I'm here!" I shouted as I burst through the door.

My husband looked up at me, smiled, and shook his head, indicating that I was too late.

"Argh! I really tried," I pleaded.

He laughed as he walked over and tenderly kissed my forehead. "I don't understand how you can be late. You work with Time," he teased me.

"Well, I can't ask Time to use his powers just so I won't be late for family night. I mean, I did, but he said no," I replied.

"I thought you were off early today."

"I was supposed to be, but there's a virus in Northeast Asia. I had to take out a whole village."

"I'm sorry, babe. Is there an end in sight?" he asked.

"Fate is tight-lipped, but judging by his demeanor, the humans should be seeing some relief soon," I happily reported.

"Good for humans and good for us. You've been working late every night this week. I miss you," he said.

"I know, I'm sorry. However, I had some time last week, but *someone* was busy fighting a flock of Fire Swans in Germany."

"Fair enough. What is it?" he said when he saw the look of concern on my face.

"Fate wouldn't look me in the eye this morning. He usually does. Do you think it means something?" I asked.

"Fate has never been the fun type. I'm sure it has nothing to do with you," he said.

"Yeah, maybe you're right. And no more talk of work," I replied with a smile.

"Yes, and I'm glad you are here now."

"So glad that you will waive the rule? I was so *close* to being on time," I begged him.

"Close doesn't cut it, Em. You know the rules: whoever is late for family night is on cleanup duty," he reminded me.

"If you agree to clean up, I'll find a way to thank you."

"What did you have in mind?" he asked.

"Maybe something like this…" I replied, then leaned in and kissed him slowly. He pulled me even closer to him and kissed me fervently. I forced myself to pull away, knowing we were not alone in the house.

"You're such a tease," he said ruefully.

"Later, promise. What happened with your mission?" I asked.

"Jay and Miku were able to subdue most of the demons, but a few got away and took human hostages with them. Rage and I followed behind, and together we were able to kill them and get the humans back safely."

"That's good, right?" I asked.

"Yeah, but the Paras had no business letting a stone that powerful out of their sights. I swear sometimes I think the Kon is sleeping on that damn throne."

"In addition to being the king of Paras, he has two boys to raise," I replied.

"At this point Bex or Hunter would make a better leader. Anyone but the guy we got right now."

"Don't say that. You know our kids play together," I reminded him.

"Yeah, but I'm not sure he's a big fan of Noru. In fact, I could swear he's jealous of the kids. Paras don't like to be upstaged in the power department."

"I agree, but whatever goes on with the adults shouldn't get in the way of the kids. Hey, does Rage have any plans this weekend?"

"I'm not sure—wait. Emmy, no!" he said sternly.

"What? I didn't say anything."

"No, but I know what you're thinking. You cannot set Rage up on another date. You promised," he said.

"Rage needs to be in a relationship."

"Emmy, leave him alone."

"He needs a girl."

"He has one. And by one I mean a hundred. Per night," he teased.

"He needs someone permanent."

"You are not allowed to set Rage up with anyone anymore."

"He's my best friend, so why not?"

"Do you remember what happened the last time you set him up?"

"It wasn't that bad," I lied.

"An hour after going out with him, she tattooed his name on her—"

"I know where she put it."

"Oh, and not to mention she called him a few hundred times. And when Rage wouldn't pick up, she started to call the team. She stalked all of us for weeks, trying to get to Rage."

"Okay, Tina was…less than a great choice," I admitted.

"Emmy, she placed herself in a Holder in front of his house and refused to leave until he agreed to be with her."

"That's romantic," I replied.

"What's romantic? The part where Paras had to come and break the Holder open or the part where the Kon had to issue what amounted to the first ever angel restraining order?" he said.

"Okay, okay. No more playing matchmaker. It's just that I want him to find someone. He can't spend his life mourning Ameana. She wouldn't want that for him."

"I know, Em. But we can't push him. He has to do this on his own terms. I don't know how long it would take me to get over you if you died—it might be…four or five…hours."

Although I knew he was joking, I picked up the nearest pillow from the sofa and hurled it at him. He ducked just in time to avoid being hit.

"You are so gonna get it!" I replied.

"Mommy!" Pryor said as she flapped her wings and flew towards me from upstairs. She could fly, but when she was excited, like now, she wobbled in the air. Her purple eyes lit up as she reached out for me with her stubby little fingers.

"There's my Carrot!" I replied as I snatched her out of the air and hugged her.

"The good news is her power to amplify fear is improving. The bad news is she used it on her babysitter," Marcus said.

"Pry, did you scare Uncle Tony?" I asked.

She smiled and nodded. We wanted to show her that we disapproved, but both Marcus and I were taken by just how proud she was to have used her powers successfully.

"How scared was Tony?" I asked as I put my baby down.

"He was in the closet, shaking." Marcus laughed.

"We shouldn't laugh. She has to control her powers," I reminded him.

"I know, but you should have seen Tony," he said, laughing even more. I knew it was wrong, but I joined him.

"Who thought it was a good idea to let us become parents?" I asked him.

"Yup, big mistake," he replied.

"Daddy, human," Pry said sternly. Pryor's favorite game was Angels & Human. When Pry shouted "human," Marcus had to pretend to be human and be "in desperate need of help." Pry then would find a way to save him.

"Okay, you guys play. I'll get us some snacks and then we can start the movie," I replied as I walked into the kitchen. I could hear them playing in the living room from where I was. Marcus complained about playing the game, but in reality, he had even more fun than Pry did.

I placed a series of snacks on a tray and prepared to watch *The Little Mermaid* for the millionth time. I think Pry loved it because the princess had the same red hair. We tried to get her to watch other things, but she was stuck on that one movie.

I didn't care what we watched, I was just glad that once a week we got to be at the house, all three of us together. That was one of the rules Marcus and I had to have in place. So no matter what was going on at work, we all found a way to get home for family movie night.

Miku and Jay had the same policy about family night. When it was Jay's turn to choose, he usually took the twins to the racetrack or a car show. And when it was Miku's turn, she took the girls shopping. Jay liked to joke that his daughters, Key and Swoop, were secretly working with evil to destroy him and were using shopping as a form of torture.

"EMMY!" Marcus called out desperately from the living room. The urgency in his tone struck fear into my very soul. I'd known Marcus forever and he rarely panicked, rarely lost it. I ran out to the living room, where I found Marcus kneeling on the floor beside Pryor. She wasn't moving.

***

We took her to a Healer and we found out that she had the Marcola: a routine virus where a trace amount of darkness penetrated your soul. Omnis allowed the virus so that angel children's bodies would grow a resistance to darkness and learn to fight it early. It was a virus that was common among angels. It was equal to what the humans called chicken pox. The Healer gave us a mixture and said it should go away in the next few hours.

However, a few days later, Pry could not get out of bed let alone run around the house like she normally did. Overnight the red veins had spread to her wings and abdomen. I was at work when Tony called me and said I needed to come home. I rushed home and held her in my arms. She looked up at me and there was no light in her eyes.

I took her back to the Healer. While she was being examined, I tried not to freak out. I called Jay, who was home with his twins, Key and Swoop. He brought them over right away.

"Jay, she's gonna be okay, right?" I asked desperately.

"Yo, you know Pry. She's stubborn and willful. She'll be fine," Jay replied.

"Jay, what if—"

"Em, don't go there. She's gonna be fine. I mean, you're Death, so if she was going to…you'd know."

"No, I wouldn't. Death never had a family before. I'm the first and only member of the council to be a parent. The way it works is that I have no knowledge of death when it comes to Marcus, Pry, or even Julian."

"Damn, I forgot. But that doesn't mean anything. Pryor will be fine," he said as he took my hand.

"Daddy! Chips!" Swoop asked as she tugged on the end of his shirt.

"Ain't gonna happen. You two already had a snack. I won't let you and your sister load up on junk giggle chips and stay up all night laughing," Jay scolded.

"Just one bag, Daddy, pleeeeeeeease!" Key begged.

"Yeah, just one. Pleeeeeeease," Swoop added.

Jay and I exchanged a quick look. I signaled to him that it was okay to let them go.

"Yes!" Swoop said as she did a backflip down the hall.

"Hey, wait for me!" Key shouted as she took to the air after her twin.

"Jay, I thought Miku was back from the mission."

"It's gonna be another three days. The Kon asked her to do him a favor and go on some peace mission to smooth things over with a group of Partials he's pissed off. She went but swears she'd rather be battling any day," Jay replied.

"Yes, your wife is very much a blood and guts kind of girl," I pointed out to him.

"There's still a little Redd in her," he replied.

"She's been able to control Redd for years now. That has to give you some peace."

"Yes, and I can't tell you how glad I am she's better. Redd was…there's a liquid pill out on the black market now called Gore. It strips you down to your most evil self for an entire hour. For most angels, that's not a big thing, but for Miku…"

"If she were given that pill, there's a chance she'd be Redd again," I replied sadly, picking up on the concern in his voice.

"Exactly, and having Redd emerge even for an hour would be deadly. So I went to the Kon and demanded he put the Paras on it. Send them out to find the demon who created the pill. Also find the Seller who is selling it and take care of them."

"What did he say?"

"You know the Kon—useless."

"Did you tell Marcus about this pill?" I reminded him.

"Yeah, but I also told him to hold off on calling the team in. I'd like to find this pill and the ones behind it without having to tell Miku."

"She'll feel bad that the team has to go on a mission just for her," I guessed.

"Hell yeah, she still holds so much guilt because of what happened the last time Redd emerged."

"I get it. The first thing I wanted to do when I saw Pry today was call Marcus. But he's on his way to fight a demon that feeds on fear; calling him to tell him Pry's sick..."

"The Crowen demon would sense his fear. Marcus would lose the battle in seconds."

"Yes, but the guilt of not calling him is killing me."

"I feel you. I'm sorry he's going off to fight by himself," Jay confirmed.

"It's not your fault. Crowen demons grow stronger the more bodies they have to feed on. Marcus can handle himself. Besides, there's no need to worry him. I mean, this whole thing could be nothing."

"I get it."

"I am not going to call him until I know for sure that Pry is in serious danger," I said mostly to myself.

The Healer walked into the hallway where Jay and I stood, and addressed us with a grave look on her face. Jay took my hand in his and spoke in a serious tone.

"Emmy, it's time to call Marcus."

***

A few hours later, Marcus met us in the clinic, with wounds on his arms and a large gash on his chest and leg. I begged him to get treated, but he couldn't have cared less about his injuries. He went into Pry's room and took her hand while the Healer explained her condition to us.

"The Marcola virus isn't very strong, and most angel toddlers can evict the virus from their bodies on their own. But the virus found itself inside the body of a Noru," she explained.

"So what does that mean?" Marcus asked.

"Think of it this way: The virus is like a really bad demon with no weapons. So while he has evil intentions, he's harmless. But in this case our demon is in the body of a being whose bloodline is nothing but power. So it not only wants to stay there, it will use its newfound power source to accomplish its goal—to kill the host."

"Wait, you're saying my baby could die from this?" I demanded.

"No, Death. I'm saying she will die. It's only a matter of when. At this point she has only a few days left. I'm sorry," the Healer replied regretfully.

"Don't tell me sorry, lady, just tell us how we save her. How do we kill this virus?" Marcus begged.

"We would need to infect someone with it and extract the vaccine that being's body would make," the Healer replied.

"Fine, then use me. Put the virus in me," I instructed.

"There are rules about infecting a council member. You know that."

"That's okay because you are going to use me. You can infect me," Marcus said.

"I can't do that," she informed him.

"Why the hell not!" Marcus blared.

"This virus is feeding off power. Do you have any idea what it would do if it were inside you, First Guardian? You'd die faster than your daughter," she reasoned.

"I don't care about dying. Just put it in me, and fix my baby," Marcus said.

"You won't live long enough to form the vaccine we need," the Healer countered.

"Then what the hell do we do? There has to be something because I will not watch my child get eaten from the inside out. So you better figure something out!" I shouted and caused the windows to shatter. Soon I was screaming and it caused the whole clinic to shake.

Marcus was trying to calm me down, but he was so distraught he could hardly keep himself from ripping the building out of the ground.

"Em, it's okay, it's okay," the Akon vowed as he restrained me.

"Miku, get Pry before the walls crumble down on her," Jay said to his wife.

"Hey, someone get this Healer chick outta here so Emmy can calm down," Rage ordered.

"I'm on it," Jay said. He picked the Healer up and breezed past us so fast he was no more than a blur.

It took hours for the team to get Marcus and me to calm down and to fix the clinic. Once everything was settled, the Healer explained what we needed to do in order to help Pry.

"We would need a being that is more powerful than the average angel but not as powerful as Death or the First Guardian, and that being would have to share Pryor's bloodline," the Healer said.

"So a sibling?" I asked.

"Yes."

"Well, she doesn't have a sibling," Marcus replied, sounding drained.

"I know. I am very sorry."

***

Two weeks later, Pry's condition worsened. My baby was barely a year old, and she couldn't move her head, legs, and arms or even flap her wings. Most days she couldn't keep her eyes open. There were red "spider vein" marks on her. They were everywhere, from the inside of her eyelids to the soles of her tiny feet. Her wings, like the rest of her, were too weak to move.

And while Marcus was treated for the wounds he got from fighting the Crowen demon, Marcus Cane was far from okay. In addition to the looming death of my baby girl, my husband—First Guardian, proud father, and love of my life—was quickly fading away from me. I always knew how strong a mother's love could be, but I didn't grow up with my father. I had no idea just how deeply our daughter's impending death would affect Marcus.

I stood outside Pry's room and watched as her father kissed her tiny hand. He stroked her fire-red hair, dropped his head, and began to weep hopelessly. I didn't cry because I would never be able to stop. I would literally flood the world. The rivers would overflow; oceans would sweep across the land and wipe out everything.

The fact was, I would be okay with that because if Pryor died, I didn't see a reason to go on at all. There was no need for life or anything else to continue. That kind of thinking was dangerous for a woman whose job it was to keep the world in balance. That was why Time and Fate carefully monitored me, to make sure I didn't lose it.

But I was losing it every day, more and more. I had gone from indescribable grief to desperate, boiling rage. It wasn't just that my only child was going to die; it was the fact that Fate knew something that could help. I knew he did because he would avoid eye contact. He wasn't just that way with me, he was that way with Marcus too.

When I approached him about it, he just kept saying how sorry he was and reminding me that his powers didn't allow him to see everything.

"I don't need you to see everything, Fate. I need you to see what I can do to help my daughter," I demanded.

"Pryor needs you in the room, beside her. Not out here in this hallway, arguing," Fate countered.

"What my daughter needs is to live past the age of one! If you know something, help me."

"You know that I can't reveal information just like that. There is a reason the council members before have not had families. Sometimes you can't be both Death and a mom."

"I don't give a damn about being Death. I am going to save my kid. And if you know something and don't tell me, Omnis help you…"

I became so desperate I tracked down a Seller and threatened to burn his entire house down with him in it if he didn't get me the Gore pill. Once the pill was in my hand, I dropped it into Miku's drink and waited for it to take effect. I knew what a terrible thing that was to do, but I would have done anything to hear my child call out for me. I knew I was crossing a line, but I also knew that I simply could not live without Pryor.

***

"I guess Fate kept his big mouth shut," Redd says, pulling me out of my thoughts as she pours herself another drink.

"It's not that he won't say, it's that he can't," I reply.

"But you don't care about that. You want to know how to make him talk," she says.

"I'm hoping in your exploits you came across something that I could use to get Fate to talk."

"I may have something that might help. But I want something in return."

"No, you can't have your powers and you can't suppress Miku."

"That's not what I want—well, it is, but for now, all I want is to lay eyes on them."

"On who?"

"The twins."

"Why?"

"What the hell do you mean why? They are my kids."

"No. They belong to Miku."

"Fine, but being suppressed is like looking at the world from the floor of the ocean. I'm here, and I would like to see them in person."

"No."

"Do you want to save your daughter's life or not?"

"I'm not going to sacrifice one kid for the other."

"You're so dramatic. I'm not asking to kill the twins. I just want to see them. I'll tell you what—you can place me in a Holder. I won't physically touch them. I just want to see them."

"No. I'm not going to allow you to see Miku's kids for advice that you may or may not have for me."

"Death, you know I can help you. That's why you went to all this trouble.

In fact, you let me see the twins and I will give you more than advice. I will give you a vial of nectar from the shadow blood flower."

"Shadow bloods are the most powerful truth-extracting flowers Omnis ever created. But he destroyed the field they grew in when demons started using them to extract sensitive information from the angels they captured."

"Yes, and there is only one left in existence, taken by a very sneaky demon who managed to walk through the flames and pluck one out of the ground. I will tell you where it is, you use it on Fate, and save your daughter. Do we have a deal?"

***

The twins are playing in the park near their home, like I knew they would be. Miku and Jay make sure that they are on a schedule so that they get a good balance of work and play. Tony-Tone is too busy preparing the kids' snack to notice us. I place Redd in a Holder and remind her that she'd better behave.

I signal for the girls to come over to me. Right away, they start to plow me with questions. Is Pry feeling better? When can they play with her? If Pry is feeling better, will Aaden come back and play with them like before?

While I answer their questions, I allow Redd to watch them. She's in a Holder with a shield that allows her to remain unseen. I don't want the girls to see their mom's alter ego. Redd studies Key very closely. It's like she's trying to look right through the little girl. When she's done, she pulls back, looking disappointed and irritated.

She then focuses her attention on Swoop. Redd leans in so close she touches the shield. She's looking into Swoop's eyes like they hold the key to everlasting life or something. She does this for several seconds. Finally, she seems to find something that not only satisfies her, but makes her howl with laughter. I send the kids back to Tony, and Redd tells me where to find the nectar. I ask Redd what's so funny. She smiles but says nothing.

***

Finding the nectar wasn't difficult since I knew where to look. And now that it's in my hand, I feel a small sense of relief, knowing I will finally get some answers. I enter the clinic and find the team, Time, and Fate all in the waiting room. I want to go check on my family, but I know that it's best if I stay focused.

I signal to Fate that I need to speak with him in private. He follows me into an empty room. Yes, he's Fate and can see what's coming, but he can't see everything. So when he closes the door behind him and I throw the oil on his face, he's shocked.

"Shadow blood, no!" he says.

"I'm sorry, but I need to know what you know."

"I knew it would be best to stay away from here. I knew something would go wrong today, but I didn't want to abandon a council member in their time of need. There will be images, flashes that will appear. I beg you, don't look at them. Don't—" His eyes start to roll to the back of his head and turn milky white. The nectar is starting to work.

"Tell me what you know about Pryor. How can I save her?" I demand. Fate was wrong. There aren't a series of images; there is just one: a little boy with wings.

"Who is that?" I demand. But Fate is powerful, and in a matter of seconds he's able to free himself from the power of the nectar.

"Damn it, Fate, who is that little boy!"

"He belongs to Marcus—your husband has no idea. His mother is Quo. Her name was Bianca, as you know. Her son's name is Jason."

"Pryor has a brother? Why didn't you tell me? I know you can't tell us everything you see. I get that. But my kid's life is on the line and you should not have held out on me."

"Discretion comes with the job, Death. You know that."

"He's the answer to our prayers."

"No, he's not."

"Fate, Jason can save Pryor."

"When you inject him, it's not just the virus going into him, it's also your blood. The blood of a council member."

"My blood will linger inside him," I reply to myself.

"Yes, leaving even a trace amount of your power is lethal in the wrong hands. This boy's soul could one day tap into it."

"But Pryor has my blood and she's fine."

"Yes, because you are her mother. But this boy's body has no connection with you. It won't instinctively know what to do with all that power. It will lie dormant, but later it could be tapped into."

"I would be his Maker," I concluded.

"Yes, you would be creating a being with powers just as strong as ours. It's like creating a fourth council member."

"But there's also a chance that Jason doesn't tap into the hidden powers. In fact, he may not even know he has them," I reply.

"Yes, but that's not the point. This kid could be the start of the end."

"His name is Jason. And you can't just assume a sweet little boy might turn evil. Yes, his mother was an outright bitch. But that's not to say her son will be as coldhearted."

"That's not his name. Jason is something humans call him. But he will grow into something else. He will be referred to by another name."

"What will his name be?" I ask.

"I don't know as of now."

"You don't even know what he will call himself and you think you know this kid's life story?"

"Who do you think you are talking to?" he says, and his voice causes the ground to tremble.

"Don't flex your power on me, Fate. I've obliterated armies on my lunch break and I have no issue taking you on."

"Emerson, I am speaking to you now as a friend. I've seen this little boy. He's small, engaging, and bright. But there is a darkness that surrounds him. I was about to tell you and Marcus of his existence, but coldness crept into my whole body and I saw a flash of darkness falling on the world the likes of which we have never seen before, not even with Lucy. That's why I didn't tell you. Maybe it's Pryor's destiny to end her life right here and now."

"The hell it is. My little girl is going to grow up, and I will fight Omnis himself if that's what it takes to ensure it," I promise him.

"This kid is not the solution."

"Maybe he is. You have seen beings with darkness inside them. But that's not what's happening here, right? The darkness is around him, and for all you know, the darkness could be his environment and not what's in his heart. You are jumping to conclusions, Fate."

"I know evil when I see it! How dare you suggest otherwise."

"My best friend was evil. He did unspeakable things. But now Rage has turned things around. You're willing to give up on a kid whose feet barely touch the ground at the dinner table."

"You cannot spin this to fit your needs. I have seen the world being sucked into a void of evil and disappear. I know it's coming, and I know it could very well start with this boy. You become his Maker and evil will follow."

"Can you vow to me right here and now that Jason will become the great evil you have seen in your visions?"

"Emerson—"

"Can you tell me that you know for sure that Marcus's son will be a threat to the world?"

"It's not certain."

"That's just it. You are not certain about Jason. But I am certain that my daughter will die. So I am going to find Jason, and I will do what I need to do to save my family."

"Death, do not do this! We each have a role to play, you know that."

"Yes, I do. And I will honor your need for discretion. I will keep the news of Marcus's son from him, even though it kills me to do so. But I'm going to save my baby," I reply as I march past him and out the door.

"Please reconsider," Fate pleads.

"If I do that, Pryor dies. And I'm not going to a funeral today," I reply as I start to ascend into the air.

He runs out and calls after me in a stern, commanding voice, "There may not be a funeral today, but tomorrow, funerals are all you will know."

BOOK I

AADEN "SILVER" CASE

When we meet real tragedy in life, we can react in two ways - either by losing hope and falling into self-destructive habits, or by using the challenge to find our inner strength,

-Dalai Lama

CHAPTER ONE:
FAULT

We listen as Death explains how she became the Maker. I think somewhere inside we all thought it was a big mistake. We all thought Spider had made that shit up just to piss us off and misguide us before his death. So much bullshit happened in such a short time…

An hour ago, New York City began crumbling under the weight of the new evil that had been created: Alago. And as hard as we tried to stop Randy from turning into an all-encompassing force of evil, he did just that. Malakaro, now having successfully gotten Randy to turn evil, reached out to touch him and end life as we know it.

Time placed a shield around each of them and froze them in place, preventing them from touching. However, the hold only lasts for twenty-four hours; like I said, that was an hour ago. So we chased the being we thought made Malakaro only to find out that the one we were looking for was Emmy.

Now, we all stand in an alley with Death. And while there is chaos all around us, the noise seems to fade in the background as Death does her best to explain the unexplainable. None of us interrupt her; she tells her story from start to finish. When she's done, I look over at my wife. Pryor's world is imploding yet again, and once again, I can't help her.

"That's how it happened. I did what I did because I needed to save you," Death says to her daughter.

"Well, I guess that makes it all better," Pryor says angrily.

"It doesn't, I know that," Death assures her.

"Do you have any idea how much you cost us?" Pryor demands.

"I do, and I'm sorry about the way things turned out. But there was no way to know what could happen."

"Fate told you not to give Jason your power, and you did it anyway."

"Pryor, you don't understand," Death pleads.

"Yes, I do; because of decisions you made, millions of people will die," Pryor shouts.

"That hasn't happened yet. We can still find a way to stop Malakaro," Death says.

"Will stopping your creation bring Key back? Will it bring back the thousands of angels, humans, and Quo that Malakaro slaughtered to get to this point?"

"Pry—"

"HOW DO WE GET THEM BACK?" Pryor rages.

"Babe, calm down," I reply as I stroke her arm.

She shakes her head, enraged, and glares at her mother as her voice trembles. "Since the day I was born, all I ever heard was that our job was to put others before ourselves. We are the ones Omnis chose to protect the humans, even if it meant our lives. But when it's time for you to pick humans, you didn't, and look what happened," Pryor continues.

"The way you were lying there in the hospital…I had no choice. What did you want me to do?"

"LET ME DIE!"

"No! I couldn't do that. I just…couldn't," Death counters firmly.

"Well, I'm alive, Mom, but half of my damn heart is missing. My dad is gone, and he didn't have to be."

"Carrot, I'm truly sorry. You know I miss Marcus every single day. I still see him when I close my eyes. I still hear his voice calling me. And there are times when I think I won't make it one more second because the pain of losing him is just too much.

"But that's when I seek you out because I can see him in you. I can see the love of my life in my daughter's eyes. That's what keeps me going: you. You have kept me alive. And I'm so sorry for what has happened with

Malakaro. But I'm not sorry I saved you. I will never be sorry for that," Death admits in a pained whisper.

The team and I exchange a glance of deep regret. Our leader softens her voice as she replies to Death.

"Mom, I get why you did it. I do. And I'm sure in time, I can get past you putting one life above everyone else, and how you nearly ruined Aunt Miku's family by bringing Redd back.

"Hell, I can even get past you enabling that sick son of a bitch Malakaro to have access to unlimited power. But if you hadn't done what you did, Dad would still be alive. It's your fault that Dad's gone."

"Pry!" East scolds.

"No, she needs to hear this, East. Mom, I love you so much, but I will never forgive you for taking my dad from me."

"Pryor, please try to understand," Death begs.

"I need to speak to my team, alone," Pryor replies.

"No, we need to talk about this," her mother insists.

"We just did," Pryor declares.

"Pryor—" Death pushes.

"Mom! Please, just...go."

I look at Pryor, and there is so much turmoil and pain in her eyes, I fear pushing her will only make things worse. So when Death goes to protest once again, I catch her eye and sadly signal that it would be best if she left. Death looks over at her daughter and reluctantly ascends into the air.

"Pry, I'm so sorry, but you shouldn't have said that to her," East says, placing a hand on her shoulder.

"Look, I hate what your mom did too. And I'm really pissed that she would use my mom like that. And yeah, maybe Key would still be alive today if Emmy didn't do what she did. But, Pry, as a mom...I get it," Swoop says carefully.

"Yeah, well, you still have your dad, so..." Pry says.

"Parents make mistakes, Pry. Trust me, I know firsthand," East offers. "Can you imagine the guilt she's dealing with? I bet she's in therapy. I mean, I would be."

"You should be," Diana quips.

"Yeah, but I think I'd need a whole team of them. You know, therapists that enjoy a challenge. And I bet they wouldn't even have to pay for it. I mean, who has better insurance than Time, Death, and Fate, right?" East says, trying to lighten the mood.

"Yeah, well, group therapy time is over," Pryor informs us.

I don't say anything because I know she needs time to cool off. I also know that once the anger dies down, there will be a tidal wave of emotions that will hit her. She's trying to avoid that pain by being in "leader" mode. And as much as I hate to say it, leader mode is exactly what we need right now.

"Well, obviously we can't try to kill the Maker," Swoop says.

"Otherwise Christmas in the Cane household will be very tense this year," East adds.

"Finding the Maker was our only plan. What now?" I ask.

"Now we have twenty-three hours to get done what we couldn't do in over three years—find a way to stop Malakaro. So go out there, get me a device, a vial, a book—hell, bring me Harry Potter's wand, anything—to kill Malakaro once and for all. But also stay together. With evil winning right now, there's no telling what demons will crawl out to challenge us," Pry orders.

"How are we supposed to get anyone to betray Malakaro?" East asks.

"Find a way. Kill and torture whoever you have to, just get me some answers," she demands.

"You mean kill any demons, right?" I reply.

"That's what I said," she counters.

"No, Pry. That is not what you said," I remind her.

"Oh, well, it's what I meant."

"Okay, you guys go get what info you can; then meet back here in a half hour. I need to talk to the First Noru," I order. The team obeys me and takes off into the growing chaos, leaving me alone with my wife.

"Pry, I'd ask if you're okay, but that would be stupid."

"I'll deal. It's just one more thing, right?" she says, looking at her phone.

"What are you doing?"

"I'm using this app to help me find where Hun's Market is today."

"You want to raid the market?"

"Yeah, it's where Sellers and demons go to trade illegal stuff, so maybe we'll get lucky and find a device or something we could use as a weapon," she replies, sounding official.

"That's a good plan and it may be worth a shot, but I need you to put down the phone for a minute," I reply.

"We don't have a minute. New York City is nearly demolished. The same thing will happen to the world if we don't figure this out," she says, continuing to avoid making eye contact.

Having no other choice, I take the phone from her. She looks up, clearly upset by my actions.

"I need my phone," she snaps.

"No, you need to talk to me."

"Aaden, I don't have—"

"Time. Yeah, I heard you. We're gonna make time."

"What is there to say? I lost my little brother. I lost my teammate. I lost my father, and now, I just lost my mom."

"No, you didn't. Your mom is still in your life."

"I can't even look at her!"

"Pryor, I'm not saying that your mom was right to do what she did. But...forget it."

"But what? Am I missing something? The woman who raised me also created the biggest evil that ever lived. And I don't have a right to be angry?"

"Yes! You have every right. But you don't know what it's like to lose a child. When I lost Sparks...Pryor, there's a separate hell that only parents face."

"Aaden, I know you miss Sparks—"

"It's not just missing your kid that tears you up; it's knowing that you failed them. Human, angel, Quo, whatever. If you have a child, it is your duty to protect them. Your kid is not a big part of your world; your kid *is* your world. And when that kid is in danger, when that kid's life is at risk…It's a pain that I wouldn't even wish on Malakaro.

"When I fly over a playground, I think about Sparks. I see a human teaching their kid to ride a bike and I think about what it would be like to teach Sparks to use her wings for the first time. And I swear to you, I would give my soul to experience what it would be like to hear her voice.

"I feel so much for a kid that never even made it out here. I can't imagine what it was like for your mom, having known you for over a year. She watched as you started to come into your own. She fell in love with you. That's what parents do—they fall in love with their kid. And if anyone gets in the way of that, anyone at all…Pryor, I would have done the same damn thing your mother did.

"I've seen the rage that comes over my own father when I'm in danger. And I didn't get it until much later. Screw the rules, screw the balance between good and evil; anyone or anything that messes with your kid should be destroyed. Because, Pry, when your kid dies, you die."

"My mother withheld this information from me for years. She broke the rules and she betrayed Aunt Miku's trust. I don't understand why you're on her side."

"I'm not on anyone's side. But, Pry, you really hurt her with what you said. I know it sucks to find out what she did, but it's done and there's no point in making her feel more like shit than she already does," I reason.

"So I'm the bad guy in this? How the hell did that happen?" she asks.

Before I can reply, my cell vibrates. I take it out of my pocket and look down at the screen. "We gotta go. East and Swoop are under attack."

"Where's Diana?" Pry asks.

"No idea, but we gotta move!" I tell her as I take off. She follows closely behind me. We find East near a construction site surrounded by demons. Pry and I attack from the air. She takes out six demons with the palms of her hands, and I set fire to the nearest scaffolding. The blaze goes up quickly, causing the towering structure to collapse and take out a dozen demons.

The demons take cover on the right side of the construction site, leaving my team to seek cover on the left. Pryor attacks the demon hitting Swoop and I tackle the bastard who impulsively flies over to our side and pins East to the ground.

We roll around in the dirt and I manage to get the upper hand. I get on top of him and start choking the life from his miserable body. But he wiggles out of my hold—literally; he transforms into a colossal serpent hybrid. It has the head of a black mamba and the body of a freaking python.

Great, this dick is a hybrid-Partial. Perfect.

The snake quickly coils itself around me and opens its gaping maw, revealing the blue-black color roof of its mouth. I'm now on my back, looking up at sharp venom-soaked fangs ready to devour me. It takes both hands for me to stop it from closing the gap between its fangs and my skin.

The snake then coils its lower body around me and tries to squeeze me to death. It's working. I'm becoming light-headed and the world starts to blur. I try to summon something—anything—that can help, but I'm losing focus.

"I'll be damned if I die at the hands of a low-ranking demon who is nothing more than a belt with teeth." I gasp.

I summon the last of my strength and manage to get a good enough grip on the serpent's head to twist it until its head bursts wide open.

"Silver, behind you!" Swoop yells.

I duck down, and black Powerballs rush by me, nearly taking my head off. I thank the two asshole demons for their gifts by sending a wall of fire their way. They cry out as they burn, but there is no time to enjoy the sight—Swoop's caught on the demon side of the battle. Her forehead is being carved open by the laser beam emitting from the eyes of the demon holding her captive.

"Bird, I'm coming!" I promise her as she screams in pain. But getting to Swoop is impossible because of the sheer number of Powerballs coming down on us. What makes matters worse are the twin demons shooting blades from their mouths at top speed. Thanks to them, it's raining knives.

"I need to get to Swoop," I shout at Pryor.

"Go! I'll cover you," she says as she starts Pulling the demons' life forces. Pry is able to kill many but not enough. And the twins are still firing at us.

"I can't kill them," Pry says.

"They are more powerful than the others. You need to get closer," East says.

“Cover me or not, I have to go get Bird. She’s dying,” I shout back.

“The sideshow-reject twins are spitting out blades quickly, but after a few rounds, they are forced to pause in order to reload. When that happens again, I have a plan,” East says.

He is right; the twins pause in between attacks. East waits until the exact moment when their mouths open again; he then unleashes his lasso. He skillfully guides the tip so that it lands inside one of the twins’ mouths. The lasso sends a jolt of electricity down the demon’s body. He shakes violently as his insides simmer; he then falls to the ground, dead.

Seeing his dead twin at his feet, the remaining brother rages and opens fire. But his blade-throwing days are done because Pryor managed to sneak up on him while he was mourning his fallen brother.

“Let’s see how you like it,” Pryor says angrily as she picks up one of the discarded knives and sinks it into the back of the demon’s skull. She twists it, hard. He groans and she kicks him to the ground. She stands over him and digs the blade further into the back of his skull with the sole of her boot.

I make my way to Swoop, who has her eyes closed and is bleeding steadily. I incinerate the asshole on top of her and look Swoop over. Relief washes over me as she opens her eyes and moans. She’s in pain, but she’s alive. I take off my shirt and use it to apply pressure to her wound. That’s all that matters.

“Pry, look out!” East yells as a Powerball aims for the back of her head. None of us are close enough to stop the ball from making contact. Yet it doesn’t make contact. A shield springs up and covers Pryor.

The shield didn’t come from East, so who the hell sent it? Before I get to ask the question out loud, a brilliant orb appears, killing every demon in sight. I turn in the direction of the light and find a group of powerful angels standing before us: the Omari.

“Since when did the Omari give a damn what happens to the Noru?” I ask.

“We came because our queen’s life was at risk,” Bellamy, the Omari leader, says.

“Where’s your queen?” Pryor says as the circular shield around her retracts.

"Right here," a voice says in a reluctant whisper.

Diana...

"I'm sorry, what just happened?" East says.

"I'm the queen of the Paras," Diana replies with a nervous smile.

"Wait, that would mean..." East can't get the words out.

"Bex and I are married."

"You and Bex are what?" Pryor shouts.

"I'm fine now. You guys can take off and get back to evacuating New York," Diana says to the Omari. They do as they are told and leave just as suddenly as they appeared. She then goes over to Swoop, takes out her pouch of mixtures, and begins to attend to her. In no time at all, Diana is able to seal up Swoop's wound and stop the bleeding completely.

"You're okay now, but it would be good to get checked out at the clinic. Just to be safe," Diana says. She indicates she needs help to move Swoop, but none of us follow. We are too taken aback to talk let alone move. And judging from the look on Swoop's face, she couldn't care less about having been hurt. She wants to know what the hell is going on just as badly as we do.

"Okay, I guess you guys need answers," Diana says, swallowing hard.

"Gee, you think?" East says.

"Diana, I don't get it. Are you being serious right now?" I ask.

"Yes," she says.

"Well, we know Bex didn't knock you up; Malakaro already did that. So...what the hell?" East says.

"Um...what he said," Swoop adds in a weak voice.

"Maybe we should get you looked at before we—"

"Diana, out with it," Swoop says as I help her prop herself up.

"We're short on time, and it's kind of a long story. I don't think I can condense it," Diana says.

"Try," Pryor snaps.

"Well—" Before Diana can go further, Pry gets a call. She picks up the phone and speaks abruptly.

"What?" she says.

"Oh, sorry, Uncle Rage. I didn't know it was—what?...When?...Are you sure?…We're on our way," she says, then she puts her cell away and looks back at me with deep concern.

"Pry, what is it? Is my dad okay?" I ask.

"Yeah, he's fine, but the Face has been attacked," she replies.

"Attacked by whom?" East pushes.

"Fate," Pryor says.

"That makes no sense. Why would Fate do that?" Swoop wonders.

"Pry, is the Face okay?" I ask.

"No. She's dead."

CHAPTER TWO
IT BINDS US

We land in the alley across the street from Buy the Word bookstore just outside of Savannah, Georgia. On the way here, we were all silent. The Face got on our nerves, but she mattered to us. When the Guardians were stuck in the light, she looked after us, whether we wanted her to or not. The Face was pushy and judgmental as hell. But she was also courageous and loyal; that's not an easy thing to find nowadays.

We enter the store and find Fate and my father standing over a table containing the Face's corpse.

"What the hell happened?" East demands.

"Did you really kill her?" Pryor shouts at Fate.

"Yes, I did," Fate says sadly as he looks over her body.

"Care to tell us why?" Swoop says, trying to control the shaking in her voice.

"Yeah, I got this," my father says to Fate bitterly.

"Dad, what happened?" I ask.

"I came in here and found Fate in the middle of striking her down. I had my hands around his damn neck when he explained what was going on."

"Which is?" Pryor replies.

"Mrs. Greenblatt decided to seek out some vital information, information that could only be obtained by accessing a hidden portal," Fate informs us.

"Since Randy isn't here, I'll ask. What do you mean hidden portal?" East says.

"There are hidden pockets throughout the world. Some are the size of a cell phone while others are as large as a city. The maker of the portal hides sensitive information there or even beings. But to access them, you have to know the right coordinates, and if you are not the original maker of the Portal, you technically can only see the Portal after you are gone from this world.

"Normally Death would be able to help, but she's busy helping Time keep Malakaro trapped. So Mrs. Greenblatt opted to drink a mixture called Lint; it simulates death. But in order to activate the mixture, you need to be struck after drinking it. That is what I was doing when the Akon entered," Fate explains.

"So she's not really dead?" Pryor asks.

"That's just it—sometimes Lint works too well and it sucks the life from your body for real. So if this chick doesn't wake up within the next three minutes…" Dad doesn't finish his sentence.

"How could you let her drink it, knowing it could kill her?" East asks Fate.

"I did as she asked, and you will rethink your tone, young man," Fate warns.

"The hell I will! She's a pushy, overbearing nag, but she was our overbearing nag and now you got her killed!" East shouts.

"East, calm down. She may pull out of it," Swoop says, taking his hand.

"And if she doesn't? What the hell do we do then?" East spits.

"East, relax. She might be okay," Diana replies.

"She lost her kid, her husband, and…just because she doesn't have any family doesn't mean you can treat her like she's disposable. What kind of shit is that?" East challenges Fate.

"I'm going to overlook your insolence because I believe it comes from a good place. However, if I were you, I would stop talking—now," Fate advises.

"You can't tell me what to do!" East declares.

"No, but I can—East, stop talking," Pryor orders.

"She could be dead and you don't care," East accuses.

"I do, but let's just wait and see if she makes it before we lose it. Okay?" Pryor replies.

East shrugs his shoulders and focuses on the Face, who lies still on the table. Pry and I exchange a look of concern. We all hate the thought of losing the Face, but for East to react this way is unexpected to say the least.

"What's inside the Portal she was trying to access?" I ask.

"We don't know. That's why she wanted to go and look," Fate says.

"You may not know what's inside the Portal, but something tells me you know who it belongs to," Pryor asks.

"It belongs to Malakaro," Fate replies.

"Malakaro has a hidden Portal and you never thought to tell us that?" Swoop says.

"We didn't know until today. We had our suspicions, but it took a while to get confirmation," Fate replies.

"You're Fate. Why the hell don't you know everything?" Dad accuses.

"That's not the way it works. I know more than most but not everything and not all at once," Fate says.

"That's just a fancy way of saying you're useless," Dad counters.

"I'm sorry that my powers aren't as impressive as yours. Omnis knows just how much the world needs a walking box of matches," Fate says sardonically.

"You want to see what a 'box of matches' can do, you piece of sh—"

"Uncle Rage!" Pryor scolds.

"Guys, if the Face doesn't wake up in the next five seconds, we've lost her," Swoop says. The room grows instantly silent.

"C'mon..." East says under his breath as he takes her hand and squeezes it.

Four seconds...

We all look at the Face and hope to Omnis she didn't just give her life to help us. The Face and I aren't best friends by any means, but it would really suck to lose her.

Three...

When I think about her, I hear a series of lectures on how reckless the team has been, the many school assignments we've missed and, of course, my foul language.

Two...

East was right; the Face is a complete nag. She's anal, talks too much, and gets into everyone's business. She'd better make it out of this.

One...

There is no movement.

C'mon, you old bat, you have a million lectures left to give us. Wake the hell up!

"Great, she's gone! Did you see that coming?" East says to Fate.

"Again, I don't see everything," Fate reminds him.

"She did this for us. We should have been here to stop her," East rages.

"Fate, there has to be something you can do to get her back," Pry pleads.

"You know there is nothing," Fate replies.

"This is bullshit!" I snap. "Mr. Case...language," someone whispers in a raspy voice. We look down at the table and the Face is sitting up slowly.

"You're okay!" East says as he rushes past us and embraces her so hard he nearly knocks her back down. We aren't the only ones taken off guard by East's reaction. The Face is so shocked it takes her a few moments to hug him back. When East finishes embracing her, he turns and finds all of us looking at him.

"What? Mrs. Greenblatt and I co-parent; we share a cat. It binds us," East says proudly.

We shake our heads and ignore East as we help the Face get to her feet. Fate hands her a glass of fizzy red liquid that appears in his hand out of thin air.

"Here, drink this. It will help get you back to full strength," Fate says.

The Face takes it and gladly drains the glass. "Thank you. I thought you would have gone to take care of something else. That's why I called someone. I thought I'd wake up alone," she says to Fate.

"Barbara, I'd never walk away when you need me," Fate says tenderly as he gazes into her eyes and strokes her hand.

Okay...

All of us look away from the two of them because it feels like we are intruding on a very private moment. My dad clears his throat and asks the

Face what she found hidden in the Portal.

"I found—nothing. Malakaro must have already cleared it out. It was empty," she replies.

"You should have come told us about the Portal the moment you found out about it. You could have died," Pryor scolds.

"Yes, I am aware. However, there is no telling what could have been in the Portal. That's why Ragual and I wanted to look into it first," the Face says.

Ragual? Since when was the Face on a first-name basis with Fate?

"I really appreciate what you tried to do for us, but this isn't your fight. Malakaro is an issue for my team and me. We are supposed to take the risks and find a way to destroy him, not you, not my mom. So please back off and let us do our jobs," Pry orders.

"You cannot do this alone. You know that," the Face reminds her.

"I'm not alone. I have a team. The same team that has survived the Forest of Remains, Mercy Island, and took on an army of Egons. So stop treating us like we're in grade school," Pryor orders as she storms out of the store. The rest of the team start to go after her, but I signal to them that I will go.

Once outside, I find her with her head in her hands, looking up at the brooding, malicious sky. Her wings are flapping furiously behind her and her face is twisted in anger.

"You know they were just trying to help, right?" I ask.

"Keeping things from us isn't helping. The odds are already stacked against us. I need to know everything so that I can find a way to stop Malakaro. When the Face, my mother, and Omnis knows who else keeps things from me, it just makes it worse.

"Everyone is saying, 'Hey, Pry, be the hero. Save the world, like your dad taught you.' But those same angels are hiding things from me. It's like they're throwing me off a cliff with my wings tied behind my back. ARGH! THAT SHIT MAKES NO SENSE TO ME!" she rages.

"I know, but you need to chill out because you're forcing me to be the levelheaded one in this marriage, and you know that is not a good role for me," I tease her.

"Maybe not, but so far, you're doing pretty well," she says, lowering her voice.

"Yeah, well, that's because I'm cheating. The entire time you're freaking out, I'm able to stay calm by thinking about my favorite place."

"What's your favorite place?" she asks.

I pull her close and whisper in her ear.

She bursts out laughing and playfully pushes me away. "You are so nasty," she scolds with a big smile.

"You knew that when you married me," I remind her.

"Hey, it's kind of why I married you. Hey! I married you," she says in wonder.

"Yeah, you did. And if you want to change your mind, you're too late," I reply as I pull her close yet again.

"No, I don't want to undo it—ever," she says, then she stands on the tips of her toes and kisses me passionately.

"I hate to interrupt, but I'm looking for my wife. Have you seen her?" Bex says as he lands a few yards away. Pryor and I pull apart and study the Kon. In the chaos of the Portal and the Face, I almost forgot the bomb that Diana dropped on us.

"So do you two know where she is?" Bex asks again.

Pryor looks up at him as if she's trying to determine if aliens got ahold of his mind and body. He looks back at her, cool and collected, but I know the Kon enough to see past that. He's still majorly pissed to see Pry and me together.

"Were the Paras able to get the humans to safety?" Pryor asks.

"Yes, we've evacuated New York City but not without casualties. And the demon world is taking advantage of the situation. We have our hands full. Have you been able to find anything that can help us destroy him, anything at all?" Bex asks.

"No," Pryor says, lowering her head.

"Well, then by all means, keep kissing; that should solve everything," Bex says snidely.

Before I know it, I'm charging at the Kon with fiery orbs in both hands.

The Kon is already armed with Powerballs, and we are about to collide when Pry gets in between us.

"Aaden, go get Diana," she instructs.

I hear her, but I don't move because all I want right now is to smell burning Kon flesh. He glares back at me with rage in his eyes.

"Aaden, I don't want to make this an order. Please," she begs.

I reluctantly head back into the bookstore, where Bex's and Pryor's voices carry. We can hear everything they say—not sure if that's good or bad right now.

"So is it true, you and Diana are married?" Pry asks, still in disbelief.

"Yeah."

"That's it? That's all I get, Bex?" she demands.

"Yeah."

"C'mon, are you kidding me? Why didn't you tell me you got married?"

"Why didn't *you* tell me you got married?" he counters pointedly.

Pry looks down at her wedding ring as if she forgot it was there and then she looks back up at her ex. "Aaden and I—"

"It doesn't matter, Pry. We're not together anymore, so it's really none of my business. But just so we are clear, it's not your business what I do with my life."

"Please tell me this isn't about us," she pleads.

"What are you talking about?"

"I'm talking about you getting with the girl that I spent most of the time disliking. And yes, we are good now, but you know Diana and I have a history."

"You think everything is about you, but it's not. I did what I did because it's my damn life."

"How is the Para world reacting to this news? I know they must be angry and looking to remove you."

"The Paras know that as their king, I want the best for them. Diana is powerful in her own right. Bringing her into the castle allows us to tap into the demon world in a way we never have before. The Paras also know that Rage is a demon and he has since become an important part of our world.

Why can't their queen do the same?"

"So how long have you been practicing that speech in the mirror?" Pry asks.

"Whatever, just stay out of this," Bex says dismissively as he starts walking away.

Pryor reaches out and breaks his stride. "Bex, I love you. I mean—not in a romantic way, but…hurting you was never the plan. I want you to be happy, I really do. Look, if you tell me you are in love with Diana, I'll back off. Promise."

"Love? Is that something I should strive for? Because if memory serves, it didn't work out so well for me the last time."

"Bex, I—"

"You know what's really messed you up? You never once considered that I married Diana to help her son. It's like Silver is the only guy you think is capable of being altruistic. Do you have any idea what could happen if it became known that Phoenix is Malakaro's son?"

"No, I hadn't. There's been a lot going on," she admits.

"Yeah, well, while you and Silver were off in wedded bliss, rumors were starting to surface about the former Kaster who may have hooked up with Malakaro. I married Diana so that no matter what happens, she and Nix have the protection of the Omari."

"Oh, I get it," she whispers almost to herself.

"So glad I could help untangle things for you," the Kon replies bitterly.

"Bex…" she calls out as he starts to take off again.

He stops and looks back at her with a pained, sad expression. "What?" he says curtly.

She goes to tell him something but then thinks better of it. "Never mind."

I turn to Diana, who has been listening quietly in the corner.

"You should go. The Kon is here to see you," I tell my ex.

"Hey, where's Fate and the Face?" I ask as Diana heads out the door.

"Judging by the heat coming off the two of them, in some alley get'n some," Swoop says with a mix of amusement and disgust.

"They went back to help Time and Death. I gotta take off too. I have a few leads, not sure if they'll pan out though."

"Okay, Dad…be careful," I reply.

"Always. But before I go, I just want you and me to be clear on something," he says.

"What's up?" I ask.

"Did you get married?" he asks.

Shit.

"Dad, with all the craziness going on, I—"

"Don't finish that sentence, Aaden Grey. Your mother and I spent thousands of hours talking about your future. Getting married is important, serious shit. I have thought about it since you were no more than a marking on your mom's palm. So the Kon better have it wrong."

"Dad, it's Pry. You love her."

"Yes, and I would love to watch her get married to my only son. I can't think of one reason why you would deny me that. Or why she would do that to her mother. What the hell were you thinking?"

"Dad, I—"

"Aaden, you and Carrot mean the world to me and Emmy. For the two of you to do this and not so much as call us…that shit really fucking hurts." The Akon takes off into the air before I can stop him.

"Damn it!" I shout as I kick a stack of books across the room.

"I've never seen Uncle Rage so angry," Swoop says.

"Great, and now my dad isn't talking to me. Perfect. Yet another problem," I reply, growing even more frustrated.

"I hate to add to the pile, but…" East says. His serious tone makes us all turn and give him our undivided attention.

"What is it?" Diana asks, standing in the doorway.

"The Face said she found nothing in Malakaro's Portal—she lied."

CHAPTER THREE
ONE SMALL THING

Diana signals for both Bex and Pryor to come back into the bookstore. As soon as they enter, East begins to explain. "First, I'm sorry for the lovefest with the Face. I was channeling Fate's emotions. Man, that guy's into her deep."

"Never mind that, why do you think the Face is lying?" Pryor asks.

"I don't have my dad's powers. I can't read your emotions like colored waves, but I take on emotions as if they were my own. Now because of how strongly Fate feels for the Face, it blocked all her feelings—except one.

"From the time the Face woke up until she left, I felt this terrible guilt. Not to mention the frenzy that's going on in her head. Something was in that Portal. I would swear my life on it," East says.

"If she knew something, why would she hide it from us?" Swoop says.

"You'd be surprise what people will hide," Bex says pointedly. Both Pryor and I decide to ignore the Kon's dig at us.

"Are you sure her guilt has to do with the Portal? Could it have been guilt over something else?" Swoop replies.

"I doubt it. I'm telling you there was something in that Portal," East confirms.

"I can't believe after everything that's happened, everyone is still keeping secrets," Diana says.

"Are we saying the Face is evil?" Bex asks.

"No, she's not evil. She's probably trying to protect us from something bad," I reply.

"I'm so over this shit," Pryor says, shaking her head.

"Yeah, it's time everyone was straight with us," East replies.

"Argh! What is so hard about being honest?" Pry snaps.

Bex looks at Pryor, gives her a snort of derision, and shakes his head in disbelief. I am really trying not to knock his rude ass to the ground, but he's making it hard. Pryor quickly looks over at Bex and decides to let yet another rude remark go by.

"We can't let this kind of thing stand anymore," Pryor says.

"I agree," East replies.

"So what are we supposed to do, throttle an old woman and make her tell us the truth?" Swoop says.

"If we have to, yes," Pryor says sadly.

"She's been in this fight with us from the beginning. I think we should give her the benefit of the doubt," Bex says.

"I don't. I mean, I want to, but we can't afford to be naïve. If there was something in the Portal and she didn't tell us, then she's working against us," Pryor reasons.

"I don't think that's really what's happening," Bex counters.

"Then tell me what's happening, because I don't understand why the Face would hold something back from us. And I certainly don't understand why we should choose to trust her," Pryor counters.

"You should trust her because she's been loyal. Something you *clearly* know nothing about," Bex accuses.

"Okay, Bex, how do you want to play this?" Pryor asks before I can say anything.

"What do you mean?" he asks.

"I MEAN WHAT THE HELL DO YOU WANT FROM ME?!" Pryor roars.

"TIME! YOU OWE ME TIME!" the Kon blares back with twice the fury. Bex has never lost control like this, never. His eyes are glowing with white-hot rage. He balls up his fist as if he wants to attack her.

"Kon, you make one move towards her and I will kill you," I vow. But the one that makes a move towards Pryor isn't Bex; it's East. He lunges at

Pry, grabs her, and slams her down to the floor. He quickly takes out his whip, wraps it around her throat, and starts to tighten it. The team is on him instantly, but East has erected a shield, stopping us from making contact with him. East is killing her.

"I loved you and you betrayed me. You said you loved me, you said I mattered to you, but how long did you wait after our breakup to hook up with the fireball, huh? Our bedsheets weren't even dry yet and you were off screwing Silver. Our relationship died because you killed it. But what's worse is you didn't even have the decency to mourn! You lying bitch!" East says as he tightens the whip around her neck, further draining the life from her.

"He's channeling Bex," Swoop says as she bangs against the shield, trying to get in. I hurl fireball after fireball at it, but it won't crack open. I know Pryor is afraid to use her power on East. If she ended up killing him, she'd never forgive herself.

"Pry, you have to fight back!" I cry out. She refuses to do what I tell her.

"Damn it, Pry, fight back! East can handle it," Diana says. But Pryor isn't taking that chance. Shit!

"East, get off her!" Bex shouts as he takes a shot at the barrier. It doesn't work. East is about to drain what little life is left in Pryor.

"I think I have a plan," Diana shouts.

"Don't explain, just do it!" I order. As soon as the words leave my mouth, Diana grabs Bex and presses her lips onto his, draining his powers hard and fast. In a matter of seconds, the Kon is so weak he falls to the floor. This severs the connection between East and Bex. East now has control over his emotions. The whip is withdrawn from Pryor's neck and the shield is lowered. I run and kneel beside her.

"Are you okay?" I plead.

She nods as I help her up off the floor.

"Pry, I'm so sorry," East begs.

"It's okay," she replies weakly.

"No, it's not. You need to control your powers, East," I scold.

"I tried. Bex—"

"I don't give a shit about Bex. You could have killed her. Malakaro is a million times worse than Bex. What's gonna happen if you tap into his rage? What will you do then? Take out the whole damn team?"

"I said I was sorry," East replies.

"I don't need you to be sorry. I need you to control your powers," I reply, seething.

"Aaden, it's okay," she calls out as she sips a vial Diana hands her.

Bex starts to stir on the floor. I look down at him and I can't remember why I've allowed him to stay alive for this long. Pryor reads the expression on my face and quickly stands in front of me, turning her body into a barrier.

"Aaden, it's okay. It's over," she says as Diana helps Bex to his feet. I glare at the Kon, knowing there's a good chance I will have to take his life.

"You're pissed off because she chose me, I get it. But you better get a fucking diary and write your feelings down. Because if they ever get out of control like that again…Diana will be a widow."

***

It's half an hour later and Bex has taken off to aid with the evacuation. Diana stayed behind to look after Pryor, who thankfully is getting the color back in her face.

East has said he's sorry about a hundred times. Pryor assures him that she's fine, but East isn't convinced.

"Are you sure you don't need a nap?" East offers.

"Maybe after we save the world," Pry replies.

"Good point. How about an energy mixture? I can go get you one—"

"East, stop. Your powers are still new to you. I get that you didn't mean to hurt me. Now let it go. That's an order," Pryor informs him.

"Does Bex really hate Pry?" Swoop asks.

"Hate? No. All I felt was…love. He loves you. He's just not sure what to do with all that love. He's hurting," East tells Pryor.

"Was there room left in there—you know, for anything aside from 'Pry-mania'?" Diana asks.

"I…I don't know. Maybe," East says.

"Okay, enough distractions. I know Bex is…I will deal with that later; right now, we need to find out what the Face saw in the Portal. Anyone have any ideas on how we do that?" Pryor says.

"Yeah, I might have a way. Why don't we just ask her?" Swoop says.

"She had a chance to tell us before," I tell her.

"Yeah, but it doesn't hurt to try again," Swoop replies.

Without warning, someone bursts through the door of the bookstore and runs to East.

"Mel, what are you doing here? Is everything okay?" East asks.

"Yeah, it's fine," she assures him.

"Then why did you come?"

"You said you'd call me back and you didn't, so…"

The team and I exchange looks of intrigue and amusement. Mel is a nice enough chick, but East may be in over his head. He tries to reason with her by lovingly placing a hand on her shoulder.

"Mel, I meant to call, but as you can imagine, it's a really busy time for the team. I mean, the end of all humanity doesn't really allow for hours of sweet talk on the phone," he reminds her.

"Yeah, I know. But you did say you would call, but you didn't. And when I called you, you didn't pick up," she says pointedly.

"Sorry I missed the call, but there's this thing we're doing called a mission," East says playfully.

"Don't do that. Don't patronize me. If you weren't going to call, you shouldn't have promised that you would," Mel counters.

"Okay, you're right. I'm sorry," he says.

"Thank you," she says with a warm smile.

"I will make it all up to you after we help Randy get back to his normal self and also after we kill the all-knowing darkness. You know how that goes."

"Maybe I should stay and help you," she suggests as she sizes up the other females in the team. She looks at Pry with mounting suspicion. Then she looks over at Diana and silently warns her to stay away from East.

"Mel, you can't stay with the team. It's not safe," East replies.

"I'm a tough girl. I can take it," she insists.

"That's not a good idea," East says.

"I don't see how me being here is doing any harm; unless you don't want me here for some reason," Mel challenges.

"Okay, we are taking a strange turn here, and I don't know what's going on. Why are you acting like this?"

"I know about Tina," Mel says, clearly upset.

"Who's Tina?" I whisper to Swoop.

She shrugs her shoulders, indicating she too is lost.

"Tina? She was a girl I dated way back."

"Yes, but there were more, right, East? There was Abby, Carla, Joy, Jenny—"

"Okay, okay. Yes, I dated a lot, but what does that have to do with this?" East pushes.

"Maybe you're not able to be around girls and not approach them. Maybe it's like something you can't help," she says, growing more and more frantic.

"Mel, we can't do this now."

"My friends are saying that you can't ever be serious and faithful to one girl. They think I should keep an eye on you."

"That's insane," East replies.

"Maybe, but it would make me feel better if I could stay here and make sure things are okay," Mel insists.

"I don't know if East has an issue with that, but I do," Pryor says.

"Oh, I see. Is there something going on with you two?" Mel asks.

"What?" East and Pryor shout in unison.

"Okay, I can see that you and Mel need to talk. You two have three minutes. I mean it, just three," Pryor warns.

The two of them step outside. East knows he needs to walk further away so that he's not overheard, but Mel doesn't seem to care; she stops just a few steps away from the window.

"Is there something going on with you and Pryor?" she demands.

"That's gross. She's like my sister."

"'Like' your sister doesn't make her your sister," she points out.

"Pryor and I are just friends. And even if I did like her, there's kind of a long line to get to that girl," he jokes.

"You don't like her, or you fear you can't get to her, so you settle for me?" she insists.

"No, that's not it."

"Then what's with you and her?" she asks.

"There's nothing going on with me and Pry. Silver would have already ripped my damn soul out if there were. So relax."

"Then is it the Kaster? She's the queen of the Paras now. Are you attracted to her?"

"Diana and I are just—okay, my friend Randy has been swallowed up by the biggest evil that ever lived. Humanity is on the brink of destruction with every passing minute, and you want to have an impromptu couples therapy session? Are you freaking kidding me right now?"

"You're gorgeous. Funny. Kind. And out of all the girls you could have, you picked me. And I need to know why. I'm trying to preempt whatever heartache comes with being with the flirt of the angel world," she admits.

"I know you've heard stories about me and other girls, but that was in the past."

"Fine, I can handle that. I just want to be around to make sure that you don't fall back into your old ways," she says.

"You can't be with me every minute of every day. Don't you trust me?" East asks.

"I want to," she says sincerely.

"But you don't?"

"No…" she whispers as tears flood her eyes.

"Then I guess this is good-bye…"

"I guess so," she says sadly as she reaches out and kisses him on the cheek. East watches as she starts to walk away. Suddenly, Pryor runs out of the bookstore and heads straight for Mel.

"How dare you do this to him?" she shouts.

"You don't understand," Mel says, taken aback by her reaction.

"Pryor, just let her go," East says angrily.

"No, you're way too deep to read her emotions, but I can see it very clearly from where I am. You love Easton. I know you do. Not long ago you were ready to take me on if it meant you could be with him. And now you're dumping him?" Pryor barks.

"It's hard to explain," Mel replies.

"No, it's not hard at all. You're dumping my friend because you're too scared to love someone who is about to go into battle. You think if you break up with him over some bullshit, then it won't hurt if something bad happens to him. But you're wrong. It will still hurt. But the only difference is the amount of guilt you will feel, knowing he died thinking you didn't want him.

"Mel, I will not lose another member of my team. You don't need to worry about East. I got him. I will protect him. That's my job. You're his girl. It's your job to love him. So go do your damn job and let me do mine," she orders.

"Is that true?" East asks as he walks up to Mel.

She avoids making eye contact and folds her arms across her chest.

"Mel, is that true? Tell me," he pleads.

She doesn't speak, but she nods slightly. He gently guides her face with his hand so that they are now eye to eye.

"I can't read your emotions. I think I'm too close to you. So if you have something you need to say to me, say it. Please," he says.

"I had a nightmare. Malakaro made you slice your own throat. You fell to the floor; there was so much blood. I tried to get to you, but I couldn't. I couldn't get to you..." she says, bursting into tears.

"It's just a dream," he assures her as he takes her hand in his.

"It felt real. I woke and I—don't die. Don't die," she says as she desperately clings to him. He holds her tightly as he looks at us over her shoulder. His eyes are clouded with worry and apprehension.

This is the first time a girl has loved him just for himself. That feeling is like a drug. But like any drug, it comes with side effects. East now has someone he has to look after; someone who risked heartbreak to be with him. And all she wants is the one thing he can't give her—a promise that he will make it out of this impending battle alive. A promise none of us can make.

When East and Mel pull apart, they look into each other's eyes and kiss each other as if they won't see each other again.

"Hey, get a room already," Swoop teases.

The couple, embarrassed, part their lips.

"Sorry," Mel whispers as she blushes.

"We suck at trying to break up," East replies.

"Yeah, we kind of do. I'm sorry I caused all this trouble. I sound like a paranoid lunatic," she says.

"You're not paranoid, Mel. In fact, you're right. What's to stop Malakaro from making us all cut our own throats? I mean, his powers don't work on Pry, but they work on the rest of us. So what will protect us?" Swoop says.

"I think I might be able to help," a familiar voice says from behind us.

I turn around and find myself staring at a striking angel with an hourglass figure, crystal blue eyes, and long free-flowing strawberry blonde hair.

Belle...

After my time at the Center, Belle and I used to hang out and find ways to keep each other entertained; that usually meant our clothes were off. We had great times. She's very much like the angel version of Diana. So it only makes sense that they hate each other.

"Well, looks like I'm just in time," she says as she looks at our worried faces.

"Who are you?" Pryor asks, on high alert.

"Come on, Pry, don't you recognize trash when you see it?" Diana asks.

Belle laughs sardonically as she gets in Diana's face. "I will try not to take anything you say personally. I mean, after all, you are being bitchy for two now," Belle says as she looks at the markings on Diana's arm.

"This is Airabella," I inform Pryor.

"Belle, please," she says with a sly smile.

"What are you doing here?" I ask.

"Not much of a greeting. I was expecting a hug or—what is that?" Belle asks as she looks down at my wedding ring.

"Aw, poor Belle. Sucks to be an afterthought, doesn't it?" Diana says.

"You got married?" Belle asks, sounding completely wounded.

"Yes, Pryor and I married. I would have told you, but—"

"Yeah, I know. Busy. Busy. Busy," she says bitterly.

"You came here for a reason. What is it?" Pryor says impatiently as she marches up to Belle.

"I know how you can defeat Malakaro," she replies.

"How?" Pryor asks.

"I'll only tell you that after I get what I want."

"And what the hell is it you want?" Pryor says, growing irritated.

"Just one small thing: your husband."

CHAPTER FOUR
RESPECT

The world falls silent. It's not just the team that's rendered speechless; nature herself seems to have been put on mute. The wind doesn't blow. The leaves don't rustle, and the birds have abandoned their song. Everyone and everything seems to be waiting for Pryor's reaction.

Pryor looks at Belle like a raging bull who's just been challenged. Her eyes are alive with fire; her nostrils flare with anger. Her jaw looks like it might unhinge at any moment and suck Belle up like a viper would a field mouse.

Pryor takes a step closer to Belle. Her movement is deliberate and calculated. Belle swallows hard but doesn't move. Pryor takes another step, and then another. The two are now face-to-face. Pryor is the first to speak. Her tone is controlled yet holds an undeniable current of ire.

"Say that again," she dares Belle.

Shit…

"I know it seems outlandish, but the information I have is very good, I assure you," Belle replies.

"Pryor—" I begin.

"You made a request. I want to hear you say it again," Pryor says, never taking her eyes off Belle.

"In exchange for very valuable information, I require some time with your husband," Belle repeats.

"He's right here; come get him," Pryor challenges as she moves out of the way so that Belle now has a clear path to me. I pray to Omnis that Belle is smart enough to stay where she is and not come closer to me. No one in his or her right mind would take a step in the direction of certain danger; but then again, Belle has never been in her right mind. She loves doing things other angels would never do.

Belle, don't do it. Don't come closer to me. For once in your life, be reasonable.

Belle walks up to me with blind confidence.

Damn it!

Pryor moves with speed that could rival Jay. She whips around and dropkicks Belle in the face. Belle falls hard on the pavement. Pryor plants one foot on top of her neck, ensuring that Belle's face stays buried in the concrete. The First Noru then gets a firm grip on Belle's wings and begins to pull them from her body.

"Pryor, no!" I shout. She doesn't listen to me. Instead she focuses all her attention on Belle.

"I have never killed an angel before, but I think right now would be the perfect time to start," she says between clenched teeth.

"Pry, if you pull on them any harder, you will tear her wings out and she kind of needs them," East reminds her.

"Belle doesn't want her wings. She doesn't want her life. What she wants is to die as painfully as possible. And I can give that to her," Pry replies as she wraps each hand around Belle's wings and begins to yank even harder. Belle's cries fill the air as Diana stands by and smiles. Belle's wings start to detach from her shoulder blades.

"Pry, stop," I shout as I try to pull her away.

"Let go of me!" my wife demands.

"You can't hurt her," I yell.

"Yes, she can! Go, Pry! Go!" Diana cheers.

"Will you stop that!" Swoop tells the former Kaster.

"Okay, Pryor, I have to admit when you kicked her in the face and threw her to the ground, that was hot. I mean like 'female-inmates-helping-each-other-take-a-soapy-shower' hot. But now that you're standing over her, pulling her wings out…it's more scary than sexy," East warns as Pryor manages to break away from me.

"Pryor, no!" I roar as I go to restrain her again.

"SILVER CASE, DO NOT MOVE! NO ONE MOVE. THAT IS AN ORDER," Pryor says in a cold and firm voice that reminds me of her father. I reluctantly stand still, as does the rest of the team. Melody, on the other hand, confronts Pryor.

"What did I just say?" Pryor asks.

"You gave your team an order. I'm not on your team," Mel reminds her.

"This has nothing to do with you. Get out of my way," Pryor replies.

"You saved me from making a big mistake a few minutes ago. Allow me to help you do the same," Mel pleads.

"This is not the same thing. Move!" Pryor orders.

"Belle has crossed the line, and I'd bitch slap the hell out of her too, but don't take her wings. Not because she doesn't deserve it, but because of how you would feel after it's done. Pryor, I don't know you very well, but I'm guessing your team follows you because they respect you. Don't throw that away for some oversexed chick with time on her hands," Mel says.

"Mel's wrong. I'd respect the hell out of you if you killed her. In fact, I'd erect a monument to you," Diana says.

I glare at her, and she shrugs her shoulders.

"Pry, don't…" Mel implores.

Pryor looks down at Belle, takes her foot off Belle's neck, and releases her wings. Belle groans and slowly starts to sit up.

"How dare you attack—" Before she can finish, Pryor decks her in the face, knocking her out completely this time. Belle is not dead, but she will be out for a while.

***

After we take Mel home, we fly to the warehouse, where we place Belle in a Holder. While we wait for her to regain consciousness, East decides to find a way to make things a little more awkward than they already are.

"Seriously, Silver, what is it you do in bed that makes you so damn wanted by the ladies? C'mon, man, share," East pushes.

"East does have a point; what is it you do to these girls?" Swoop asks.

"We're not discussing this," I inform them.

"Silver, it's me—Bird. You can tell me," she says, flashing her most beguiling smile.

"Do you see what you've started?" I ask East.

"Swoop has a right to ask questions," East replies.

"Yeah, just tell me. What makes you so hot in bed? Is it rhythm, extended foreplay, acrobatics? Wait, are there props?" Swoop says.

"Bird, we are not doing this," I reply.

"Is it candles? Oils? Costumes? Chains?" she replies.

"You are being ridiculous," I reply.

"You tell me stuff all the time. Why can't you tell me this?" she pleads.

"You seriously don't know why?" I ask.

"I'm not three years old anymore. I'm a grown woman, Silver. Look, grown woman boobs," she teases as she cups her breasts and aims them at me playfully.

"Argh! Stop it," I reply as I turn away. She laughs, knowing how much I hate to think of her as anything other than my kid sister.

"And I have curves, hips, and as far as whips go—"

"Bird!" I snap.

"Okay, okay, you better stop, Swoop. Silver's head is gonna explode," East says.

"Diana, go inside the Holder and tend to Belle. I don't want her to bleed out before she tells us what she knows," Pry orders.

Diana reluctantly obeys.

"Swoop, call the Face and see if we can get her over here," the leader says.

"What if she doesn't want to come?" Swoop asks.

"What is it that makes you think I'm *asking* her to come?" Pryor counters.

"Okay, boss, I'm on it," Swoop replies as she takes out her cell phone and walks over to the far end of the warehouse.

"What do you need me to do?" East asks.

"Control your powers," Pry reminds him.

"Oh. Yeah, sorry. Again," he says.

"Go into one of the training rooms in the back and practice. We really can't have you losing control at this point."

"Didn't you almost kill our only lead?" East says.

"Yes. But that wasn't because I couldn't control myself. That's because I didn't want to. Now move," Pryor instructs. Once the others are no longer in hearing distance, she leans on the wall and rakes her hands through her hair, exhausted.

"You okay?" I ask.

"Yeah, I'm having a blast."

"Sorry about Belle. I don't know what's going on with her. You know that she and I were a long time ago and—"

"Aaden, after everything we've been through, I'm not threatened by another girl. I know you belong to me, just like I belong to you."

"Then why did you nearly strip her of her wings?" I ask.

"That wasn't about you; that was about me. I've endured too much, seen too much, and hurt way too much to be disrespected. And I sure as hell won't allow anyone to disrespect our marriage. Period."

"Oh, really?" I reply with a smirk.

"What's that smile about?" she asks.

"It's funny that you reacted so violently because when I see Bex stepping out of line and I fight him, you go all crazy about it."

"That's different."

"How so?"

"I don't know, but it is. Belle was out of line. But Bex...he's hurting. You two can't be at odds for the rest of your lives. You do know that, right?" she says.

"You know how things are with me and that guy—he's just like his uncle."

"That's not fair. Bex has his good qualities," she insists.

"I'd have to take your word for it," I reply.

"You guys need to see this," Diana calls out. We all run over to the center of the warehouse, where Belle's Holder has been placed.

"What is it?" I ask.

"Belle has on several layers of Kofi," Diana says from inside the Holder. I remove the bubble-like prison and allow it to turn back into its original form—which in this case is a chain. We walk towards Diana as she points out spots on Belle's body.

"This bluish glow is from a mixture called Kofi. It hides scars. But when it's starting to fade and needs to be reapplied, it glows."

"I've used Kofi before, but I've never seen it used throughout the body. She's glowing everywhere. How many scars could Belle possibly have that would require using so much?" I wonder.

"The Kofi is fading quickly. Soon we'll see what she's been hiding," Diana replies.

In a matter of seconds, the bluish glow engulfs Belle's body. When it fades, it reveals Belle's scars. We look on in horror as wounds appear all over Belle's body. Parts of her face are fractured like a weathered-down, battered stone statue. There are large gashes all over her body, gaping flesh wounds and burn spots. There's no doubt about it; someone has been torturing her.

"Oh my Omnis!" Swoop gasps.

"Who did that to her?" Pry asks.

"Let's find out. That way I know who to send flowers to," Diana says as she takes out a small vial and spills three drops on top of Belle's chest. Belle bolts upright as if she's been electrocuted. I run over to her.

"Belle, who did this to you?"

"You can't take off the Kofi without asking me, you spiteful bitch! I look hideous," Belle accuses Diana.

"Yes, you do," Diana says with glee.

"I can't believe I didn't kill you when I had the chance," Belle swears.

"Well, I'm free now. You can go anytime you want," Diana offers.

"You've always been jealous of me, you bitter piece of—"

"ENOUGH!" I shout. The two of them fall silent.

"Airabelle, who did this to you and why?" I demand.

"You want to know why? I'll tell you. I was tortured and tormented because of you, Silver," she declares.

"What the hell are you talking about?" Pryor asks before I can.

"I was held captive by a Quo who ambushed me in Rome. She wanted to know all there was to know about you, Silver. Not just you but your whole team. She knew that the two of us had hooked up for years, and she wouldn't stop cutting into me until I told her everything.

"She placed me on a table, held me down with Samson string, and carved into me until I passed out. She'd revive me only to hurt me again. After a while she grew impatient and started to electrocute me. I tried to hold out, but I couldn't. I told her everything I knew about you and your team," she says, crying frantically.

"What do you mean everything?" I ask.

"I've kept up with you and the team, you know; it's what I do. I know where you guys go to be alone, what weapons you use, who is in love with whom—everything," Belle says.

"And you told her all you know about us?" Swoop says.

"Yes," Belle replies.

"You said you know everything—does that mean you know about RJ? My mom was going to take him back to the humans this morning. Did you tell the Quo where my son lives?" Swoop says as her eyes widen in terror.

"Yes—I'm sorry. I tried to hold out, but I was in so much pain—"

"Bitch, you have no idea what pain is! If this Quo chick comes near my son because of information you gave her, I will feast on your flesh with my teeth. And slurp down your soul like soup," Swoop says as she grabs Belle's face in between her hands.

"Swoop, go check on RJ—call us at the first sign of trouble. We'll take care of this," Pryor orders. Swoop takes off into the air frantically.

"Why did she want to know so much about us?" East asks.

"All she said was that she had plans for your team," Belle adds.

"How did you escape?" Pryor asks.

"I didn't. She let me go. She held me for two days. Then she walked into the tunnel where she held me and said I could go. She said she found what she wanted and that she didn't need to chase the team; the team would come to her. Right before she released me, she placed her hand on my chest; I thought she was going to kill me.

"But she let me go. It was only a few hours later that the mark started to appear on my chest," Belle says as she slides down her shirt to reveal a black orchid symbol seared into her flesh.

Diana looks at the mark and exchanges a look with Belle. I have no idea what the black flower means, but judging by the look on Belle's face, it's not good.

"What does that mark mean?" Pryor asks.

"It's the symbol left behind by one of the most powerful Quos on Earth—Ever Knight. She's literally a walking virus. Her touch is lethal. When she wants to kill instantly, she breathes out and blows toxin into her victim's face. But when she wants to torture and taunt her victims, she brands them with the image of a black bleeding-heart orchid. At first, only a small piece of the flower appears on the skin. But in a matter of days, the flower is fully formed. Once that happens, the victim dies an agonizing death," Diana explains.

"The flower is complete," East says as he studies the image closer.

"Yeah, I know. That's why I came to see you, Silver. You know, one last ride for old times' sake," Belle says as she looks at me.

"Keep pushing it, blondie. Terminal or not, I'll rip your damn head off," Pryor vows.

"You should have come to us earlier," I reply as I take her hand.

"It wouldn't have mattered. There's no cure for an Ever virus. All you can do is prolong the inevitable," Diana replies, sounding somewhat saddened by the news.

"Sorry, I lied about knowing how to stop your brother," Belle tells Pryor.

"Why did you?" Pryor asks.

"I guess…I didn't want to die alone," she says as tears fill her eyes.

"Belle, you didn't have to do that. I would have helped you. You know that," I reply as I kneel before her.

"The old Silver would have, but now…you're different now. Happy," Belle says.

"We'll fix this, okay?" I assure her, her hand in mine.

"You can't. Silver, you asked me once if I ever wanted to settle down with one being. You remember what I said?" Belle wonders.

"Hell no, party forever," I reply.

"I lied. You could have been my forever—or at least the top five in the rotation," she teases.

"It's an honor just being on your list," I reply, not sure what else to say.

"I know I screwed you guys over, but I can tell you something that might help."

"What is it, Belle?" East asks.

"I know it doesn't make up for misleading you, but here's a heads-up: Malakaro knows about Phoenix. He knows that he's his son. He knows you've been giving him a mixture to sever the connection," she says to Diana.

"How? How does he know?" Diana asks, terrified.

"He has demons everywhere, tracking the team's every move."

"Oh no! Oh no!" Diana begins to panic and pace up and down the warehouse. We try to calm her down, but the thought that Malakaro could have access to her kid is too much. Pryor takes Diana's hand and vows that we will not let anything happen to her son.

"What mixture have you been giving Nix?" Pryor asks.

"It's a light supplement that stops him from connecting with his father. It was the only thing I could think of to keep that kind of evil out," Diana replies.

"So far it's worked. There's no indication that Malakaro and Nix are communicating," East reminds her.

"Not yet, but I'm sure he's working on getting to that kid," Belle says.

"Are you trying to make Diana crazy or what?" Pryor snaps.

"Hey, I'm just trying to help," Belle counters.

"You wanna help? Fine, tell us what else you know," East says.

"I was with a friend, and he confided in me that on his travels, he happened upon a creature that many thought no longer existed," Belle confides to us.

"So you were hooking up with some loser and he told you a secret so you wouldn't lose interest in him. You know that's pathetic, right?" Diana counters.

"Really? Is it as pathetic as you trying to trap Silver into being with you by getting pregnant?" she asks.

"Game. Set. Match," East whispers as Diana glares at him.

"Belle, go on," Pryor says.

"Anyway, this angel confided in me that he had come across a Craven," Belle insists.

"Bullshit. All the Cravens were killed off years ago," Diana counters.

"We read about Cravens in school. They are beings with two powers. They can extract your deepest desire and they are neutralizers. Anytime they were around, demons were rendered powerless. That's what made them so important," East tells us.

"Yeah, that's also why they were all slaughtered. I remember my dad talking about it. They were killed off by a group of demons who wanted to take over their territory," Pry replies.

"I thought they were all dead too. There is one left. The oldest and most powerful of them all—Bya," Belle says.

"You think this angel was telling you the truth? You think he really did spot a Craven?" I ask.

"This guy would never lie to me. I had him wrapped around my—finger," she says, catching herself. Diana and Pryor roll their eyes in unison.

"If it's true, if there is a Craven still out there, we would have the perfect weapon against Malakaro," East says excitedly.

"It's not just any Craven that the angel spotted, it's Bya, the leader, the oldest and most powerful Craven that ever lived. With her by your side, you could take out Malakaro easily," Belle informs us.

"Okay, it's worth checking out. Where did your friend spot Bya? Where can we find her?" I ask.

"Oh, now c'mon, I have given up nearly everything I know. And so far all I've gotten in return is insulted, beaten, and mocked. So if you want Bya's location, it's time to show me some gratitude," Belle says.

Pryor, growing angry again, marches up to Belle. I place a hand on her shoulder, signaling for her to stay calm.

"What are you going to threaten me with, First Noru? I'm already dying," Belle reminds her.

"Yeah, but not nearly fast enough, but I can fix that!" Pryor threatens.

"Hey, let's just hear her out," East replies.

"Thank you. I get how that asking to spend the night with him could be perceived as pushing it. So let's compromise: I'll give you the location of the Craven, and in exchange, you allow me one kiss from Silver" Belle offers.

"No," Pryor says.

"All it takes is one kiss to save the world and your best friend, yet you won't do it? Really, Noru?" Belle pushes.

"Belle, there has to be something else that you want," I reply impatiently.

"What I want is...this is the deal. Take it or leave it," Belle replies.

"We'll leave it," Pryor announces.

"Belle, give us a minute," East says as he signals for us to step away from Belle and confer in private. We all gather a few feet away.

"Look, I know this is not ideal, but I think we should take her up on it," East says.

"The hell we will," Pry replies.

"She's dying. It's not like she stands a chance of coming back and asking for more. And there may be another way to get her to talk, but the fact is time is not on our side," East reasons.

"What do you think?" Pryor asks me.

"I can't ask you to be okay with this because I sure as hell wouldn't be okay with another guy kissing you—ever," I counter.

"Yeah, but, Silver, you're not the leader. And right now, that's who Pryor needs to be," Diana replies.

"She's right. This is the fastest way," Pry says softly.

"Are you sure?" I ask.

"Yeah, I am," she confirms.

"This is a bad idea, Pry. This could get messy. You know that," I reply.

"It's already messy," she reasons.

"Are you certain this is what you want me to do?" I push again.

"No, but I'm certain it's what has to happen. So, yeah. Do it," she says.

"Alright. But you should step outside. That way you don't have to watch," I propose.

"No, I'm not leaving you alone with that she-creature," Pry says.

"You should not watch this," East reasons.

"I'm watching. Now let's go," the leader orders.

"Okay," I reply, trying to ignore the sharp blade of guilt poking at my chest. We walk back towards Belle. East helps her stand up and she demands that Diana give her a bottle of Kofi so that she can look as flawless as she did when we first saw her.

Diana grudgingly hands her the bluish mixture. She drinks, and in a matter of seconds, all her marks are gone. I reach out for her to give her a quick peck, but she pulls away.

"Let's be clear, this is the last kiss I am ever going to have. I don't want you to kiss me like you're kissing your grandmother," she warns.

"Fine," I reply.

"I mean it, Silver. You hold back and the deal is off!"

"Yeah, I got it," I scold, glaring at her.

"Hey, don't look at me like that. I know I'm asking for a lot. But when this is over, all of you will go back to your lives. I don't have that. I know I am not a model angel. But I was here. I lived. I laughed. And I even saved you once, Silver. So kiss me good-bye—kiss me like I mattered to you. Because I think at one point I did," Belle reasons.

"You do matter to me. I'm sorry about the virus," I reply.

"Then show me you're sorry this is my last day. Show me. Kiss me like...like you did when we were in Bali," she says.

"We were in Bali?" I ask.

"You don't even remember being in Indonesia with me?" she says. She shakes her head with a mix of frustration and sadness. Before I can reply, she walks over to the nearby metal chest filled with weapons and sits on top of it, looking crestfallen.

"Belle..." I call out softly, not really sure what to say.

"Silver, you don't think I know how pathetic this whole situation is? Having to beg for a kiss? Me? I could destroy an angel from across the room with one smile. One touch and he'd surrender everything.

"I've been with kings, Paras, even Originals. But the one time I felt really, truly alive was in Bali with you. The world saw our actions and decided we weren't worthy of a normal life. But we saw each other, you and me. We looked past each other's mistakes and bad choices. I saw you, the real you, and you saw me.

"I always thought somehow life would bring us back together. Maybe not as husband and wife but as two professional drifters who had no real home. But it seems you found your home now. And I thought maybe in time I would too. But I'm out of time. So I thought at least I can recapture that night in Bali, a night you apparently don't even remember."

"We were chasing a Seller who had stolen a case of Coy Dark we had. We chased him to a little town in Bali called Uluwatu. It started to rain so hard, spotting the Seller became too difficult. So we ended up spending the night in an abandoned temple on the edge of the cliff. There, we saw the most stunning sunset Omnis had ever created," I reply as I walk over and sit beside her.

"You remember?" she asks.

"Yes, I do. Your hair was down, like this..." I reply as I reach over and release the clip that held her hair up. Her hair now falls all around her, framing her face.

"We were so cold," she says with a smile.

"But we couldn't walk away from that sunset. We had to watch every moment of it," I recall.

"We were soaking wet and shivering. But we just stood there like idiots, too awestruck to move."

"But then we did move, didn't we?" I reply, looking into her eyes.

"Yes, we did..." she says as she looks even deeper into my eyes.

"We went back into the temple and we..."

"Yeah, we did," she says as she swallows hard and parts her lips slightly.

"And I think it started something like this..." I reply as I place my hand under her chin and tilt her head slightly to the side. I skim the surface of her lips with my tongue as I part her mouth. Her response is primal and urgent. She ensnares my tongue with hers and delights in our entanglement. She leans even further into the kiss and growls with desire. She moves to intensify the kiss yet again, but I pull away.

"Thank you," Belle says with light in her eyes. I look over at Pryor, not sure what her reaction will be. I can't tell because she's avoiding me.

"Okay, you got what you wanted. Where is the Craven?" Pryor says in a stern voice.

"She lives in a town house off the coast of Maine," Belle says. Pryor makes her give us the exact location.

"Is there anything else we need to know?" East asks.

"I don't—" Belle can't finish her thought; her body starts jerking up and down uncontrollably. I call out her name, but there's no calming her down. The vines from the black orchid come to life underneath her skin. It grows and travels through her body in every direction.

She rocks violently and cries out as the virus spreads. The stem of the flower wraps around her neck, then up through her nose, and punctures out her eyeballs. A black liquid oozes from her mouth, eyes, and nose. Suddenly Belle's body is very still. Belle is dead.

"Silver, I'm sorry," East says as we look down at Belle's corpse.

"Yeah, me too," I reply as I close her eyes.

"We need to get going. We have to go find the Craven," Pryor orders.

"I'm gonna call Swoop and give her an update. If everything is okay, do you want her to meet us back here?" East asks his leader.

"No, give her the address and have her meet us in Maine," Pryor replies.

East agrees and walks away to call his cousin. Diana, sensing that Pryor and I need to talk, makes an excuse and heads to one of the training rooms.

"So are we…okay?" I ask awkwardly.

"I don't know. I guess," she says.

"You know that kiss meant nothing. I just had to make sure she gave us the info we needed," I remind her.

"You were so…convincing," she says almost to herself.

"I'm not sure what to say about that," I confess.

"There's nothing you can say. You're just really good at…making girls want you," she says as she turns away from me. I reach out to wrap my arms around her. She flinches and moves away.

"So you're mad at me?" I ask.

"No. Yes. No—a little. I don't know," she admits.

"You told me to do this," I remind her.

"Yes, I did. But that doesn't mean it was easy to watch."

"I told you not to watch. I pleaded with you."

"I know that, but if I didn't, then it would create a picture in my head far worse than what actually happened."

"Are we gonna get past this?" I ask.

"It's been four minutes. Can I get some time?"

"Fine," I snap as I start walking away.

"Why are you upset with me? I'm sorry if I can't bounce back and embrace you after watching you kiss another woman."

"Did you think I enjoyed that? Because I didn't," I reply.

"It's hard to tell if you were having fun or not. I was distracted by the intricate dance your tongues were doing. If there is an Olympic event that involves kissing, you two can pack your bags and head to Tokyo. I guarantee you both will win gold."

"Well, that would be kind of hard to do since she's gone," I counter.

Pryor looks over at Belle's body as if for the first time. She goes into one of the rooms and comes back with the thick blanket that usually covers our training gear. She opens it up and starts to cover Belle. I quietly help her. When we are done, we look over at each other.

"So…you come here often," she jokes.

"All the time," I reply.

"You're kinda cute. Are you taken?" Pry asks.

"Very much."

"Maybe I could lure you away from her," Pry says as she places her arm around my neck.

"I doubt it. My wife is pretty badass. She'd hunt you down and kill you."

"Damn right," she says as she laughs.

"I'm sorry you had to watch that," I tell her when the laughter dies down.

"It's okay. Let's just focus on getting to the Craven," Pryor says.

"Focusing on the Craven would be a mistake," someone says behind us. We turn around and find the Face stepping off a Port. She walks towards us.

"What do you know about the Craven?" Pryor says.

"For one thing, she's dead."

CHAPTER FIVE
WORTH IT

Pryor calls Swoop and tells her that plans have changed and that she needs to meet us in the warehouse. In the meantime, we dispose of Belle's body. Normally, we'd give her a proper send-off, but the fact is, we are at war with Malakaro and we just don't have the time. Once Swoop lands, she tells us that RJ is safe and that her parents placed a shield around the human home where he is now being looked after.

"Good, I'm so glad he's okay. I know it's hard on you, Swoop; you'd prefer Uncle Jay and Miku to be watching him," Pryor says as we head to the table that's been placed in the center of the warehouse.

"What I would prefer is to be his mother full-time. I would like to be the one protecting him," Swoop says pointedly.

"Keeping you from RJ isn't something I'm happy about. I want the two of you to be together. I love that kid; we all do. But we need you. I need you," Pryor says sincerely.

"Yeah, I know. It's just hard to hold his little face in my hands and then take off only moments later. I feel like I'm letting him down. Like I'm a bad mom because I'm not there," Swoop admits.

"You are protecting him by being here and fighting to make the world safe. You are doing that for him. If evil does win today, there will be nowhere to hide RJ. You being here is what a good mother would do," Diana replies.

Swoop doesn't say anything, but she does place her hand on top of Diana's hand. Now that the two of them are moms, they are connecting on a new level.

Once we are seated at the table, all of our eyes are set on the "guest of honor," the Face. She looks out at us, and it's easy to see that she's lost in thought. She seems uncertain as to how to start this meeting. But judging by our faces, she can tell she needs to start immediately. So she takes a deep breath and begins.

"It's clear that all of you think I have been withholding information from you. You are right, I have," the Face says.

"Why have you been keeping things from us?" I ask.

"Some subjects are difficult to discuss," she reasons.

"That may be so, but we still need to know," Swoop says.

"I agree," she says in a soft voice.

"How do you know the Craven is dead?" Pryor asks.

"Because I did some research and also because Ever told me she was," the Face says.

"Really, and exactly how close are you two?" East says angrily.

"We're not close at all, unfortunately," she says to herself.

"Okay, why don't you take it from the top. And try not to leave anything out. Because if you do…just don't lie to us again," Pryor warns.

"Ever Knight's real name is Everly-Ann Knight; she's my baby sister. She's a powerful Quo and she had a good heart. Years ago, she fell in love with someone she couldn't have. She begged me to speak to him and try to convince him to be with her. I went to him—many times. And in the process we fell in love with each other. We didn't plan it. It just happened. And we were only 'together' for one night.

"I didn't regret having been with him, but I did regret hurting my sister. So I decided to be honest with Ever. I told her what happened, and something in her snapped," the Face says, sounding far away.

"The being she was in love with, it was Fate, wasn't it?" East asks.

"Yes."

"You stole Fate from your sister?" Swoop asks.

"It was foolish because Fate isn't…you can't have a normal life with a member of the council. I knew that and so did he. But we were young and very foolish. Anyway, it ended nearly as soon as it started," the Face says.

"Okay, so you pissed off your sister a long time ago by taking her guy. What does that have to do with us now?" Diana says.

"Ever let her pain take over her life. She was lured to evil thanks to her anger and bitterness. She began to offer her powers up to the highest bidder. She became a 'hired gun,' as the humans would say. She spreads death and agony on behalf of whoever is willing to pay her price," the Face adds.

"So your sister is an assassin for hire?" East says.

"Yes. She does that because she's hurting. She's not a bad person," the Face replies.

"If Belle were here, I'd think she'd disagree," I bark.

"I know, she's lost her way," the Face says.

"Gee, you think?" East whispers under his breath.

"Why is she coming after us?" Pryor asks.

"For two reasons: one, because someone is paying her to do so," the Face admits.

"And what's the second reason?" Swoop asks.

"This isn't just a gig for her. She's relishing this because she has finally found my weakness—this team," the Face says.

"What do you mean?" I ask.

"She has been looking for a way to get back at me for years. When she learned that I was watching over all of you years ago, she paid me a visit. She threatened to hurt you all. I acted like I didn't care about the team, so she left all of you alone. But over the years it became clear that you all mattered to me.

"I begged her to just walk away and let it go. But the more I fought for her to stay away from you, the more she wanted to harm you. So I tried pretending like I didn't care anymore. I assured her that your team had disappointed me and that you were more of a burden than anything," the Face tells us.

"But she wasn't buying," Pry concludes.

"No, she wasn't. So I told her if she so much as *thought* about harming you all, I'd kick her ass. I cursed. That's how strongly I felt about it."

"Careful, we might start to think you care," East teases.

"Don't get me wrong, you are all insolent, impulsive little balls of hormones. You are always pushing the limit, going off your emotions and generally making poor choices. But however misguided you all may be, you are mine to look after. I know all your parents are back, but I still feel as if you all are…my family," she confesses, unable to look us in the eye.

"What did Ever say about that?" I ask.

"She loved it because it meant I had something she could take away. I didn't know how she planned to hurt any of you. Then years passed, and I thought she was finally ready to let it go."

"But she wasn't, was she?" Diana says.

"No. I realized that when I looked into the Portal and I found a box with my sister's calling card—the black orchid. In addition to the flower, I found a few reddish specks of dust in the corner of the box. I did some research, and the red specks are ashes of a species long thought dead—the Craven. As it turns out, Malakaro found the Craven Bya and burned her alive. He then kept the ashes in the Portal," the Face adds.

"Why would he do that?" Swoop asks.

"Craven ash is powerful. If you can gather it and add it to a mixture, you'd be able to harness its power," Diana replies.

"Exactly. Malakaro did that so that should a bigger evil appear, he could use it to neutralize them," the Face says.

"But Ever got to the ashes first and she took them and left you the orchid so you'd know it was her. Why didn't you tell us this in the beginning?" East says.

"That's what she wanted me to do. She wanted me to tell all of you that she has what you need to defeat Malakaro. Then the team would go after her. I didn't want anything to happen to you all. So I kept it to myself and I went to her to talk her into giving back the ashes. I really tried to reason with her."

"I take it she wasn't in a 'reasonable' mood?" Diana replies.

"No, she wasn't. She said she couldn't wait to take away the beings that I love. And that she would relish killing you all. And as far as the ashes go, even if she had them, she wouldn't return them."

"Ever doesn't have the ashes?" Pryor snaps.

"No. She said she gave the ashes to her employer already—I have no idea who that is. But if you want to get your hands on them, you will have to face her," the Face says.

"Is that it? Is that all?" I ask.

"Okay, so let me see if I got this right: the Craven's ashes were in the Portal, but your loving baby sister took them and gave them to the being who hired her to steal them. Baby sis won't tell us who she gave them to unless we go over there and make her," Pryor concludes.

"So your only son was killed. Your ex-husband ran the Center. And your little sister is an assassin for hire. How is it you're not drunk, like, *all* the time?" East asks earnestly. For the first time since she's been here, the Face smiles despite herself.

"You cost us a lot of time; time we don't have," Pryor says firmly.

"I know," the Face says.

"You want us to believe you didn't tell us about the contents of the Portal because you didn't want us to go after Ever and get hurt, but I suspect it's more than that. I think you didn't want us to go after her because you know we could very well kill her," our leader replies.

"She's my baby sister. You try to put all of that aside, but..."

"Well, thank you for finally being up front with us. And for the record, you matter to us too. We love you. All of us. But I need you to know two things: if you ever lie to us again, we will be done with you. In every way possible. Do you understand?" Pryor asks in a voice that leaves no room for argument.

"Yes, I do," the Face replies.

"And second, you will tell us where to find Ever. And when we do, if she doesn't tell us who hired her, we will not hesitate to end her life."

***

The Face agrees to tell us where to find her sister; however, when we get there, the entire estate is gone. Ever placed her home in a Whirlwind. That means that her location is always changing. It's as if she's living inside a twister and has no fixed location.

"Why would Ever hide if she wants us to find her?" I ask.

"According to the Face, her sister enjoys making everything as hard as possible. No doubt the Whirlwind is difficult to track," East says.

"Difficult but not impossible. We need to find someone who can track the entrance of the Whirlwind and do it fast," Diana says.

"That could take hours. Randy doesn't have that kind of time," Pryor replies.

"Unless you find an angel who is obsessed with Whirlwinds and knows all about them," East says, looking pointedly at Swoop.

"Really?" Swoop says begrudgingly.

"This is for all of mankind and Randy, your favorite nerd candy," East reminds her.

She sighs deeply and tells us to follow her. The team takes to the air and lands in the business district of downtown Los Angeles. Palm trees and reflective-surfaced skyscrapers surround us. We enter a glass elevator and Swoop presses the button that will lead us to the penthouse floor. Once the elevator door opens, we step out and head for the only apartment on the floor. As we walk up to the mahogany double doors, Pryor asks what we are all thinking.

"What are we doing here?"

"We're here to see this guy; he knows a lot about Whirlwinds. He knows…everything," Swoop says, avoiding eye contact with us.

"What does this guy do?" Diana asks.

"He's an angel historian by day and a gadget geek by night. He will be able to help us track Ever," Swoop replies.

"How do you know him?" I ask.

"It's complicated…" she says as she braces herself and knocks on the door. A tall, muscular angel with dark eyes opens the door. He's wearing dark-rimmed glasses, a gray sweater over a white collared shirt, and jeans.

He only focuses on Swoop. We all seem to fade into nothing; all that's left is the two of them. Swoop looks like she wants to leap into his embrace, yet I can see a sense of panic behind her eyes; some part of her also wants to run away.

"Dylan," she whispers, in the most feminine voice I've ever heard coming out of Swoop. We all exchange looks of curiosity.

Who is this guy?

"Hello, Kiana," he says as he takes in the girl before him. The tension in the hallway is palpable. It feels like we walked in on a private moment.

"I need…I would like your help with something," Swoop says carefully.

"Do you need help learning to use the phone?" he asks. Although his words are biting, it's easy to see he'd give anything to let her in.

"I know you called a few times—"

"Seven," he corrects her.

"Okay, seven."

"You never returned any of my calls," he replies, masking his hurt with irritation.

"I know," she replies gently.

"You have no idea," he corrects her.

"So does that mean we can't come in?" she asks.

He reluctantly steps back and lets us enter the penthouse. It's filled with high-tech gear and row after row of books and vials. There's a large glass table in the center of the room. After we enter, he motions for us to take seats at the table. We tell him what we need, but the whole time we are talking, he's looking over at Swoop.

"Hey, Bird, can I talk to you for a sec?" I ask as I get up and head over to her. She follows me back into the hallway.

"Okay, start talking," I demand.

"We're friends. I mean in the beginning. Pry sent me to do some research and I sought him out. I didn't think we'd have anything in common, but somehow we hit it off."

"What happened?" I push.

"We spent the weekend together. I liked him. I really like him, Silver."

"Did he break up with you?"

"No. I left before he woke up. And I didn't call or anything, ever again."

"Why?"

"Because my last boyfriend was second in command to the biggest evil in the world. Silver, I have evil inside me. I'm attracted to evil. That's who I am. Dylan may be nice now, but what would have happened if he was tangled up in my life? What if Raven is never really gone? What if somewhere inside me, I'm still evil?"

"Bird, there is no darkness in you, not anymore. And you can't keep pushing guys away because you're afraid."

"I hurt so many people…I don't want to add him to the list," she confesses.

"Look, he knows about your past. And it's clear he's good with it. Don't make this decision without talking to him. He deserves a say in this," I argue.

"I think I have the equipment that you guys will need to track the Quo," Dylan says as he enters the hallway.

"Great, we'll give you two a minute," I reply, not giving them a chance to object. I leave the two of them in the hallway and walk back to the table, where Dylan has laid out a large crystal map and placed it on the table.

"Is my cousin okay?" East asks.

"Yeah, they just need a few minutes," I reply.

"Um, is it just me or…" Before Diana can finish, Pryor joins in.

"It's not just you; Dylan is 'geek hottie' goodness," Pryor adds with a smile. East and I roll our eyes and try to ignore them.

"Aren't historians supposed to be dusty old men with shaky hands and bad eyesight?" Diana asks Pry.

"His lips are perfect, and he has the bluest eyes I've ever seen," Pryor mutters under her breath.

"I know! And did you see his pecs—damn," Diana adds.

"I'm *loving* that no-shave stubble thing," Pryor replies.

"Calm down, ladies. He's a historian; his only function is to read," East says.

"I wish I was a book in his collection. He'd grab me off the shelf, slam me down on the table, glide his fingers over me, and *read* me all night," Diana mumbles suggestively.

"Hmm, I hope he reads *slow*…" Pryor says before she can stop herself. She and Diana share a laugh. I look at her, and she quickly says she's just playing around. I look over at East and we shake our heads, silently agreeing women are crazy.

When Swoop and Dylan come back in, there is still tension but not nearly as much as there was in the beginning. He tells us he can track her, but that it will take up to an hour to pinpoint Ever's exact location.

"Please do what you can. We need to find her so we can track down whoever hired her. Once we do that, we can get our hands on the ashes," Pryor says.

"Malakaro isn't an easy foe. Surely a handful of ashes won't stop him," Dylan cautions.

"No, but combined with the ashes, my team and I can destroy him," Pryor replies.

"Do you want me to go on the mission with you, Kiana?" he asks.

"No, but thanks for the offer. We got this," Swoop says, blushing.

Wait, is Bird really a grown woman? When the hell did that happen? I guess it happened at the same time my wife was growing up. My wife...

"Can you explain to us how you are trying to track her?" Diana asks as she looks at the blinking light on the glass map.

***

(MATURE CONTENT AHEAD. YOUNGER READERS CAN SKIP TO THE NEXT CHAPTER WITHOUT MISSING PLOT POINTS.)

As Dylan goes over the logistics of tracking down Ever, I look across the room and spot my wife in deep thought. She's so fucking sexy when she's in leader mode. She has laser focus and absolute concentration. She sits next to Diana and listens attentively as Dylan speaks. She crosses her legs, and in the process, I glimpse her black satin panties.

Damn...

It's been less than a day since we were in bed together, but I swear it feels like years. I know it's inappropriate, but I don't care. I pull out my cell and discreetly text her.

"I watched you cross your legs. Now I'm hungry…"

She looks at her cell and reads my message. She doesn't break out of leader mode. She doesn't look my way or even pause. Instead she continues to give orders and assemble a plan of attack. But a few seconds later I get a text from her.

"I hope you're thirsty too because the thought of you inside me is making me wet…"

An image flashes in my head of the last time we were in bed together. Her legs wrapped around my waist. Her nails digging into my back as I inserted myself so deep inside her, she gasped.

"Aaden!" Swoop calls out loud, pulling me out of my flashback.

"What?" I ask.

"Dylan asked if you want a glass of Coy," Swoop says, looking at me strangely.

"Yeah, sure. Thanks," I reply, trying to suppress the urge to fly across the room, grab Pry, and rip her clothes off. Dylan comes from the kitchen with a large bottle of Coy and passes out the wineglasses. He says something, but I'm not sure what it is because I'm too busy looking at Pryor. She suggestively circles the rim of her glass with her index finger, dips it into the sweet liquid, then discreetly sucks on it.

I try to focus on the meeting. But it's just not possible. She crosses her legs again, this time making sure that the material of her skirt doesn't cover up her thigh completely. I bite my lower lip and swallow hard. She walks over and brushes up against me as she looks over Dylan's tracking equipment. She then goes back to her seat and texts me.

"Right pocket. You're welcome."

I turn away and sneak a glance at the right pocket of my jacket; I pull out a pair of black satin panties. Knowing where the soft material had been makes my head spin. I stroke the fabric with my hand. The last time I felt something that smooth and silky—I was traveling down the slope of her breasts with my tongue.

I recall what it was like to kiss the middle panel of her panties and listen as she begged me to remove the last fabric barrier that stood between us. When I removed it and had complete access to her, I experienced levels of pleasure I didn't know existed. She began grinding her hips against my mouth.

Unable to stand it any longer, I embedded myself deep inside her. I was in so deep, it caused a violent surge of passion to zoom down both of our bodies. That one little piece of clothing brought back my favorite moments—moments that I need to relive—right now. I text her as I walk out of the room.

"Parking garage."

She texts me back: *"Mr. Case, I'm working."*

I reply: *"Now."*

I walk out to the parking garage; I don't know what she told the team, but five seconds later, Pryor comes running out. She leaps into my arms and wraps her legs around me. I grab hold of her and we kiss feverishly. I don't know how else to explain what it's like to taste her, other than to say it's the closest thing to perfection.

The frenzy of our kisses reaches heights far beyond what we are used to. We devour each other as if we had only seconds left to be together. I slam her against a gray concrete pillar, tear her shirt open, and peel her satin bra off with my teeth. She pulls my face into her bare breasts, puts her hand behind my head, and arches her back so that I can suckle on her nipples until I have enough. But that is not possible; there is no such thing as enough.

Unable to contain myself, I place one hand under her skirt and explore the space between her legs. She rolls her eyes in the back of her head and curses as the sensations overwhelm her. As I fondle and stroke her slippery, wet folds, now I too am overwhelmed.

She glides her nails across my back as she strips me of my shirt and tosses it towards the row of nearby parked cars. Soon she's exploring me with her lips and leaving a trail of kisses on my chest. I can't handle the pleasure surging through me and still keep my balance. So I pull her off the pillar and lay her on top of the sports car behind us. For several minutes, we intertwine our bodies and frantically taste each other. I'm dying to pull her skirt past her thighs and strip her naked, but I don't want her to feel exposed. So I apply pressure to the car door and pry it open.

I then lay her down on the backseat. But by now, I'm craving her so much, I don't want to take the time to lower her skirt; instead I put my head under it and drink. She writhes in ecstasy and stutters my name. She latches onto a handful of my hair and pulls tightly as my tongue grazes her swollen tip.

"Ohmyomnis. Ohmyomnis. Oh. My. Omnis—shiiiiiiit!" she pleads as her hips jerk up and down uncontrollably. She glares at me as if to say it's her turn. She slides down off the seat and out of the car. Then she pushes me down so that I am now the one who's seated. She unzips me, pulls my jeans off, and discards them.

She puts me inside her mouth so slowly that by the time she reaches the base, I'm panting. She maintains an airtight seal along my core. Her strokes are rhythmic, skillful and dangerous. Her movements are aggressive, yet graceful. She wraps her mouth around me like she's an extension of me.

She then breaks the seal and opens her mouth. Soon she's using another weapon in her arsenal of pleasure: her tongue. She rubs, slides, and rotates it in ways my body can't comprehend. She makes me gasp one swear word after another. It's not long before I'm too deep in the grip of pleasure to remember my name. She brings me to the brink of desire, and I beg her to take me over the edge.

She grants my wish by placing the tip of my member between her lips and humming. The more she hums, the more of me she inserts in her mouth. By the time she gets to the stem, my whole body is vibrating. Just as I am about to reach the pinnacle, she pulls away. Having her mouth taken away brings me physical pain. I need her. I need her.

I'm drunk with relief when seconds later she impales herself onto me. My length penetrates deep inside her. My thrusts are powerful. Hard. Possessive. Her hip movements are hypnotic, fluid, and passionate.

She rides me with the same skill and fearlessness she shows in battle. And much like in battle, she has no mercy. So as her bouncy, beautiful breasts move up and down, I cup her ass and hold on for dear life.

We thrust deeper, harder, and faster; we are wrecking the shit out of this car. But I don't care about that. There's only one thing I care about right now: her nipples. They are distended, taut, and rosy. They call out to me in my ecstasy-filled haze. I ache to taste them. I lick my lips, anticipating what it would feel like to suckle on such exquisite fruit.

She looks down at me. Her hair is dripping wet from sweat and her body is shivering with pleasure. She knows what I want. And judging by the deep arch in her back and her raspy breathless voice, it's what she wants too.

"Eat," she orders.

I feast on her nipples until she's beside herself with pleasure. I can't stop or even pull myself away from her flesh for a moment. So we don't stop. We keep colliding into each other, keep moving.

Thrust. Thrust. Thrust. Brace for impact.

Shit!

"Baby—fuck!" I pant.

Thrust. Thrust. Thrust. Grind.

"OHSHITOHSHITOHSHIT," she cries.

Thrust. Thrust. Milk.

"AAAAAAADEN!" she yells.

We grip each other tightly as the biggest Outer Arc orgasm we've ever known crashes down on us. It shatters the car window, expands beyond us, and one by one, shatters every car window in the parking lot. The blast sets off dozens of car alarms all at once.

My wife and I look over at each other, surrounded by glass and chaos. She's thinking the same thing I am.

This was so worth it...

CHAPTER SIX
BE READY

"We are so irresponsible," Pryor says with a big smile as she peels a piece of broken glass off her bare flesh.

"No, we're not," I reply as I help her put her bra back on. I then reach for my shirt and put it on. My jeans, however, are outside the car.

"Aaden, what kind of beings stop to make love in the middle of saving the world?" she asks.

"Smart ones," I reply. We look over at each other and burst out laughing. She's right; it's ludicrous to stop and do what we did. In fact, I'm guessing we broke some kind of rule, but again, so worth it.

"We have to be the worst saviors of mankind ever," she replies.

"Yeah, I don't think we're getting a parade once this is all done."

"Screw the parade. I want a vacation," she declares.

"Really?"

"Yes. We kick evil's ass, bring my best friend back to his old self, and then take a vacation."

"Where are we going?" I ask.

"When I was little, right before I started my first training session, I was beyond scared. I had to lead a team of angels, all of whom were older than me, not to mention taller. I tried to put on a brave face and act like I had it all handled. Looking back, I'm sure my parents could tell I was in a panic. My legs wobbled, my voice shook, and when it was time to fly to class, I looked out the window, eyes wide in terror. So my dad took my hand and said, 'Carrot, we're gonna stop off somewhere before your training.'"

"I never knew that. Where did he take you?" I ask.

"He took me to see this huge waterfall in the Philippines called Summit Falls. It's hidden and nearly impossible to find. When we got there, he took my hand and we walked onto the edge of the bank.

"The water was so pure, it was as if it sprang from the palm of Omnis's hand. It cascaded off the side of the mountain like a graceful bird. The surface of the water reflected the sky perfectly. The flowers and plants were so vivid and so stunning; I still see them when I close my eyes.

"My dad said to look around and listen to the sound of the waterfall. I said I couldn't really hear anything, just softly flowing water. Then we swam down to the deepest depths of the water, and the currents were overwhelming. When we got back to the surface, my dad spoke to me.

"'Pryor, I know you're smaller than the other kids on the team. But that doesn't matter. This waterfall is small compared to the others. Other falls have raging waters that roar loudly, announcing their presence. But while the surface of Summit Falls is calm and peaceful, underneath it's strong, powerful, and ferocious. It's not what people see on the surface, it's what is going on deep down that matters. And deep down, you are a force of nature.'

"My parents had the Green Mountains. It was their place as a couple. But when my dad needed to be alone and to reflect on his own, as a leader, he went there. And he shared that with me not as my dad, but as one leader to another. For him, Summit Falls embodied what a leader should have: quiet strength. And I could use a little of that," she says.

"Then you got it, one trip to the magical waterfall," I assure her.

"Perfect! Now we have a problem that's almost as bad as facing the end of humanity," she says grimly.

"What's the problem?"

"How do I get out of this car without a shirt on?" she says as she eyes her shirt on the cement floor outside the car.

"Fate said it would be wise for me to enter the parking garage backwards and to come with extra clothing," a familiar voice says from the entrance closest to us.

"Mom!" Pryor shouts as she ducks down to hide her nearly naked body.

"Hi, Carrot. Here," she says as she hands Pryor a bag of clothes while still looking away.

I reach out the window and take the bag from Death. I even manage to get ahold of my jeans. I'm trying not to laugh, but this is just too crazy. Death waits patiently while we get dressed in the car before she approaches.

"Aaden, can you give us a moment?" my mother-in-law asks.

Pryor looks at me as if to say, "Don't you dare agree to go." But it's time the two of them work things out, so I reply, "Yeah, sure," as I start to walk away.

I look back at my wife. I'm sure this is the last time I am going to have sex with her because she is going to kill me for forcing her and her mom to talk alone. I walk through the double doors, fully intending to go back into the penthouse, but I hear no sound coming from Pry or her mother. Worried, I turn back and look through the glass, hoping they will get past their issues and really work things out.

"So...did you and Aaden kill all these cars?" Emmy asks awkwardly.

"Yeah, guess the humans will be upset," Pryor says, equally uncomfortable.

"So will your uncle Jay. These are top-of-the-line cars. I can hear him crying now," she jokes.

"What are you doing here? Aren't you supposed to be helping Time hold up the barrier?" Pry asks.

"Yes, but Fate is filling in. Malakaro hasn't broken through yet, but with every passing moment, he gets closer. I didn't think he'd be this strong."

"No, you didn't think..." Pry looks away.

"Wow, you must be livid with me—you're tapping your finger against your leg. You always did that when you were angry. The faster you tapped, the more upset you were. And judging by how fast your index finger is going...you really don't like me right now.

"The last time I saw you that upset was when you were five and I wouldn't let you throw a human out the window to see if you could catch them in time. You tapped your little finger, poked out your bottom lip, and scrunched your little face. You were so cute. I can hear you now.

"'Mom, I have to know if I'm fast enough to catch a human.' Your father and I asked you what would happen if you weren't fast enough yet and the human died. You shook your head impatiently, placed your hands on your hips, and said, 'Duh, Mom, Omnis would bring them back so I could try again,'" Emmy says, smiling to herself.

"I don't remember that," Pry mumbles.

"I know…"

"Did you come to tell me something?" Pry asks.

"Yes, I did. I came here on official business—mostly."

"Fine, what is it?" Pryor asks as she shifts her weight and forces herself to sound official.

"Barbara told us what was happening with Ever. As you know, Fate doesn't know everything. He was just as surprised as we were that Ever's hatred had driven her this far. I know Barbara regrets holding anything back from you, Pry."

"It seems to be the theme of the day," Pry replies under her breath.

Emmy decides to let her daughter's comment go and continues, "I know you're going after Ever. And since you're here, I'm guessing you're checking with Dylan about the Whirlwind."

"How did you know about that?"

"Dylan is a top-of-the-line tracker. He's also brilliant when it comes to angel history. The council chose him to be lead historian because he has an unending hunger for knowledge. Normally we like to keep angels like him out of battle, but in this case…"

"You think we should take Dylan with us?" Pryor asks.

"If he's willing to go. There are creatures out there that your team hasn't heard about, and it would be wise to have a guide."

"Great, so there are monsters that you and the council didn't tell us about. That's just perfect, Mom."

"Every day there are new inventions made by the Paras. Good continues to advance. Did you think that advancement was an ability only given to angels? The demon world has advanced too. They have new creatures, new weapons, and new ways to inflict pain. That's why you should take Dylan with you. He will be able to sort out what kind of evil lies ahead," Emmy reasons.

"I don't think Swoop is going to like him coming along."

"Miku told me about that. Swoop is afraid she'll hurt him by being in his life," Death replies.

"So Swoop and her mom talk. Must be nice," Pryor replies pointedly.

"Carrot, you and I talk. We have a good relationship."

"That's what I thought too. Then I find out..." Pryor bows her head in disappointment.

"I know you're hurt that I didn't tell you I was the Maker. I was wrong. I am so sorry that I caused you any sadness. But that doesn't mean our whole relationship is gone. You're my daughter, the love of my life."

"I don't...what am I supposed to say, Mom? How do I wrap my head around the fact that I am the reason this is all happening? Yes, you saved me and that was on you, but I'm the one who got sick, it's all my fault."

"You were a baby. How could it be your fault?"

"I know it logically, but in my heart...I just wish you hadn't done it."

"You wish I let you die? Is that really the outcome you wish?" Death asks.

"No, it's not, but...it would have meant one death as opposed to thousands."

"Losing your baby is a pain far worse than anything else in this world. I hope that kind of pain never touches you. Now, I know you are upset that I didn't tell you, but I will not stand here and have you scold me for saving you. I know a few angels who are glad I did. Your father, your team, not to mention your husband," Death snaps.

Pryor looks at her with wide eyes and a troubled expression. Death lowers her tone and speaks with great sincerity.

"How could you get married and not tell me?" Emmy says in a pained whisper.

Okay, so it's official: we are the worst offspring in the history of the world.

"Mom...we didn't get married to cause problems. We just wanted to be together."

"That's what I wanted for the two of you. That's what we all wanted. And after years of false starts and misfortune, we deserved to see it happen. You robbed us of that. Rage and I will get past it. That's what parents do, get past things even if they hurt like hell."

***

When Pryor and I go back inside the penthouse, Dylan agrees to go with us. As expected, Swoop does not take kindly to that idea.

"No! He's in academia. His power is to appear and disappear at will. He'll be useless in battle," Swoop says.

Ouch.

As soon as the words leave Swoop's mouth, I can tell she regrets it. But it's too late. We can almost feel Swoop's words slicing into Dylan's ego and working their way into his pride. Swoop's statement was more than just embarrassing for the historian; it really hurt.

"Nice to know you think so highly of me," Dylan says in a tight voice.

"I do—I didn't mean…"

"Kiana, I know what you meant. You don't think I'm strong enough to help your team. In fact, you don't think I'm strong enough to handle anything; that's why you left without saying good-bye the last time, right?"

"No, it's not that," she assures him.

"Yeah, whatever. It's fine. I don't need to go," Dylan replies, turning his back towards Swoop as he attends to his books.

Diana nudges Swoop forward and signals for her to say something to the historian.

"I didn't mean that the way it sounded," Swoop says.

"It sounded like you think I'm useless," Dylan says, frustrated.

"No, you're very useful. And that's why I'd like to keep you out of harm's way. You help me see the world in a logical way. You have a million facts and statistics that make me feel like maybe nothing is random, like there's a point to all this. And after losing Key, I need that anchor. I don't want to lose you on a mission. I've lost so much already," Swoop admits.

"Kiana, I get what you're saying, but I want to do my part and help keep you safe," Dylan replies.

"I can protect myself," Swoop reminds him.

"Okay, then what about the humans? And your friend Randall?" he asks.

"Hey, I know you want to help, but you can't be with us in battle. East, say something," Swoop pushes.

"My girl wanted to go too, and I told her she couldn't. It's really not safe," East adds.

"Melody is human. I'm an angel. And just because I spend the majority of my time in study doesn't mean I can't help. But if you don't want me to go, Kiana, then okay."

"Thank you. It would just be better if you stayed here where it's safe. Any luck on finding Ever?" Swoop asks, relieved.

"Yes. She's in an abandoned cemetery in New Orleans, commonly referred to as 'Cracked Soul' Cemetery," Dylan says.

"Great, we'll go get her," Swoop replies.

"You have no idea what's waiting for you there. I have a layout of the cemetery, and thanks to meticulous record keeping, I have lots of information on the creatures you will find there."

"What creatures?" Diana asks.

"For one thing, Fawns have been spotted in that area," he says.

"Fawn?" East replies.

"A Fawn is a creature that is over fourteen feet tall and has a curved back. Its skin is slick gray and spreads thinly across its skeletal frame. Their eye sockets are sunken pools of yellowish pus. The creature's bare skull is exposed and elongated like that of a horse; there are massive spiked horns protruding from its head. The entire lower half of the creature's face consists of jagged fangs, eager to tear into its prey."

"We've come across similar creatures before in the Forest of Flesh and Bone," I reply.

"I'm sorry to say but Fawns are one of a kind," Dylan adds.

"And why is that?" Pryor asks.

"They are the physical embodiment of rage and wrath. Their claws are sloped down and curved so that it's easier for them to gut their victims. The only way to kill them is to cut their head clean off. They are superior hunters. They don't lose in a hunt. Ever," Dylan warns.

"Okay, so we have to prepare for Fawns. Got it. Anything else?" Swoop says.

"A Wintuk. It's a black, scaly, pixie-like creature about seven inches long with red bulging eyes, pointy ears, and translucent wings. It's the mosquito of the demon world," Dylan replies.

"Mosquitos don't strike me as being dangerous," Swoop says.

"Actually, they are the most dangerous insects in the humans' world. They are responsible for spreading malaria, yellow fever, and the West Nile virus. All in all, they have killed millions of humans. It's estimated that every thirty seconds, they take yet another victim," Dylan adds.

"How do you know that?" Swoop says, beside herself.

"I read it somewhere," he says shyly.

"I can't remember the last book I read," Swoop admits.

"That's okay, you have other gifts," he says, unable to take his eyes off hers.

"Like what?" she asks.

"Like that," he says, signing towards the smile on her face.

"Hey, Beyoncé and Jay Z, I hate to interrupt this moment, but can you tell us more about the Wintuks before you two set out on your star-crossed lovers tour?" East asks.

"Oh yeah, sorry. The Wintuks have multiple tentacles in their throats that leap out when they open their mouths. It latches on to the nearest life form, sprays a chemical that liquefies bones, then sucks up the remains. They love it. That's why they are always lurking in cemeteries. They have a thing about 'bone' juice."

"Okay, did 'Jay Z' just say 'bone' juice?" East asks Swoop.

"Yup," she replies.

"How do we kill them?" I ask.

"You squeeze them to death. But that's also the best way for them to kill you. Because if they manage to put their tentacles on you, it's juicing time," Dylan replies.

"He has a way with words," Diana mumbles to Swoop.

"Okay, got it. Anything else?" I ask.

"Yeah, please look out for Kiana," he says sincerely.

"We will do our best," East says.

Dylan smiles, but it's easy to see he's troubled. He looks like he's about to say something but can't quite get it out.

"Dylan, what is it?" Pryor pushes.

"Ever didn't just pick this place at random. She picked a place where she knew she would have the advantage," he replies.

"In what way?" I ask.

"Ever has spent years perfecting her powers and *adding* to them. She's an assassin of the highest caliber. But my research shows that often in exchange for her services, Ever would receive mixtures to enhance her powers. If you go into that cemetery thinking you are facing a mere Quo, you and your team will not make it back alive."

Pryor turns and looks at Swoop sadly. She doesn't say a word, but judging from her expression, she is going to go against Swoop's wishes and take Dylan with us. Swoop folds her arms across her chest and shakes her head angrily. Dylan goes up to Swoop and stands beside her.

"Kiana, I know we haven't known each other long, but you have ownership of a very large portion of my heart. If it's your wish that I stay behind, I will. I have found that it's pointless to go against your heart. But I also know that in times like these, times where darkness threatens to eradicate everything and everyone we love, we have to find it in us to be brave."

"You don't know what these missions can be like. You don't know what they can take from you," Swoop pleads.

"I am no fool. I would never brave the darkness without any light. So if you allow me, I will go on the mission but stay next to you, my light."

"You promise not to be brave or heroic? Or anything stupid like that?" Swoop demands.

"I vow to be an utter coward," Dylan replies.

"Well…okay," she mumbles. He gives her a quick kiss on the cheek, and she tries to downplay it, but she's blushing.

"I think we'll have a few more angels on this mission," Diana says as she looks at her cell.

"Is that Bex?" Pryor asks.

"Yeah, I updated him. He wants to come, but there are riots breaking out all over the UK. Demons are celebrating their impending victory by setting humans on fire. He thinks it's better that he help the Paras regain control. But he's sending four of his top guards to help us on the mission to catch Ever. They are waiting downstairs," Diana replies.

"Great, let's go," Pryor replies as she heads for the door.

"I have a few things that might help along the way," Dylan says as he grabs a backpack and slings it over his shoulder.

When we get downstairs, we find four larger-than-life Paras waiting for us. They look like carbon copies of each other. They are dressed in designer white robes and everything about them is annoyingly perfect.

"Everyone, say hello to the newest members of our team. Otherwise known as One Direction," East jokes.

The Paras glare at East but remain silent as they bow to Diana. She returns their greeting and thanks them for helping us.

"We do as our king asks," the dark-haired one replies.

Dylan addresses the group as we take off. "We're headed to Cracked Soul Cemetery. It's a no-fly zone, so…be ready."

***

We land in New Orleans not long after. We find ourselves standing at the base of a broken, weather-beaten, concrete staircase. The moment we touch the ground, our wings disappear and the sun is swallowed by a horde of dark ominous clouds. It must have rained earlier because the smell of wet earth fills our nostrils. We are surrounded by overgrown weeds and trees in various stages of death.

There's a chipped stone statue off to the side of the staircase, depicting an angel on her knees, praying as two demons on either side of her feast on the "meat" of her soul.

"Charming," East whispers as we walk past it.

At the top of the steps, there stands a black wrought-iron gate with an upside-down symbol of the council. Beyond the gate is a vast cemetery with multiple headstones portraying enraged demons, weeping humans, and tormented angels.

"I think she's in there, waiting for us," Pryor says, motioning towards the back of the graveyard. We follow her gaze and spot a small concrete mausoleum. The humble structure has been ravaged by time. Its walls are water stained, cracked, and mildewed. The only source of light comes from the small broken circular window above the fractured archway.

The darkness deepens as we cautiously make our way across the cemetery. A few feet away, three black crows break the eerie silence by crying out as they take flight. Something with a thin tail and beady eyes darts past us. We survey the area on high alert. I spot movement near Swoop's feet—or at least I think I did. I look again and there's nothing there.

No, something moved just now. I'm just not sure what it was.

It moves again.

What the hell is it?

There's subtle movement on my left. It could have been a leaf or another critter. Maybe I'm being paranoid. This place calls for that kind of crazy thinking.

Wait—there it is again.

This time, there's movement to my right. I turn quickly but miss it yet again. It takes a few tries, but finally I am fast enough to spot where the activity is coming from—the headstones. The headstones are turning in the direction we are headed. Before I can call out a warning, the headstone near Swoop's foot morphs into a vortex.

"Bird, look out!" I yell.

There's no time for her to heed my warning. The headstone sucks up the air around Swoop and tries to pull her into its cavernous mouth. Soon, she's swept off her feet and dangling sideways in the air. She reaches out for me; I grab her with one hand and attach my other hand to the nearest tree. But the vortex is so powerful; I can barely keep myself from getting pulled in.

"Swoop, hold on!" Pryor shouts.

We all band together and desperately hold on to her; unfortunately, the sheer force of the void makes rescuing Swoop almost impossible. The vortex rips the surrounding trees from the ground by their roots and swallows them whole. Small furry rodents and debris go hurtling past Swoop's head as they tumble into the abyss.

"It's a Runt, a hidden portal that takes you directly to the house of fire. If you let her go, she is gone forever," Dylan says in a panic.

"Shut up and pull," East shouts between clenched teeth. The Runt is winning the tug-of-war. Swoop can't hold on with both hands anymore; the suction is just too strong. She can't help it; she lets go of my hand.

"No!" I cry out as I watch the last Noru twin tumble towards her demise.

CHAPTER SEVEN
EVER KNIGHT

Swoop manages to cling to the side of the gravestone seconds before it inhales her. She's holding on by sheer will. The suction is so strong now, all of us are swept off our feet and holding on to headstones and tree trunks. Dylan scrambles to reach his backpack while still holding on to the tree that anchors him. But he can't quite reach it.

Pryor gets the tip of her foot around the strap and drags it over to Dylan. She's not sure what his plan is, but she knows anything is better than watching Swoop die. Dylan uses his teeth and his free hand to open the backpack. He takes out a small glass orb the size of a baseball. Then the historian does the last thing we would have expected—he lets go of his anchor.

We watch in complete horror as both Swoop and Dylan are sucked into the void. The hole closes up and returns to its original state as a harmless headstone. Everything that was airborne drops to the ground, including us.

"What just—did Swoop—how did…" East can't begin to comprehend what's just taken place.

"OHMYOMNIS!" Diana cries out. The four Paras immediately express their condolences. Pryor and I look over at each other, speechless. This can't be happening, not to Bird. And certainly not like this.

"We need to keep going," the dark-haired Para reminds us.

"I agree. We need to keep moving," the blond Para replies.

The other two Paras, with the long hair, add their two cents to the conversation. "The others are right. Let's go," they insist.

"You don't tell my team when to move; I do. And we are not going anywhere without them," Pryor affirms. She doesn't finish the rest of her thought, but she looks at me and right away I know what she's thinking—it can't end like this for Bird.

"You need to be reasonable and keep your team in line, First Noru," the blond Para suggests.

"You are done talking," I warn the blond.

"There has to be a way to get them back," Pryor says frantically.

"They are down in the house of fire now. There's nothing more to be done," the dark-haired Para says.

"We do not abandon members of the team, Para. You need to get that, or you can go back," Diana informs him.

"My Queen, you don't understand—"

"Screw you and the rest of One Direction. My cousin was just killed and—"

A massive fiery explosion erupts from the center of the headstone. The blast lights up the night sky and sends us flying backward into the iron gate. Among the chunks of rubble is an injured but very alive Noru and a rattled but breathing historian. We run over to them and Diana quickly begins to attend to the couple.

"I thought we lost you!" East says, pulling Swoop into his embrace.

"East, it's okay. We're okay," Swoop mumbles. East finally lets her go. She looks down at her arms and legs; she's sustained large cuts and burns all over her body. But Diana confirms none of Swoop's injuries are life threatening.

"How about you, Dylan? Are you okay?" Pryor asks.

"He'll be fine, but when we get out of here, they both should go to the clinic," Diana says as she applies a purple mixture to their wounds.

"How did you get out of the vortex? What caused the explosion?" East asks.

"He used an orb designed to ignite in the presence of evil. It's called the Lady, and it's a forbidden object," the dark-haired Para scolds.

"Yeah, about that…" Dylan says carefully.

"Why is it forbidden? That sucker worked great!" Diana replies.

"It could just as easily have wiped out all of New Orleans. It's unstable. That's why it was outlawed," the blond says.

"To be fair, it wasn't outlawed. It is merely frowned upon," Dylan replies.

"I don't care. You saved Swoop, thank you. How did you know it would work?" East asks.

"I knew that going to the house of fire meant we'd be surrounded by evil and it would go off," Dylan explains.

"So you set it off as you were falling, hoping the blast would be big enough to reopen the void?" Diana says.

"Exactly, and it was. I was right," Dylan replies breathlessly with relief and newfound confidence.

"Thank you for saving her," Pryor says.

"I'm just glad Kiana's all right," he says as he places his bloody hand on top of hers.

Swoop looks over at him, and I don't know what it is Dylan is expecting to see, but it's not what he gets. She glares at him and pulls her hand away; she is seriously pissed off.

"You're not upset, are you?" he asks her.

"Ten minutes! That's how long it took for you to break your promise to me!" Swoop declares.

"Wait—I did what I did for you," Dylan replies.

"You said you would not be a hero; then you get yourself sucked into a void that leads to hell to save me! How is that okay?" Swoop demands.

"I couldn't let you die," Dylan says.

"That is not the deal we had! How could you break your promise to me?" Swoop asks.

"Hey, what's the name of that tree over there? It looks really familiar," East says.

"It wasn't easy for me to do, but I wasn't going to stand by and let you get hurt. And since when is it a crime to come to the rescue? Silver does that all the time for the First Noru. When we get married, that's the way things are going to play out," Dylan replies, paying no attention to East's question.

"Married?! You see, that's the trouble with you. You are always going too fast. You make plans without talking to me," Swoop shouts.

"How can I talk to you? You're always running away," Dylan counters.

"That is so not fair!" Swoop spits.

"There's something about the tree. Where do I remember it from?" East says to himself.

I look over at the tree he's referring to, and right away, I know what the tree is and why it's important.

Oh no...

"Is that a Devil's tongue tree?" I ask Dylan.

"Yeah, it is," he says, taking a quick look in the direction of the tree, then going back to his argument.

"You are always running from us, and I—oh no! That's a Devil's tongue tree!" Dylan says, finally understanding.

"Wait, the same tree that was in Mercy Island? The tree whose sap takes away an angel's powers?" East says.

None of us reply. The four Paras look at each other, and for once they too are silent. The first one to try their power is Pryor. Nothing happens. The rest of us try as well and still nothing. Even Diana has no powers, thanks to Phoenix, whose angel markings are all over her.

"We have no powers!" Swoop says.

"That's why Ever wanted your team to meet her here. You guys are defenseless," Dylan says.

"We need to regroup and figure out—" Before the blond Para finishes his thought, I spot a large creature with horns and curved, bladelike claws headed in our direction at top speed.

"Fawns! We need to go, now!" I shout as I help the team get Swoop and Dylan back on their feet. In a matter of seconds, we are off and running for our lives. We run at breakneck speed, but there's no escaping them. But no matter how fast we are, the Fawns are only a breath away.

The blond Para shouts that he has a Holder, but Pryor warns him to keep running because throwing the Holder will slow him down and get him killed.

"I know what I'm doing, Noru!" the blond shouts back. He turns around and prepares to throw the Holder and imprison the Fawn. But in the time it takes him to raise his hand in the air, the Fawn is already on top of him, slicing into his chest like a blade through butter.

The Para dies with his eyes and mouth wide open.

The dark-haired Para slows down, contemplating going back for his friend. Diana grabs his arm and forces him to keep going. The more we run, the more Fawns begin to appear out of the darkness. There are two of them and then a third who's just joined the hunt. They growl and roar into the night as they gallop towards us.

"We won't make it to the mausoleum. It's too far," I shout to Pryor.

She looks around anxiously for another option. She signals towards a small toolshed hidden behind a cluster of trees. I can feel the Fawn's hot breath on my back as we race towards the shed. We make it to the dilapidated wooden structure, and together, we bash in the door and scour for weapons. "Grab something, anything!" East orders.

Diana and East each grab a shovel. Swoop gets hold of a pickax and hands it to Dylan. She then takes a hammer for herself. The two long-haired Paras wield rakes. The dark-haired one finds a pitchfork. Pry settles on a pair of large pruning shears that are nearly as big as her. I raid an old box of tools in the corner. I settle for a pair of large axes.

Our makeshift weapons would have been great to work with ten years ago. Today, they are all dull and rusted over. But it doesn't matter because there's no time left—the Fawns attack the shed. They come through the ceiling, the side windows, and door. The roof caves in just as we flee.

The Fawn closest to Diana runs after her with unparalleled rage. She takes off down the broken path as fast as she can. The Fawn swings its claw through the air, severing a tree in half. The tree topples over and heads straight for Diana. The dark-haired Para tackles his queen, removing her from the path of the tree. Unfortunately, it places him right in front of the Fawn that was chasing Diana.

The dark-haired Para strikes the beast in the leg with the pitchfork. It howls in pain but doesn't slow down at all. It swings its claws into the air once again, this time managing to make contact. East tries to get over to the

Para, but it's too late—the Fawn skewers him on the tip of his claw.

Seeing this, the last two remaining Paras, now fully enraged, avenge their friend by smashing their rakes into the Fawn's already wounded leg, slowing the creature down. The Paras break the rakes in half and use the handles to jab the Fawn in the knee.

It tumbles down to the ground, but it still has the use of its claws, so East and Diana use their shovels and beat down on the Fawn's wrists until its claws are severed from its hands. The Paras grab the shovels from Diana and East, and together they plunge the shovels into the Fawn's neck and use such force they are able to cut its head off completely on the first try.

A few yards away, a Fawn has Dylan backed up against a tree with nowhere to go. Swoop takes her hammer to the back of the Fawn's leg, but she isn't wielding enough strength to get his attention. The Fawn sees the terror in Dylan's eyes and enjoys it so much he makes the terror last longer by getting within inches of Dylan's face and roaring thunderously.

I run to help them, but another Fawn rams into me from the side and sends me flying headfirst into a headstone. Blood gushes out from my forehead like a damn spring. My vision starts to blur, and when I try to get up, I fall back to the ground. I force myself to focus on finding my weapon as the Fawn that attacked gears up for a second strike.

Fuck! Where the hell is the ax?

The Fawn charges towards me like a pissed-off bull on steroids. That's when I spot one of the axes lying on the ground behind the Fawn.

Seriously?

I have only one move to make. I ignore the pain in my head and the screaming muscles in my body, gather up all my strength, and stand up. I cry out in frustration and anger as I run towards the Fawn as fast as I can.

The Fawn, fed up with playing with its food, opens both claws and swings. Just before we crash into each other, I drop down to the ground, slide between the creature's legs, and reach for the ax. As the Fawn turns around for round three, I fling the ax with everything I have left in me and hope to Omnis it lands. It does, right in the center of that bastard's head.

Round three, my ass!

I look towards Dylan, fearful that Swoop was not able to save him. Swoop couldn't get Dylan to safety, so she placed herself in front of him. The Fawn bears down on her; it lowers its head and rams her with its horn.

"Swoop!" Dylan cries out behind her. Swoop's body starts to go limp. As I run over to them, I spot Pryor quickly climbing the top of the tree near Swoop and Dylan. She leaps off the tree, shears in hand, and lands on top of the Fawn's head. The creature shakes wildly in an attempt to throw her down to the ground. Pry holds on but drops her shears. She improvises by snapping a branch off the tree and stabbing the Fawn in the eye.

The pain makes the creature even more volatile. It throws Pryor off and sends her down to the ground. She falls hard on her back and calls out in pain. The Fawn, no longer concerned with Swoop and Dylan, focuses on Pryor. It cuts through the air with its claws then stops midstride. It looks down at the pool of black blood dripping from between its legs. Pryor found the shears. The Fawn collapses. East stomps on it hard with all his might, and the Fawn's head cracks open like a watermelon.

***

Diana stabilizes Swoop enough so that she can be moved. Together, we head towards the mausoleum. We are about a yard away when Dylan stops us and points to a trail of pixie-like creatures invading the corpse of a crow. They open their mouths, and their tentacles leap out and turn the crow's body into an empty shell.

"We should be fine. They're busy with the bird. Just don't step on them. They have an inner alarm system. When one of them is killed, they all track the source and invade it. So whatever you do, don't step—" We hear a *crunch*, like crispy leaves crushed under the weight of a shoe. But there are no leaves near us. We all look down at Dylan's foot. He raises it, and under his shoe is the remains of a Wintuk.

The army of critters turns in unison towards the sound of their fallen friend. They immediately take to the air and come after Dylan. They swarm him like hyped-up, psychotic bees. They emit chirp-like sounds as their tentacles pop out and latch on to Dylan's face.

We snatch them off Dylan as fast as we can, but when we get rid of one Wintuk, three more appear in its place. Dylan lets out a bloodcurdling scream, and a Wintuk latches on to his eyeballs and starts to drain him. I yank the bastard off Dylan's eyes and squeeze it until its eyes pop out.

The colony of Wintuks double their efforts to eliminate us. They send a cry into the air and hundreds more Wintuks appear from every direction and swarm us. They aren't just on Dylan; they are attacking all of us. When their tentacles attach to my skin, it feels like getting kissed by a chainsaw.

The more they suck, the weaker we're getting. We are being forced down to our knees. We fight them off as hard as we can, kill hundreds of them, but there are just far too many to make a difference. If we don't find a way to kill them all—fast—we will die here. The being that's most affected by the Wintuks is the Para with the longest hair. He must have been weak already from the battle with the Fawn, and now his body has given up the struggle almost completely.

The Wintuks pick up on that and send out a hideous cry to alert the others to triple their efforts on the weakened Para. Soon, thousands of Wintuks are descending upon him. There are so many of them on him, we can't see him anymore.

"GET AWAY FROM HIM," Diana rages.

She grabs hold of the sharpest twig she can find and jabs herself in the leg, so deep we can see right through to the bone. She hollers in pain, but her plan works. The Wintuks are drawn to the sight and smell of her bare bones. They flock to her and leave the weak Para behind. But by then it's too late. The Para is nothing more than a layer of skin.

Without warning, the Wintuks start to flee. They scatter in the air and fly away as fast as they can. They leave in droves and don't even look back at the corpse they were feasting on. We look around, shocked by the creatures' sudden departure. The last Para runs to tend to Diana. Pryor helps him while I look everyone else over.

"What the hell made them run away so fast?" East asks.

"Aw, I'm afraid that was my fault," someone says pleasantly above us.

We look up and there's an extremely pale woman hovering in the air. She has on bloodred lipstick, with matching eye shadow. Her hair is dyed sterling silver and swept up in a stylish bun. She wears drop diamond earrings and a spiderweb-patterned necklace that wraps around her throat and is encrusted in rubies. Her flowing red satin dress highlights her devilish figure. I would never have known she was related to the Face, if it wasn't for her eyes. They both have the very same eyes.

"The Wintuks fled because they have a very keen sense of death. They know that there is going to be a whole lot of death here very soon," Ever says as she lands a few feet away.

Pryor marches up to her, and before she can get close, Ever flicks her wrist and a current of red lightning leaps from her palm and lands in the center of Pryor's chest.

"Pry," I shout as I run over to her.

She mumbles that she's okay.

"Of course she's okay. What fun would it be to kill her in one little zap?" Ever asks innocently.

"Just because we know your sister doesn't mean we won't kill you," I warn her.

"My sister…everyone thinks she's so proper and so righteous. Ha! She's a first-class, grade A bitch!" Ever informs us.

"Okay, she took Fate from you, but that was forever ago. Can't you let it go?" Diana shouts between labored breaths.

"Oh, I can. And I will. Because I have something she loves. And I'm going to destroy it in front of her. Oh, Barbara, come on out, honey!" she shouts towards the mausoleum. She swings both her hands wide in the air and all four of the mausoleum walls come tumbling down. Standing in the middle of the tomb, tied to a cement pillar, is Ever's sister, the Face.

Right away we run to help her, but Ever sends her red lightning straight for us. It picks us up off the ground and binds our hands, feet, and wings in the air. Nothing we do loosens the red current holding us captive.

"Barbara, don't fall asleep now. I know the mixture I gave you is strong, but you're gonna want to see this for yourself," Ever informs her sister. She then turns and focuses on us.

"Now, my employer said to keep you all alive because he wants to have the pleasure of killing you. But I don't know if I can resist," Ever admits.

"Screw you and your demon boyfriend, Malakaro. I will kill him. I promise you!" Pryor screams.

"Malakaro? No, no, no, dear. He's stuck in that little bubble. I'm sure he'll get out and be very upset that my boss got to you all before he did, but, hey, if Malakaro wanted the Noru dead, he should have hired me," she says with a bright smile.

"Then who hired you?" East demands.

"You know, I really didn't come to answer questions. I came to put on a show," Ever replies with a cold laugh.

"You're gonna end us anyway, so just tell us," Diana says.

"Fine. My boss is the guy who wants to bathe in your blood. The guy who has earned his retribution the same way I earned mine," Ever replies.

"So does this dick have a name or what?" I push as Pryor silently signals to me.

"He's referred to as the Architect, and he wants all of you so bad…it's a shame, there won't be much left when I'm done," Ever says sadly. She then turns her attention to the Face.

"Alright, Babs, it's showtime!" she says as she sends a strong current at her sister's chest, shocking her from her mixture-induced haze. The Face wakes up and is horrified to find us bound in midair, about to be killed.

"Ever, don't. Please!" the Face begs in a weak voice.

"Begging! Yes, that's good, Babs, but let's start out properly. Let's let the kids know what they're in for. I hear we have a historian with us. Dylan, is it?" Ever asks.

Dylan glares at her but doesn't respond. Ever zaps Swoop with such force, she howls in agony. "Okay, okay, I'll do whatever you want. Please don't hurt her," Dylan replies.

"See, there. That wasn't so hard. Now, over the years, I have acquired some very useful powers. But none of them are as much fun as the power I was born with. The humans actually have a garden that replicates my power very well. Care to tell them about it?" Ever says.

"There's a garden in north London called Alnwick Garden. It's comprised of the most lethal plants in the world. It has everything from hemlock to ricin. The plants and flowers there are so poisonous, visitors are forbidden to smell, touch, or taste anything. It's so dangerous that the humans place the plants behind a cage," Dylan replies.

"And what does that really mean, historian?" Ever asks.

"Ever has a million different kinds of virus inside her. The merciful ones kill instantly. But there are some that could leave you paralyzed; some that could make you hallucinate or, worse, drive you insane," Dylan adds.

The Face begins to beg Ever again to let us go. Ever enjoys the torment in her sister's voice and smiles like she's getting her picture taken.

But as Ever continues to bask in the glow of her evil, something odd starts to happen to me. My strength is returning. I can feel sparks of fire igniting between my fingers. I turn to Pry and right away I can tell she's feeling the same thing. Her powers are also returning. I look down at the ground and then I begin to understand. We are no longer on the ground, so the sap that inhibits our powers is no longer affecting us. In her eagerness to capture us, Ever took away her advantage without realizing it. Pryor signals to me and wants to know if I'm ready. I'm stronger but still need a little more time. I shake my head no. So she nods and tries to buy us more time.

"I can see why Fate picked her over you. You're kind of an asshole," Pryor says.

Ever blasts her with two hands. I go to retaliate, but even in her pain, Pry shakes her head no. She knows we need more time for our powers to return. But the sound of Pry screaming as her body is electrocuted is pure hell for me.

I will make sure this chick dies screaming.

"Ever! Please. I'm sorry. I'm sorry I hurt you. Please…" the Face begs yet again.

"It's so unfair to pay all this attention to only one angel. There are so many of you. But don't worry, I have enough love for you all," Ever says as she summons a flood of red plasma-like waves at all of us. Our screams fill the sky and make Ever downright giddy.

"Yes! That's it, kids, let's have fun!" she says as she blasts us yet again.

"Everly-Ann, take me. Hurt me. Not them. They're just kids. Please, please," the Face says, howling for mercy on our behalf.

That's when I feel it—the spark in my body now has the capacity to be a full-on fireball. I signal to Pryor and she silently agrees—it's time to strike. She signals to Diana, who starts to tease Ever.

"Hey, bag of crazy, did you ever ask your sister what it is she does better than you? I mean, what does she have that you don't? I'm guessing a lot of things. For one, she must have killer moves in bed. I mean, Fate is still chasing her ass," Diana taunts.

Ever, newly enraged, turns to the Face and physically starts to bash in her face.

"Aaden, now!" Pry orders.

I send two fiery orbs at Ever. She dives down to the ground just in time to avoid being set on fire. East, now able to access his whip, throws it out and catches Ever by her neck. He starts to drain her strength.

"We can't get down. If we do, we'll lose our powers again," Diana says.

"I can hold you up, but I need help," the Face says weakly.

"I got it," the last Para replies as he forms a glowing orb and sends it towards the Face. The orb strengthens the Face and adds to her ability to move objects. The Face is now removing the red current that binds us and is keeping us airborne.

"You're a booster. You can enhance other angels' powers?" East says to the last Para.

"Yeah. Why? Can't all boy-band members do that?" the Para says bitterly.

The Face places us down on top of the concrete rubble that used to be the walls of the tomb. "You should be okay here," the Face says, exhausted. We help free her and make sure she's okay.

Pryor drags Ever by the whip around her neck. "Now, let's talk," Pryor says.

"You think it's over? You don't know anything. My boss is going to drink your blood and make you pay!" Ever shouts.

"Maybe, but not today. Today, you're going to tell us where we can find your boss and get the ashes back," I warn her.

"I'd rather die," Ever spits.

"Ever, please. Talk," the Face says.

"Screw. You," Ever says hysterically.

I grab her by her neck. "You watch how you talk to your sister," I bark.

"Silver, my favorite tortured soul. The Architect likes you best of all."

"What the hell are you talking about?" I demand.

"He's very fond of you. The two of you share such a deep connection."

"I've never met anyone called the Architect. I don't have any idea who he is," I shout back at her.

"No, but you are very familiar with his work."

"Ever, where are the ashes we need to defeat Malakaro?" East roars as he tightens his hold on her.

"You'll never get it out of me," she vows.

Pryor kneels down on the ground beside her, their faces only inches apart. "If you don't tell me who the Architect is and what he did with the ashes, I will kill you. Right here, right now," Pryor promises.

"You're prettier up close. I can see why the Akon offspring married you. You think he loves you, don't you? Idiot. They don't know how to love. No one does. Guess I'll have to show you," she says as she blows Pryor a kiss. She exhales, and red snowflake-like fragments emerge from her mouth and land on Pryor's face. We are expecting blood and guts or whatever crazy things her viruses do. But nothing happens.

"That's it? That's the best you got?" Pryor says.

Ever just laughs.

"I really tried with you, Ever, I really did. You just couldn't bring yourself to let go," the Face says sadly.

Ever looks up at her older sister with ire and shouts from the depths of her soul.

"It's been years. You are my little sister. I love you. Why? Why can't you let this go?" the Face pleads.

"I LOVED HIM AND YOU TOOK HIM FROM ME! I WON'T STOP HUNTING THE NORU DOWN BECAUSE YOU CARE ABOUT THEM. I WILL KILL THEM. IF NOT TODAY, THEN TOMORROW

OR THE NEXT DAY. I WILL NEVER STOP! I DON'T CARE HOW LONG—" A pair of large shears cuts through the air with deadly precision and embeds itself in the middle of her forehead. I look over at the being who fatally stabbed Ever—the Face.

She looks back at us and explains her actions in a sad, but resolved tone. "No one threatens my family."

As we start to gather Swoop and Diana, both of whom are badly wounded, my conversation with Ever comes back to me. And as we make our way to the clinic in Hawaii, I can't help but think there's something I'm missing. Ever's words come back to me.

"Silver, my favorite tortured soul. The Architect likes you best of all."

"What the hell are you talking about?" I demand.

"The Architect is very fond of you. The two of you share such a deep connection."

"I've never met anyone called the Architect. I don't have any idea who he is," I shout back at her.

"No, but you are very familiar with his work."

We enter the clinic and right away the Healers begin to tend to us. But my mind is still on Ever. What did she mean when she said I was familiar with the Architect's work? The answer comes to me suddenly. It brings with it a sharp coldness. I'm shaking, but I don't realize it until East points it out. The room is going in circles. There's a pain in my chest that makes it hard to remain standing. Pryor walks over to me.

"Aaden, what's wrong? What is it?"

"The Architect," I reply breathlessly.

"You know who the Architect is?" Diana asks as the Healer fusses over her wounds.

"No, I don't know who he is, but I know what he designed..." I reply as the color drains from my face.

Pryor makes me sit down; she places her hand in mine. She speaks with a deeply concerned voice. "Aaden, tell me; what did the Architect design?"

"The White Room."

CHAPTER EIGHT
GET READY!

Flashes of the White Room bombard me. I try to block them out and focus on the present. I remind myself that the Center has been destroyed and that everything is fine now. But that doesn't stop my thoughts from traveling back. Suddenly, in my mind, I see the stark white room where I was forced to watch Pryor die over and over again.

I flash back to all the times she "died" in the cruel simulations played out in the White Room. There were times Pry died by fire. Times she died of blood loss and other times where there were pieces of her on the ground. I run to her and press my hand against her wound, but I can't stop the bleeding. I see her blood spreading out on the cold floor, and in the middle of the puddle, I spot my reflection laughing at me. It's repeating the same thing over and over again.

"You will always lose what you love. Always."

"AADEN!" Pryor shouts, ripping me back from my horrid thoughts.

"I'm here," I reply, looking around the room. The Healers are fussing over us. They've managed to fix our wounds and stop the bleeding but warn us as they exit the room.

"Your team needs to recuperate," the head Healer suggests.

"Yeah, we will," Swoop replies.

"Are you okay?" Pry asks me.

"Yes, I'm good," I mumble.

"Are you sure the Architect built the White Room?" Diana asks.

"Yes, I'm sure," I reply.

"That means this guy is skilled with mind games and we are screwed," Swoop says.

"I feel like we haven't gotten anywhere," East confesses.

"We know who Ever was working for, and we can use that info to our advantage," Diana replies.

"Diana's right. We need to comb the streets and see what we can find out about the Architect. Who is this guy? Why does he want to kill us?" Swoop says.

"Whatever his reasons, they must be personal," Pryor says.

"I was thinking the same thing. The Architect went through a lot of trouble to get the ashes and draw your team to him. I'm guessing he has plans for you all," Dylan adds.

"And you've never heard of him before?" Diana asks Dylan.

"No, but I can go back and check my files again," he offers.

"That would be good, but I also need you to see what you can find out about the virus that Ever gave to Pry," I reply.

"The Healers looked me over and they said I'm fine. I show no signs of a virus at all," Pryor reminds me.

"That doesn't mean you're okay. I know she did something to you. She's a walking poison garden. She wouldn't have bothered to blow you a kiss if it wasn't going to hurt you in some way," I reason.

"Silver has a point, Pry. She blew you a kiss and we saw red snowflakes, and I'm guessing they weren't there to wish you a merry Christmas. Dylan, please go and have a look for us," Swoop says.

"Absolutely. Oh, and about what I said in the graveyard about us getting married…" Dylan begins.

"Yes?" Swoop says as if expecting him to change his mind.

"How do you feel about a winter wedding? I mean, everyone likes spring, but winter has always held more wonder in my opinion. What do you think?" he asks her.

"I think we really need that info. Please, can you go find out for us?" she says gently.

"Okay, but we're not done," he says with a sly smile as he leans in and gives her a quick kiss. He takes off and tells us he'll come back as soon as he finds something. Once he's gone, we all turn to Swoop.

"What? C'mon, we don't have enough going on? Do we need to plunge into my love life?" she says.

"You're right. It would be childish to stop in the middle of this mission and ask you what's up with you two. But guess what? I'm feeling very immature," East says with a big grin.

"Me too! Immature all the way!" Diana replies.

"I can't marry him," she says.

"Why not?" Pryor asks.

"Because…I just can't," Swoop says, shifting her weight.

"So you want to, but something's holding you back. What would that be?" East pushes.

"Yeah, Swoop, out with it. Tell us why you're pushing him away," Diana says.

"He's so sweet and he knows just about everything. And did I say he was yummy? Because he is," Pryor adds.

"And he saved our asses on the mission, Swoop. He's perfect," East says.

"Say yes to him," Pry says.

Diana quickly chimes in, "Oh, it would be nice to have a winter wedding. I have the perfect dress—"

"There isn't going to be a wedding," Swoop snaps.

"Bird, what's wrong?" I ask.

"What's wrong is we all live together, work together, fight together—that's fine—but once in a while, we need our space. *I* need my space, a part of my life that's just mine. So please, just back off," Swoop says, and she starts to storm off when Diana shrieks.

We all turn and look at her in total confusion.

"What is it?" I ask.

"Nix! He's ready! I mean, I'm ready. He is—I'm—OHMYOMNIS!" Diana says as she holds out her palm. We look at the markings; they are complete. Her son is ready to come out of his protective shell and join the world. The Healer, having heard Diana shouting, enters the room.

"Come, we'll take you to the Original who will help you match the pattern on your hand to your son's cocoon," she says.

Diana gets out of bed and beams back at us.

"Do you want us to go with you?" I ask.

"Yeah, but you guys should stay and finish getting Pryor checked out. And also we need to stay on track and find the Architect," she says.

"You shouldn't be alone," East says.

"Yeah, and we want to see Phoenix as soon as he opens his little eyes," Swoop says.

"You will. Bex and I will get him and be back here as soon as we can," she promises.

The Healer takes her hand and the two of them start to walk out. But just as she passes through the doorway, Diana turns back. She looks at me with a sad smile. It's like she thinks this is all too good to be true. I know that feeling very well.

"Hey, it's okay. You did it. You protected Nix. He's all yours now. Yours to love and take care of. And Sparks would have been so proud of you," I whisper as I lean in. Diana and I had always been close, but after losing a child together, we formed a bond that could not be put into words. I hug her and congratulate her. The next time we see the former Kaster, she will be someone's mom.

***

The news of Nix's impending arrival is all anyone in the room can talk about. But given what still needs to be done, we are forced to contain our excitement and get back to business. Pryor orders Swoop and East to scour the streets for information while Dylan is looking over past journals in his penthouse.

I want to hit the street and see what I can find, especially since nearly an hour has passed since we have been here. But I have a feeling my wife would leave the clinic as soon as I turn my back. That can't happen. We need to be a hundred percent sure that Ever's virus is really nothing.

Pry doesn't share my concern. She keeps rolling her eyes and sighing dramatically. I ignore her and continue with what I'm doing—looking at her arms and legs in search of any marks. Finally she has had enough and pulls my hand away from her.

"There are no marks on my body. I am fine. Maybe the virus Ever sent me failed because she was dying. Maybe I'm too strong to be affected. Or maybe Omnis cut us a break," she says.

"Were you always this impossible to take?" I ask.

"No, I had to grow into this. It took time," she teases.

"Okay, okay. I will stop, but you can't leave that bed until Dylan comes back and says he didn't find anything," I reply.

"Fine. Hey, I've been calling your dad and he's not getting back to me. Is he okay?" she asks.

"Yeah, but he's really pissed at us for getting married without him and your mom present."

"Did you tell him it was all your idea and that the blame is yours?" she asks.

"What? Why would I do that?" I ask.

"Honey, your father is already mad at you. Do we really need him to be mad at me too? C'mon, take one for the team." She laughs.

I shake my head and smile at her. "I think we should get married again—just for them. That way they don't, you know, kill us," I suggest.

"That sounds like a good idea. It'll be nice," she says.

"Okay, I'll tell our parents and hope that gets us off their shit list."

"Speaking of parents, I've been thinking about us having kids," she says carefully.

"Really?"

"How can I not? I'm surrounded by new moms."

"Okay, so what are your thoughts on the issue?" I ask.

"We just got married. We have so much going on. And demons don't ever stop. It would be totally illogical to even think about having a kid right now," she says.

"Oh…yeah, well, that makes sense," I whisper. Her words make my chest tighten and my heart sink. I was only a father for a short time, but it changed my life. I want to feel that again as soon as we can. I think we would be good parents. Pryor and I are almost always on the same page, and we've known each other all our lives.

"Aaden, I'm kidding. Let's be illogical," she says with a sly smile.

"Seriously? You want us to have a kid? I mean, I know we've talked about it before, but you're saying you really want to?"

"Well, we already had sex with no Tam. Was that an accident?" she asks.

"I wasn't thinking about it; turns out seeing you naked makes it hard to focus. So blame your breasts," I reply.

She laughs and places her hand in mine. She tells me that she remembered the Tam and that it was okay not using it. In fact, she was more than okay.

"So we are really gonna have kids?" I reply with a stupid grin.

"Yes, right after we save the world and Randy. And if we happen to get a visit from a certain bird before then, we will deal with it. With our luck Alexi will come right in the middle of a battle," she jokes.

"I could see that happening. You'd have a Powerball in one hand and Alexi in the other," I reply.

"I know it's crazy to do it so fast, but we got married fast. And well, it's always going to be something. The fact is all we have is now. And right now, I want to have your Sib. She'd have your smile and my eyes. She'll joined an all-boys sports team and crush it! She'll be amazing," Pry says gleefully.

"Why do you think our first kid is going to be a girl? It could be a boy," I remind her.

"Nope, us girls are stronger. We're warriors. And that's what our child will be. I'm good with a boy too, but I gotta tell you, I'm thinking our first will be a girl."

"Well, it doesn't matter if we have a boy or a girl, I just know one thing: our baby will have to face a difficult, unreasonable horror," I warn her.

"Yeah, I know. Demons at every turn—"

"I'm not talking about demons; I'm talking about something far worse—Comic-Con. Randy will force our kid to go with him every year. How can we put a kid through that?" I tease.

She laughs and vows that she will not let Randy dress our kid up in anything with a cape. "I can see Randy now—'Pry, Wonder Woman is an icon. We have to let your daughter wear the cape,'" Pryor says, doing her best Randy impression. We laugh together. But then she grows quiet.

"You okay?" I ask softly.

"Yeah, I just really miss him. I want him to be in our lives, Aaden. I want him to give our child the same thing he gave me: an indestructible friendship. I want our daughter to run to him when she thinks we're being unfair—which, if she's anything like me, will be all the time."

"She's going to have that because we are going to save Randy. I have no doubt about that at all. He's gonna have keys to the house and insist on taking our daughter to get her very first gaming system. I can see her jumping up and down, excited. Destroying everything in Roslyn because Uncle Randy is gonna take her out," I reply.

"She's going to wreck the house and crash into things as she learns to fly. Only Omnis knows what her powers will be, but whatever they are, it will be a major headache. I can't wait!" she tells me.

I study her face. She's glowing with happiness at the mere suggestion of being a mom.

I've watched her grow from an emotional little girl to a strong-willed leader. There were times I wasn't sure she'd be able to handle all the heartache that came with being Noru. But she did it. She endured losing her baby brother, a member of her team, and now her father, the light of her life. But she fought so hard to come back from all of that. She worked to get past the pain, no matter how much there was of it. If our kid is a tenth as strong as her mother, I'll be happy.

Speaking of Marcus...

"Hey, I have the perfect name for our kid," I inform her.

"Oh really?" she says suspiciously.

"Yeah, I think you'll like it."

"And it works for a girl or a boy?" she asks.

"Yup, got you covered."

"Okay, Noru. Spill it. What will you name our first child?" she pushes.

"I thought we could name her something that has a special meaning to you, something to honor Marcus. Our first child's name will be...Summit."

Tears spring to her eyes in a matter of seconds and she reaches out for me and wraps her arms around my neck. She's shaking as she cries in my arms.

"Does that mean you like it?" I ask as I wipe away her tears.

She nods, too overcome to talk. I give her a few moments so she can collect herself. Soon, she's beaming.

"Aaden, Summit is perfect! It's just absolutely perfect. My dad would love that we're naming our kid after a place that meant so much to him," she says.

"Your dad said *summit* represents 'quiet strength.' I can't think of a better message to send our kid into the world with than those two words. She'll have her father's rage and wrath, but her mother's heart and courage," I reply.

She places her hand on the side of my face and pulls me into her all-consuming kiss.

"Hey, hey, stop that. If I can't get some because we're stuck on a mission, then neither of you can," East playfully informs us as he enters.

"Sorry, we're just celebrating being parents," Pryor says.

"OHMYOMNIS! Where is she? Where's Alexi? We need to get ready!" East says in a panic as he looks for the silver bird around the room. We lovingly laugh at him.

"Calm down, East. Alexi is not here. We're just thinking ahead," I reply.

"Oh, please, you two can't keep your hands off each other. It's a wonder Alexi isn't perched on top of Pry's skull right now," East replies.

"We haven't been that bad," I counter.

"Are you kidding me? The only way I've been able to practice my new power is by working on blocking your attraction to Pry. Silver, if I wasn't exercising some serious control over my powers, I'd be tapping into your hormones. If that happened, you'd need the Omari to pry me off your wife."

"Hey!" I warn.

"What? I'm just saying I'm mastering my powers and you two—need to get a room," East jokes.

Swoop enters the room, excited. She starts speaking right away and can barely contain herself. "Guess what? I know where to start looking for that creepy designer bastard! But first, I'm sorry about yelling at you guys before. I was just stressed out," she says.

"It's okay, Bird. We get it. Tell us, what did you find out? Did Dylan come across something?" I reply.

"I haven't heard anything from him yet, but one of my other contacts did come through," Swoop says.

"Does your contact know who he is?" East asks.

"No, but he told me about a demon who was hired to get materials for the Center. And that's what he called his boss—the Architect. He told me where I could find the demon," she replies.

"Yes! This is our first good lead. Let's go," Pry says as she hops out of bed.

"We still don't know if you're okay," I remind her.

"Aaden Grey, look at me. I'm fine. We need to go. Now," she says, sounding official.

"Okay, but when this mission is over, we're coming back here to make sure you're really fine and that the virus didn't take," I assure her.

Dylan enters the room, looking concerned. He tells us he didn't find anything that would help us find the Architect.

"Don't worry, Swoop has a lead," I tell him.

"That's good," he says, sounding preoccupied as he walks closer to Pry and focuses all his attention on her.

"Dylan, what's up?" Pryor asks.

"I didn't find out anything about the creator of the White Room, but I did find out about Ever's virus," he says.

"And?" I ask.

"First, just give me a second," Dylan says as he takes Pryor's hair and lifts it off her neck, allowing us to view a small mark embedded there. It's a small wavy line with three slashes going through it. Dylan looks at it and sighs deeply.

"What is that?" I push.

"That's the mark of a very rare and very powerful virus, one nearly as old as time itself. It's called Sheba's kiss, named after the vicious demon who invented it," Dylan says.

"Is it—I mean, is she…" I can't bring myself to finish the thought.

"No, this virus won't kill her," Dylan says.

"Okay, that's good," I reply, relieved beyond belief.

"Will it hurt Pry in any way?" Swoop asks.

"No, there is no physical pain to Sheba's kiss," Dylan says.

"Then why do you look so stricken?" Pryor asks.

"Um…it doesn't give you any pain, but it does something else," Dylan says.

"Dylan, please! Just come out and say it! What does Ever's good-bye virus do?" Pryor demands.

"It prevents you from having children—ever."

CHAPTER NINE
TAKE EVERYTHING

"Aaden, let him go!" Swoop screams frantically. It's only after hearing Bird's voice that I realize what's happened. In a blind rage, I tackled Dylan and pinned him to the wall by his throat. My face is inches away from his; the fury that swells up inside me is more than enough to destroy him.

"You're lying! You're lying!" I shout as I squeeze him even harder. His face is pale and his eyes are bulging out of his head. He struggles to move his head and signal to me that he's not mistaken. But he has to be wrong; he has to be wrong.

"Silver, he's not lying. I can sense him. He's sorry. He's very sorry, but it's the truth. The virus does what he said it does," East reasons.

I look into Dylan's eyes and see that he is sincere. This is really happening. I let go of him and back away.

I can feel the flames rising from every inch of my body. Blue fireballs spring to my palms and threaten to engulf everyone around me. I pull the door handle with such force the concrete around the doorframe starts caving in. I storm out to the hallway, and by the time I get to the window, I am engulfed in blue flames. I take off into the sky with absolutely no idea where I am going.

I end up somewhere in Russia, in the middle of a dense forest. I can't remember burning so many things down so quickly. As I set the forest on fire, I curse Omnis to hell. I hurl my anger out into the heavens above. I vow to Omnis that I will hate him so long as I am alive.

"This is bullshit! This is complete bullshit!" I shout to the bastard in the sky.

"YOU TAKE EVERYTHING FROM ME! EVERYTHING! ARGH!" I yell as I kick, stomp, split, and smash everything in sight. I load up to incinerate another acre of land, but before I can strike, I spot a demon land a few feet away.

"Dad, go away!" I order him.

"I can't. You need me," the Akon replies.

"No! What I need is a way to get to Omnis. That sick fuck has taken so much from me, from Pryor. From all of us!"

"I know, son."

"You don't know. You have no idea."

"Pryor texted me, said it was an emergency. I called her back and she explained what happened."

"Really? Then explain it to me. Because I really don't understand this shit. All we do is try to help people. Why does he keep punishing us for it? Huh? What kind of sick fuck is Omnis? He only gets off when he's taking things away from us."

"Yeah, I've gone a few rounds with those same thoughts. I get it, Aaden, you know I do."

"I just need to know why. Why does he hate me so much? What did he get by taking Sparks from me? Why did he take my little girl? And now that I finally put my life together, now that I finally get to be with the girl I love, why would he take away the possibility of having another child?" I demand as I set a trail of flames blazing through the woods. I can't break or set anything else on fire. I'm exhausted. But I don't know what else to do. So I keep destroying things, the same way Omnis keeps destroying me.

"I don't know why this crap is happening. But you can handle it. I know you can. You're my son; that means you can handle anything. Don't forget that."

"We named her—Summit. Pryor and I we were just talking about…we *named* her."

"I'm sorry. I know about losing the ones you love. I grieve for your mom every day. Every day. It would have been easier to lose my damn wings than to have her taken from me. But I found some good in this world too."

"Really? And what would that be? Because from where I stand, this is all shit! All we ever get to experience is death, blood, and more death. So tell me, Dad, what's good about it? Because I can't see the good. Since Mom died, what has made your life worth living?"

"You."

I start laughing ironically. The weight of everything comes down on me—hard. I drop to my knees and cry out in utter despair and frustration.

"Dad, just go…let me be gutted and miserable by myself."

"You can be as down and out as you want. You can even set the world on fire if that's the shit that needs to happen. But you will never be by yourself," he says as he sits beside me on the ground silently as the forest burns around us. He smiles sadly and mutters something to himself.

"Summit Case, she would have been something."

***

A short while later, I make my way back to the clinic. I enter the room with the busted door and find the team gathered around Pryor. When I enter, all eyes are on me. I turn to Dylan and address him.

"About what happened earlier…" I begin.

"It's okay. Don't worry about it. The body processes anger and disappointment in a myriad of different ways. It's totally normal," Dylan replies.

Okay…

"Yeah, well, it was a crappy thing to do and I could have hurt you, so…sorry," I reply.

"I can take it," he says, trying to add bass to his voice.

I turn to Pryor, who is looking out the window and has been ever since I came in.

"I need a minute alone with Pryor," I announce.

"Yeah, we'll go ahead to the location of the demon and look around, make sure there are no nasty surprises for us," Swoop offers.

"No, I don't want you guys going without us. We have to do this as a team in case things go wrong. Hang out in the hallway. We'll be out soon," Pry says.

"Got it, boss!" Swoop says as she leads everyone out of the room.

Pryor and I are officially alone. I walk over to her, and although she's only inches away from me, I can't read her face. I have no idea what she's thinking and that troubles me.

"I shouldn't have taken off like that. It was…stupid," I admit.

"Is anything left standing in the forest?" she asks.

"Some…"

"I think the demon we're headed to meet is a strong lead, but I don't want us to put all our hopes on him. We should also seek out the demon's friends and associates. That way we have options," Pry tells me.

"That's a good idea. Babe, can we talk now?"

"We are talking," she reminds me.

"No, I mean can we address what Dylan told us?"

"Yeah, it sucks."

"That's it?" I ask.

"What else is there to say?" she asks.

"I don't know…I just thought you'd want to discuss it."

"Well, you took off before Dylan finished telling us everything. The virus latches itself onto the part of the soul that is responsible for creating Sibs. So when we had sex in the car, if a Sib was forming, the virus would stop it from reaching the point of growth needed to get Alexi to come to us. So…I guess that's it. No baby. It's okay, they can be kind of a time suck, actually," she says casually.

"Pry, why are you saying that?"

"It's true. I mean, I wanted one, but…hey, it's no big deal. Now, let's go kick some demon ass, okay?" she says as she races for the door.

I stop her and turn her towards me. "Pry, you don't have to do this with me. I know how hurt you are. I am too. Don't shut me out."

"I'm not. I'm just choosing not to be a wreck about this. That's all. The girl was just an idea and it didn't pan out."

"Summit."

"What?" she says, confused.

"Her name would have been Summit."

"Oh, yeah. Right. Okay, let's go," she says as she exits the room.

I follow her out into the hallway, where we find Diana and Bex waiting in the center of a crowd full of Healers and the team. But the being the crowd is interested in is not Diana, it's the baby angel she holds in her arms—Nix.

Phoenix Cane looks exactly like his father, or what I picture Malakaro must have looked like as a kid. His big dark eyes are full of life. And as he looks at the world around him, they light up with glee. He has plump chubby cheeks, just ripe for squeezing. And his stubby little fingers point to everything with fascination and wonder. He's wearing a white onesie with gold trim. On the front of his outfit, it says, "I rule. No, seriously. I do."

He bounces up and down excitedly as he meets the team. He longs to be set free so he can explore everything around him. He pouts when he realizes he won't be able to escape his mother's hold. The only thing cuter than this kid's smile is his angry face. He scrunches his forehead, determine to show us he's upset, but doesn't quite make it.

"I know, Nix, I know. But I can't let you go. Your wings aren't strong enough yet," Diana reasons with her son.

Nix points at two birds flying just outside the window. He summons them to him and they enter, ready to do his bidding. We laugh as we watch Nix try to figure out a way to use the birds' wings to support his efforts to fly away from his mom.

"Okay, okay. Here, play with this," Diana says as she hands him a glass box with a small orb. If you focus enough, the orb will turn into various shapes.

But Nix is not ready to give up his dream of flying away from his mom's hold, so he tries to get more birds from outside to join us. When he can't see them through the trees, he points his finger at them and turns the trees into dust. Now he has full access to the birds that were hiding there.

"Nix! That's not nice. Leave the birds alone. They have to play too," Diana says as she kisses her infant's forehead. She gently blows on his face, and he starts giggling. While he's strong enough to reduce timber into sawdust, he's not strong enough to maintain his displeasure with his mom. In fact, he soon gives in and is in full laughter mode.

Diana passes Nix around and the team are instantly in love. When Diana hands him to Pryor, she declines but smiles and says he's adorable.

"You don't want to hold him?" Diana asks, sounding wounded.

"I just…yeah, sure. Of course," Pryor says as she opens her arms and Diana places Nix against her chest. He is fascinated with the color of her hair. He runs his fingers through it and starts cooing with excitement. He reaches out for her, trying to get higher and closer so he can get a good look at the main attraction—Pryor's purple eyes.

She holds him closer like he wants and his mouth opens wide in shock. Pryor's eyes seem to offer the biggest surprise for Nix. He puckers up and kisses his auntie and then beams at her. Tears begin to well up in Pryor's eyes. She rushes over and hands him back to Diana.

She takes off out the window and I follow her. She lands somewhere in New York City. We're only a few miles from where Malakaro and the Alago are being held. Pry scours the area, looking for something or someone. When I ask her what she's looking for, the pain in her voice is undeniable.

"My mom. I know she's here somewhere. I have to tell her—"

"Pry, what is it? What happened?" Death says as she lands near us.

"How did you—"

"Fate. I think he's trying to make up for what happened with Ever. He said to be here at this time. Talk to me, honey, what's wrong?" Death asks.

"I'm sorry I was such a jerk to you. I didn't get how much you could love someone and how awful it would be to lose them. I took it for granted that my mom saved my life. And now Omnis is punishing me. He won't let me have babies. But I already saw her, Mom, I saw her in my head. She's beautiful. She has pretty eyes like you and long hair and she loves me…Summit loves me and I will never get to meet her," Pryor says as she sobs in her mother's arms.

I knew it bothered her to hear the news about not being able to have children. And as hard as she tried to act unaffected, it's killing her. I step far enough away that the two of them can talk but stay close enough in case she needs me.

Pryor explains everything to her mother and confesses that she's shocked by how much the news hurts her.

"It's stupid, I know. I mean, it's not like I have to have a kid to be valuable," Pryor says.

"No, you don't," Emmy says.

"Then why do I feel so…empty?"

"Motherhood is a gift. But not having children doesn't make you any less important."

"I just keep seeing her out in limbo somewhere, waiting for parents she's never going to have. A family she will never know…it wasn't supposed to go this way. What did I do wrong?" she cries.

"You didn't do anything wrong. This isn't a punishment. Sometimes things just…my baby, come here," Death says as she holds her weeping daughter tightly.

"I just want to meet her, Mom. Even for a few minutes."

"I know. And there was nothing that could be done?" Emmy asks.

"No. The virus latches onto my soul. We can't pull it out of me—wait! I have an idea!" Pry shouts.

"What is it?" Emmy says.

"Aaden, gather the team at the warehouse. Moments after we execute my plan, we'll go look for the demon," Pryor shouts to me.

"Wait! What plan?" I shout as she takes to the air.

"The plan to save our daughter!"

***

On our way to the warehouse, Diana reluctantly drops Nix off with Mrs. Maybelle. It's hard for her to fly away from him, but Swoop takes her hand and assures her she's doing the right thing. Mrs. Maybelle has looked after a bunch of kids and she'd give her life if it meant saving one of them: angel, demon, whatever. Mrs. Maybelle loves kids.

By the time we land in front of the warehouse, I've called and texted Pryor three times. She says she's on her way and not to worry. But the fact that she has to tell me not to worry…worries me.

When we enter the warehouse, a figure appears from the corner and walks towards us. We are all on high alert and ready to strike, when we realize the being in front of us is a friend. He's one of the most powerful angels of our time. He's an Original angel. I've always liked him; he isn't as rigid or stuffy as the others. In fact, he's a die-hard gadget lover.

"Raphael, what are you doing here?" I ask.

"I came to see the Kon," he says.

"What is it?" Bex asks in a commanding voice.

"It's about your son—the one who isn't really yours," the Original says.

Bex and Diana look at each other in a sudden state of panic. Bex walks up to the Original with certainty and claims Nix as his son. Raphael smiles a little but says nothing.

"If you have an issue with my son, then say it," Diana says protectively.

"Not at all. I saw the little Toren. I can see why he's worth all this trouble," he replies.

"What's a Toren?" Swoop asks.

"That is what the angel world is calling the children of the Noru. Although to be honest, we didn't think we'd need to find a name so quickly. You know there's no shame in waiting to become parents," he says.

"You're right. It's not like life is short or anything," Swoop says, rolling her eyes.

"You're right, and life will be even shorter for your son if the angel world learns who his father really is. But that's exactly what will happen once the demon Kador gets done shouting to the world that Phoenix belongs to Malakaro."

"Who's Kador?" Bex asks Diana.

"He's a friend of Kill's. He threatened to expose the truth, so I killed him. But he said he had an accomplice that would tell my secret," Diana replies.

"Why didn't you tell me about that?" Bex says.

"I thought he was lying. I had no idea his friend was real or that he would really expose Nix. Are they out to get him? The angels? Do they want my baby? What's gonna happen to him—I have to go!" Diana says as she prepares to take off.

"Wait!" Raphael says as he takes her arm and gently brings her back towards the team.

"Kador approached the Originals with his claim that Nix doesn't belong to Bex. It's easy enough to prove. Since Nix would be a Kon, there is an internal mark that will shine from within him, proving his royal bloodline. Nix will not have that mark," he replies.

"What do we do? Can we replicate the mark at all?" East asks.

"You would need a special pendant called a Lure. And it's been like a hundred years since anyone has seen one," Dylan says.

"Maybe we can find it," Swoop says.

"But we don't have time for that," East reminds her.

"So, what? Let the Paras do what they will with Nix?" Diana says.

"You know I won't let anything happen to Nix. Why don't you trust that by now?" Bex asks.

"Because I don't know how far your desire to stick it to Pryor really goes," Diana says.

"What are you talking about?" Bex pushes.

"You're keeping me and Nix safe because you want to show Pryor that she picked the wrong guy. That you're the good guy. But how far is that desire going to extend?" Diana says.

"You really think that's why I'm helping you?" Bex says.

"How could I think anything else? Everything you do has to do with her. I figured this did too," Diana adds.

"Wow, thanks so much for letting me know what kind of angel you think I am," Bex says angrily.

"You have helped us so much. I am grateful. But it's like you only think about Pryor and not about us. By that I…I mean Nix," she says, avoiding his eyes.

It's then that Bex finally gets it. Diana hasn't been pretending at all. Being with Bex has been real for her. Real in ways he never even thought about until now.

"Diana, are you…" He doesn't finish. He just looks at her, not sure what else to say.

"Hey, I'm sorry to cut short our weekly episode of 'things everyone realized but Bex,' but how are we going to protect Nix?" East says.

"When do they want to test him to see if his markings are like that of a Kon?" I ask.

"It's already been done. They got an Original to officiate the process at Mrs. Maybelle's the moment you dropped him off," Raphael says.

"What did they do to him? Is he hurt?" Diana demands.

"No, he's fine. It's not painful," the Original swears.

"Who did the procedure?" Bex asks.

"I did. That's how I know he's not really a Kon," he replies.

"You told them he's not a Para?" Bex says.

"No, the pendant I referred to has been in my family for some time now. Once I saw Nix had no markings, I distracted everyone and used it to simulate the symbol. Kador was killed for lying to the Originals and trying to cast doubt on the Kon," Raphael explains.

"You did that? You saved my son?" Diana asks.

"The Noru have dealt with a lot. You guys don't ever get a break. I know what that feels like. I'm a gamer; I know pressure," he says proudly.

"Thank you for helping Nix," Diana replies.

"There's always going to be rumors about Nix not belonging to the Kon, but nothing that can be proven. In fact, I'm guessing the Toren will have a whole new shit storm to face," Raphael replies.

"Raphael!" Pryor shouts as she flies into the warehouse.

"Carrot!" he says as he embraces her. Pryor's family has always been fond of Raphael because he helped out the Guardians when they desperately needed him. In fact, without him, they would never have been able to save the world.

The very same world we are in danger of losing yet again.

Raphael heads back to help the rest of the Originals fight a band of demons who are attacking in the Middle East. As soon as he's gone, Pryor turns to us and we give her an update. As soon as she's caught up, she takes my hand and addresses me with newfound excitement.

"I think I got it!" she says with a big smile.

"Got what?" I ask.

"What did Raphael call the next generation of Noru again?" she asks.

"Toren," I reply.

"Well, there are two Torens now: RJ and Nix. But if this works, someday, hopefully soon, there will be a third Toren." She beams.

"What are you talking about?" I ask.

"I found a way to beat the virus," Pryor says as she wraps her arms around me.

"How?" Dylan asks before I can.

"So this Sheba virus latches on to part of my soul and that stops it from creating any Sibs. And there's no way to pull it off me, right?" Pryor asks Dylan and Diana.

They nod their heads in agreement.

"But what if we don't pull it out, what if we destroy it by sending something after it?" Pryor says.

"You mean a mixture to dissolve it somehow?" Dylan says.

"Pry, there are no mixtures that can do that. I checked after I learned about your condition," Diana adds sadly.

"Not a mixture—a creature," Pry says carefully.

I have no idea where she's going with this, but I'm sure I won't like it. I walk closer to her and look in her eyes.

Yeah, I'm sure as hell that I will not like this.

"Pry, how do you plan to get rid of the virus?" I ask.

She takes out a glass vial the size of her index finger. Inside it is one of the most lethal weapons ever created—a Sive. It's a chrome-like spider that eats through flesh and bone to get to the soul. Once released, it's unstoppable.

"And what do you plan on doing with that thing?" I ask.

"Swallow it."

CHAPTER TEN
OMNIS KNOWS

I look at my wife, fearing that she has truly lost her mind. The Cane women have been known to do crazy, risky things; Emmy once leaped off a building with no powers at all in order to help on a mission. But this, *this* is insane.

"Pry, are you suggesting we stand by and watch you ingest a Sive?" Swoop asks.

"If you look closely, you'll see a bluish glow in the creature. I had it submerged in a liquid tracker. That way when it goes inside my body, we can track its movement and know where it is at all times. Once it gets to the center of my soul, it will eat the virus, and the mark that represents the virus will fade," she says as if it's no big deal.

"And how are we supposed to get it out of you?" Diana asks.

"Use this suction tube," Pryor says, holding out a foot-long glass tube to show us.

"Do you have any idea how many things are wrong with what you just said?" I ask.

"No, this will work. Diana, tell him," Pry pleads.

"Technically, it could…" she replies.

"You can't be serious," Swoop scolds Diana.

"I'm not saying we should do it; I'm saying it's possible that it may work," Diana offers.

"The Healer is right, a Sive could eat away at the virus, but that doesn't mean you should take it. It could eat faster than you anticipate, and it would then end up killing you," Dylan reasons.

"Or it could work and we get to save Summit," Pry says.

"I can't believe we're even having this conversation. Pry, you're not doing this. We are not risking your life," I protest.

"You don't want to save our child?" she accuses.

"There is no child. Summit is an idea," I remind her gently.

"Really? So you burned down the world for just an idea," Pry counters.

"Pry, I want us to have a kid too. I want us to be a family, but I am not willing to risk your life for someone that doesn't exist. This is crazy."

"Aaden, you don't get it. Summit could be amazing…" Pry says.

"We had sex in the car with no Tam. That was before we encountered Ever. There's a chance you might already be pregnant," I reply.

"If you'd stuck around, you would have heard all the details of the virus. Tell him, Dylan," Pryor urges.

Dylan turns to me and speaks with great reluctance, given what happened to him the last time he gave me bad news. "Even if a Sib was conceived during your last…intimate encounter, the virus would stop the Sib from growing large enough to be detected by Alexi. So even if the First Noru did get pregnant in the car, you two will never see that child. If the Sib isn't allowed to grow, it will get smaller and smaller until…" Dylan says, bracing himself for my reaction.

I rake my hands through my hair in frustration.

"So it's possible that we would have a kid, but she's being blocked," Pryor says as she reaches out to me.

"But it's also possible nothing happened. It's possible Alexi was never coming for us," I reply.

"So what? Maybe I didn't get pregnant from what we did before, but what about the next time or the time after that?"

"Pryor—"

"No! Look, I'm not baby crazy. If we can't have one now, that's okay. We have our whole lives ahead of us. But Sheba's kiss doesn't mean we can't have kids now. It means we can never have one. NEVER!" Pryor shouts.

"Baby, I know how hard this is on you. Believe me. But I can't let you do this. I can't let you inhale something that will kill you. Don't ask me to do that," I plead as I take her face in my hands.

She steps away and shakes her head. "This is the only way. I have to do this. Please support me," she begs.

"I can't. Pryor, you are not taking that Sive," I demand.

"I have given everything to these missions—my family to missions, my friends, my whole life. I will not give up my future. That's what Summit is, Aaden. She's a symbol of life after the team."

"Pry, stop."

"Can't you see her now, squeezing her hands into fists as she tries with all her might to soar in the sky but only getting as high as your knee? She'll look at you with pretty purple eyes and beg to learn to fly as high as Daddy. And you'll teach her, just like you did for Swoop."

"Pry…stop it," I reply again, trying to block out all the images she's pushing on me.

"We'll raise her in the house you built for me. I'll train her on the same field my dad trained me. Maybe she'll have your power over flames, maybe she'll inject fear into her enemies with just a look, or maybe she'll move things with her mind like your mother. Aaden…don't you want to meet our baby?"

"I SAID STOP IT!" I rage as I pick up the nearest chair and hurl it across the room. I throw it with such force it embeds itself into the wall. Everyone in the warehouse is startled, including me. I didn't stop to think about what I was doing, I just wanted her to stop putting images in my head. The same images I would have to watch disappear once the reality set in.

"You. Are not. Swallowing. A Sive," I inform her in no uncertain terms.

"You can say whatever you want, but you and I both know you want me to do this," she counters.

"I want you to risk your life?" I shout incredulously.

"Yes, because you want that feeling back. The feeling you had when Diana told you that you were going to be a dad. At first you freaked out, but then, it made you happy. It's like a light came on inside you. And you looked at Diana with this glow of admiration, it was more than romantic love, it was a never-ending, eternal love. The kind that comes from sharing a child."

"I won't stand here and act like I'm good with Sparks being gone or act like

I'm okay with us never having a kid. But I am sure not okay with letting you die for something that may or may not work," I reply, trying to calm down.

"Please, please let me try this," she begs.

Seeing the pain in her eyes makes me want to concede and give her whatever she wants. But I can't do that, and it's fucking killing me. "Pryor, give me the Sive," I order as I reach my hand out.

"Fine, I'll give it to you if you answer just one question," she offers.

"What is it?"

"Does not having children change how you see us?" she asks.

"Pry, I love you. That's not gonna change," I vow.

"Answer the question: does this virus change how you view us?"

"Well…no."

"DON'T LIE TO ME! JUST SAY IT! SAY THIS CHANGES US! THIS CHANGES EVERYTHING!" she yells.

"Alright, fine! It does change us. I had the same picture in my head that you did. I saw the same things and I wanted them too. Now that picture has changed. I wish we could undo what the virus did but not like this. Not with your life on the line," I snap.

"My life is always on the line! Just once I want to risk my life for something other than the world. Something just for me, for us," she counters.

"I know it hurts like hell. I can't even begin to explain how familiar I am with what you're feeling. But you are not taking that Sive," I assure her.

"Yes, I am. This is our future," she calls out desperately.

"You ingest that Sive and there is no future. You will die. I can cope with never being a dad again, but I cannot live without you. Now hand over the Sive," I reply.

"But Aaden, I—"

"Pryor, hand me the vial. Now," I order.

She angrily throws the vial at me. I catch it before it hits the ground and put it in my back pocket. She leans against the wall and softly cries. The team quietly steps outside so we can be alone. I walk up to her; she pushes me away. I come back again. And again, she pushes me away. That doesn't stop me. I keep coming towards her.

She rages and cries out, saying she hates me. She pounds her fists into my chest furiously and demands that I stay away from her. But I keep trying until I am finally close enough to hold her against my chest. She struggles for a few moments, but then she gives in. She sobs as she buries her head in my chest. We cling to the only thing we have left, each other.

***

Pryor asks for a few moments alone. I hate walking away, but I know what it's like to want space. So I leave her inside. The team looks concerned as they watch me exit the warehouse alone. I assure them everything is fine and that Pry just needs a few minutes.

"What about you? Are you okay?" Diana asks.

"No, but I'll deal with that later. We are really behind on this mission, and if we don't speed things up, it could be our last one," I warn.

"If it helps, you can spoil Nix all you want," Diana offers.

"Thanks," I reply.

"I'm sorry I could not find a way to fix this. I looked over all the records pertaining to the virus. It's just so rare," Dylan says.

"You know what, let's just get off this subject and focus on finding the demon we need to get to the Architect. Here, Diana, take the vial of Sive. I don't want it to fall into the wrong hands," I instruct as I go into my back pocket to fetch the Sive. There's nothing there. Alarm washes over me as I dig into my pocket once again.

"Damn it!" I shout as I race back towards the entrance of the warehouse. The team follows close behind and asks what's going on.

"Pryor took the Sive from my pocket," I shout as I try to open the door. It's locked.

"Pry, open the door!" I yell as I pound my fist against it. The door is made to withstand massive amounts of pressure just in case we are invaded. There is a panel in the center of the door, where I can place the tip of my wing and the door will recognize that I am a member of the team. It will then open and let me in. However, that's not happening right now.

"She must have jammed it from the inside," Swoop says as the rest of the team pleads with Pryor to open the door.

"I'll go around back," Bex says as he races past us. He tells us she's locked all the windows.

"This is crazy, Pry! You know we'll get in there sooner or later," East reminds her.

"I know, I'm counting on that," Pry shouts from behind the window in the center of the door.

"Pry, don't do this. Don't take the Sive!" I beg as I pound even harder.

"I'm sorry, I have to," she says as she raises the vial up to her face and studies it. The chrome spider moves around excitedly as if it knows it's about to feast on a Noru soul.

I slam my body against the warehouse door as hard as I can. It shakes, but the door doesn't give way. Bex sends one Powerball after another at the door, but it's holding steady.

"I can make a larger orb. It would be far more powerful and it will take the door down," Bex tells Diana.

"It'll also take the First Noru down with it," Diana reasons.

I look at Pryor's desperate face through the reinforced glass window. "Pry, please, please don't do this," I reason.

"Monitor me and make sure you don't pull out the Sive until the mark of the virus is gone. Please," she says.

"It's gonna kill you, Pry. Don't do it. If you love me, baby, you won't do this," I plead as I place my hand against the cold glass. She places her hand against mine and mouths the word "sorry." She then opens the vial, takes the Sive out, and holds it between her fingers. She leans her head back, opens her mouth, and swallows the Sive.

"NOOOOOOO!" I scream. She falls to the ground and can no longer be seen through the window. The interference she was causing to the door is gone. I can now enter using the tip of my wing. I quickly rush into the warehouse and find Pry on the floor, convulsing.

"We have to steady her so the Sive doesn't run wild in her system," Diana says as she tries to pin her down.

"Get the tube. We have to get this thing out of her," I shout.

"Silver, she's already ingested it. You might as well try it her way," East reasons.

"No! This thing has been inside her for seconds and she's shaking from the pain!" I reply.

"She wants this to happen," Diana says.

"I don't care what she wants. I am not letting her die!" I reply as I reach for the glass tube and try to find the perfect extraction point.

"No! If you pull it out of her right there, it will tear through her stomach and she will bleed out," Diana says.

"The Healer is right," Dylan says.

"Then help me, help me save her," I beg.

The Sive is moving quickly through Pry's body. It leaves a faint blue trail in its wake. Diana tries to track the movement of the Sive, but that bastard is moving so fast, it's nearly impossible to nail it. The Sive slides down Pry's upper body, hungrily eating its way through flesh and bone. Pry twists and writhes in agony. She screams like she's being eaten alive, which is exactly what's happening on the inside. I can hear the bones in her body breaking as the Sive makes its way towards her chest. East tells us that the mark of the virus is starting to fade. I don't care, because at this rate, Pry won't live long enough to be a mom.

Pryor is gray because of the internal bleeding. Her body can't process the amount of pain that's surging through her, so it tries to find salvation the only way it can—by trying to black out. But fading to black is a luxury the Sive will not allow. Pry bangs her head against the hard cement floor even harder. There's no denying it, she would rather die than experience the agony she's drowning in.

I hold her head so that she doesn't crack it open. East and Swoop try to keep her body steady. Bex and Dylan try to find a steady point on Pry's body to aim the tube and suck out the Sive, but again it's moving faster than they can aim. Every time they target a location, the Sive turns in a different direction. The Sive is eating away the virus, but it's also eating away at her soul, just like we feared.

"Wait! It's slowing down," Dylan says, relieved. Diana studies the shadow of the Sive under Pry's skin closely. Something strange is happening. The Sive is going right and left at the same time.

"No, no, no, no, no!" Diana shouts at the creature.

"What's happening?" Swoop yells.

"The Sive—it's splitting itself in two," Diana says.

"It replicated itself! I didn't know they could do that," East says.

"It's growing so much from her soul, it's now strong enough to do just that," Dylan says.

"That means she's gonna die twice as fast," East whispers to himself. I tune him out. I tune everyone out and focus on Pryor.

Diana shouts, "I got it!" as she manages to pin one of the Sives with the tube in her hand. She presses it against Pry's skin and the tube begins to suck out the Sive. It's fighting like hell to stay inside Pry. The more the creature struggles, the more pain Pry is in.

"She can't take much more. If we don't get both of them out of her right now, she's dead," Dylan says.

I don't think about what I'm about to do, I just do it and hope it's not a mistake. I summon a sharp blade and it appears in my hand in seconds. I raise it above my head and bring it down on my wife's chest, cutting her open.

She is immediately bathed in blood. But we now have a clear view of the two Sives. I dig the tip of the blade into Pry's body and scoop out the two Sives. Bex catches them and places them in the vial as I pick Pryor up and take to the air. But as I look at her nearly lifeless body, I know she will die before I can make it to the clinic. I have no choice but to land at the nearest human hospital.

I race towards the entrance and burst through the double doors. When the humans see me enter with a bloody body in my arms, they are shocked. And since Pry has no control over her body, she can't conceal her wings. This makes the humans lose their shit. They go into full-on panic mode. Some of them scream for their lives. Some of them faint at the sight, and others get on their knees and pray.

I place Pry's body on the counter and beg them to save her. They just look back at me as if they are in some bizarre nightmare.

"HELP HER!" I yell, shaking with rage and desperation. The nurses and doctors are snapped out of their shock and quickly go into action. They place her on a gurney and wheel her into the operating room.

"EVERYONE STAND STILL," someone orders from the entrance.

I turn around and see Fate at the door. He has paused the entire hospital. He signals for me to look behind him; he has come with six Healers. He orders them to the room where Pryor was taken. He instructs them to be quick and stabilize her enough so that she can be taken to a clinic. The Healers agree and get to work.

***

It takes almost half an hour for the Healers to get Pryor stable enough to be transported. Fate sends the Paras to wipe out the humans' memories and clean up. I arrive in the clinic as the Healers race to get Pryor ready to be worked on. The team shows up moments later. They bombard me with questions. I don't reply. I hear and see them, but it's like the team is far away, too far for my voice to reach them.

"Silver!" East says loudly.

I turn to him in a complete daze.

"They are prepping her for surgery to try to repair what's left of her soul. Do you hear me?" he asks.

I nod but say nothing. I walk towards the operating room, but Diana stops me.

"They can't have you in there," she says.

"I have to be there…I…I have to…"

"They can't let you in there because you're soaked in blood. So let Swoop help you change and then you can come back," Bex says.

Swoop takes my hand and guides me into an empty hospital room with a private restroom. She hands me fresh clothes she just purchased. The blood on my shirt makes it stick to my skin. As I peel it off me, flashes of Pryor's blood-soaked body invade my mind. I lean forward on the sink and close my eyes, hoping the flashes will go away. They don't.

Swoop helps me take off my shirt and she keeps telling me that it will be okay. But we both know she's lying. I look down at my hands. They are dripping with Pry's blood. I hear someone crying. It takes a second to realize it's me. Sorrow drags me down to the cold floor, sobbing. Swoop holds me tightly. I cry out from the deepest depths of grief.

"Bird, Omnis knows how much I love her, so he's gonna take her from me. Just like he took my mom, Sparks, and Marcus…He's gonna take her away…"

BOOK II

PRYOR REESE CASE

"To handle yourself, use your head; to handle others, use your heart."

-Eleanor Roosevelt

CHAPTER ELEVEN
THE REAL WORLD

"Randy, you seriously can't tell me that you have room for yet another hamburger," I scold. He smiles as he unwraps the fourth burger and takes a large bite. I shake my head and wonder where the hell he stores all that junk food.

"If you don't slow down, you'll choke," I warn.

"Hey, my body and I have an agreement. It accepts the fact that I like McDonald's, and I accept the fact that no matter how much I work out, no part of my body will ever be muscle," he replies.

"You're impossible," I tell him as I pluck a fry from his tray and dip it into the clump of bright red ketchup. As I soak the fry, I could swear the ketchup was human blood. I tell Randy about it. He dips his finger into the red sauce and tastes it.

"Nope! Just plain old ketchup. Are you sure you're okay?" he asks.

"Yeah, just imagining things, I guess."

"I think today is the day—I'm gonna ask Key to marry me," he says with certainty.

"Wow, really?"

"Yeah, I won't have another chance like this," he says.

"What's so special about today?" I ask. He doesn't reply; he just grins and shoves more food into his mouth.

"Before I go talk to Key, can I get a jetpack that propels me into the air like Iron Man? But I don't want it to be red. I think that's a little…flashy. Wait, you know what, let's do flashy! Screw it! Get me a red jetpack," Randy says.

"And where would I get a—" Before I can finish my thought, a shiny red

jetpack appears in the center of McDonald's dining area. Randy runs up to it and starts to strap it on.

"Wait, where did that come from?" I ask.

"From you, the best BFF that ever lived. Thanks, Pry!" he says.

"No, seriously, Randy. How did that get here?" I push.

"Pry, I asked you for it, and you made it happen. This is your world. You get whatever you want."

"I don't understand. Okay, whatever. Randy, my chest hurts," I reply as I place my hand against my chest.

"Oh, don't worry about that. I'm off to propose to Key. Any words of advice for me?" he asks.

"Um...I don't know," I admit.

"You could say good luck," he replies.

"Yeah, good luck."

"Like I need it. She will always say yes because you want me to be happy. And Key makes me happy."

"But I thought Key was..."

"Dead? Yeah, she was and now she's not. Thanks, Pry!" Randy says as he takes off on the jetpack.

"No fair! Where is my jetpack?" someone asks behind me.

I turn and see Sam standing in front of me. My heart races as I run to him. I pick him up in the air and spin him around with tears in my eyes. Suddenly the McDonald's is no longer there. We are now in the Guardian home. We're inside Sam's room, and he's putting his PJs on for bedtime.

"I thought something happened to you," I say as I go to hold him again.

"Not me. You. You're bleeding," he says.

I look down at my shirt and it's soaked in blood. But I can't tell where the blood is coming from. I want to go check my wounds, but I don't want to leave my little brother alone. Suddenly I hear a familiar chuckle behind me.

"Hey, Carrot! You can go. I'll watch the little guy," the voice says.

"Tony!" I shout as I hug him. Tony-Tone has always been our fave babysitter. He let me skip bedtime, eat all kinds of angel junk food, and taught me how to play poker. He smiles and tells me Sam is in good hands with him. Sam is already jumping up and down with excitement at the thought of hanging out with Uncle Tony.

"Okay, I'll be right back, Sam! And, Tony, his bedtime is in exactly ten minutes," I warn him.

"Yeah, I got it. Bedtime, half hour," Tony replies.

"Tony..." I scold. But the two of them are already playing, so I decide to let it go.

As I leave the room to clean up, Sam calls after me. "Pry," he says in his sweet, soft voice.

"What is it, Sam?"

"Dad wants to talk to you. You better hurry or you'll miss him. He's going on a mission," Sam says before he rolls over in the bed and falls asleep. I run out of his room and down the steps to where my parents are saying good-bye.

"Dad! You're here!" I say as I run to him and embrace him.

"Wow, I've never gotten this big a hug from you. What rule have you broken?" he says, smiling.

"I haven't broken any rule. I just miss you, that's all," I reply, still holding him.

"Carrot, don't lie to your dad," Mom says.

"What did she do?" my dad asks.

"She keeps trying to change the death list," Mom replies.

"Pry, the death list is not a game. If someone is on it, you have to leave them on it. Otherwise—"

"Marcus, you have to go. The team is waiting for you. You know how much Rio hates when you're late. He sulks and gets in a foul mood," my mom reminds him.

"Yeah, he's so temperamental. You'd think Winter would have had a calming effect on him," Dad replies.

"I'll talk to her about calming him down when I see her at the charity event," Mom says.

"Is Ameana going to be there?" Dad says.

"She better be. We already told her she needs to take a cold shower. Her and Rage hardly leave their bedroom. I swear those two are in heat all the time," Mom says.

"Okay, I gotta go. We're headed for a no-fly zone and Jay's driving. That puts far more fear in me than any demon ever did," Dad says as he starts to take off.

"Dad, wait! Stay with me," I beg.

"I'm always with you. Always. But you need to say good-bye," he says.

"I don't want to say good-bye to you," I reply.

"Me? No, I'm already gone. Say good-bye to him," he says as he takes off into the air.

I look in my arms and a baby suddenly appears.

"Who is this?" I ask.

"This is Summit. Or at least that's what Aaden said. Summit. A boy. Strange," Mom says.

"This is Summit? This is my son?"

"Naturally," Mom replies.

"Is he the one I have to say good-bye to? I can't. I can't say good-bye to him. Mom, help me!" I reply as the baby starts to fade away.

"Did you forget about Jason?" Mom asks.

"Is he the reason the baby is fading? You tell Malakaro this: I will kill his son if it means saving mine..."

"Now, Pry, that's not very nice. And anyway, Summit won't exist because you refuse to stop playing around with the list. You want to save Summit and save everyone, then say good-bye," she orders.

"Say good-bye to who?" I beg as the baby dissolves into nothingness.

"Him," Mom replies as she changes my surroundings and sends us into the middle of a pond in the forest. There are dozens of frogs hopping around from one lily pad to the next.

"What are we doing here?" I shout. But my mom is gone. I'm in the woods by myself. A dark looming figure comes before me. It's Aaden. I call out to him, but he walks past me and goes into the pond. There's a dark void in the center of the water; Aaden is headed straight for it.

I run to stop him, but I'm stuck on the muddy shore. I can't move my feet. I call out to Aaden, I beg him to stop, but he walks into the void and disappears.

"NO!" I cry out. Someone appears next to me suddenly. It's Fate.

"Please, help me!" I shout.

"First, you should close that, you're letting all the flies in," he says.

"Close what?" I ask.

"Your chest," he says.

I look down and my chest has been carved open. My guts are seeping out and sliding down my body. The flies are making a feast of my organs. The frogs spot me standing on the shore and they start hopping towards me. Soon, I'm being invaded by hundreds of frogs and flies. I fall backwards onto the muddy ground. I try to throw the creatures off me, but they are ravenous.

Fate calls out to me just before he disappears. "Say good-bye to one, or say good-bye to all."

The thing that yanks me out of my dream is pain. It reaches into my skull and digs its razor-sharp claws into me, dragging me kicking and screaming back to the real world. And in the real world, I am severely injured.

There are bones in my body that were once connected to each other, but now no longer touch. There's sharp and intense pain traveling through my chest; it hurts so much, I'm a few seconds away from calling for my mom. I try to calm my mind and focus on the figures in the room. I can make out the team but not much else. Soon, I am overwhelmed by the pain and am forced to give in to the darkness.

***

I don't know how much time has passed since I blacked out. There are no clocks on the wall. It could have been hours or just a few minutes. It's hard to say. My chest feels better, but certainly not back to normal. There's a dull ache that serves as a reminder of the severe pain that came before.

I feel like a thousand Soul Chasers tore into me, rendering me with no more strength than that of a toddler. I can't pick up my own head, let alone defend myself, should a demon attack. It takes all my strength to open my eyes.

The first face I see is that of my husband. The angel who I let down when I decided to swallow a Sive. He's relieved that my eyes are open and that I'm alive. But behind his relief, there's a rage that is strong; it's damn near bouncing off him. The rest of the team stand around my bed, looking worried and concerned.

"I'm okay," I tell them. I wanted my voice to sound strong and clear. Instead, it sounds weak and raspy.

"You scared us," East says, sounding very upset.

"Didn't mean to. Sorry," I reply, finding the sheer act of talking almost too daunting.

"It was so stupid to do what you did without us being by your side," Diana scolds.

"I know," I reply.

"You tell me you need me on the team, you make me stay away from my son, then you go and put your life on the line for a kid who doesn't even exist?" Swoop says, deeply disappointed.

Summit...

The first thing I want to do is ask if the Sive worked. Did I manage to get rid of the virus? But I don't ask. I'm afraid of what the answer will be. What if the Healers come in here and tell us nothing's changed? Should I just have someone look to see if the mark of the virus is still there? No. I don't want an answer now. I mean, not right this second.

"I know I said we should go together, but given the circumstances, you guys should go after the demon without me. If he leads you to the Architect, send me the info and I'll join you at the location," I reply. From the corner of my eye, I can see Aaden shaking his head, irritated as hell.

"I know I'm not strong right now, but I will be by the time you guys come back from tracking the demon," I assure him.

"Pry, we already went to look for the demon. Silver instructed us to go while the Healers were working on you," Swoop says.

"Did you find him?" I ask.

"We got there too late. He found out we were looking for him and went into hiding," Diana says.

"Shit! Can't we have the Paras look for him? Better yet, the Omari?" I ask.

"The Omari have their hands full. They've lost three members of their team in a battle on the border between China and North Korea. Evil has always had a strong hold in that region but now, things are completely out of hand. In the two hours you were knocked out, thousands of angels have died, not to mention humans and Quo," Bex says regretfully.

"Bex, I'm so sorry," I reply.

"Yeah…I just came to make sure you were okay. But I can't stay, I have to get back to the front lines," he says.

"You need to take a rest or at least drink a few vials to give you energy," Diana says to Bex, sounding very concerned.

"It's fine. I can handle it," Bex replies.

"I know you can. But still, drink this. It'll keep you strong. I don't have time to come save your royal ass," she teases as she hands him a vial. Bex laughs despite himself. The two of them look at each other in an odd way. It's like they forget we're in the room for a few moments. Bex tells me to do whatever the Healer says and then he takes off.

"So our only lead is gone?" I ask.

"Yeah," Dylan says sadly.

"Damn…" I mutter softly to myself.

"ASK ABOUT THE DAMN VIRUS!" Aaden shouts at me.

"Silver!" Diana says.

"WHAT? THE VIRUS IS ALL SHE CARES ABOUT! SHE RISKED HER LIFE AND THE WELL-BEING OF THE ENTIRE WORLD, AND NOW SHE DOESN'T EVEN WANT TO KNOW?" he demands, full of wrath.

"I do. I just wasn't sure I would get the right answer," I admit.

"It wouldn't matter. You'd just keep going until you got the right one. That's just…who you are," he says bitterly as he stomps out of the room and slams the door behind him.

"These past few hours have been rough on him," Diana says.

"On account of you totally playing him and doing the one thing he told you not to do, and forcing him to have to stab you in order to save you. And essentially forcing him to come face-to-face with the most horrible situation he's ever had to face," East says. We all look at him.

"What? Hey, Randy isn't here, so it falls on me to recap. You're welcome," East replies.

"I know Aaden's upset. I get it. I'll talk to him. Guys, what about the mark? Is it still there?" I ask, unable to wait any longer.

"It's gone," Swoop says.

"Really?" I shout happily.

"Yeah, the Healer said she'll come explain everything to you after she's done running more tests," Dylan says.

"So no virus?" I ask.

"Doesn't look that way. But if we don't stop Malakaro…" Dylan says.

"Then none of it matters. I know. Okay, you guys go back out there and see what you can find. It doesn't matter how small the lead is; we need something. As soon as I talk to the Healer, I'll join you guys," I promise them.

Aaden enters again and tells us a Seller located in Denmark says he might have the info we need, if we are willing to pay him.

That's just like a Seller—all they care about is money. They died as humans while doing something heroic. But they never do enough good to become angels. That is except for Tony-Tone, but he was rare.

"Let's go before the Seller changes his mind," Diana says.

"Are you okay here alone?" Swoop asks. I can tell by her tone she's still mad at me, but at least she cares enough to ask. Aaden hasn't asked how I am feeling at all.

"Yeah, I'm good. You guys should go—hurry!" I reply. As the team takes off, I ask Aaden to stay behind. The team exchange knowing glances with each other. They then take off, leaving me alone with my second-in-command.

"The virus is gone! Did you know that?" I ask.

"Yeah."

"That's great! Isn't it?" I ask.

"Yeah, Pry. That's terrific," he says sardonically as he heads for the door.

"Hold on, can we talk?" I ask.

"I should be out there with the team."

"Yeah, I know, but I just need a few minutes," I reply.

"We can't stop and talk right now, Pryor. There's just too much to be done," he says, sounding more official than ever.

Damn, he must be really pissed off if his tone is that cold. There has to be a way to get him to talk to me. I mean, he can't be that upset. I am okay, after all. And he knows I had good reason to do what I did.

"I really would like it if you stayed—for a few minutes," I tell him.

"Is this an order?" he asks.

"Wow, does it have to be?"

"Is it an order or not?" he restates.

"No, it's not an order."

"Good, then I have to go," he says.

"Aaden!" I call out as he opens the door.

"What?" he says, not bothering to turn around.

"Do I have to beg you to stay and talk to me?"

"Begging and pleading never work on you, maybe it's time they stopped working on me," he counters.

"Look, it's obvious you're upset that I swallowed the Sive. Let's just talk about it," I offer.

"How is that going to help anything?" he asks.

"Can you just close the door and come over here?"

"That's what you need from me, right, huh? You need me to set everything aside and listen to you. But when I needed you to listen to me, you told me to fuck off and you did what you wanted," he says as he closes the door and faces me.

"I never said that."

"You didn't have to. Your actions did all the talking for you. We agreed you wouldn't use the Sive and you did it anyway," he reminds me.

"I know you're mad, but for the record, I never agreed. You agreed."

"Really? You want to argue semantics with me, right now?!" he snaps.

"I'm sorry I upset you by taking the Sive. That wasn't my intention," I promise him.

"Upset? You think this whole thing 'upsets' me?" he asks in disbelief.

"Okay, then tell me. What did this whole thing make you feel?"

He bites his lower lip and shakes his head angrily. He glares at me, then heads back towards the exit.

"Oh, okay. I guess this is the part where you do what you're good at—

run away. Argh! I hate when you do that! If something goes wrong, you just walk out on me, on us. Just this once, can't you stay and face our issues? Why are you running away? I wish you would just grow a set and say what you need to say."

"I'm not running away. I'm going to help the team," he replies curtly.

"That's an excuse and you know it. Damn it, just say what's on your mind already!"

"You want to know what's on my mind? Okay. Here it is," he says, coming towards me. When he speaks, his tone is harsh and arctic. The level of anger behind his words makes his voice tremble.

"You are willful, selfish, and cruel. When I was at the Center, I experienced unimaginable levels of torture. But *nothing* I experienced can compare to what you made me witness two hours ago. YOU ALMOST DIED!"

"Aaden—"

"I am not done! You *knew* what they did to me in there and you took me right back to that place by putting your life in danger needlessly. The worst moments of my life and you made me relive them. How could you do that to me? How could you put me through that shit? I am standing over your open chest and all I can do is watch your life slip away from me. What kind of sick, sadistic bullshit is that?"

"I'm sorry."

"No! You're not sorry. Sorry is when you do something without knowing the consequences, but that's not what this is. You knew what this would do to me. You knew what it would do to us, but you didn't care. You didn't care that I could not live without you. You didn't care that my fucking soul was dying right along with yours. You did whatever the hell you wanted and left me alone to figure it out," he accuses.

"I wasn't trying to hurt you, you have to know that. I wanted a baby for us. This was all for us."

"BULLSHIT! THIS WAS ALL FOR YOU."

"What? How can you say that?" I ask, unable to hide my hurt.

"We were both devastated about the virus. We could have grieved together. We could have handled this together. But you went off on your own because you have some dumbass notion that I won't love you if you don't bear my child."

"Would you?" I counter.

"Argh! How can you ask that?" he demands.

"You said yourself things between us would change," I remind him.

"I said it would change us, I didn't say it would end us."

"I did what I did because I wanted to help us," I reply.

"Pryor, stop lying."

"I'm not lying!"

"This whole thing is about you competing with Diana. Ever since Sparks was conceived, you've had this notion in your head that fatherhood is all I need to be happy."

"Isn't it?"

"No! I didn't just want *a* family; I wanted one with *you.* The virus took something very important away from us, but we still had each other. But you went off on your own and you did what you always do—you put us in second."

"I didn't do that," I protest.

"Yeah, Pry, you did. You put your needs, your desires, and your plans before us. Well, congratulations, you managed to do what the Center could not—you broke me."

"Don't say that. You know that's not what I wanted," I beg.

"How could you do that? How could you make me watch the life drain from your body? I would *never* put you through that."

"I'm sorry. You know I am," I reply as my voice trembles.

"I don't know that. I don't know anything when it comes to you."

"Yes, you do. You know that I love you," I reply.

"You made me watch as the ground soaked up your blood. I had to sink a blade into your chest. You lay lifeless in my arms and I begged Omnis not to take you away from me. And when it looked like you were going to die, I made a list in my head of the places I could go to end my life. Because I knew I would not, *could not* survive without you."

"Aaden, I'm so—"

"Don't you dare say you're sorry, don't tell me it was for us, and don't say you love me."

"But I do. Aaden, I do love you."

"I thought you did, but I was wrong. I don't think you know how to love—anyone."

I place my hands on top of my mouth to stop from crying, but it doesn't work. I burst into tears as he walks away.

CHAPTER TWELVE
PERFECT

I hear someone at the door a few minutes later. I quickly wipe away my tears and try to compose myself as the Healer enters. I clear my throat and try to act like everything is fine. The reality is nothing is fine. Yeah, I'm sorry that I hurt Aaden and it sucks that he had to watch me almost die. But I'm almost pissed at him for saying all those awful things to me. He said that shit just to hurt me.

Or maybe he meant it. Maybe he meant that I didn't know how to love. What does that mean for us? Is it true?

I hear the door open. I'm sure everyone in the clinic heard Aaden and I arguing, but still, I don't want the Healers to see me like this. I try to fix myself up. But the being that enters isn't a Healer. It's a human. A boy I miss so very much. Randy.

"Hi, Carrot," he says with a big grin.

"Hi," I reply with a sad smile.

"Okay, no time for pleasantries. We have so much TV to catch up on. But before we do that, talk to me. How could you swallow that Sive? Are you nuts? Seriously, are you losing your mind? That happened a few times on Star Trek. *So if you are going crazy, I might have a way to save you," he says.*

"Aw, thanks, but I'm not going crazy."

"You swallowed a deadly spider and you're talking to an imaginary friend," he points out.

"No, I'm talking to an imaginary best friend. I miss you, Randy."

"Same here. But you'll save me. I know you will. Do I look worried?" he asks.

"No, you look great."

"Yeah, and that's thanks to you. You gave me pecs and a six-pack! Look at this. I'm hot," he says as he studies his reflection in the mirror.

I laugh as he sits on the bed next to me.

"Are you okay?" he asks as he reaches for my hand.

"No," I reply softly.

"Don't worry, you and Silver will work things out. He's just upset."

"No, he's more than upset. He's really hurting. I wish he'd understand why I did what I did," I reply.

"You guys will work it out. It may take time. But so what, it's not like this is the end of the world," he teases gently.

"Yeah, I guess."

"Pry, don't be sad. Silver loves you."

"Things with me and Aaden are really bad right now. I mean scary bad. But that's not why I'm sad."

"Then what's wrong?" Randy asks. I tell him my dream. He listens carefully until I'm done.

"Wow, I wish I could explain the dream to you, but I'm not sure what it means," Randy confesses.

"I do—I know what the dream means," I admit reluctantly.

"Well, come on! Out with it! What does the dream mean?" he asks.

"It means…it means I have to say good-bye to the one I love. The one who was my real-life 'Mr. Frog.'"

"What do you mean?" he says.

"You were slated to die. You were on my mom's list and I kept trying to stop that from happening. It means it's time to face reality. Randy, I have to kill you."

I'm jarred out of my dream and bolt upright in my bed. The Healer next to me places her hand on mine. I look around the room and she's the only one here. She explains that she gave me a mixture to help me Recharge. She says she walked in and found me crying and thought rest was what I needed.

"Oh, um…sorry about that," I reply awkwardly.

"It's okay. Been there. I'm Joan," she says with a warm smile.

"Joan, you know if my team landed in Denmark yet?"

"Yeah, a few minutes ago."

"I need to be in touch with them. I can't just stay here and—"

"Here, we figured the only way we could get you to lie still and rest was to make sure you had this," she says as she hands me a flat device the size of a cell phone. "It's called an Eagle Eye. It's connected to the tracker you placed on your team. It will give you a live feed so you can see everything."

"How did you know I put a tracker on the team?" I ask.

"You're very much like your dad that way," she says.

"Thank you for this. I just want to make sure they're okay," I reply as I wait for the screen to turn on.

"When will the Healer be done with her tests?" I ask.

"She only has one more to perform. So sit tight, watch your team, and try not to get too excited," she says as she heads for the door.

"Joan?"

"Yes?"

"When Aaden left my room and walked down the hallway, did he…turn around at all?"

"No."

"Oh, okay. Thanks," I reply as my heart slinks to the floor.

My husband thinks I don't know how to love. My team is away without me, and I may have to kill my best friend. Perfect. Just, perfect.

When the Eagle Eye device springs to life, I'm grateful to have something else to focus on. At first the image is blurry, but soon it clears up and reveals the current location of the team.

***

They are standing in front of an abandoned factory covered with crude graffiti. The three-level antiquated building is made up of eroded metal and large blown-out windows. There are numerous gutted cars in front of the property, suggesting the building was once used to manufacture automobiles.

The team carefully surveys the area. There are two entrances; Aaden divides the team, making sure each entrance is covered. Swoop, Dylan, and Diana take the main entrance. Aaden and East go around the back. Aaden looks through the nearest window and indicates to East that it's clear to go inside.

The inside of the factory looks even creepier than the outside. There are mountains of scrap metal everywhere. The walls are spray painted with skulls, and the cement pillars look far too fragile. There are cars on every level. Some of them are hidden under filthy, dusty covers; some have been stripped down to the steel frame. As they look around, East leans into Aaden and speaks softly.

"So what's going on with you and the missus?" he asks.

Argh! East! Why?

Aaden doesn't reply. He continues to investigate the area. East looks him over and decides, very foolishly, to try again.

"How bad was the argument? Do you need a hug? You can ask, man, I'm here," East says.

Aaden glares at him but doesn't say anything.

"Hey, I'm just trying to look out for you. You know we're practically brothers. Our parents are together. I mean, it's kind of official from what I hear," East adds.

"Easton," he warns.

"Hey, my mom wants us to get along. I'm just trying to help."

"You want to help, stay focused on what we came to do. I don't see any sign of the Seller. Help me find him," Aaden says as he spots the rest of the team on the other side of the vast room.

"Do you think our parents will get married?" East asks.

"Easton! Focus."

"Just tell me, do you think they will?"

"I don't know. I don't get into my dad's love life."

"Do you want them to?" East pushes.

"I want him to be happy. If that's with Winter, then fine; if that's with a hundred other women, then that's fine too."

"Other women? Is there something you're trying to tell me? Your dad better not be playing my mom. I swear to Omnis, I won't let him hurt her," East warns.

"Shhh, keep your damn voice down," Aaden scolds.

"Is he cheating on her or what?" East demands.

Aaden has no choice but to stop and address his very pissed off teammate. "Look, I don't get into who my dad is hooking up with, that's his business. But if it helps, I have never seen him as happy as he is with your mom. And I don't think he's out to hurt her. There, now can we get back to why we're here?" Aaden asks.

"One more thing."

"What is it?" Aaden snaps.

"Are you and Pry gonna be okay?" East asks sincerely.

Aaden is about to reply when he spots something that makes his eyes widen with shock.

"Oh shit, get down!" Aaden shouts as he tackles East and throws them both onto the concrete floor. They look up, and the spot where they were standing is now a giant crater.

"What the hell was that?" East asks.

Aaden signals towards a demon on the third-level balcony. I recognize him because of his badly burned, peeling face. His name is Reign. He has the ability to generate powerful plasma filled with acid. He sends it towards his target and obliterates them on the spot. Anything the plasma touches is immediately wiped off the face of the earth—there's no blood, no bones, nothing.

Aaden sends a series of fireballs after Reign. He manages to dodge all of them. East whips out his lasso and manages to make contact with the demon. The lasso coils around Reign's hand, but before East can drag him off the balcony, Reign sends an orb that eats right through his lasso. East quickly pulls away what's left of his weapon.

"We gotta find cover," Aaden says as Reign prepares to fire again. East puts up his shield, but in a matter of seconds, the orb penetrates it and they are once again vulnerable.

"Get behind that van, hurry!" Aaden says as he provides cover fire for East. While East seeks safety, Swoop flips and leaps her way to the third floor in hopes of stopping Reign. Before she gets to him, a demon with a ghostly white skin tone takes off after her.

"That's Arctic. Don't let him touch you!" Diana shouts. However, it's too late. The ice demon grabs Swoop in the middle of a handstand. She is frozen solid, upside down with her legs up in the air.

"Silver, you have to warm her up or she'll die. Go!" Diana shouts.

"I got this, Silver. Go get Swoop," East replies as he sends his lasso cutting through the air and aims it at Reign.

Aaden flies up to the third level and forms a controlled orb of fire. He aims it at Swoop; the ice that is encasing her starts to melt. But before Aaden can free her completely, a demon with a Mohawk flies through the window and tackles him. The two of them tumble over the iron balcony and exchange blows as they crash down to the ground. The demon lands on top of Aaden and takes advantage by pounding his fist into Aaden's face repeatedly.

"Come here, handsome. Give me a kiss," Diana says as she climbs on top of the demon, yanks his head backwards, and sucks out his life force with her mouth. The demon falls back on the ground, lifeless.

"Diana, look out!" East yells as Reign manages to break free of the lasso once again and sends his orb of acid right for Diana. Seconds before the acid bomb hits Diana's face, Aaden grabs her into his embrace and takes flight. The acid lands and devours everything in its path.

Dylan uses his power and disappears. When he reappears again, he's on the third floor, next to Swoop. He grabs a metal rod and smashes it repeatedly against the ice casing keeping Swoop captive. He's too focused on Swoop to spot the demon behind him.

The demon has olive skin and conjures up a large shadow serpent between his hands. The shadow coils itself around Dylan and begins choking him to death. Dylan clutches at his throat desperately, trying to loosen the grip of the shadow snake.

Aaden sends Diana to help Dylan and Swoop. Diana dropkicks Swoop, sending her right into the wall. The force she throws her with allows the remaining ice to fracture. Swoop is now free. Diana goes to help Dylan, but Swoop assures her she's got it.

I've never seen Swoop attack with such rage. She grabs the shadow demon from behind, flips him over her head, and slams him to the ground. She then viciously snaps his neck. He dies and so does his shadow serpent. Dylan, exhausted and nearly drained of life, leans on the wall for support.

There are two more demons that have entered the factory. Diana and East band together to restrain and kill them both. Meanwhile, Aaden takes on Reign by aiming his fireballs at the metal platform Reign is standing on. It quickly melts it away and sends the demon plummeting down to the ground floor. He grabs two long rusty metal rods and stabs Reign in the palm of each hand, pinning him to the ground. He then sends an ocean of fire to engulf Reign. The acid-soaked bastard dies screaming.

Arctic quickly comes to avenge his demon friend. He brings forth a surge of deadly frost, and Aaden counters with a wave of flames. The two of them go head-to-head and sparks surround the factory. It looks like Aaden might lose to Arctic; the frost is coming closer and is about to overwhelm him.

Arctic laughs as the ice from his palm threatens to swallow all of Aaden's fire. But the demon's laughter is cut short when Aaden goes into overdrive and sends a surge of blue flames at him. Arctic's mouth drops in horror as the sea of blue fire bathes him. The explosion kills him and takes out the right side of the building. The blast hurls the team into the air and drops them down on a pile of metal debris.

"Everyone okay?" Aaden asks. The team grumps about being launched into a mountain of metal and junk, but all in all, they assure him they are okay. I breathe a sigh of relief and thank Omnis no one is seriously hurt—yet. I wish I were there to help out. I should be there; I should have their back. What if there are more demons?

"There might be more of them, so stay sharp," Aaden says as if hearing my thoughts.

"Seller! Come out! We know you're here," Swoop says.

"Maybe the blast took him out too," East replies.

"I doubt it. I'm sure that piece of trash is somewhere around here, watching," Aaden says.

"You think he told the demons we would be here?" Diana asks.

"Hell yeah. I'm sure he agreed to let the demons know we were here if they paid him a small sum," Aaden says, disgusted.

"Actually it was a very large sum. And can you blame a guy for wanting to support his family?" a figure says as he appears in the entrance. The Seller is tall and lanky. He has a dark mustache and beady eyes.

Aaden takes to the air quickly and tackles him. In a matter of seconds, he has the Seller on the floor and his foot on the guy's neck.

"You sold us out!" Aaden says angrily as a fireball springs from his right hand.

"I have six kids to support and three ex-wives," the Seller gasps.

"You wanna try again?" East says, studying his emotions.

"Okay, I have three kids and two ex-wives," the Seller says.

Easton signals to Aaden that the Seller is lying yet again. Aaden summons a fireball with his other hand. He now has two fiery orbs ready to go. The Seller suddenly finds himself rethinking his previous statement.

"Okay, okay. I have no kids and my ex-wife pays me alimony. Happy?" he says.

Easton sneers at him.

"Hey, don't look at me like that. I am a businessman—a businessman with a big gambling problem and a bookie that doesn't take IOUs," he replies.

"I don't really want to kill you, but in the past few hours, I've had to do a lot of things I didn't want to do," Aaden warns him.

"How about you give him a reason not to hurt you?" Swoop says.

"For starters, I know who the Architect is," he reminds them.

"What's your name?" Diana asks.

"Orkin," he says.

"Well, Orkin, since you tried to get us killed, we're going to need a little more than just the identity of the Architect. We will need his exact location," Diana replies.

"That wasn't part of the deal," Orkin protests.

Aaden holds his hands high above his head and lowers the orbs of fire down onto Orkin's face.

"Okay! Okay!" Orkin begs.

Aaden stops just inches away from making contact with the Seller's skin.

The Seller gets up and dusts himself off.

"All I wanted was to make a little money from you guys. And then make a little more money from the demons who wanted your location. I knew they wouldn't kill you guys. I always had faith in you," he lies.

"Orkin, start talking—as if your life depends on it," Swoop warns.

"Alright, alright. For starters, the Architect is not his real name."

"Yeah, we kind of figured that," East says sardonically.

"His real name is Apex, and he has been around for a long time," Orkin says.

"Apex. I know that name," Dylan says.

"I figured you would, historian," Orkin replies.

"We can get the history later. Right now, we need to know what he looks like and where we can find him," Aaden says.

"Can you describe him?" Diana asks.

"I can do better than that. We had dealings a few years ago, and I keep a log and a picture of everyone I do business with. I have his picture right here with me. I can give it to you—for a small fee," Orkin says.

Before the team can respond, Dylan disappears and reappears behind Orkin. He snatches the picture from him with ease.

"Hey! That's my property. You can't—" Orkin is in the middle of bitching when the building starts to shake. Without warning, the ceiling collapses.

"Guys, get out! Get out!" I shout as if they could hear me. But it's too late, the ceiling falls and crushes the team—or it would have had it not been for Aaden holding a large slab of the concrete up above his head.

"Hurry!" Aaden says between clenched teeth. The team grabs Orkin and races towards the exit. They make it out of the factory just as it crumbles to the ground. Everyone has escaped except Aaden. I don't see him anywhere.

"Where are you? Aaden, I can't see you! Where are you?" I shout frantically at the screen. The team is also freaking out. They search the area but see no sign of the second-in-command.

"Silver! Silver!" Swoop shouts at the mountain of rubble. Swoop and the rest of the team turn over large chunks of debris, hoping to find Aaden under it. But the search is cut short when the ground cracks open and the entire block starts to shake.

"Up there!" Dylan says as he points towards a figure looming in the sky. Argh! I know that asshole! He is Stone, a highly skilled demon with the ability to manipulate earth.

"We gotta get out of here!" Orkin says.

"Why? Don't you and Stone have an agreement? Didn't he pay your greedy ass to betray us?" Swoop accuses.

"No! I didn't take money from him. Apex sent him. He must know what we're doing here. We have to go!" Orkin begs.

"Not without Silver!" East says as the ground continues to shake uncontrollably.

"Do what you want, but I'm getting on my Port and—" Orkin is struck by a large slab of concrete. It hits him with such force it splits his head open, killing him instantly. Dylan grabs hold of Orkin's collar and shakes him furiously.

"No! Don't die! Where is Apex? Where is he?!" Dylan begs.

"Dylan, he's gone. We have to find Silver," Swoop yells.

"Diana and I will take on Stone. The rest of you stay down here and look for Silver," East says as he takes off into the sky. Diana quickly follows behind.

Aaden, where are you?

As the team looks for Aaden, I turn my attention to the battle in the sky. East gets the lasso around Stone and, together with Diana, manages to drag him out of the sky. But as soon as he's on solid ground, Stone naturally has the advantage. He summons the surrounding tree branches and makes them come to life. He silently orders them to ensnare Diana and East. The two of them struggle to break free but have no luck.

Stone pulls the lasso from his waist before it can drain his energy. He discards it and continues to strangle East and Diana. Dylan finds a rusty, jagged piece of metal a few feet away. He grabs it and disappears. When he pops up again, he's in front of Stone. He stabs the demon in the eye, causing him to lose control of the branches. Diana and East quickly free themselves.

"I found Silver!" Swoop shouts.

Please be alive. Please be alive.

"Is he okay?" Diana shouts as she runs towards him.

"He's alive, but I can't move him by myself," Swoop says.

"Hang on!" East says as he ties his lasso around Stone's neck. This time he knots it repeatedly so that it stays on and saps all of Stone's strength. Stone is still howling in pain from Dylan's attack, making East's job easy. Once Stone is bound, they all run over to Swoop and Aaden.

Aaden managed to make it out of the building before it fell, but the blast propelled him right into a rusty spike. The jagged metal went right through his left leg and took a large chunk of flesh with it. The team tries to help, but when they lift his leg and try to separate it from the spike, Aaden groans and a flood of blood oozes out of him at an alarming rate.

"No! He'll bleed out if you remove the spike," Diana says.

"What do we do?" Dylan asks.

"Whatever it is, we need to hurry. Stone called for reinforcements," East says as he directs their attention to the swarm of demons in the air, heading straight for them.

"Go! Take off!" Aaden growls.

"No! We're not leaving you. We're gonna pull your leg off the spike," East insists.

"If we do, he will bleed way too much. He could die," Diana says again.

I can feel my heart leaping into my throat. I've never been this terrified in all my life, not once. I want to turn away from the screen, but at the same time, I'd kill anyone who tried to separate me from what's happening.

"Diana, we have no choice. He *might* die from blood loss, but he will *certainly* die if the demons get to us. We are outnumbered. We need to go," East reasons. Meanwhile Aaden keeps ordering the team to leave him behind.

Thankfully the team ignores his pleas and yanks the spike from his leg. I ball my hands in a fist in front of my mouth and bite down on the tip of my tongue. The blood oozing out of Aaden's leg seems to flow forever. By the time he is finally free, the demons are a breath away. With no more time left to spare, the team helps Aaden take to the air. Stone regains his powers, and together with the other demons, they call upon the city to cave in on itself. Denmark crumbles into an avalanche of dust.

As soon as the team arrives, the Healers quickly attend to Aaden. They assure us that they can fix him up. Dylan flies off to see what he can find out about Apex. He's positive that now that we know his real name, we should be able to learn more about him. The team tells me how sorry they are that they didn't bring Orkin back alive. But I remind them the mission was a success.

"Pry, we still don't know where to find Apex," Swoop reminds me.

"No, but we know who he is and what he looks like. We got this. I know we do. You guys did so well. I'm so proud of you." They smile, and I can't help but smile back.

The fact is, for the first time since this awful day started, we actually have something to celebrate. The team got out alive, and even though we don't know *where* Apex is, we know *who* he is and what he looks like. For once, the Noru catch a break.

It's about damn time!

CHAPTER THIRTEEN
MY WHITE ROOM

I stand in his hospital room, watching him sleep. Knowing that he's laid up from an injury, however minor, reminds me of just how much I love him. And how losing him would absolutely end me. I want to crawl in bed with him just to be next to him and hold him close. But I don't dare because I'm not sure what his reaction would be. What if he pushes me away? What if there simply isn't enough space on the bed for both our issues and us?

I knew that we wouldn't be in the "honeymoon" stage forever. I knew we'd argue about one thing or another. But I was hoping it would be something minor. Something like us not spending enough quality time together or whose turn it is to pick the movie we watch. Yeah, I know, that would never be a real issue with us. Honestly, I thought working with beings we used to date would be our big issue. But I'm getting along with Diana, and right now, I'm pretty sure Aaden likes Bex far more than he likes me.

I want to talk to him, but I feel like no matter what happens, we'll end up arguing. Maybe I should give him some time. Or maybe I should confront the issue? Argh! How am I supposed to know what's the right thing to do? Where the hell is the instruction manual? My mom and dad argued but not very often. They had so much drama when they were dating that by the time they got married, they had already been through so much, very little rattled them.

Did Aaden and I get married too soon?

I don't feel like we did. If I had it to do over again, I'd do the same damn thing. Maybe I should wake him up and tell him that. I should tell him that he's my world and we can fix whatever is broken with us.

According to him, I'm what is broken...

Panic and worry settle over me. Suddenly I'm not sure being here is the right thing. I turn around and slowly begin to exit my husband's room.

"Where are you going?" he says as he opens his eyes.

Crap!

"I...I thought you should rest," I reply.

"I'm fine," he says.

"Good, good," I reply, then I clear my throat and look around the room and avoid his eyes.

"Where's the team?" he asks.

"Dylan went to do some research on Apex. Diana went to Mrs. Maybelle's to check on Nix. And the Healers are examining the rest of the team. We should find out who Apex really is and why he hates us, soon," I reply.

"Okay. How...I mean...what did the head Healer say about you? Are you okay?"

"She has one more test to do, and then she'll come see me," I inform him.

"How are you feeling?" he asks.

"Great!" I reply with the enthusiasm of a cheerleader. Argh, why did I say it like that?

"So in other words, you're still feeling weak?" he says.

"Yeah, a little," I confess.

"Are you taking the mixture the Healer made for you?"

"Yes, I'm being a good little patient. Turns out I'm good at a lot of things—well, except being a good wife. I've apparently failed at that, dismally."

Shit! Why did I say that? Why couldn't I just let it go? Maybe he won't take the bait. Maybe he'll let it go.

"I never said you weren't a good wife," he says.

"Oh, you're right. You just said that I am incapable of love," I reply.

Pryor, shut up! Shut up! Please, Omnis, let him be more mature than me; let him move on to another subject so we don't have to talk about this.

"Did Bird get a chance to check up on RJ?" he asks.

Great! He's changing the subject…wait! Why is he changing the subject? So, what, he doesn't want to talk about it? I know why I don't want to talk. He hurt my feelings and said some really awful things to me. But why doesn't he want to talk? Hey, I should be the one who doesn't want to talk, not him!

Pryor, does it matter? He's giving you a way out of a conversation you both don't want to have. Let it go.

"So you really don't want to talk about us? Seriously?" I snap.

So much for letting it go…fuck!

"Are you sure you want to do this now?" he asks.

No!

"Yes," I reply out loud.

"Okay, well, I don't."

"I'm new to this marriage thing, but I'm guessing the two beings in the relationship have to talk things out at some point."

"I'm sure they do, just not now," he says curtly.

"Seriously? So, what, now you get to dictate how our marriage will work?" I bark at him.

"We don't have enough going on? We aren't nearly as far ahead as we should be on this mission—"

"Don't do that! Don't act like we're not talking because of work. We're not talking because you decided to ice me out."

"No, we're not talking because I don't know what to say to someone who is okay with dying. Someone who puts everyone's feelings aside and only focuses on her goal."

"Is that really what you think of me?"

"What else am I supposed to think, Pryor? Tell me, when you ingest something that can kill you and do it with a smile, what the fuck am I supposed to think?"

"So now you're lying there, sorry that you married me? Is that what you're saying?" I demand.

"No, I'm not sorry I married you. But I am sorry that I'm not the leader of this team. Because if I were in charge and I commanded you not to swallow the Sive, you would have heard me and done what I asked. And it pissed me off to no end to know that the only way I can get through to you is to be 'official' about it. Why can't I have a say with you as your husband?"

"So because we're married now, I have to blindly do what you say? Is that what I'm supposed to do?"

"NO! WHAT YOU'RE SUPPOSED TO DO IS NOT MAKE ME HAVE TO CUT YOUR DAMN CHEST OPEN IN THE MIDDLE OF A WAREHOUSE!"

"I said I'm sorry."

"Stop saying that! You don't think I know you? You think I can't see that you're lying to me?"

"I am not lying. I told you already I am sorry for what happened. What else do you want me to do?"

"You're sorry? Okay. Let me ask you this: If we could somehow go back, if we could be in the warehouse, holding each other, and you had a chance to change what you did, would you? If you could go back and leave the Sive in my pocket, would you? Or would you do the very same thing?"

I don't even need to think about it. I know the answer even before he's done with the question. What's worse is that he knows what my answer will be.

"Pryor! Would you do the same thing all over again? Would you swallow the Sive?" he demands.

"Yes…yes, I would."

"Look, I love you. I really do, but right now…I just want to be alone."

"Aaden—"

"Pryor, I need you to go."

I nod slowly, lower my head, and start to walk away. But just as I place my hand on the doorknob, a thought occurs to me. I walk back to Aaden and speak my new revelation softly.

"You have every right to be angry with me. I made your worst fears come to the surface. Hurting you may have been the result, but it was never the goal. I wanted something for us, something more than missions, grief, and bloodshed. But you were right, it wasn't just about us. There's someone else I thought about when I did what I did, and no, it's not Diana," I inform him.

"Who is it, then?" he asks.

"My father. He gave me the middle name of someone he loved and cared about. He said my having their name meant they would also live on. When I was a kid, that made absolutely no sense. Ever since my dad died, there's been this hole inside me. Some days, the hole is as wide as an ocean; other days, it's the size of a pinprick.

"But no matter how small it got, it was always there. It stayed with me every minute of every day. But then you told me about Summit. And suddenly, I got it. I understood what my father was talking about. Naming our child—even our make-believe child—after something he believed in meant my dad would somehow live on. Then I found out about the virus, and it was like I was losing him all over again. And I couldn't let that happen. I couldn't lose my dad twice."

I can feel a lump forming in my throat. The more I talk, the more my voice trembles. I force myself to stay calm. I am not going to break down now, that's not the point of this conversation.

Aaden looks at me. He's torn between his concern for me and his ever-present anger for what I did.

"We don't have to talk about this now," he says, looking away.

"Yeah, we do. I need to clear the air. You told me how you felt about what I did. And now, I want you to know how I feel," I reply, regaining a steady tone.

"Okay, fine," he mutters.

"You told me that I broke you today. That may be true, but you broke me years ago. You took large chunks of my heart with you every time you disappeared without a trace. You knew I loved you, yet you traveled the world, sleeping with everything and anything with wings. Every girl I heard about, every one-night stand tore me apart."

"We weren't together then," he reminds me.

"Do you think that made it hurt less? You knew I loved you. And you loved me. You knew where you should have been—with me. But you weren't. You used sex and distance to try to make everything okay. Every girl you were with and every mile you put between us crushed me."

"Pryor—"

"I'm not done. When we finally got together, your past caught up with you—with us. And suddenly, you were going to be someone's father. That's not an easy mixture to swallow, believe me. But I learned to love Sparks and I learned to care about Diana. The truth is you could have come with a hundred kids and I would be okay with it because they are part of you. I made space for you in my heart and in my life. I accepted you and your past, even though that past kept biting me in the ass. When we got married, I thought I would finally have you all to myself, but I was wrong. I lost you again. I lost you to your other love."

"What 'other love'? What are you talking about?" he pushes.

"I'm talking about the one thing you love more than me—distance. It lures you in and you disappear and leave me to figure it out on my own. I thought now that we are married, you would never go back to craving 'her.' But you love her. You love 'distance,' and when things get hard, you reach for her and not me."

"That's not true. I didn't take off on you. Okay, I did. But I came back soon after. I wasn't away for long," he protests.

"You shouldn't have been away at all. Minutes after we talked about having a child, we learn that we can't. So what's your solution? Take off. And just when I needed you the most. You did what you always do—run. You run as far as you can as fast as you can."

"I needed time to process, okay?"

"No! That's not okay. We were in it together. You wanted to set the world on fire, you wanted to shout to the heavens and cry. That's fine, but you should have done that with me. You and I are the only ones in this relationship. Not your dad, not my mom, just us. Yet you turned away from me and just took off."

"I wouldn't have been any use to you," he says.

"You were falling apart. Well, me too. But we should have fallen apart together. Instead, you did what was best for you. Not best for me or us, best for you. So maybe I am selfish, but so are you."

"I didn't leave you to hurt you. You know that."

"No, I didn't. Not right away. At first I wanted to fly after you and bite your damn head off. I mean what kind of husband flies away when his wife is devastated? And what kind of angel takes off when he's most needed?" I ask bitterly.

He doesn't answer. There's so much going on behind his eyes. There's frustration, pain, and uncertainty. He's pissed off, but I'm not sure if it's with himself or with me. It may be both.

"Do you know why I didn't go after you, Aaden? Because I knew what you needed from me more than anything was my understanding. And as hard as it was to do, I gave it to you. I didn't yell, argue, or make you feel like shit because you took off," I snap angrily.

Again, he doesn't say anything. I can't tell what he's thinking, and right now, I don't care. He had his say and I will have mine.

"Aaden, you can say a million things about me. Omnis knows I'm not perfect. You can say that I'm stubborn, difficult, impulsive and, yeah, maybe selfish. But you have no right to say that I can't love. You run away from us, you put up walls, and you have a short fuse. But I loved through that.

"I had to swallow that Sive. That's who I am. I'm Marcus Cane's daughter…he never taught me how to give up. Yes, I've messed up as a leader, as a daughter, and certainly as a friend. But I have loved you and that love has never faltered, even when I was with Bex. I think you said I couldn't love anyone because you wanted to hurt me. And that is cruel.

"Aaden, today I made your worst nightmare come true. And I am sorry for that. But every time we argue or things get hard, I think to myself, 'Is this the day he takes off again?' That's my nightmare. That's my White Room…"

***

Diana returns to the clinic and tells us Nix is safe and that there hasn't been any contact made with Malakaro through the newborn. Dylan returns not long after and asks us to gather in my room, which is slowly starting to feel like more like a prison cell.

The last one to enter the room is Swoop. She had a video call with RJ. I heard them earlier, singing a song that Swoop had taught him. They sounded too cute for words. It made my heart hurt a little. Even though the mark is gone, meaning I can have kids, the way things are with Aaden right now, I don't see that for us.

"Okay, what did you learn about Apex?" I ask once we're all together.

"Apex is an angel with an extraordinary gift—vision. He had the ability to see days into the future. It was a gift only given to Fate at the time. Granted, Apex could not see as far as Fate could; still, his gift was impressive," Dylan explains.

"What happened to him? Can he still see the future?" Diana asks.

"No. At some point in his life, Apex grew weary of only being able to see part of the future and was envious that Fate could see so much more. He asked Omnis to expand his power and insisted that it would be for the betterment of humanity. Omnis said that the gift of foresight should go to the rare beings that understood that there are consequences for knowing things before their time. And Apex was simply too immature to understand. So he was denied," Dylan says.

"Let me guess, Apex took it very well and let this be," East says cynically.

"No, he went out on his own and tried to increase his powers," Dylan adds.

"Was he able to do it?" Aaden asks.

"Yes and no. He put together a series of very dangerous and forbidden mixtures; they allowed him to see the next two thousand years for mankind."

"Apex knows what's going to happen to mankind for the next two thousand years?" Swoop says.

"He saw all the events that would happen. But in doing so, it scrambled his brain," Dylan tells us.

"I don't get it. He was a powerful angel, why did seeing the future mess with his head?" I ask.

"Think of it this way: seeing what will happen before it actually happens is like spotting a ray of sun that no one else can see or feel. It's warm, bright, and inviting. But increase that ability and all of a sudden you're not gazing at the sun from a safe distance. You're actually standing right in front of it.

"So what was once warming your skin is now melting your flesh. The slightly wondrous glare of the sun is now a brutal assault on your eyes. And the awe-inspiring beam of light that you cherished is now an unstoppable surge of power that will render you blind," Dylan explains.

"So seeing too much made him insane?" Aaden says.

"Yes. Now he can't see the future. He can't even see five seconds ahead. So now he's…"

"Now he's bat-crap crazy," East says, helping Dylan, who was at a loss for words.

"Yes," Dylan replies.

"But why didn't Fate go crazy? He sees everything," Swoop says.

"That's a misconception. Fate doesn't see everything. He sees more than any other being but not everything. And the reason Fate didn't lose his mind is because Omnis equipped him with the ability to handle his power. In other words, Fate has protection. He won't go nuts," Dylan adds.

"What happened after that?" I ask.

"When Apex could no longer see the future, he went off the deep end. He attacked everyone—good, bad, or indifferent. They finally had to put him away. Years later they learned that while Apex is crazy, he had also gained some powers thanks to all the mixtures. He could read people's deep desires and fears. He also has the ability to build vast make-believe worlds in his mind. And bring them to life. The fact is while Apex is insane, he's also brilliant. He has a talent for sniffing out the pain in others. He is the 'Omnis' of the torture and torment world."

"Dylan, why would they let an angel like that exist?" I ask.

"They lost track of him. After he helped build Bliss, the angel prison, he went underground. Only a few beings knew how to get in contact with him. The owner of the Center was one of those beings. He used Apex to create the Center and the White Room. He's done other jobs. If there's a structure designed to inflict pain, Apex is the creator."

"So he lost his mind and turned evil," Swoop concludes.

"No, Apex isn't really good or bad," Dylan says.

"Really? That's your take on it?" Aaden says.

"Silver, what I mean by that is this: Apex is the textbook definition of insane. He doesn't do things that are right and wrong. He does things that make sense in his head. For example, when he created the prison, all he asked for in return was a bottle of giggle-flavored Coy. That made sense in his head.

"Conversely, when he built the White Room, he demanded everything of value that Bishop owned. Apex once went into a bar and cut out an angel's eyes because he thought that angel was blinking curses at him in a secret language. He's unstable and unpredictable," Dylan says.

"So to him, building the White Room could have been the same as being asked to build a playroom?" I ask.

"Yes. His morals and his ability to gauge good and evil are seriously impaired," Dylan adds.

"Wow…what else?" East asks.

"He's always been hard to find, but a few years back, he went into complete seclusion. Some angels say he contracted a serious virus, some think he was held prisoner by someone he helped torture, and a few angels think he fell in love and gave up the life. I don't know, but I think once we know what happened in those missing years, we'll know what drives him and why he's after all of you."

"And I take it you have no idea where to find him?" Aaden says.

"Sorry. I passed this picture around to everyone I could find," he says as he takes the fragile picture from his pocket and places it on the nightstand by my bed.

"So we're back to having nothing," I say to myself.

"I'm sorry," Dylan says.

"Hey, you were amazing. We would not have gotten this far without you," Swoop says as she leans in and kisses him on the cheek. Dylan blushes and tries hard to hide how much Swoop's approval means to him.

Without warning, a being pops up in my room, on a Port. He is human but has a stern expression that could rival any demon. He is clearly angry.

"Grandpa!" I shout, overjoyed as I make my way to him.

"Not so fast, missy! We have some talking to do. Actually, I have some yelling to do. Then some more yelling," Grandpa Julian says loudly.

"Um…I'm sorry, I have been meaning to call. Things have been really busy," I reply, hoping my explanation is enough.

"I don't give a care how busy you are," he counters as he gets off the Port.

"How did you know we were here?" I ask.

"I have my ways. I didn't think I'd need to use them. I thought my family would share information with me," Julian scolds.

"It wasn't intentional," Aaden replies.

"You are not talking, demon," he replies.

"Grandpa! What's wrong with you? You like Aaden," I remind him.

"I did until he went and married my grandbaby without sending me so much as an email!" he spits.

"Yeah, we got the lecture already. We're sorry about that," Aaden says.

"Sorry don't mean shit. I should have your balls in a blender!"

Someone kill me now!

"Grandpa, please, we have so much to deal with right now. Can't you just let this go?" I beg.

"Sorry, I can't. What in the hell has been happening with this team anyway? Swallowing Sives, making deals with trash like Orkin, and going to a damn graveyard knowing your powers won't work!" he snaps.

"We didn't know that at the time," Diana reasons.

"That's why you send out a scout. You do your research. What the hell is this about going into a mission blind? Is that what I taught you? Is that what your father taught you?" he pushes.

"No," I reply.

"What about the rest of you? Did your parents teach you to work a mission this way?"

The team mumbles no under their breaths.

"Now, Omnis knows me and Marcus have gone a few rounds, but he led his team well and he taught you to do the same. And what about Emmy? I know she taught you better than this, Carrot," he says gravely.

"Grandpa, I'm glad you're here. I missed you, but if you came to yell at me for…whatever, it's gonna have to wait," I reply firmly.

"Hell no. I didn't come to yell."

"Said the guy yelling," East mumbles.

"Well, I didn't come just to yell. You all are important to me. It makes me good and mad to see all of you in so much danger. And then—oh, great! You all decided to make things worse by contacting this psycho," Grandpa says as he picks up the picture of Apex on the table.

"You know Apex?" East asks.

"Of course I do. That guy is crazy as hell. I've dealt with him before. I tell you, it's a wonder his kid turned out normal," he says.

"Apex has a kid?" I ask.

"He has two. One of them was as crazy as he was and the other, well, you know…" Julian says factually.

"Actually, we don't," I confess.

"Pry, you really don't know who the Architect is?" Julian asks, stunned.

"No, who is he?"

"The Architect is Randy's real father."

CHAPTER FOURTEEN
BE CRAZY

Grandpa is about to fill us in when East asks for him to pause. We all look at him like he's crazy, but he disappears into the sky and comes back a few moments later with a dozen bottles of Coy.

"You made us wait so you could get a drink?" Diana says.

"Damn right!" he says.

"That's insane!" Swoop replies.

"Really? Who here *doesn't* need a drink?" East asks. He looks around, and even Grandpa is game for a drink. East passes them out and we all drink. I'm not sure I should with the mixtures I'm taking, but hey, it's too late now.

"Okay, before you continue, Julian, I just want to make sure we are on the same twisted page. So the Architect's real name is Apex. He is an angel who went mad. Apex found love with a woman, who then gave birth to twins: Alfred, also known as Spider, and Randy, also known as Pry's BFF. Is that right?" East asks.

"Yes," Grandpa says.

"Okay, just wanted to be sure I had reason enough to drink this third bottle of Coy," East says, then drains the bottle in one gulp.

"So why is Apex out to get us?" I ask.

"You're asking me to explain the reasoning of a madman. All I know is that even if you don't raise your kids, you still rain down all hell on the ones who mess with them. Your team killed his son Spider," Grandpa says.

"Yeah, but we saved his other son. We saved Randy a dozen times," Swoop replies.

"I know. And maybe that will count for something," Grandpa adds.

"Or maybe it won't and Apex picks and chooses which facts he will pay attention to," Dylan says.

"Did he have it out for me from the beginning?" Aaden asks.

"No, he was impressed by you."

"Julian, what do you mean?" Aaden says.

"He created the White Room, a place of pure hell, and you lasted a year. No one had ever done that before. The more you withstood, the more excited Apex was to break you. It was his twisted way of showing you respect."

"Great, and this is the guy who has the ashes we need to save the world?" Diana says.

"Yes," Grandpa replies.

"We can also save Randy with them. So why would he take them from us?" I ask.

"I don't know. But something tells me he's going to make it his mission to meet with you and your team. He went to a lot of trouble; I'm guessing he's designing something especially cruel for all of you," Grandpa adds.

"Or he could just as easily be planning an ice cream party for us," East says.

"Exactly. But since you don't need any prep work for ice cream, I suggest you all get ready for a battle."

"So you know where he is, Grandpa?"

"I have a few ideas. I'll check it out and get back to you."

"The team will go with you," I reply.

"No, I got this. There are only three places he could be. I'll find the location and report back. In the meantime, I have a cabin in the Andes Mountains full of weapons from past battles. You should go and take what you need," Grandpa suggests.

"Okay, but be careful, and if you see Apex, don't engage," I reply.

"Look at you, giving me orders," Grandpa says with pride. He tells the team the exact location of the cabin; then he takes me aside. "I wanna talk to you."

"I know you hate the way I'm running this team, and I'm not the great leader my dad was."

"That is not what I was going to say."

"It's not?" I reply, confused.

"No. It so happens, I'm proud of my grandbaby and her team."

"Why? We aren't nearly as far as we need to be on this mission. And we never would have figured out who Apex was had it not been for you. Why didn't we just come to you in the first place?" I ask myself.

"Because all your life you watched your mom and she never involved me. So you grew up not thinking of me as an option."

"Hey, why didn't Mom come to you more often?" I ask.

"She wanted me and your grandmother to have a normal life. She knows how much the angel world has messed with the two of us. She wants us to be free of it all."

"Is that what you want, Grandpa?"

"Yeah, I hate the angel world. But I love you. So if you need me, just let me know. And if anyone messes with you, you send them to me," he vows.

"You don't have any powers, Grandpa," I remind him gently.

"Who needs powers? I can still kick ass, you know."

"Yeah, I know," I reply with a huge grin as I embrace him. He holds me very tightly and calls me Baby Carrot.

"Grandpa, you can't do that. I'm all grown up!" I remind him.

"The hell, you are always going to be a little bitty thing to me. You okay with that?" he asks.

"Yeah, I am."

"Good! I'll go see what I can find out about Apex's location. Don't you worry, we'll find it."

"Thank you."

"And hey, you got a good team. They are brave, strong, and they look ready to follow you into hell itself," he says.

"Well, I guess that's part of the job," I reply.

"No, that's not. They aren't following you because of your title. They follow you because they respect you—not because you are Marcus's daughter, but because your courage is matched only by your heart. You are more powerful than you know. Never forget that," he says as he kisses me on the forehead.

"I'll try. Some days are easier than others," I admit.

"Must be even harder fighting with your husband—yes, that's right. It's not hard to tell you two been going at it. The way you both try to avoid making eye contact," he says.

"Yeah, it's been rough," I reply.

"Let me guess. He told you not to take the Sive and you did anyway?"

"Kind of. How did you know?"

"You may have Marcus's strength, but you got your mother's iron will. She'd do the same thing. Drove me and Marcus crazy."

"Yeah, I've heard the stories." I laugh.

"She didn't know how to sit back and let others help her. Had to do it all on her own."

"Guess I'm the same way," I reply.

"Well, stop it. Marriage ain't easy, but it ain't got to be hard neither. Talk to him. Find a way to push through the crazy. Be a unit. Got it?"

"I'll try."

"Look, Pry, I know I'm hard on you all, but I just want all of you to come back home safe. I know firsthand what kind of wicked assholes the angel world has and what kind of evil they can bring down on you. It's not the demons you need to worry about. It's the damn angels, if you ask me."

"You sound like Uncle Rage," I shout.

"Well, that bastard ain't far off," he replies. Grandpa then gets on his Port and calls out to me just before he disappears, "You kids have a lot of power, and that is dangerous on both sides. So be careful and be vigilant. Don't let those bastards get the best of you."

***

The team is about to take off for the Andes Mountains. It sucks that they will take flight yet again without me. Thankfully before they go, the head Healer tells me she's done running all the tests and that she'd like to see me in my room. The team asks if they can stay for a few minutes to hear the results.

"It might be prudent to discuss this matter with my patient and her husband, alone," the head Healer says.

"No, everyone here is my family. You can talk in front of them," I reply, trying not to give in to the nervous energy swelling inside me as we all enter my hospital room.

"Well, it's highly unusual, but if you insist. I ran a series of tests and—"

"Wait!" Aaden says as he stands up and addresses me. "I need to see you outside."

"Right now?" I ask.

"Yeah, right now," he says with certainty.

I tell the head Healer that I will return in a few minutes, and then I step out into the hallway with Aaden.

"What is it?" I ask as I study his serious expression.

"I don't know what that Healer lady is gonna say. It could be good news or really bad news. The only thing I do know is that I don't want us to go back in there and be at each other's throats. I have no idea what it is we're supposed to do or say to get back on track, I just figured whatever has to happen should happen before we get your test results," he says sincerely.

"When you say 'whatever has to happen' you mean…you want us to end this? Is that a possibility? Or a certainty at this point?" I dare ask.

"No! I don't want us to end this—wait, do you want to end this?" he asks.

"No!"

"Okay, so that bomb isn't gonna go off, good to know." He sounds relieved. He isn't the only one. The thought of us breaking up is just too devastating to imagine.

"Do you really think I don't know how to love?" I ask in a whisper, unable to look him in the eye.

"I didn't mean that," he insists.

"Then why did you say it?"

"I wanted to hurt you because you hurt me," he admits.

"Aaden, we can't do that to each other. We can't—"

"I know, Pry. I know. You're right. It was a crappy thing to do. Even as I was saying those words to you, I knew it wasn't true. But I couldn't stop myself. I was destroyed when I thought I lost you, and when you woke up, I just lost it.

"Don't get me wrong, I don't agree with what you did. And I had every right to be angry, but I didn't have a right to attack you like I did. I should have handled it better. And I certainly shouldn't have taken off on you. It's a reflex. I had no idea my leaving made you question if I would return or not. It never occurred to me to go away forever. I am always going to come back. Always."

"Aaden, I don't want to be married to a guy who always comes back. I want to spend the rest of my life with the guy who never leaves. Can you be that guy? Can you be the guy who stays no matter what?" I ask, turning to face him.

"For you, yes. Yes, I can be the guy who stays. From now on, we stay in the room. No walking or flying away. Promise. Okay?"

"Yeah, okay," I whisper.

"I didn't know how strong your connection was to the idea of Summit. I didn't know how much you had attached it to your dad," he admits.

"I should have told you from the beginning. I hid that part because I felt foolish. Just hanging on to an idea, like that idea would bring him back. I didn't want you to think I was crazy."

"Baby, if you can't be crazy with me, if you can't stop being in leader mode with me or be vulnerable with me, then how is our relationship different from your relationship with the rest of the world?" he pleads.

"I didn't say the thing about my dad because I didn't want to be the little girl who missed her daddy. I'm the First Noru and can't be that girl."

"Yeah, Pry, you can. You can be that girl with me," he vows.

"I guess I should have; it would have helped you understand. I am sorry. Our marriage is important to me. And I made it collateral damage. But we can fix it, right?"

"We have to—we already have the tattoo, remember?" he says with a smile.

"Yeah, and it's expensive to get it lasered off," I reply.

"Well, our tattoos say 'no bullshit.' So maybe it's time we really lived by that. If we agree not to do something, we can't turn around and break that agreement. We have to be able to trust each other."

"Okay, deal. But you promise that if something does happen to me, you will live out your life," I reply.

"Fine, I will live out my life. And get remarried and stuff."

"What? No! You are to mourn for me for the rest of your life," I order playfully.

"Okay, deal."

"Aaden…I'm serious. If something happens to me, promise you won't take your life. Please."

"I promise. And you promise me that we will make major decisions together."

"Yes."

"Come here, I've wanted to do this since you woke up from the warehouse," he says as he pulls me close. He places my face in between his hands and kisses me hungrily. When he pulls away, I feel a sharp pang of disappointment. I want more of him. Not just his kisses, I want more of his love, his compassion, his light.

Please let the virus be gone. Let me have a chance to have his daughter someday.

***

Once we are all back in the room, the Healer asks again if we wouldn't like to have some privacy. I assure her that my team is cleared to hear what's going on with me. Aaden sits beside me and takes my hand, and together we brace ourselves.

"As you well know, you were brought in here having lost a fair amount of blood. In fact, had you not had the strength of a Noru, you would have died," she concludes.

"Thank you for all your help; you saved our leader," Swoop says.

"It's our pleasure. However, there's more. The virus, as you can tell, is gone, hence the mark fading from your skin. I take it before the battle with

Ever, you and Silver were 'together'?" the Healer says.

"Yeah, they were together all right. That's what caused the earthquakes. It had nothing to do with the end of the world. It was just these two going at it," East jokes. I grab a pillow and throw it at him; East ducks just in time.

"Well, the good news is, there was a Sib made in the process," the Healer informs us.

Aaden and I look at each other, both too overwhelmed with happiness to speak. But then his expression quickly changes.

"You said there 'was' a Sib. Is the Sib gone? Did we lose..." Aaden can't bring himself to finish his thought.

"Let me see if I can explain this in a way you can understand. Most angels think that they are pregnant when the Alexi lands at their feet. But the Sib comes before the bird. The Sib forms in minutes or in days, it varies. But it gets here first. It sends a beacon to the Alexi, letting the creature know that it is ready for travel. When you were struck with the virus, the Sib was not strong enough to send out a beacon as of yet. Then the virus hit, and whatever strength the Sib had was all but drained," the Healer says.

"But the virus is gone now. Summit can regain her strength, right?" I plead.

"Summit?" the Healer replies.

"They named her already," Diana explains sadly.

"Okay, well...Summit was already small to begin with, hence not being able to call to the Alexi. But after the virus, she went from small to possibly not existing at all," the Healer says gently.

"What do you mean 'possibly'? We need to know for sure," I push.

"Like a human fetus, a Sib excretes a chemical in the blood of the mother. Our equipment was able to detect that chemical. But only a trace amount."

"What does that mean?" Aaden asks.

"It means in a few hours, if the Sib was strong enough to hold on, Alexi will come. But if it wasn't..." The Healer stops speaking and bites her lower lip.

"So we have to wait and hope Summit gains enough strength? Is there a way we can give her more strength? Is there a way we can make her stronger?" I beg.

"No, all you can do is wait and see. I'm sorry," the Healer replies.

"It's gonna be okay. She's strong. I know that in my heart. She'll be okay," I reply as I look at Aaden. He kisses my hand and agrees with me.

"Summit will find a way to get to us," Aaden replies.

"I wish that was all the news I had," the Healer says.

"There's more?" East asks.

"Yes. The two Sives that were in your body were queens. Much like a beehive has its rulers, so do Sives. Only queen Sives can split into two. That means they were extra powerful and ate very quickly. The damage most Sives do in hours, they did in minutes. That is why you are so weak," she says.

"Okay, so is there a mixture to make me stronger?" I ask.

"You don't understand. The Sives ate almost eighty-five percent of your soul."

"What? How can that be? Shouldn't she be knocked out if that was the case?" East shouts, in great distress.

"Normally, yes. But again, she's a Noru. So the remaining fifteen percent is working really hard to pick up the slack," the Healer adds.

"So what do we do? How do we fix this?" Aaden pleads with her.

"Here's what you need to know: There's a new procedure called Sempra. It's the process in which we create a synthetic soul and incorporate it into the existing one," the Healer replies.

"Does it really work?" I ask.

"Yes, we've had great success with it. You would have your strength back almost immediately. If you are no longer pregnant, this procedure should work very well. However, if you are..."

"I'm sorry, I don't get it. Just explain it to us as plainly as you can," I reply, desperate to stay calm.

"Right now, the Sib—Summit—if she is still inside you, she has a forty percent chance of growing strong enough to signal to Alexi. Now, if we do the procedure, the trauma to you would be minimal, but it would lower Summit's chances for survival."

"You said she had a forty percent chance of survival. How much lower would her chances be?" Diana asks.

"It would go from forty percent to five."

"Then no, we won't do the procedure, right?" I reply, turning to Aaden.

"My wife is right, no procedure," he says.

"I understand. But you should know that right now you are very weak, Pryor. You would not, *could* not survive an attack," the Healer warns.

"So if a demon attacked me, I wouldn't be able to take a hit. Got it. I'll just make sure they never get the drop on me," I reply.

"Pryor, you aren't getting it. Forget about a demon, or even a Quo, hitting you. If a human walked in here and punched you in the face hard enough, you'd die—instantly. That is how weak you are," the Healer replies.

"That can't be—I'm the First Noru."

"You are an angel with most of her soul missing. If you don't get this procedure done right now, your days as the First Noru are over."

CHAPTER FIFTEEN
ANYTHING YOU WANT

In the past few years we have encountered situations that I never thought we would. I can say that very little surprises me at this point. But sitting here listening to the Healer tell me that my days as leader are over…I never saw this coming. I can't begin to wrap my head around what she's saying. It's one thing to have to choose between Summit and the team. But choosing between Summit and the world is just not fair.

"Pry, are you okay?" East asks.

"Yeah, fine," I reply as Aaden and I exchange looks of concern.

"Is there any way you could be wrong about this?" Diana asks.

"I wish I were. I ran multiple tests. The results are the same. Pryor can stay weak and give Summit a good chance at being born or she can get the procedure, get back her strength, and battle evil again. However, she would be giving her child a five percent chance of survival at that point," the Healer replies regretfully.

"There has to be something else you can do. There has to be another way. She shouldn't have to make this choice," Swoop pleads.

"I'm sorry. But I really do want to impress upon you the time aspect of this decision. If we are going to do the procedure, it should be as soon as possible," the Healer reminds us.

The team asks her a bunch of questions, but in the end, there is no getting around it: it has to be Summit or the world.

I know that the team needs to get back to the mission. Even in my daze, I know that time is being wasted. I should be the one to order the team to get back to work, but I can't find the strength. Aaden can see that in my eyes, as both my husband and the second in command. He tells the team to go to the cabin and get the weapons my grandfather has in the mountains.

"Guys, we need to stick to the plan. You need to go get the weapons," Aaden says.

"We can't leave Pry like this. We have to help you guys," Swoop says as she sadly places her head on Aaden's chest.

"I know, Bird. But the fact is we are quickly running out of time. Regardless of what Pry and I decide, we still need you to get the ashes from Apex. So let's stick to the plan. You guys get going. Head for the mountains."

"Fine, but before we go, there has to be a quiet place around here where the couple can make up their minds," Diana says.

"Well…yes, I suppose so. There's a garden out back. It should be fairly peaceful," the Healer says.

"Okay, we'll talk things over and be right back," Aaden replies as he places a soft, thick blanket around me. Dylan holds the door for us and we head out into the hallway.

***

We walk into the garden and immediately encounter the scent of jasmine and lilies. The garden is small but well maintained. It's illuminated by small floating beams of light that hover above the stone pathway. In the center of the garden is a little cascading stone pond full of fish. The only sound we hear is the water streaming through the rocks as it makes its way to the center of the pond. Along the pathway is a bright red bench that looks out onto the water. Aaden and I hold hands, make our way to the bench, and sit down.

"It's really quiet out here. You'd never know we are at war," he says.

"Yeah, maybe we can find somewhere in this garden to hide so reality doesn't find us," I reply.

"I have a feeling it would," he says sadly.

"Yeah, probably," I say mostly to myself.

"Babe, we can figure this out together. Okay?" he offers.

"Yeah, okay," I reply, unable to meet his eyes. He gently turns my head so that I am facing him. I didn't want him to see me cry, but it's too late now.

"I know, I know…" he says as he pulls me close and lets me sob on his chest. When I am finally able to talk, he wipes my tears away and reminds me that I am not alone.

"Whatever you want to do, I'm behind you," he vows.

"Our daughter is a fighter; for her to hang on as hard as she's been doing…she's already amazing. And the thought of doing anything that could cause her to die before we even meet her…" I reply as I shake my head in disbelief.

"I agree. I do. But we can't leave you in this weakened state," he says desperately.

"You remember the first battle tournament we had in school? Where we had to battle in front of a crowd and get graded on it?" I ask.

"Yeah, it was a big deal. My dad fought to be allowed in. He watched me battle with this big grin on his face. He was so proud," Aaden recalls.

"Yeah, my dad was too. Uncle Jay and Miku came to see the twins, and Easton's mom came to see him. The only one who wasn't there was my mom. She had to be on the front line of a battle with some evil entity that was sucking souls out of humans as they slept. I was so disappointed and hurt that she didn't show up."

"I remember that. Your dad tried to cheer you up, but it didn't work," Aaden replies.

"No, it didn't. I was seven, so that hurt and disappointment came in the form of rudeness and anger. When my mom got home later, I shouted at her that she didn't love me and that I wanted a different mom. It destroyed her at the time.

"She looked me in the eye and said, 'Carrot, I love you. I love you more than anything else in this world. And I am so sorry I could not be there for you today. But the truth is there will be days when you cannot be both a good mother and a leader. There will be days when you will have to choose between your duty and your family. Saving humanity is my duty. And sometimes it means breaking my children's hearts.'"

"What did you say to her?" he asks.

"Nothing. I stopped talking to her for a whole week because I didn't get it then. She said that I would understand one day. And now I do. I understand that today. Because as much as I love Summit, as much as I want to see her little face, and as much as I want to hold her in my arms, I know I can't allow humanity to suffer. There are millions of children out there, millions of moms who don't have anyone to stand between them and total annihilation. They have to come first," I reply, trying to steady my voice.

"I know, but, Pry, she's here. Summit is real. We have a kid. She's ours. How can we let her die? I know it's wrong to let millions get killed, but I can't lose another little girl. I don't know how to get past that. Not again," he pleads.

"Aaden, I will not make this decision without you. If you want me to give up the team, I will. If you want me to leave the battle to you, I will. But you have to know that there are humans out there who have no one. And everyone we know who was killed, dead in service to humanity, including your mom—if we let this happen…it was all for nothing."

"Pry, I can't. I can't say it's okay to take away our daughter's chance at life. I can't say it's okay to kill her. Please don't ask me to do that," he begs.

"You don't have to say it. You just take my hand and I'll do what we have to do," I whisper. Aaden's hands are at his sides, unable to move and connect with mine. He cannot bring himself to do what has to be done.

"Listen, there is a five percent chance that Summit will be strong enough to summon Alexi. She's your child and mine. That means she's powerful. And that five percent may be all she needs. But if I don't fight, there is a one hundred percent chance that everything ends. Summit might not live. But if we do nothing about Malakaro, humanity will *certainly* not live."

"You think she can survive with a five percent chance?" he says, sounding pained and overwhelmed.

"I think if any kid can, it's her. We have to have a little faith, okay? Have faith in our little girl."

"Pry…losing Sparks was so hard. It was so…"

"I know, I know. But Summit is the First Torian. She's the child of a First

Noru. And she's Rage's granddaughter. Not to mention being the offspring of the second most powerful angel in the world. We need to stop acting like this is the end for Summit. She is from a long line of pigheaded and strong women. She will make it. She will beat the odds. We have to believe that," I push.

"Omnis could take her away from me…he has never given me anything," he says pensively.

"Aaden, Omnis has given you more than he has anyone. He gave you a great father. He gave you a team that would die for you and a wife who would quickly give her soul to be beside you. He gave you Sparks, and even though that time was short, it changed you. It made you a better angel.

"And I know it's hard to see it sometimes, but he gave you the Center. Your time there made you strong. It let you see just how powerful you really are. You were in that hell for a whole year and you didn't give in. You didn't give up, so let's not do that now. She has a five percent chance. That's all she needs. Don't give up on our baby," I implore.

"She is from a long line of stubborn women. And if anyone can do the impossible, it would have to be your kid…but what if she needs more time? What if she's almost strong enough to call Alexi and then we shut everything down by doing the procedure?" he says.

"We will give Summit as much time as we can. You and the team will face Apex, and I will stay here in case Alexi comes. If Alexi doesn't come by the time the team is done with Apex, I will get the procedure done," I explain.

"Summit might already have Alexi in the air right now, headed our way, right?" he asks hopefully.

"Right," I reply as we look up at the night sky. Had this been a book or a movie, the Alexi would come right here and now. But this is real life, so there is nothing in the sky. All we can do is buy Summit an hour or so. Then we will have to reduce her chances and hope for the best.

"There's nothing up there," Aaden says, sounding gutted.

"Not yet, but there will be. Summit will bring Alexi to us. Have faith in her. In us," I reply as I hold out my hand. He takes it, signaling that he's okay with the decision we made together.

Sweetheart, please come to us. We love you so much already. Daddy wants to meet you, and your mom, she's aching to have you in her arms. Summit, come home…

***

When we come back into the room, the team is still there. I can't be angry with them; I know they are just worried about us. We tell the Healer what we have decided. She's glad that we agree to the procedure, but she's unhappy with us waiting until the team comes back with the ashes.

"You will keep growing weaker," the Healer stresses.

"I know, but while we can't give Summit all the time she needs, we are certainly going to give her whatever time we have. So the team will go get the ashes and I will stay behind and hope that Summit can bring Alexi to us. And if she can't do that by the time the team comes back, we will do the operation and get my strength back," I reply.

"Is this what you two have decided?" the Healer asks.

"Yes, we are both in agreement," Aaden says.

"Okay, I'll get the mixtures ready," the Healer says as she walks out of the room.

"I'm so sorry, guys," Swoop says.

"Yeah, we are too. But Summit is a fighter. We have to have a little faith," Aaden says as he looks over at me.

"Well, we're gonna take off and be back as soon as we can," East says.

"Hopefully Julian will have Apex's location by the time we are done collecting the weapons," Swoop says.

"Diana, I need you to find Bex. I know he's in the middle of a battle, but I think we're going to need him for the mission to find Apex. Can you go get him?" Aaden asks.

"Yeah, sure," Diana says, taken aback by Aaden's willingness to involve the Kon.

"Also, Dylan, can you stay with my wife?" Aaden asks.

"Ah…yeah, okay," Dylan replies, looking slightly disappointed.

"I feel better knowing she's being looked after by someone capable," Aaden says, trying to appeal to the angel's ego. It works. Dylan smiles and sits beside me on the bed. Swoop gives him a kiss and thanks him as she flies out the window. Everyone on the team takes off except Aaden; I know he's having difficulty leaving me.

"I'll be back as soon as we get the ashes," he promises as he tucks me back into bed.

"Please be careful," I reply.

"I will. Look, I know it's hard for you to sit back and watch yet another mission take place without you, but I promise I will take care of the team. You lie here and rest. Take care of our daughter."

"Deal," I reply.

"I know you will be watching everything. Just don't get too excited," Aaden warns.

"I got it, Mom," I tease.

"Dylan, watch her," Aaden says, then kisses my forehead and flies away. Dylan helps me prep the device while we wait for it to turn on.

"I'm sorry you're stuck here with me," I tell him as he mounts the device onto the rail of the bed.

"It's okay. I think Swoop is happy that I'm not coming," Dylan replies.

"She wants you to be safe."

"I get that. But if being in battle is the only way I get to be around her..."

"You really love her, don't you?" I ask.

"Yeah, but I don't know if that's enough," he admits.

"So what is it with you two? Why is she putting up such a big fight?" I wonder.

"She won't admit it, but I think it's because of Raven, her alter ego. She thinks that she doesn't deserve to be happy because she has an evil side. She thinks she should be punished for hurting so many innocent people."

"That's crazy. Swoop couldn't help herself. It wasn't on purpose," I reply.

"I tried to tell her that, but it didn't work. She thinks she should be punished, not rewarded with a relationship."

"Did you tell her she was wrong?" I ask.

"I did. I said, 'Swoop, believe me, I'm no prize,'" he jokes. He makes me smile. That is not an easy thing to do right now. So I thank him.

"It's my pleasure. I've always wondered what it would feel like to be part of a team. And now I know it's pretty nice. Now, I only have two other things on my bucket list," he says.

"What's a 'bucket list'?" I ask.

"Something humans do. They write a list of things they want to do before they die," he says.

"Wow, that doesn't sound ominous at all," I tease, trying to keep my mind off Alexi.

"It's a little nuts, but I kind of like it," Dylan says.

"So what else is on your list?" I ask.

"Get Swoop to marry me. And see an Echo up close and personal."

"What's an Echo?" I ask.

"It's a—never mind. I'm talking too much. Swoop always jokes that I'm like Google's annoying cousin," he jokes.

"No, please. Keep talking. The team is still in flight and the device is not up yet, so I can't see what they're doing. And if I lie here and look out the window, waiting for Alexi without a distraction, I'll go mad. Please, go on," I plead.

"Um…okay. An Echo is a being that is chosen by Omnis to replace another powerful being. So let's say Time is destined to be replaced someday. If there is a being strong enough to harbor multiple powers and someone who has a strong character, Omnis chooses them and allows them to be the replacement."

"So an Echo is a being that will take over for another powerful being?" I ask.

"Yes."

"But how do you know when an Echo is born?" I ask.

"The Alexi is a different color than it normally would be. As you know, Alexi are silver. But if it's carrying a Sib that's slated to become an Echo, the Alexi's color will change."

"Wait, I've heard about colorful Alexi before, but I thought that was just a story, a legend. Are you saying it's real?" I ask.

"Oh yes, Echos are real. They are just…very rare. Like never happened before ever kind of rare. I read about it an obscure journal I found years ago," Dylan admits.

"So it could just as easily be a lie," I reply gently.

"Okay, maybe—but it's not. I just believe that somewhere out there is an Echo. A perfectly powerful being slated to take the place of Time, Fate, or whoever. I just have faith that such a thing exists."

"Fair enough. What color is the Alexi once it makes contact with an Echo?" I wonder.

"The color of Alexi depends on who the Echo is here to replace. Let's say Fate is dying and Omnis picked a being to replace him. The Alexi would turn sapphire in color. If the Sib were going to replace Time, it would be ruby colored. And if it was supposed to replace Death, it would then be onyx."

"So that's your dream? To see a colorful Alexi?" I ask.

"It's not just that. An Echo is rarer than the Hale-Bopp comet. That's a comet that's like a thousand times brighter than Halley's comet. It's absolutely perfect. Anyway, the comet is nothing compared to an Echo. And Echo is a being that is handpicked by Omnis to replace someone powerful. Could you imagine being handpicked? Think about it, you are just sitting here and suddenly a red Alexi comes to you," he says.

"Honestly, right now I'd settle for just the common everyday silver Alexi. That would be enough of a miracle for me," I admit sadly.

"Oh, right. Sorry. I'll go get more blankets. You look cold," he says as he hustles out of the room. He's embarrassed that he went on and on like he did. I smile to myself as I watch him leave. We have to get Swoop to give him a chance. Dylan is so sweet—awkward, but sweet.

I look out the window, as if Alexi had scheduled an appointment with me. There's nothing in the air. I tap my fingers on the bed restlessly. I then rake my hands through my hair and sigh loudly. I look at the sky again. Nothing.

C'mon, Alexi! Where the hell are you?

***

(MATURE CONTENT AHEAD. YOUNGER READERS CAN SKIP TO THE NEXT CHAPTER WITHOUT MISSING ANY PLOT POINTS.)

Just when I think I'm about to lose it, the Eagle Eye device comes on. It's feeding from Diana's tracker. It shows me a clear picture of her in a small town in China, talking to her army of Paras. She asks for Bex and they tell her he's in one of the small hotels along the street. They ask her if there is anything they can do for her. She thanks them for doing a great job driving out the demons that were overrunning the town. She warns them to be vigilant, as the fight is far from over.

She walks towards the quaint hotel and enters. The property is painted light yellow with white trim. There are large vases of fading roses throughout the hotel; the front lobby has shabby but charming furniture that gives the place an old "faded romance" vibe. Diana calls out to Bex but doesn't get a reply. So she heads up to the third floor, where the Omari said he'd be. She enters the only room with the light on and finds Bex wet and naked, fresh from his shower.

Her eyes are wide with surprise and she turns her head away, embarrassed. She quickly explains that I sent her and updates him. She does this all while looking at the floor. I never took Diana for the type to be rattled by naked flesh. In fact, everything I know about her says she is the opposite. Yet here she is bowing her head like she's never laid eyes on a naked angel before.

"Is Pryor okay?" he asks.

"Yup, she is just waiting on Alexi," Diana says.

"Good. Are you going to avert your eyes the whole time?" he asks.

"Oh, I'm sorry. I didn't know—I mean—I should go," she mumbles as Bex grabs a towel and places it around his waist.

"Or you could stay..." he says as he walks over to her and closes the door.

She stares at his wet, bare chest and seems to be mesmerized by it. She shakes herself out of the trance by clearing her throat and making herself look into Bex's eyes instead. That doesn't help. Bex has eyes that pull you in and make you want to stay there. He looks at her with a serious, intense gaze.

"I shouldn't be here," she says mostly to herself.

"What if I want you here?" he says in a gravelly voice.

"Bex, I don't want a one-night stand—not with you," she confesses.

"What do you want?"

"You're going to laugh at me, but...I want a 'movie' kind of love," she says, looking away.

He smiles and slowly nods.

"What? It's stupid, right? I mean girls like me generally get one-night stand offers only," she says.

"I know all about one-night stands. I've had a few of them lately. And when I think about you, I don't want you to be in that category," he says.

"You think about me?" she asks, taken aback.

"When we're in battle, I always look around to see where you are in relation to where I am. Just in case you need me. But you never need me."

"Oh..."

"When I think about you, I can't help but be impressed. You're fearless, resourceful, and given everything you've been through...you amaze me," he says softly.

"Thank you," she mumbles, unable to hide from his ardent stare.

"You've been on my mind, but in the past I fought against it."

"And now?" she asks.

"Now, I have another reason to dislike Silver—he saw you naked."

"Silver never loved me, at least not like he loved her. We spent a hundred nights together, entangled in the most scandalous ways. But nothing Silver and I did alone in a bedroom could compare to the simple act of him holding Pryor's hand."

"Do you wish he was here instead of me?" Bex asks.

She walks over to the double glass doors that lead out to the balcony. I can tell she wants to go outside. The rain hasn't let up; in fact, it's pouring even more than before. Diana looks at her reflection in the glass door and sees Bex standing behind her.

"Diana, do you wish Silver was here instead of me?" he asks again.

"No, I don't wish that. But I am afraid," Diana confesses.

"What are you afraid of?" he asks.

"Falling for a guy who wants my friend and not me—again."

"That's not what's happening right now," he assures her.

"Then what's happening?" she asks.

Bex takes a small vial of Tam and gives it to Diana. She drinks it, never taking her eyes off him.

"The guy who was too stupid, too dense, and too blind to see you is finally coming to his senses. And all he wants to do is make love to you—if you let him," he says.

She addresses his reflection on the glass door but doesn't turn to face him. "Bex?" she calls out softly.

"Yes?"

"Don't hurt me," she says. It isn't a warning; it is a plea. I didn't realize just how much she loves him. I don't think she did either, at least not until this moment. Diana is a powerful, resourceful, and dangerous demon. But right now, she's just a girl who's seriously in fear of getting her heart broken.

Bex leans into her and whispers a promise in her ear. "My love won't ever hurt."

I should look away, but I can't. Maybe I'm just nosy. Maybe I'm a pervert who loves to watch, or maybe it makes me happy to watch two beings finally get the happiness they deserve. Either way, I look on and watch the Kon and the Kaster make love for the very first time.

He stands behind her, and she watches his movements in the glass door. I think she's expecting him to pull her close and kiss her. But he doesn't. Bex has his own plans. He's going to give her what she's been wanting for so long—"movie" love.

He glides his hands up and down her arms slowly. His movements are smooth and gentle. He doesn't rush; he takes his time as he kisses her collarbone and grazes her neck with his lips. When he reaches her lips, he skillfully parts them with his tongue, all the while continuously stroking her. I can practically feel Diana shiver from the heat generated by Bex's touch.

The subtle, light touch of his tongue on the nape of her neck is sending a flood of pleasure through her body, so much so that she sighs heavily. She lifts her hair up so he can unbutton her blouse. He does exactly as she wishes and removes it; the soft material flows down to the floor. With her back now exposed, he unhooks her bra and leaves behind a trail of tender, soft kisses. The kisses start at the back of her neck and go down to the space between her shoulder blades. When the bra becomes a hindrance, he peels it off her and lets it fall to the floor as well.

He teases her by whisking the tip of his fingers against her stiff nipples. She arches her back. He uses both hands to massage her breasts and send her into overdrive. She hooks her arms around his neck while still facing the glass door. Bex works her upper body over with the same determination he has in battle. He kneads her breasts until her eyes roll to the back of her head and her knees start to buckle.

He reaches under her skirt and slides her white lace panties off her. The dampness in the middle panel of her underwear makes him growl. He places his hand between her legs and explores the area he just stripped bare. Once his fingers are inside her, he gasps loudly.

"Damn, baby, you're so wet..." He groans with pleasure.

No longer able to contain himself, he takes her skirt off, turns her around to face him, and carries her to the bed. He gently lays her down, removes his towel, and stands above her. But as much as he longs for her, he's smart enough to take his time. He admires her body with a heated, sincere gaze.

Bex is genuinely taken by how stunning the girl on the bed really is. Diana's been ravished before, but this isn't that. This is something new, something wondrous, and that frightens her. Diana quickly sits up and covers her breasts with the white blanket. There's alarm in her eyes and tension in her shoulders.

"Diana, I don't want to stop touching you. When I drink from your lips, it feels like I'm drinking straight from the light. Just now, I begged Omnis to end my life because I knew I would never feel as good as I did when my fingers were inside you. But if you want me to stop, I will," he vows.

"The guy I was with before I died—Sebastian—I felt about him the way I feel about you. I thought he was a good guy, but he stood by as his father raped me. I survived it by telling myself that sex is nothing, it's no big deal. I told myself over and over again. I started to believe it. It helped make the pain stop, and now…now you're here and it's special…special scares me," she admits with tears in her eyes.

"Then we can stop," he says as he puts the towel back on and sits down beside her.

"Are you sure?"

"Yes," he says as he gently kisses her forehead.

"I'm sorry. I've never had to stop before."

"Don't be sorry. Don't ever be sorry for that. We don't have to have sex. We don't have to do anything but be here with each other," he says as he positions himself so that her head is resting on his chest. He holds her close and lovingly strokes her hair.

"I've wanted this for a long time now—can't believe I'm blowing it," she says mostly to herself.

"You're not. I like having you near me. I'll take you any way I can get," he says.

"I had a choice of outfits," she says, sounding distant.

"What do you mean?" he asks.

"That night, the night of the rape, I could have gone with a longer skirt. I could have gone with a looser shirt or—"

"Diana, stop. It wasn't your fault. None of it was your fault."

"I know that most of the time. Once in a while—"

"I get it. It's okay. When you start to feel that way, you let me know. I'll help you push that thought away," he replies.

She sits up and turns to face him. "You really do have feelings for me."

"I do."

"Can we try again?" she says.

"Diana, we don't have to—"

"I know, I want to. I want us to make love…"

He doesn't jump right back in. Instead, he plants light, tender kisses on her lips. He kisses her eyelashes, the tip of her nose, and her knees. She learns that she's ticklish. She starts to giggle; soon the two of them are laughing out loud. But once he starts slowly licking the area below her breasts, above her waist, the laughing stops. Her breathing gets choppy; the moaning begins.

He kisses every exposed inch of her, turns her over, and grazes his lips between her shoulder blades and down to her lower back. He gently runs his fingers, lips, and tongue across her entire body in slow, concentric circles. Judging by her incoherent moans and shaking, Diana is soaking wet and on the edge of ecstasy. Unable to take it anymore, she begs him to be inside her.

But Bex has found a thrill in making love to Diana that he has not found with anyone else. I can tell because he's looking at her like she's a treasure he's found, one he would rather die than watch get taken away.

Bex doesn't want it to end. He doesn't want to stop touching the places that are making her writhe in ecstasy. The only thing the Kon wants to do is get as close to Diana as he can. So he parts her knees and "drinks" from her center. It only takes a few minutes for Diana to start convulsing with pleasure.

She cries out in frenzied lust and begs once again for Bex to have mercy on her. Bex, unable and unwilling to stop, dives deeper inside her with his tongue. Diana cries out as she tries to close her legs and get away from the overwhelming sea of pleasure she's drowning in.

Bex won't allow her to escape. She moves her hips off the bed, she squirms, and she bucks back and forth. But Bex is able to keep up with her. She's so taken by lust and pleasure she slams her palm against the side of the bed. By the time Bex is ready to stop, Diana is a weak and trembling, blissful mess.

Bex lies next to her, and she summons all the energy she has left and straddles him. They take turns exploring each other. Bex suckles on her fingers and she groans. She catches his nipples between her lips and flicks them with her tongue until Bex's eyes glaze over. She glides her lips over his taut abs and pecs. She lowers her head and takes him into her mouth. He starts speaking a language no one has ever heard before. Diana starts to hum softly with Bex in her mouth; the vibrations send the Kon into orbit.

"Diana—anything—anything you want—just don't stop! Don't stop—oh shit!"

He grabs Diana roughly by her shoulders, lifts her up in the air, and impales her onto him. She rides with a passion and desire that can only come from being in love. They thrust against each other repeatedly; each time they collide, it causes a rush of ecstasy that makes them both cry out.

They lock hands as the final wave of passion comes over them. The Inner Arc is strong and jarring. The orgasm rocks them both to the core. Diana bites his shoulder, and he grabs her throat and squeezes as the ecstasy engulfs them both. They lie there. Naked. Exhausted. Happy.

"What are you doing all the way over there?" he asks when he sees that Diana has placed several feet between them.

"I don't know. I guess this is usually the part where I flee the scene. Or the part where the guy wants to go."

"Get over here," he says. Her back is to him, but she closes some of the gap between them.

"Closer," he orders gently.

She does as he asks.

"Closer," he says again. They are now so close there is no air between them. She is right up against his body as they spoon each other. He brushes the hair from her face, kisses her temple, and covers his girl with his wings.

CHAPTER SIXTEEN
ANYTHING FOR YOU

Dylan enters the room as I throw a sheet over the device and hang my head in shame. He looks at me and asks if I'm okay. He thinks this is about Summit or the team, but he's wrong. This is about the stupid thing that I just did.

"Pryor, what happened?" he asks.

"I'm a pervert. That's what happened. I'm a peeper, like a creepy old man in a stalker movie," I reply.

"No, you're not. Why would you say that?" he says.

"The device came on and I saw Diana and Bex having...you know."

"Oh, and you didn't turn away?" he asks.

"Are you kidding? I was two seconds away from getting popcorn and batteries! Who does that? What kind of perv am I? Why didn't I turn away?" I ask as I bury my head in my pillow.

"I could think of a few reasons."

"Me too. I'm demented and creepy," I reply.

"Well...on the surface. But there's more to it than that. There's research that says people become voyeurs because it makes them feel alive."

"That's no excuse. Dylan, it was a really intimate moment between two beings, and I should not have been there. And if Diana and Bex find out I watched, they would be mortified," I reply.

"Don't be so hard on yourself. Looking at another couple is forbidden; everyone likes things that are forbidden. Also, I suspect that had it not been the Kon and the queen, you would have turned away."

"Great, so I'm only a pervert when it comes to them. Awesome."

"Pryor, I can think of three really good non-pervert reasons as to why you watched your ex and his new girl have sex."

"Okay, lay it on me," I reply, eager for an explanation.

"You are waiting to find out if your child is going to be born. You are in need of a distraction in the worst way. And I bet the whole time you were watching, you didn't think about Alexi or look out the window to see if she was coming."

"Well, yeah. It did take my mind off everything for a while," I admit.

"Also, I know you and the Kon used to be together. I'm gonna take a wild guess here and say that he wasn't the one that broke it off."

"No, I ended things with Bex," I mumble.

"You have a big heart and hurting him made you feel really bad. But watching him find a new love, a new source of enjoyment, it assuaged your guilt," Dylan says.

"Yeah, it made me feel better to know he was happy…"

"Exactly."

"What's the third reason?" I ask.

"The third is a little…dark. You know that some pregnant angels have died while Alexi sucks up the Sib inside them. It's a major stress to the body. If Summit gets enough strength to summon Alexi, that doesn't mean that you will be strong enough to endure Alexi cutting you open to suck Summit out of you. You could very well die in childbirth," he says grimly.

"I know that can happen…don't ask me to talk about that. I can't," I admit.

"Yeah, I guessed that. That takes us back to reason number three: it's easier to watch two beings having hot sex than to wait for the bird that may essentially kill you," he says gently.

Thankfully I don't have to reply to that because just then I get a phone call. I pick up and speak to my grandpa briefly. Once I'm off the phone, I update Dylan and let him know that Grandpa found Apex's location.

"Grandpa called Aaden and gave him all the info," I conclude.

"So everyone is headed there now?" Dylan asks.

"Yes," I reply.

"And where exactly is 'there'? Where's Apex's home?"

"In the center of the Black Forest in Germany," I inform him.

"Do you really think it's a good idea that they go into the forest?" Dylan asks.

"Yes, the forest is safe, nurturing, and fills me with ease," I reply sardonically.

"Guess I touched a nerve. Sorry," he says.

"No, it's not you. I just hate to think of them out there with some crazy angel hell-bent on revenge. And the forest has never been good to us. I think Apex knows that. I think he knew exactly what he was doing when he stole the ashes and placed them in a forest of all places. I have a bad feeling about this," I reply.

"Me too, but we don't have a choice. We only have two hours left until Malakaro breaks free," he reminds me.

"That's why they have to go in and hope for the best. And I have to just sit here, helpless, and watch," I reply miserably.

"I talked to Swoop, and if it helps, some of the weapons they found in the mountains are really cool."

"What did they find?" I ask.

"A coin that turns into a sword—the sword of Avery! It was so named after the queen of the Paras centuries ago. She used it to single-handedly save the day. The Omari were in a battle, they were losing to evil, and she took up the sword and managed to slay them all," Dylan says.

"I heard about her in school. She was a real badass. It's said that sword can cut through anything," I reply excitedly.

"Well, almost anything. It can't harm an angel because it was made by angels."

"Damn it! So I can't use it against Malakaro?" I ask.

"No. But it would be the perfect weapon for—"

"Alago. So Swoop found the weapon for me to use to kill my best friend?"

"Yeah. Basically. But it can also slay demons," he says, trying to cheer me up.

"What else did they find?"

"The Blade of Alkar. It takes in any substance you place it in. So once we get the ashes, we scatter them over the dagger, and the blade will take on the power of the ash. It will strip Malakaro of his powers."

"So a sword to kill Alago and a dagger to weaken Malakaro. Sounds easy," I lie.

"How bad is it that Apex wants to meet in a forest?" he asks, unable to hide his worry.

"It's really bad," I admit.

He looks out the window as worry creeps into his eyes and makes its way through his body. He looks like he could take to the sky at any moment to go help Swoop. In fact, I'm pretty sure he will take off if I don't find a way to distract him from the dangers the team is about to face.

"Hey, don't worry, Dylan, I have Easton's password for HBO GO! We have more than enough thinly veiled porn to get us through the night," I tease. We share a much-needed laugh.

"Hey, the device just turned on," Dylan says as he spots the light coming from under the sheet. I grab the device and place it so that we both have a view of the Black Forest. Dylan and I share the same silent prayer: Dear Omnis, let them all make it out of there alive…

***

The team lands in Germany not long after receiving the coordinates; Bex and Diana have now joined them. They find themselves in the front yard of an estate that's been carved right into the mountain. It resembles a small castle. It's made of large stone, curved archways, and wide spiral stone steps. It looks like something out of a dark fairy tale. Beyond the castle is a vast, dense forest that spans thousands of acres. There is a long white table set up with a linen tablecloth, napkins, and antique chairs. The table is set for six.

"A dining table set on top of a mountain, with a dark and mysterious forest looming just beyond us. This looks like it's gonna go very well," East quips.

"Yup, this has 'lovely evening' written all over it," Swoop says.

"Keep your eyes open. I have no doubt Apex knows we're here," Aaden says.

"Judging by his table decor, he's expecting us," Bex replies.

"He may be a madman, but his taste in dinnerware is flawless," Diana says as she picks up a champagne flute and studies it up close.

"Naturally, my love, anything for you and your team. I am sorry to hear your leader will not be joining us. I had plans for her," someone says at the top of the stone staircase. They look up in the direction the voice came from and find a tall, slim angel with sharp facial features. He has bone-straight, long blond hair and wears a long gray button-down, suede jacket. He looks like he belongs in another time period.

"Who the hell are you?" Aaden demands.

"My dear sir, I do believe you have wandered onto my property, so I believe it is I who should ask the questions," he says as he makes his way down the staircase. His style is elegant, his movement graceful, but something about his clear blue eyes disturbs me.

"Are you Apex?" Bex calls out.

"Kon, it hurts me that you do not recall who I am. But then again you were so young when we met. I shall make allowances for your ignorance and I will not be offended," Apex replies, clearly proud of himself.

"Where is the vial of ash? Give it to us now and we will let you live," Aaden offers.

"Silver, I must admit I happen to be a big fan. How is it that you survived all those awful days and nights at the Center? I have to admit, at first, I was upset that a mere child was outdoing my creation. But then I started to understand that you, Silver, were a gift. You pushed me to work harder, to stretch the boundaries of pain and torment. You, my friend, are an inspiration. And I'd like to think that today, today I will make you proud," Apex says.

Aaden is about to tackle him, but Bex wisely holds him back. Suddenly five glass cylinders appear behind all but one of the chairs at the table. They contain human beings with Samson strings around their necks.

"These humans are also guests of mine. Originally I had six, but since your leader couldn't join us, I've had to retire one of them. But don't fret, angels and angel sympathizers, you can still rescue all five humans and get the ashes you came for."

"And how exactly are we supposed to do that?" Swoop asks as she eyes the humans desperately banging on their see-through cages. We can't hear what they're saying, but it's not hard to see how scared they are.

"That's easy, my dear. All you have to do is simply follow instructions. If you do not, I will be very unhappy, and the ropes around the humans' necks are linked to my mood. Should I be distressed, they will start to tighten around the humans until they too are put out of their misery. So I think the key word here is *manners*. Your team simply must mind their manners," Apex says with a cheerful smile.

"It's obvious you wanted to meet us, so we are here. What the hell do you want?" East says.

Apex frowns, and right away, the ropes around the humans' necks begin to tighten.

"Okay, okay! My cousin is sorry. Now stop hurting the humans," Swoop pleads.

Apex relaxes, as do the ropes around the necks of his prisoners.

"I am so glad we understand each other. Now, please, everyone, have a seat. Dinner will be served shortly," he says as he makes his way to the table. Aaden and the rest of the team reluctantly follow.

"We don't have time to play demonic tea party with the Joker from *Batman*," East whispers to Aaden.

"I agree, but we do anything to him and the humans are dead," Aaden replies as he takes a seat.

"Better five humans than five billion, right?" Diana asks.

"Let's not go down that road just yet. We need to hear him out," Bex says.

"You want us to have a heart-to-heart with the guy who's dressed like a demented extra from *Mad Men*," East replies.

"Until we find out where the ashes are and free the humans, yes. That is exactly what we have to do," Aaden says tightly.

"Okay," East says as he takes a seat alongside the team. Apex sits at the head of the table and casually waves his hand. Shadow Servants appear out of thin air and start to pour Coy into all the glasses. When they are done, they disappear. Apex looks at his guests and raises his glass high in the air, signaling for the team to do the same. The team does as he wishes.

"I would like to propose a toast to family. Be they ever so dimwitted, ill mannered, and vicious, they still belong to us and must be protected. To family!" Apex says as he swallows the glass of Coy in one big gulp. The team doesn't drink. Apex glares at them and silently reminds them of the consequences. They put their drinks to their lips and slowly sip.

"Now, I know you are all wondering why it is you are here," Apex says.

"We came for the ashes," Aaden replies, trying hard not to sound as pissed as he really is.

"The ashes, the humans in the glass tubes, these are all secondary things. I consider them motivational tools in order for us to get together and talk. So often people ignore invites, no matter how beautifully crafted they are. Now that I have gotten you here, I will tell you what this is about," Apex says as the table fills up with various angel-flavored foods. Apex has ordered everything for his guests from mood-elevating fruits to memory-inducing "meats."

"It would be great to know what the purpose of this...dinner really is," Bex says, trying to play along.

"I want to fillet your entire team. I would like your insides spread among the forest for the savage creatures of the night to feast on," he says as if he's reciting a beautiful love poem.

"And what did we do to deserve such special attention from you?" Swoop asks politely.

"You killed my sons," Apex says as he cuts into a loaf of bread.

"If you cared so much about them, why didn't you fight for them?" Aaden asks.

"You allowed your daughter to be killed. Does that mean you didn't care for her?" Apex says.

Aaden clenches his jaw. He's seconds away from beating the shit out of Apex. Swoop places a hand on Aaden's shoulder, hoping it's enough to calm him down—it is, for now.

"I must admit, while I was desperately in love with their mother, the twins didn't really mean anything to me. They were more of a time suck, really. I looked in on them here and there, but I never cared one way or the other," Apex admits.

"And what changed?" East asks, full of disdain.

"Nothing, I still don't really care," Apex says.

"Then why did you bring us here? Why are you trying to kill us if you don't care about what we did to Spider and Randy?" Swoop says.

"Do try not to refer to him as Spider. For Omnis' sake, I would rather you call him Alfred. I think that's more of a gentleman's name," Apex says.

"Fine, why are you avenging Alfred?" East asks.

"Because he belonged to me. Granted I never much cared for him, but I find that having something taken away from me, want it or not, is very upsetting. You killed him, and he had my blood in him. I'm not a good father, but I'm not completely void of paternal feelings. You beat my son to death; I think it only fair I return the favor," Apex says.

"What about Randy? All we've done is try to help him. We've saved his life many times. He isn't just a friend to us; he's a member of the team. We have protected him for years," Diana replies.

"Ah yes! Let us see what it means to be protected by the Noru team, shall we?" Apex says as he waves his hand and illuminates the night sky with images of the team's past missions.

We see countless images of Randy being chased by demons, attacked by Powerballs, hurled across the sky, and finally an image of Randy's body being invaded by spiders.

"We tried to protect him, you have to believe that," Swoop says.

"I do; I also believe you failed," Apex says calmly.

"You are such a damn hypocrite. You abandon your kids, treat them like shit, and you think you can bring us here to scold us? Screw you!" East says as he stands up.

Apex waves his hand, and the human in the glass tube behind him is strangled to death in seconds.

"You bastard!" East says as he charges ahead and tries to tackle Apex. Aaden manages to block him in time to stop him. But East isn't ready to back down. He struggles against the hold that Aaden has on him.

Apex picks up the two forks on either side of him, bangs them on the table hard, and cries out, "Manners! Manners! There will be manners at my table!"

Apex is holding on to the forks so tight, the sharp points sink into his flesh and blood oozes out of both hands. He looks at the blood dripping from his hands down to the tablecloth; he goes berserk. He starts talking to someone who isn't there.

"You see, Penny, I can't be held responsible for my actions. These ingrates drive me to distraction!" he bellows.

The team look at each other, confused. They search everywhere but can't see who Apex is talking to.

"No, no, you can't make it better. We have rude guests and they must all be killed…well, yes, I did invite them…they are not behaving very well, Penny…yes, I suppose youth has some part in it…yes, we have worked hard to plan this…but why can't we just kill them all right here and now? They killed Ever, you know…yes, she was a bit batty. Still, we should kill them.

"Yes, I supposed there would be a huge cleanup…okay, all right then. But can I at least strike the insolent one? Yes, he is very much like his father, Rio, full of opinions…you're right, they will all be dead anyway…thank you, Penny, you always ease my mind…" Apex says as he reaches up and kisses the air.

"Look, I love a Lindsay Lohan-style breakdown just as much as the next angel, but we are trying to save all of humanity, including your son. Why aren't you helping us?" East says.

"I don't care about humanity, although I must say I will really miss Tom Cruise. He makes such interesting movies," Apex says.

"Wow, you really are bat-shit crazy…" Diana says.

"Yes, I think so," Apex says seriously, taking time to reflect on the question.

"Alfred is gone, but you can help Randy. There is still hope for him," Swoop says.

"You think my son—a human—is still alive after having been taken over by the second most powerful evil that ever lived? Yet I'm the one who's crazy?" Apex asks.

"Apex, can we speak to Penny?" Aaden asks.

"No! You are all so very rude! She doesn't like that. She has civility. Something you and your team might want to try," Apex says as he gathers himself.

"How long have you and Penny been friends?" Swoop asks.

"Ever since I tried to see the entire future. She came to me and made things better—the blinding headaches, the dizziness, and the screaming. She makes that all better," Apex informs them.

"How does she do that?" Bex asks.

"She talks to me. She lets me know that these things are not my fault. Randall already had a father; he didn't need me. Alfred was going to be evil no matter what, so he didn't need me. I was right to stay away. I was right. Penny reminds me of that," Apex says.

"Penny told you not to kill us?" Bex asks.

"No, she would never say that. She told me not to be so impulsive. I have planned your deaths meticulously. It would be a shame to waste it," Apex replies, now back to "normal."

"What does that mean?" East says, trying not to lose it again.

"Randall was fond of all of you despite the things you all allowed to happen to him. So because of that, I will give you and your team a chance to find what you seek—the ashes. Granted, you will all most likely die in your quest, but still, it's better than killing you all here and now," Apex reasons.

"You're going to make us search for the ashes? We don't have time for that!" Swoop says.

"You don't need to search; the ashes are right behind you," Apex says as he takes a bite of joy-flavored bread.

They turn and spot an object the size of a basketball hovering in the air. It's clear with silver and black markings embedded in it. It's shaped like a pentagon; all five sides have a slot where an old-fashioned key would be placed. Inside the pentagon there is a vial of ashes floating in a sea of blue plasma.

"That lovely little thing is called a Tidum. It's a safe that opens when all the keys have been inserted into it. However, this Tidum is on a timer, hence the blue liquid. Once the box is filled, whatever is inside it self-destructs. To be fair, I got that last part from the *Mission Impossible* franchise. I tell you, Tom does great work. Although that last one…it felt like he was phoning it in," Apex says as he continues to enjoy his meal.

"How do we open the box?" Bex says.

"You need to go get the five keys. I would have thought that was obvious. Duh," Apex says. His behavior is baffling to everyone. On one hand he's stylish and sophisticated, but then he turns and acts out like an immature kid.

"How much time do we have until the box is destroyed?" East says.

"Ten minutes. You should start heading into the forest now," Apex says as he eats.

"That's bullshit! There's no way we can search the entire forest in ten minutes!" Swoop says.

"First of all, that is the last outburst I will allow. Second, who said anything about the keys being in the forest? I said head in that direction. There will be a different adventure waiting for each member of your team. But fair warning, if all of you don't make it back in time to place a key in the lock, the ashes will be gone—forever," Apex informs them.

"This isn't happening! We don't have time for this!" Diana cries out.

"You now have nine minutes and thirty seconds…" Apex says.

"We need the ashes, but you also need something from us. You need us to play your stupid little game. And we aren't going to do that so long as the humans are held captive," Aaden says.

"You act as if you have a choice," Apex counters.

"This movie only works if the hero is motivated enough to try to save the world. I've been through a lot, and maybe I'm okay with watching it all go to hell. Maybe I'm not. But all I know is that my team will do as I say. And

I say we sit here until you free the humans," Aaden demands.

He signals for the team to sit back down at the table. It's hard for them to obey, knowing what's at stake, but they do as Aaden says.

"You're wasting time!" Apex shouts.

The team remains seated. Aaden was right. Apex has planned specific deaths for all of them and he doesn't want his plan to go to waste.

"FINE! FREE THE STUPID HUMANS!" Apex barks as he waves and brings back the Shadow Servants.

"Put them on a Port and send them back where they came from," Aaden demands.

Apex does as he's told. All the humans are safe, apart from the one that died.

"You now have seven minutes," Apex says with a smile. The team runs into the woods, not sure what awaits them.

They get to the center of the forest, where the trees are so thick they can barely make out anything ahead of them. There are animals howling and hissing everywhere. Small winged creatures fly back and forth overhead, and scaly, slimy things move on the forest floor. However, the team don't concern themselves with any of the above. Their attention goes right where Apex wanted it to: the five large red doors hovering just above the forest floor. Each door bears a team member's name. Below the names, the same message is etched.

"And Fear said unto them, 'Feast, my friends! Feast!'"

The five doors open all at once. Large, foul-looking creatures made of smoke and shadow come through the openings and pull each of them into the door with their name on it. I watch in horror as my entire team disappears.

CHAPTER SEVENTEEN
RED DOOR TRIALS

"Pryor, please. If you don't want to calm down for yourself or for Summit, do it for me," Dylan says as I rush to put my street clothes on.

"What do you mean do it for you?" I ask as I look for my shoes.

"I told Silver that I would stay here and watch over you. If he comes back and you are off somewhere trying to stop Apex, he's going to kill me. Do you want my death on your head?" Dylan asks.

"Look, I understand what you're saying, but my team just disappeared into a world created by an angel who is so nuts he makes me miss Raven. I have to go and help."

"Pry, you go out the window and you are risking Summit's health, not to mention your own."

"I can't let them get killed. They are my family, Dylan. I love them," I reply.

"I know that. I also know that your team is very trained and skilled. I get that it's hard for you; it's hard for me too. But everyone has a role to play. The team will defeat Apex, Summit will grow strong, and you will stay calm and wait for Alexi. Don't give up on your team. Have some faith."

"I just said that to Aaden before he left," I admit.

"Well, follow your own advice. Come back to bed, and we can watch from here. We can cheer from here and let them know we are with them," Dylan says as he guides me back to bed.

"They won't be able to hear us," I remind him.

"No, but they will feel us rooting for them. Your team supports each other no matter what. That's something you taught them. Look, I'll be honest. I didn't always like your team. There's so much drama and scandal...it's crazy. But I have had a chance to watch you all in action, and I am amazed. At the end of the day, no matter what has happened, everyone has each other's back. They will make it through this. And so will you," Dylan says with confidence.

"If Swoop won't take you, I will," I tease as I kiss him on the forehead.

He smiles and sets up the device so that there are five split screens. We look on and hope that the team can make it through this. Just before the first part of the screen comes on, Dylan places his watch at the edge of the device and puts seven minutes on the timer; each team member will have seven minutes to make it out of whatever hell Apex has dreamed up for them. The first part of the screen lights up.

Okay, here we go...

The first one to play Apex's wicked game is Swoop. We look on as she is dropped into a small town somewhere in America. There are pristine tree-lined streets, mom-and-pop shops, a charming red brick library, and a coffee shop with the flavor of the day handwritten on a chalkboard out front. It's a clear, crisp day in what looks to be the perfect town. Swoop scouts and tries to adjust to the change in environment.

She starts walking around the neighborhood and is just as baffled as I am; so far this place looks harmless. But then Swoop asks herself the same question I would: where is everyone? She enters the shops and looks around for signs of life; there is nothing. She runs to the library and finds that the place is empty.

"Hello?! Hello?!" she calls out as she searches up and down the street for any signs of life. From the corner of her eye, she spots movement coming from the attic of one of the houses. She rushes over to the bright green-and-white home and sees a little girl in the window, playing. She rushes up the steps and bursts through the attic door.

She finds a room full of dead humans. Some of them have been stabbed; some have been shot, while others appear to have suffered massive head trauma.

In the corner of the room, a little girl stands beside the window, wearing a pink dress. Her hair is in a neat ponytail. The girl looks to be about five years old. She's human and has a big smile. She's playing with a set of angel figurines that I could have sworn I have seen before. The same thing goes for the pink dress the girl is wearing. This girl is oddly familiar. I think Swoop recognizes her too, but she doesn't say anything.

"What happened?" Swoop asks her.

"They got to escape," she says.

"Escape what?" Swoop says as she comes closer to the child.

"The darkness," she replies.

"What darkness?"

"The one that comes to town to kill everyone. Where have you been?" the girl asks.

"I'm not from around here. What's your name?" Swoop asks.

"I don't have one," she says with a smile.

"Okay, can you tell me more about this darkness?"

"It gets inside the homes in the town and kills everyone. The town had a lot of people before the darkness. But every day it would come and kill someone. So now the town decided they would rather die their own way than let darkness choose how they should die. Everyone has already chosen a way to die, everyone but me. What do you think, jump out the window or knife to the neck?" the girl asks.

"No, none of them," Swoop says, horrified.

"But I have to choose a way to die or it will choose it for me. And that will hurt—a lot," the little girl reasons.

"Okay, well, sweetie, I won't let the darkness get to you. I'll protect you," Swoop says.

"Do you promise?" she asks.

"Yes, I promise," Swoop says as she reaches out for the little girl's hand. The two of them make their way past the bodies and head out to the main street. Suddenly the skies darken, and thunder and lightning roar all around them.

"It's coming! It's coming!" the girl yells as tears spring to her eyes. Swoop tries to use her wings, but nothing happens. She quickly scoops the girl into her arms and begins to run.

A stream of dark smoke emerges from the sky and fills the street. Everywhere the smoke reaches is suddenly decayed. Soon, the town is ravaged by a black mold-like substance that grows and attaches itself to everything around them. The darkness is coming for them at impossible speed.

Swoop runs with the girl as fast as she can. They duck behind the abandoned post office. The little girl rolls herself up into a ball in Swoop's arms. She's crying uncontrollably. It takes several attempts for Swoop to finally get her to calm down. When she does, the little girl thanks her for rescuing her.

"You're welcome, but we're not safe yet. The darkness is catching up," Swoop says.

"Well, of course it is. It never goes away. It just hides until it's ready to come out. It will kill us, but at least we have a few minutes," she says.

"We are not going to die," Swoop assures her.

"Yeah, we are, but this is a very nice dress to die in."

"No! We will outrun the darkness. We'll fight it, okay? I promise you that," Swoop says.

The little girl laughs.

"Why is that funny?" Swoop asks as she watches for any signs of danger. She spots the looming darkness headed towards them.

"We gotta go, now!" Swoop says as she drags her along.

As they run for their lives, the darkness quickly begins to catch up. The ground beneath them splits open; the sky parts, allowing a bigger flow of dark energy to invade the town. Swoop drags the girl behind a bakery and hides under a series of large crates.

"Tell me about the darkness. When did it start?" Swoop asks.

"It's always been here. It won't ever go away," the girl says.

"There has to be a reason why it's here. I think if we find out, we can get rid of it. Tell me what you know about the darkness, anything at all," Swoop pleads.

"It kills anything it touches, it hurts everyone, and it won't ever stop," the girl cries.

"It's okay, sweetie, everything will be okay. We'll get out of this and I'll let you meet my son. You two can play together," Swoop says.

"You have a son? Where is he? Is he gonna die here with us too?" she asks.

"No, he's far away from this place. And you will be too. I just need to figure out how to kill it," Swoop says. "Everyone in town has been hurt but you. Why is that?"

"That's because you saved me," she says.

"What did I save you from? What is the name of the darkness coming for us?" Swoop asks.

The little girl gives her a sinister smile. She suddenly morphs into Swoop's malevolent alter ego, Raven.

Swoop jumps up and runs into the street. Raven follows. The two of them face off in the street. Raven studies her and shakes her head in disgust.

"Did you really think there could be an end to me? Did you really think you could ever erase me?!" Raven demands.

She holds both hands out and blasts Swoop across the street and right into the front window of the bakery. Before Swoop can recover, Raven jumps down on her and blasts her into the shop. She yanks Swoop by her hair and slams her head into the mailbox.

"YOU WILL NEVER BEAT ME!" Raven rants as she kicks Swoop in the face. She grabs her by the collar of her shirt and drags her to her feet. She rams her into the wall of the bakery. Swoop lies on the ground, bloody and in pain. Raven yanks the handle off the large oven and starts beating Swoop in the head.

As Raven goes in for the final blow, she bends down to the floor and hisses at her, "You never had a chance. You're weak, foolish! And you will die today!" She rages. As Raven is beating Swoop, Swoop spots Raven's pendant. It's shaped like a key and has an inscription on it.

"What's in a name?"

"What's in a name…name…her name," Swoop mumbles to herself.

"It's time to die once and for all!" Raven shouts.

"I KNOW HER NAME!" Swoop shouts just as the rod is about to crack her head open.

"WHAT?" Raven says, stopping midway angrily.

"The little girl was just a smaller version of you when I was a kid. That's why she had the same toys I did. That's why she wore her hair the same way I did. I felt you in me, but I denied it. That gave you power. Not anymore. The little girl has a name. The darkness has a name," Swoop says.

"You don't have the guts to say it out loud!" Raven says as she sends a large double-door refrigerator down on Swoop's head. Swoop barely gets out of the way in time. She quickly gets up and tackles Raven. They both roll around on the floor, each trying to get the upper hand. Raven is too powerful to be controlled. Time is running out; I can tell because the world around Swoop is starting to disappear. The town outside the window is fading, the post office is gone, the street and the park are both gone. I look at the clock on the screen. Swoop has only ten seconds left to get the key from Raven and escape.

"Swoop, hurry!" I shout, knowing she can't hear me. Dylan is in shock at what's taken place and can't talk, let alone shout. Swoop now has five seconds remaining.

Four seconds…

"YOU'LL NEVER GET RID OF ME. I'M ETERNAL, BITCH!" Raven shouts as she rams Swoop's head into the floor. She comes close to Swoop's face and gloats for the last time.

Three seconds…

"I told you you'd never have the guts to say it!" Raven laughs.

Two seconds…

Raven gets Swoop in the corner and is about to finish her off with a final blast.

One second…

"KIANA! THE GIRL'S NAME IS KIANA!" Swoop yells as she rips the necklace off Raven. Raven lets out a shrill cry as the darkness engulfs her and carries her away. Swoop's vision starts to blur. Moments later she wakes up on the forest floor in front of the red door, key in hand. Admitting to herself that she has a dark side saved her life, but what about the others? Will they be as lucky as Swoop?

***

The next being to show up on the device is East. He's been dropped into a one-room cabin in the woods. It's sparsely decorated with a table and two chairs. On the table there are bottles of Coy and East's favorite brand of flavored snack chips. The room has low lighting, so it takes East a moment to realize he's not alone.

There's a tall, lanky male angel, with almond-shaped eyes, perfect eyebrows, and spiky red hair, standing in the corner. I recognize him at once from the pictures in my mom's photo album. He's Rio, a former member of the Guardians' team.

"Dad?" East gasps.

"You don't know how long I waited to meet you," Rio says. Rio hugs his son tightly and refuses to let go. When the two finally break apart, Rio and East are both noticeably emotional.

"I don't understand. How are you here?" East asks.

"You know there are a million mixtures in the angel world; I finally found the one that allows me to come back to you. My son. My greatest joy," Rio says.

"This is some trick," East says.

"Maybe it is, but I'm here. So we might as well get to know each other."

"I can't. I don't have time. I have to find a key and get back to the forest," East says.

"I've wanted nothing more than to get to know you. Please, give me a few minutes," Rio begs.

"Yeah, yeah, I guess," East says, pulling up a seat at the table next to his biological father. "I have dreamed of meeting you. I have so much to ask you."

"Me too! There's a lot that I want to say to you. And a question that I wanted forever to ask."

"Ask me anything," East says, excited.

"How does it feel to be a walking disappointment?" Rio asks.

"What?" East says in disbelief.

"I'm a powerful Guardian. I battled and killed thousands of demons. I saved the world every other day, and my offspring is you?"

"Dad, I have done a good job. I have helped the Noru team."

"Helped them? They are doing you a favor by letting you stay on the team. You are the weakest member; they only allow you on the team because of who you are related to. Had you not been my son, they would never even talk to you."

"That's not true. I have helped. I am important to the team," East shouts as he stands up and backs away from the table. Suddenly East's stepfather appears in the corner of the room. He sees East and starts laughing.

"I told you before, you are nothing! You are a mistake! I told you that, and now your own biological father is saying that to you!" Frank rants.

"No! This isn't real. This is some kind of trick! My real father would never say that to me," East shouts.

"You are a total letdown. Your mother is disappointed in you, just like the team. Don't you get it, Easton? You are worthless," Frank says.

"No! No!" he blares at the top of his lungs.

"What are you gonna do? You gonna shut me up?" Frank demands.

"Son, drink this. It will give you everything you don't have: inner strength, power, and respect from the angel world. Drink this and you will finally be someone worthy of love," Rio says as he hands East a bottle of water.

However, as soon as he touches the bottle, it turns into a Soul Chaser. The more East drinks from it, the more soul is being drained from him. But East must be hallucinating because he keeps treating it as if it were a bottle of water. East's desire for acceptance is about to kill him.

"East, put it down!" I yell. But he continues to drink and his energy starts to diminish. Soon, East can no longer stand up. He's on his knees and the color is draining from his face. Yet the bottle is securely latched onto his lips. East is going to die.

The other males in the room laugh at East as death comes closer and closer to him. East is starting to realize what's happening. He tries to pull the bottle away from his lips, but he's too weak. He desperately looks around the room for some way to get out of the mess he's in. He looks at the ceiling, the floor, and all around the cabin; he can't find anything that can help. Just as he is about to close his eyes forever, East spots the label on the wrapper of the snack that has fallen to the floor. The company is called "Key Stone," and there is a quote at the bottom of the bag.

"I am not bound to succeed; I am bound to live by the light that I have..."

East starts to smile as the last sign of life is being drained from him. He reaches for the wrapper, clutches it in his hand, and chokes out his last words:

"My light. Not yours, Dad, mine," East says. The moment the words come out of his mouth, the Soul Chaser disappears, as do Rio and Frank. The wrapper transforms into a key, and East is back in the forest, safe and sound in front of the red door.

***

Dylan and I watch with bated breath as the third screen comes on. It's Diana's turn. She finds herself in a small boat floating on a river located deep inside a series of caves. There are dozens of other boats like hers, each with a person inside. Everyone around Diana is paddling furiously, trying to get away from whatever they left behind. They try desperately to reach the shore, where angels are eagerly waiting for them.

Diana keeps looking around in search of the danger that is causing everyone to flee. She looks back in the direction they came from but doesn't see anything other than the dark river. She looks off to the side, and still, there is no danger. Yet the people around her are scared to death.

Diana is out of ideas. She can't understand why everyone needs to go ashore so badly—that is until she looks in the water. She sees a blue light glowing from beneath the surface of the river. The bluish glow is coming closer and closer to the surface. People are now screaming for their lives.

"What the hell is in the water?" Diana asks out loud as she tries to make out the danger below. She puts her face right up to the surface of the river and comes face-to-face with the fire-blue eyes of an Egan!

Oh shit!

Egans are the demonic equivalent of Paras. They have blue flames in their eye sockets, a skeletal frame, and can't be killed. If they catch you, you are as good as dead. Suddenly all around Diana are hundreds and hundreds of Egans; their bony skulls peer out from under the water. Diana starts to paddle as fast as she can, but there is no avoiding the Egans.

All around her people are being dragged off their boats and thrown into the water, where they are being devoured. They scream as they are dismembered and mutilated. The Egans reach their cold, bony hands into Diana's boat. She manages to kick them away, but soon more Egans latch themselves onto her vessel.

"Get away from me!" Diana shouts as she tries to steer away from them. It's no use; they are everywhere. Diana is spinning her boat around in circles, trying to fend them off.

I don't get it. Why isn't she trying to reach the shore where the angels are? Why doesn't she seek shelter like the others are doing?

There are beings that have made it to the shore and are now being greeted by the angels. They are taken to the safety and bliss of the light. But while some beings are saved once they step on the strip of land, others escape the troubled water just to end up bursting into flames as soon as they pass the large boulder at the water's edge. Dylan turns my attention towards a message carved into the boulder next to the angels.

"Only the virtuous."

So according to the rock, if anyone steps foot on land but isn't pure in spirit, they will burst into flames. That must be why some of the people on the boats are hesitating to get off and go ashore, people like Diana. Yet the ones who stay in the boats are being devoured by the Egans. If Diana doesn't get off the boat, she will die like the others.

"Diana, you can go on land! You can do this!" I shout at the device.

Diana uses her oar to bash an Egan in the head; it slows him down but not for long. Soon the Egan is crawling onto the side of the vessel. While she's fighting to keep him at bay, another five latch on to the back of the boat.

"C'mon, Diana, go ashore!" Dylan shouts.

An Egan sticks his hand out of the water and grabs on to Diana's ankle. He tries to drag her into the water, but she kicks and punches her way out of his grip. Diana's victory is short lived, as the Egans are now in the boat with her.

Diana strikes one of them with her paddle again, but this time she misses. He grabs it away from her and tosses it into the lake. The boat is now overrun with Egans, and they are seconds from ripping into Diana. There are angels on the shore, calling for her to come to them. But that offers Diana no comfort because they called the others who ended up bursting into flames too. Diana is deathly afraid of going onto shore and finding out she is not among the worthy. The boat is now rocking so hard, there is no doubt about it: Diana is about to go overboard.

The boat shifts quickly and is upside down in seconds. Diana makes a big splash as she lands in the water, surrounded by an army of predators. She has no choice now but to try to swim to shore. But the Egans will not allow her to get away so easily. They paw and grab at her from all sides. They tear at her clothes and rip into the flesh of her hands and feet.

Diana keeps moving despite being brutally attacked. She fights her way through the mob of vicious creatures and frantically makes her way to the water's edge. She is now only a few feet from touching the shore, only a few feet away from the large stone where others have turned to flames.

All she needs to do is run from the edge of the water and right into the arms of the awaiting angel. But in order to do that, she has to get past the boulder. Diana's hesitating. Fear and doubt are preventing her from getting any closer. Dylan and I yell at her to hurry and run, but the fact is, she's afraid. To be fair, Diana only pauses for a few seconds, but it's one second too long. An Egan leaps up from the water behind her, grabs her, and pulls her back into the middle of the lake.

The Egans pull Diana to the floor of the murky river. She struggles to break free, but the longer she's down at the bottom, the weaker she gets. As she starts giving in to her inevitable death, she looks at her right arm and glides her hand over it. She's heartbroken and sad. She must be thinking about what she's leaving behind: Nix.

Realizing she would be turning her son into an orphan, Diana tries one last time to fight off the Egans. She struggles with the rage of a Kaster. She manages to make a small opening in the dense mob of Egans around her. She swims for dear life and reaches the surface. This time she does not stop. She does not hesitate. She jumps out of the water and bolts past the boulder. Diana does not encounter any flames or any fireworks whatsoever.

"YES!" Dylan and I yell at the same time once Diana is safely on land.

However, the Egans are not done. They come out of the water, and unlike the other beings, they follow Diana onto land. Suddenly the angels who were there start fading away. The bright light begins to dim. The river is now gone. Diana is running out of time. Everything is fading except the Egans.

"The key! She hasn't found the key," Dylan cries out. Diana realizes her error at the same time that Dylan does. She looks all over the cave and the strip of land but can't find the key. The Egans are now all out of the water and coming for her once again. This time there is no escape. There is nowhere to run to.

She gets as far back as she can while she scours the area. She doesn't see anything that looks like a key. She's running out of space to back up into. The Egans have her back to the wall, literally. The first Egan to touch her slices into her arm with his bony fingertip. She begins to bleed profusely. The others come in closer for their pound of flesh.

Just as they reach out for her, a bird makes its way onto the shore—a Phoenix. Diana reaches out for the bird but is only able to grab a feather. She holds it out in front of her and cries out to the heavens, "Phoenix! My son! He's the key. He's my key!"

Seconds later Diana is on the floor of the forest, with a bloody feather-shaped key in hand.

CHAPTER EIGHTEEN
RED DOOR TRIALS (PART 2)

When Bex's screen turns on, we find him in the middle of his castle without his wings, standing before his mother. She has glowing skin, dark eyes, and red lips. She's poured her enviable full figure into a gorgeous beaded silver ball gown that drapes down to the floor. She sits on the throne and studies Bex with an undeniable sense of disapproval.

"Mom, what's going on? What's happened?" Bex asks as he looks around for possible danger.

"Well, son, from what I can gather, Apex is testing you," she says.

"How, by draining some of my powers? I feel weak," Bex asks.

"It's more than that. Apex has rendered you human."

"Why?" Bex replies.

"He wants to see if you can make it through this little adventure with no powers at all. He took every drop of Kon strength you had and placed it somewhere else," she says.

"Where did he put my powers?"

"In your hands, Bexington."

Bex looks down, and a thirty-two-ounce glass mason jar appears in the palms of his hands. Inside the jar is a brilliant golden light that illuminates it.

"What is this?" Bex asks.

"It's a mason jar containing your powers. If you can make it out of this with the mason jar unbroken, you will regain your powers. But if the jar breaks or gets opened before you get back to the forest, you will lose all your powers."

"Alright, I'll take care of it," Bex says as he holds the jar securely against his chest.

"You know this Apex being has me perplexed," she admits.

"How so?"

"He wants to test you and find out if you can hold on to your powers. But what he really should be asking himself is if you are worthy of them in the first place," she says sincerely.

"I know, Mom, I'm not good enough in your eyes. I never have been, especially after Dad died."

"After you got him killed," she corrects him.

"I was a kid. I made a mistake."

"Oh, Bexington, how I wish it were only that one mistake."

"What are you talking about?" Bex demands.

"I'm talking about you allowing your brother to get killed. I'm talking about you letting the castle burn to the ground while you sexed the First Noru. And most of all, I'm talking about the delusion you have of bringing a demon into this palace!"

"Diana is not evil. She has risked her life—"

"BEXINGTON, PERHAPS I AM NOT MAKING MYSELF CLEAR: I WANT THAT DEMON OUT OF MY CASTLE!" she says as she holds out her hands and sends a torrent of violent wind at Bex. He holds on tightly to the jar as he's literally being blown out of the castle and out onto an endless battlefield perched on a cliff covered with angels, thousands of them, lying on the ground lifeless.

Bex is devastated as he looks around the field. Judging by the look on his face as he examines the bodies, many of them were Paras that were known to him personally. He knows he has to keep going and that he can't settle here, but he can't help but stop and say a silent prayer to honor his people. He sits down on the ground with the jar in hand and closes his eyes.

That's not a good idea…

One of the dead Paras a few yards away suddenly sits up. The corpse of the angel is rotten and parts of its face have been hollowed out. It turns its head towards Bex. Judging by what's left of the creature's face, I think it was a female angel.

"Bex, open your eyes!" I shout.

Bex does as I ask, but he does not turn around. He's too busy lamenting his fallen friends. The corpse stands up and slowly makes her way towards Bex.

What the hell? Really, Apex? Walking Dead, *the angel version? Argh!*

"Bex, turn around!" I shout again.

"C'mon, Kon, look behind you!" Dylan demands.

Bex finally turns and sees the corpse headed for him. But he's not afraid. He's not running away or even getting ready to battle. Instead, he looks on with happiness and wonder.

What's happening?

The corpse comes right up to Bex and they hold hands. He is lost in emotion as the corpse greets him.

"Hello, Bear," she says.

"Key, I've missed you," he admits.

Key! I can't believe I didn't recognize her. Even with the trauma to her body, I should have been able to see who she really is.

"I guess I look like hell, huh?" she says.

"Well…it's not my favorite look on you, but you're still beautiful to me," Bex says.

"You aren't shocked to see me?" Key asks.

"No. Apex would use what's important to me to try to mess with me. And you are very important to me."

"Bex, why didn't you save me?" she asks.

"I couldn't. You know I would have if it were possible. Please don't tell me you're here to say you hate me."

"I wish you had tried to save me. I wish it had all been different. But I don't blame you. I guess there was nothing you could do—back then. But now, now you can help me," she says, filled with hope.

"How? Tell me. I'll do anything," Bex says anxiously.

"You can help me get back to the forest with you. I can leave this place."

"How?" Bex says.

"With that," Key says as she motions towards the jar.

Bex looks down at the container and anguish spreads across his face. "Key, that's my power. If I give it to you, I will go back to our world powerless," he says.

"Yes, but you'll be alive and I'll be alive."

"Key, I can't—"

"You said you would do anything, Bex. Anything."

"I would, but I—"

"YOU DON'T EVEN DESERVE THESE POWERS! ALL YOU HAVE DONE AS KON IS GET THE ONES WHO LOVE YOU KILLED! GIVE ME THAT JAR! NOW!" Key leaps on top of Bex and starts to tear into his flesh. He struggles to pull her off him and hold on to the jar. Suddenly another corpse springs up and starts walking towards them. This one is less decomposed and easier to make out—Hunter.

Damn it! Bex seeing his little brother will totally screw with his head.

"C'mon, big brother, you know you never earned these powers, give them to us!" Hunter rages as he tackles Bex. The two of them gang up on Bex, and no matter how hard he tries, he can't get them off him. A few moments later his childhood caregiver, Mrs. Doris, joins in. Her eyes are red with rage and she points her bony fingers at him.

"You let them murder me! You let me suffer! You should be here rotting with us!" Mrs. Doris yells as she hops onto Bex's back and sinks her teeth into his neck. Dylan points my attention to a tree filled with black birds and tells me there were seven but now there are five.

"That's his timer. Bex has to get out of there!" I reply.

Bex getting out of the battlefield becomes less and less likely due to the number of corpses that are now on their feet. In a matter of seconds, Bex is inundated from all sides. The whole battlefield has come to life. In the chaos and craziness, Key manages to get to Bex and yanks the jar out of his hands. She takes off running and tries to get the lid open. Bex takes off after her but can't get far because of the sheer number of corpses now pulling on him. Key is about to open the jar and take away Bex's powers forever.

"No!" Bex says as he tries to free himself from the horde.

Before Key can open the jar, Hunter comes up behind her and bashes in what's left of her skull; Key falls down. The glass jar goes flying into the air. Hunter reaches for it but gets knocked down by the corpse closest to him. The jar gets kicked out of that corpse's hand and goes right into Mrs. Doris's. A new corpse runs alongside Mrs. Doris and snaps her neck. The jar is air bound once again.

Bex makes a play for the jar, ignoring the pain of his injuries. His fingers make contact with the surface but not enough to grab onto it. A corpse on the ground yanks at Bex's feet and sends the Kon hurtling towards the ground. Bex stomps on the corpse who impeded his attempt and tries to back up. Bex succeeds; he gets back on his feet—just in time to watch as the jar goes over the cliff. "NOOOOOOO!" Bex screams as he hurls himself down after it.

Bex falls for what feels like a lifetime. Without any wings, I fear this is the end of him. Amazingly enough, he lands in a puddle of water in a dark alley, unhurt. Thankfully, he also managed to grab onto the jar and shield it from breaking with his body. He looks around the alley and curses at Apex. I think I know why. This is the alley where his father died.

"Hello, son," a voice calls out from a few yards away.

Bex runs towards the voice and sees the corpse of his father propped up against a dumpster. His face is gaunt and pale. Bex tears up at the sight of his dad. He runs up to him and takes his hand.

"Dad, I never thought I'd see you again," Bex says.

"It's not much to see, son," the former Kon replies.

"I've missed you so much. I'm so sorry I let you get hurt. I didn't know what would happen that night. I didn't know you would get killed," Bex pleads. There's a puddle near them, and three black birds land by it.

Bex has three minutes.

"I don't have a lot of time. Dad, have you seen a key somewhere? I need it," Bex says.

"I see a lot of things, son. Things you may not be ready to see," he says with a smile.

"Dad, help me."

"I will if I can. But first, son, I need you to give me the jar."

"Dad, I can't," Bex says, sounding more hurt than I've ever heard him before.

"I can give you something in return. You give me the jar, let me come back and rule the kingdom of Paras once again, and I will give you something you have wanted all your life—forgiveness."

"What?" Bex gasps.

"I will forgive you for getting me killed and butchered in this alley. Give me the jar and I will forgive all of it," his father vows.

Bex slowly starts to hand his father the jar.

"No! Bex, you can't!" I yell. A bird takes flight, leaving only two left.

Two minutes remaining...

Bex stops midway, and his father calls out his name.

"Give it to me, son."

Bex continues to hand it over, but just as he is about to make contact with his father's hand, he sees a small light coming from something on the ground near the trash. He looks closer and sees a piece of broken mirror. The jagged fragment has a key crudely carved on its surface.

One bird left...

One minute...

"Dad! Don't!" Bex says, coming to his senses; it's too late! His father is about to open the jar. Bex quickly reaches out to stop him. His father hurls him across the alley. Bex goes flying into the air and lands in the puddle; the jar lands next to him—shattered.

"Damn it!" he shouts.

His father curses and laughs at him. He tells Bex that he will never have power again.

Bex doesn't have time to focus on the loss of power; he grabs the mirror fragment and holds it out before him. Nothing happens. The mirror fragment, although it has a key etched on it, is not the key.

AGRH!

"What am I missing?" Bex says out loud. He looks at the mirror as if hoping to see a sign.

Twelve seconds...

"C'mon, there has to be something I'm missing! What do I do with a damn mirror?"

"Fuck! What's the key?" he yells at the sky above.

Nine seconds…

"I have to live with no power and now I can't even open the damn gateway? Damn you, Apex!"

"Damn it! Why isn't Diana here? She knows what to do with a mirror. She'd look at herself all day," he jokes in desperation.

Five seconds…

"That's it! 'Self.' The one in the mirror is the key. Me. I control my powers. Not the jar. Me. I'm the damn key," Bex says as he waves his hand and watches the contents of the jar gather from the ground and enter his body. His powers return, as do his wings.

One…

He looks over at his dad and says, "I don't need you to forgive me anymore. *I* forgive me."

The moment the words come out of his mouth, a clearing appears in the wall and Bex jumps into it. The Kon is back in the forest, with his team, where he belongs.

***

The final screen comes on and shows us Aaden in bed, sound asleep in a bright and sunny bedroom. He's wearing boxers and a T-shirt while lying on plush, crisp white bedding. The room is decorated in light, calming blues, grays, and white. There's a framed picture on the nightstand, but it's turned away from the screen so I can't make out who is in it. The window is open, allowing us to hear birds chirping and the neighbors greeting each other with, "Good morning."

The sunlight beams across Aaden's face, waking him up. As he checks out his surroundings, he remains on high alert. He gets out of bed, opens the closet door, and finds his clothes neatly hung up and ready to be worn. He quickly changes into jeans and a shirt. Just as he's done getting dressed, he hears someone cry out, "Oh no! Please don't kill me!" Aaden runs out the door, down the well-lit hallway, and down the stairs, ready to attack.

He finds a little girl with bright amber eyes who looks like the spitting image of Diana. She's about four years old and has Aaden's eyes. The little girl is in the living room, playing a handheld video game. She has on a jean jumper with big yellow sunflowers stitched on the front panel; under the jumper is a yellow shirt. The front of her hair is gathered on top of her head and held in place by a sunflower hairpin. The remaining hair flows down her back.

When she sees him come down the staircase, she holds both her hands out and away from her body in an over-the-top gesture and sighs dramatically.

"Daddy! I die again!" she says, tossing the game on the sofa.

"Sparks…" Aaden gasps in utter disbelief.

"I know, I know, no games on a school day. But I went to wake you up for school and I asked you, 'Daddy, can I play my game before school?' You did not say yes, but you did not say no. So I played. Am I in trouble?"

"Sparks…" Aaden whispers as he comes close and studies her.

"Am I in trouble, Daddy?" she asks.

He picks her up and scoops her into his arms. He holds her so tight that she complains. He holds her high up in the air at arm's length and is on the verge of tears.

"Daddy, we gotta go. We're gonna be late for school!" she scolds.

"Um…yeah, yeah. Okay. School," he says.

"Can you put me down?" she asks.

"Oh, yeah. Okay," he says as he puts her back down on the floor. She gathers her notebooks and papers and says she's ready. Aaden is still trying to take it all in.

"Dad, look! I painted my nails! I put letters on them," she says, showing off her colorful nails. She painted both the skin and the nails, but she is so proud, Aaden tells her they look great.

"Thank you! And, Daddy, do you like my rain boots?" she says.

He looks down at her hot pink rain boots and says he loves them.

"You do?" she replies.

"Yes, but, honey, it's not raining," he tells her.

"I know, but they were lonely. So I had to wear them," she explains.

"Oh, naturally," he says, suppressing a smile.

"And tomorrow, I'm gonna wear my snowsuit and my red Minnie Mouse sandals," she says confidently.

"Let me guess, they are lonely too?" Aaden asks, unable to stop smiling.

"Yup!" she says in her very best "official" tone.

"We should get you off to school, honey," he says.

She takes his hand and the two of them head for the door. Once outside, Aaden finds himself on an active block full of angels, Quo, and humans. Everyone is greeting everyone as they go off to school or work. But Sparks stops suddenly and makes a big announcement.

"Dad! I forgot my coloring book on my bed! Be right back!" she says as she runs to the house.

Aaden stands in front of the house and looks around the neighborhood. He watches as seven figures with ash gray smooth, dome-shaped heads jog by wearing long black robes. There are three large, deep, and wide gashes where their eyes should be. They jog in a straight line, one behind the other, in perfect rhythm.

"Oh, don't mind them," a short slim man with glasses says as he walks over to Aaden.

"Who are they?" Aaden asks.

"They're called Tick-Ticks. Very annoying."

"Are they dangerous? What are their powers? Sparks, come out here now!" Aaden says as he peeks into the house.

"No, they aren't dangerous at all. They just run around like that all the time. After a while you get used to it. We haven't met before; I'm Marshall. Did you just move in?" he asks.

"Ah, yeah. What is this place?" Aaden asks, getting antsy as he walks back into the house, searching for Sparks.

"Safe Haven," the man says.

"Dad! Let's go! It's the first day of school!" Sparks says as she blows past the two of them and runs down the street.

"Headed for school, huh?" Marshall asks as Aaden follows.

"Yeah, I think so," Aaden replies, still not able to trust his eyes. He calls out to Sparks and tells her to wait for him.

"C'mon, Dad!" she says. He catches up with her and takes her hand. The school is only two blocks away. They fly together and land moments later. The two of them enter the front gate of the three-story schoolhouse. There are kids running into class from all directions. The Tick-Tick joggers are across the street, but this time there are only six of them.

"Very subtle, Apex," Aaden says under his breath. I am relieved to hear him say Apex's name. That means he knows that this world is made up. He knows that he has a real world that he has to get back to. But why is he playing along with the little girl?

Because she's his daughter and even a simulation of her is better than not having her around at all.

My heart aches for Aaden. He knows deep inside that this whole "perfect" life thing isn't real, but it hurts too much for him to walk away and not take part in it. I could kill that asshole Apex for making him face such a heart-wrenching past.

"Sparks, you know that I can't stay with you, right?" Aaden says in a pained voice.

"Yes, you have to go on a mission," she replies.

He kneels down in front of her so that they are eye to eye. "It's kind of a mission, yes. And I will have to leave you. But I love you and I will always keep you with me in my heart. I promise."

"Can you stay with me for a little bit?" she asks as her eyes start to tear.

He looks up and sees there are now four joggers. He knows he is down to only four minutes. "I'll stay as long as I can. But I need your help. Have you seen a key around here?"

"Here, it's my favorite, but you can have it," she says as she opens her backpack and takes out a colorful sticker with a key on it.

Aaden grins and thanks her for the gift.

"Can you come to class with me? Everyone wants to meet you, Daddy! You're their favorite Noru," she begs.

He pulls her in and embraces her once again. He wipes away her tears and tells her that everything will be okay. “I don’t want to leave you alone. Is there someone who will take care of you?” Aaden says, knowing how strange it is to ask that in a world that doesn’t really exist.

Sparks gathers herself and tries to be brave. “I will be okay, Daddy. I’ll make friends in my class,” she says, trying very hard to sound mature.

“I’m sure you will. You’re so smart and so pretty. You’ll have a lot of friends,” he says, trying like hell to keep it together.

I swear to Omnis I’m gonna kick Apex’s demented ass!

“Dad, don’t worry. I’ll be fine. I’m a big girl. I flew to the store all by myself once.”

“You did?” he says, pretending to be shocked.

“And I picked out my clothes too! Just like today!” she proclaims.

“You are a very big girl, then. And I don’t have to worry about you at all, now do I?”

“Nope! I got this, Dad,” she assures him. My heart is breaking right along with Aaden’s.

“Dad, the train is here. It’s here for you!” she says.

Aaden turns and finds a three-car train has appeared a few blocks from the school. The joggers pass by; there are three of them now. Aaden does his best to end the visit on a good note; he kisses her cheek and embraces her.

“I love you. I love you. I love you,” Aaden vows as he holds his daughter for the last time and strokes her hair. He has done better than any of us could have expected. He woke up knowing as soon as he saw her, he’d have to let her go.

“I have to go. Class has started. Here, you can have this picture we took at the open house. You can take it with you on your mission,” Sparks says as she takes out a wrinkled sheet of paper and hands it to him. Aaden gladly takes it, stands up, and says good-bye to his child.

“Dad! Run! The train is leaving!”

Aaden looks and sees the train is flashing, signaling it’s ready for departure.

Aaden takes one last look and then starts running for the train. As soon as he heads for the train, his wings disappear. It doesn't matter because I am confident he can make it to the train on foot. As Aaden darts down the street, he takes a quick glance at the picture Sparks gave him. It's a photo of her and some other kids standing in a group in front of the school. There is a banner draped across the front of the school that reads:

"Welcome to the Center (School for Angel Reconditioning).

Founded by Professor Colton Bishop."

Oh. My. Omnis. Aaden has just surrendered Sparks to the Center! Aaden stops dead in his tracks and turns back towards Sparks. She's being yanked into the school by guards I recognize from when the Center kidnapped me. Aaden runs back towards Sparks at speeds I can't begin to comprehend.

He calls out her name and curses the guards. He vows to kill them all if they don't let her go. But they continue to pull her and drag her kicking and screaming inside. She drops her backpack in the struggle and kicks off her boots. She cries out and begs for her daddy, but the guards have no mercy.

Aaden gets to her and snatches the guards off her. He picks them apart one by one, casting them off left and right. But the more of them he takes on, the more guards appear. Sparks is sobbing and begging for Aaden to save her. She calls out for him again and again. Each time is like a dagger in Aaden's chest.

"Daddy! Daddy!" she shrieks at the top of her lungs.

"GETOFFMYKID!GETOFFMYKID!I'LLKILLYOU!I'LLKILLYOU!" **Aaden rages as he picks one of the guards up over his head and slams him down onto the sidewalk. Aaden kills the guards faster than I have ever seen done before. But they manage to get Sparks inside the school grounds.**

"Take her to the White Room!" Bishop says as he walks towards them with an evil smile.

"Give her to me now, or I'll kill the rest of them!" Aaden says between blows.

"You should have listened to me. You should have stayed away in order to protect the ones you love. Better yet, you should have just died. But no, you tried to make a family. You tried to be normal. You are a curse on all their lives. Anyone who loves you pays dearly. Including the girl," he says, signaling towards Sparks, who is now passed out and being prepped for the White Room.

Aaden starts throwing guards into the building and using their bodies to break through windows in an attempt to get in. Sparks is calling out for him again. He tries to get to her, but there are hundreds and hundreds of guards. And for some reason, his power isn't working. From the corner of his eye, Aaden sees the last jogger run past the front window.

Shit! Time! We're out of time!

The last jogger means the last minute. Aaden has sixty seconds to make a run for the train or he will never come back to the real world. Aaden doesn't care; he barrels his way inside the school. It may look different on the outside, but inside, it's the Center. Aaden makes it past hordes of guards while they beat down on him.

They kick him in the ribs, bash him over the head, use large pieces of shattered glass to stab him—nothing can stop him from getting to Sparks. We hear the train announcement from inside the building as if it were right next door.

"Safe Haven Express is leaving for the Black Forest; all passengers please get on board."

Aaden makes it to the White Room, and although he's bleeding and very broken, he manages to reach Sparks. But try as he might, he can't unlatch the Samson string that holds her hostage. He fights with his daughter's restraints as if he is fighting for his life.

The guards now have backup—demons, lots of demons. Before Aaden can stop it from happening, the White Room becomes a battlefield of Powerballs, blood, and mayhem. And still he can't summon his own powers or untie Sparks.

"Daddy! Please! Please!" she begs again.

Aaden is crying and shaking as he begs for Omnis to please help him.

"The Safe Haven Express will depart for the Black Forest in thirty seconds; all aboard!"

"Aaden, you have to go!" I shout at the device. I hate to tell him to leave his baby girl, but she's not real and he can't give his life up for an illusion.

But even as I cry out, I know in my heart Aaden is never going to leave her in a place like the Center. He's never coming back to the forest, back to us.

"Aaden, please," I beg him. Dylan urgently points to his watch.

Fifteen seconds.

Aaden keeps struggling with the ropes, and they refuse to give in. He gets down on his knees and holds his daughter's hand. He bows his head in defeat and tells her he's sorry.

"Daddy! Listen to me! Please," she says. But before she can tell him what she wants to say, the demons tie her mouth. She struggles and tries to break free. Aaden holds her hand tighter than before and looks at her tiny fingers. He looks closely at her nail polish and finds that each finger has a letter on it, just like she said. He didn't pay attention before, but now he places her fingers together and reads the message.

"L-E-T" is written on the first three fingers.

"G-O" is written on the last two.

Both hands have the same message:

"Let Go."

Although Sparks can't speak, it's hard to deny the compassion in her eyes. She silently assures her father that leaving is the right thing to do. Aaden nods and does the hardest thing he's ever had to do in his life: walk away from his kid. Every step he takes hurts him in ways I can't put into words. He makes it out of the room and runs into the hallway.

Ten seconds remaining...

The demons have multiplied and have no intention of letting Aaden go. They chase him down the hall as he races out of the building. He makes it outside and bolts down the street; there are only seven seconds remaining. He gets to the platform, but there's a demon who has managed to keep up with him.

The demon blasts Aaden with a series of Powerballs. One lands right on Aaden's back. He cries out as the pain nearly cripples him.

Five seconds...

Aaden reaches out for the closing doors of the train, but the demon yanks him back onto the platform.

Four seconds...

"Come get me, asshole!" Aaden yells. The demon sneers as he heads straight for him. Aaden moves out of the way swiftly, allowing the demon to plow headfirst into the lamppost. The demon gets back up quickly, but by then Aaden is already reaching the door.

Three seconds...

The demon doesn't give up. He hurls a Powerball at Aaden's head. Aaden dodges it, but not quickly enough; he gets hit in the shoulder.

"Fuck!" Aaden says as the pain rips into his flesh. The hit causes him to lose his grip on the train doors.

Two seconds.

The train doors are closing.

One...

Aaden lets out a primal scream as he hurls himself onto the train and lands face-first on the train floor. The doors close; the train takes off. The world around Aaden quickly dissipates, leaving him on the forest floor a few feet in front of the red door, his daughter's gift in his hand.

The team is overjoyed to see Aaden and to know that he survived. Aaden doesn't say anything. He doesn't make eye contact with anyone. He gets up from the ground, wounded and bloody. He marches towards the front of the castle, where Apex stands a few feet from the dining table.

"Well, I must say Penny and I are surprised you made it out, Silver! We never thought—"

Before Apex can finish his statement, Aaden takes the nearest butter knife on the table and jams it into his chest.

Apex is so shocked his eyes are as big as saucers. Aaden angrily thrusts the knife deeper; blood spills from Apex's mouth like water from a spring. He falls to the ground in a bloody heap. Apex, aka the Architect, is dead.

Without saying a word, the team goes over to the glass pentagon, with mere seconds remaining, and each places their key in the lock. The blue liquid dries up; they take the vial of ashes out of the safe and behold it with wonder.

Finally, the weapon to destroy Malakaro is in hand.

CHAPTER NINETEEN
READY

I don't know if it was wrong or right, but when Dylan and I watched Apex die, we cheered almost as loud as the humans did in Chicago when their favorite baseball team won the World Series. Normally we can't conceive of a reason to cheer at the death of an angel, but this time, that bastard had earned it. And if Aaden hadn't killed him, I'm pretty damn sure I would have. Dylan and I rejoiced like never before, and it felt glorious. We were so loud, at one point the Healer came in to scold us. We promised her we would keep the noise down.

"Is that the team texting you?" Dylan asks once things quiet down.

"Yeah, they said they'd be back here shortly," I reply as I walk over to the window for the millionth time. The dark sky has no mercy in it and certainly no Alexi.

"Still nothing?" Dylan asks.

"No. I was hoping after all they've been through, when they came back, I'd have something good to tell them, but I don't. The only thing that made watching Aaden say good-bye to Sparks in such a heartbreaking way all right was knowing that Summit might be here. But they'll be back soon, and I have no good news for him," I reply as I cross my arms in front of my chest and look at the sky yet again.

"I'm sorry. How can I help?" Dylan asks.

"You've done enough already. Thank you," I reply as I embrace him. My cell goes off; I rush to take the call. It's Mrs. Maybelle.

"What? When? How do you know? Okay, I'll be right there. Don't worry.

I'll take care of it," I reply into the phone right before I hang up.

"What's going on?" Dylan says.

"Mrs. Maybelle, Nix's caregiver, says Malakaro is making contact with him right now!"

"He broke out of his prison?"

"No. He's projecting himself into the room. But I don't know how," I admit.

"He's using astral projection. He's still trapped by Time, but he's amassed enough power to will his spirit somewhere else," Dylan says.

"We have to go and protect Nix. Malakaro can't get to him," I reply as I start getting ready to leave.

"I don't think you have to worry. Normally, a being can't touch anyone in that state."

"Dylan, there is nothing normal about Malakaro. He has powers no one else does. Even if he can't reach out and touch Nix, it doesn't mean he hasn't figured out a way to sap Nix's strength and use it for himself. I can't take that chance."

"You're right, but you can't go. Call Diana and the team. They can take care of it."

"Look, my team has just been through their own custom-made hell. They have done enough."

"Pryor, you can't go off and face Malakaro by yourself!"

"I'm not facing him. I'm facing a hologram of him. And all I'm going to do is talk to him. If things get out of hand, I'll figure something out."

"No, you shouldn't go."

"Dylan, I don't have time to argue with you."

"What if Alexi comes in the meantime?"

"Alexi will follow me wherever I go. It's what they do."

"And you want Alexi to find you while you are interacting with the greatest evil that ever lived?"

"No..."

"Then stay here."

"I can't sit here and do nothing. It's just not in me," I confess.

“I have an idea,” Dylan says as he tinkers with the Eagle Eye device.

“What are you doing?” I ask.

“Eagle Eyes are preset to a certain frequency. If I can find the frequency that Malakaro is on, I can match it and project a replica over to him. You would be projected into the room along with him and Nix, all the while keeping you right here in this room.”

“Can you do that? Seriously?” I shout.

“If I have to come back in that room one more time, I’m turning off all the lights and making everyone go to sleep! I mean it!” the Healer calls out from the hallway.

“Sorry!” Dylan and I say in unison as we lower our voices.

“Your body will remain here, but it will go limp. It can be very taxing for you physically, so you only have a few minutes to get in there and find out what Malakaro wants with Nix.”

“I already know: he’s trying to suck power from his son so he can free himself sooner.”

“Well, you have a few minutes to convince him not to do that. Hurry.” Dylan takes the device and aims it at me. Suddenly everything around me starts to blur. I hear Dylan’s fading voice; he’s begging me to please make it back before Silver gets to the clinic.

Mrs. Maybelle’s home soon comes into view. Every inch of her house is right out of a Southern comfort magazine. I love this place. I enter and see Mrs. Maybelle guiding the other kids away from the room with Nix and Malakaro. I signal to her that I will handle everything; she looks worried but agrees to let me enter the baby’s room.

There is a mural of humans, angels, and Quo kids playing together. Mrs. Maybelle even added a few “happy”-looking demons because she hates when kids are excluded. The room is cheerful and sunny. In the center is a crib where Nix lies bundled up and sleeping. Standing over the crib, reaching out for him, is the astral projection of evil incarnate.

“Don’t touch him!” I warn.

Malakaro looks over at me and smiles, very pleased to have me in front of him. He pulls back and doesn’t touch Nix.

"Well, what a time for a family reunion," he says.

"Get away from him," I insist.

"Why? He does belong to me, doesn't he?"

"The hell he does. He belongs to his mother," I correct him.

"Ah yes, the former Kaster. Tell me, how is Ruin?"

"Her name is Diana. And she's just fine. But if you don't step away from her kid, you'll regret it," I promise him.

"I won't hurt him."

"Why should I trust you?"

"You shouldn't. However, that does not change what I just said."

"Why would you spare him?"

"Oh no, that's not what I'm doing at all. Today is the last day for humanity. If you and his mother want him to be alive long enough to watch the world end, then so be it. However, I find it rather…cruel."

"Well, you could give up this whole 'end the world' thing. Then he'd be just fine," I suggest.

"Now, what kind of lesson is that to teach my son? I would like him to be persistent. If the goal is to end the world, one should keep going until that goal is met," he reasons.

"We won't let you destroy everything. I know for a fact that we will stop you."

"Because you've been so successful thus far?" he asks.

"You just don't get how much I hate to lose," I reply.

"Well, I guess that's a family trait, now isn't it?"

"I guess so," I admit.

"I could use his powers and strengthen myself," he says.

"Wow, and you call my father an awful dad," I quip.

"Fair enough, I could maybe leave him as he is until the world falls. However, I'd like something in return."

"I won't help you get out of the barrier Time has placed you in."

"I have more than a few ideas on how to break free. Using the child was just one of many," he admits.

"Then what do you want?" I push.

"I want to know his name."

"Phoenix."

"As in 'rising from the ashes.' Another something we have in common," Malakaro says as he looks down at the baby.

"They call him Nix for short. He talks to animals and can reduce objects to dust," I reply, not sure why I'm giving him any info.

"And people? Can he do the same thing to them?"

"I guess, maybe as he gets older."

"I see," he says.

"So what, that makes you proud? You want him to be the new source of all evil? If that's what you want, then you are in for the shock of your life. This kid is going to be good. He's going to be—"

"Wanted?" he asks.

"Yes."

"Well, then maybe evil isn't in his future," he says to himself.

"It doesn't have to be in yours either, Mal—Jason. We don't have to be enemies. Our father loved us both," I reply, trying to find a drop of humanity in him.

"Yes, but he only left one of us. He only pushed away one of us. And he only forgot about one of us," he spits.

"So that's it? You will try to end the world, and we try to stop you and in the process save your son?" I ask. Before he can reply, Nix stirs awake and starts to fuss. Malakaro comes closer to him.

"I said stay away!" I snap.

"His eyes—he has my eyes…"

"Yeah, it looks like it," I reply evenly.

"I didn't think he'd have my eyes…" he says, astonished.

I decide to take a big risk. If I am wrong about this, Diana will kill me. But it's worth a shot. "Jason…if you're capable, you can hold him, if you want."

"Of course I am capable," he says, offended. He reaches into the crib and takes Nix into his arms. He studies his son closely. Nix reaches his chubby hands out to him and tries to touch him. He doesn't reach out a hand for

Nix to latch onto, but he does not pull away either. A few moments later, Malakaro turns his attention back to me.

"I could end him right now and suck out his power like marrow from the bone," he threatens.

"If you were going to hurt him, you would have done so already," I reply.

"But I will hurt him. I will end the planet he's on. He will never get older."

"Taking out a million nameless faces may be easy for you, but I'm betting one face, one face with your eyes, is a lot harder. Even for the great Malakaro," I remark.

He smiles and puts Nix down. "You believe you have found an…opening."

"I hope…"

"Yes, you angels do a lot of that," he says sardonically.

"It helps," I reply.

"You look…weak. Tired. Perhaps this is all too much for you," he says.

"Nope, I'm great. I will be seeing you soon—in the real world."

"Pryor, you will not win. It will all crumble around you. And as I said before, it was cruel to bring a life into a world that is just about over. But so be it. The day my son is born and the day he dies will be one and the same," he says.

"What if it's not? I know you think you will win, but let's say for argument's sake that you don't win. Let's say my team wins and you are wiped off the face of this earth. What then? What will happen to your son?"

"I know that like his mother, you will protect him. You will care for him," he says as he begins to fade.

"Jason! What do you want him to know about you? If you don't survive this like you think you will, what do we say to Nix about his father?" I ask.

Malakaro's response surprises me.

***

I make it back mere seconds ahead of the team. In fact, as they are coming in for a landing, I'm getting back in the bed. Once they enter the room,

Aaden quickly rushes to my side and Swoop leaps into Dylan's arms.

"Are you okay?" Aaden asks as he searches the room for some indication that Alexi came.

"Yes, I'm good," I reply, exchanging a look with Dylan.

"You haven't been overdoing it, have you?" my husband says.

"Aaden, I never left this room," I assure him.

"I find that hard to believe," East says.

"Okay, fine. Dylan and I sat here, cheered you guys on loudly, watched porn, and then I projected myself into a room to chat with Malakaro," I reply in a joking tone. Dylan has to press his lips together in order to keep from laughing.

"Very funny," Swoop says as she embraces Dylan.

"You guys did an amazing job. I am so proud of you all. You guys dealt with some really crazy stuff. No matter what happens tonight, I want you all to know—and that includes Dylan—I am honored to fight alongside you, and if we die, we do so as a team, as a family," I say as I embrace them all.

The Healer enters and tells the team to follow her so that she can treat their wounds. She tells me that she will return so that the procedure can be done.

"Wait! Don't we have any time left? Is there a chance we could give Summit some more time?" Aaden asks.

"Hey, can you guys—"

"Yeah, Pry, we'll give you two a minute," Diana says.

"When I come back, we have to work on you. It's now or never," the Healer says as she and the team head out to the hallway.

Aaden and I are alone in the room. He walks over to the window and looks up to the sky. There is nothing out there. He takes a seat in the chair next to the window and looks out into darkness. I run my hand through his hair and sit on his lap.

"So…no Alexi, huh?" he says, sounding worn and weary.

"No, I'm sorry, baby."

"Yeah, me too," he says as he holds me close.

"I watched you walk away from Sparks; she was your heart. I couldn't begin to understand what that felt like. I wish I was there with you," I reply.

"You were. I knew you were watching. I knew you needed me to come back. But it didn't make it easier to go and leave her there—even if it wasn't real. It ripped me apart."

"And you came back thinking we'd find Alexi. I feel like I let you down. Did I let you down?"

"No, you didn't. Not in the least. And just so you know, you are reason enough to come back. Even without Alexi."

"I love you," I reply as I look into his face. He embraces me. When it's time to let go, he won't. He needs more time. When we do pull apart, I try my hardest to lighten the mood.

"There is some good news," I tell him.

"What is it?"

"When this is over and we kick Malakaro's ass, you and I will have nothing but time to try to get Alexi to come to our house," I reply suggestively.

"Are you ready to try all day and all night?" he jokes.

"It's a hard job, but I'm up to it. And I've learned some new moves from watching—TV. And stuff," I lie.

He studies me and shakes his head. "What have you been up to?" he wonders.

"Me? I'm an innocent First Noru. I have no idea what you're talking about," I tease.

The Healer comes into the room with a stricken look on her face.

"What is it?" I ask as I jump to my feet.

"We just got word, someone has broken out of the barrier," she says.

"Malakaro is free? We have an hour left," Aaden says.

"He was much more powerful than the council thought—and it's not Malakaro that's free. It's Alago. He's free and trying like hell to do the same for his partner!"

The Healer quickly gets me set up so she can repair my soul. That means Summit will only have a five percent chance of surviving now. I want to indulge in the fantasy that she can make it past this, but the time for fantasy is over. There are other babies, other families out there, and they need to be saved. Aaden wants to be with me, but I convince him to go get the group ready so that when I am done, we can fly straight into what's left of New York City.

The operation is painless, thank Omnis. I just lie down and drink the mixture that she gives me. It puts me to sleep in seconds. When I wake up, there is a silver glow spread out across my chest. The Healer explains it's normal to have the glow after and that it will fade. She tells me that it worked, but I didn't need her to say it. I feel a hundred percent better. My strength is back and I am ready to battle. Time to end this once and for all.

***

As we fly into what's left of the New York City skyline, we see two enormous plasma orbs looming over the city: the orb that holds Malakaro captive, and the other orb that is now empty. It's true, Alago is out, but Time, Fate, and Death are trying to hold him with a surge of power wrapped around his body.

Alago has muscles the size of small mountains, translucent skin, and flames where his heart and chest used to be. His mouth is crammed with jagged fangs, and since the last time we saw him, he's grown flesh-colored spikes throughout his body. Alago's massive hands are like claws, and his arms, legs, and neck are bulging with muscles. The beast pounds against the plasma holding him hostage.

"Let the Alago out!" I shout down to the council. They exchange worried glances. I shout down to them once again, assuring them that we know what we are doing. The council reluctantly let go; they now move their focus to Malakaro's orb. The instant Alago is free, he rages and roars so violently, he shakes all of New York City.

Alago sees us flying above his head and attacks with the fury of a thousand demons. He reaches out to snatch us from the sky; we swiftly move out of range, causing him to smash the side of the Empire State Building. It comes tumbling down in a landslide of metal and concrete.

Alago rips what's left of the Empire State Building out of the ground and uses it as a makeshift bat. He takes a swing at us with everything he has. We dodge the attack by mere inches. Unfortunately there are still humans on the ground, and they aren't as lucky. They get caught in the crossfire, causing a confetti of human blood, metal, and debris to fall down on the city.

East tries to get close enough to wrap the lasso around him, but Alago catches the tip of the electric rope and hurls East towards him. Swoop tries to catch him before Alago can, but she fails. East is catapulted right into Alago's hand. East literally slips between the creature's giant fingers, but before he can take flight, Alago plucks him from the air by his leg and drags him back to the ground. He struggles but is unable to stop Alago from slamming him down onto a row of brick homes.

Aaden comes from behind and grabs Alago by the neck. But the creature is too large and too angry to be suppressed. As Aaden struggles, Alago throws East away like a piece of soiled tissue. East goes flying into a nearby building. His head hits the glass and he slides down a hundred stories with nothing to break his fall.

I quickly dive down to save East, but he's falling faster than I can fly. East looks like a broken leaf at the mercy of the wind, helpless in every way. As hard as I am trying to catch up, I know for a fact that I am going to miss him. He's going to hit the ground and there is nothing I can do to stop it. Seconds before it happens, Bex swoops in and catches him.

I don't have time to register the relief I feel because in the corner of my eye I spot Aaden struggling to subdue Alago. I fly over to help, but before I get there, the beast throws Aaden to the ground. He growls and rages at Aaden as he goes in to attack.

Aaden sends a surge of blue fire at him, but instead of hurting Alago, it serves as his meal. Alago inhales the fire like liquid through a straw. It feeds him and gives him even more power. The newfound power is converted into fuel. Alago hurls a sea of blue flames back at Aaden, who rolls away seconds before it hits him. Alago goes to strike again; this time I am close enough to stop him.

I hold out both palms and start to pull his life force. However, he's too strong for me to have an effect on. He swats me away like I am an inconvenient fly. I go flying headfirst into a nearby post office. As soon as I land, I take off again, determined to stop Alago. The creature kicks Aaden in the ribs, sending him catapulting into downtown Manhattan. He then turns his attention on me.

"Randy, I don't want to hurt you. Please, stop!" I beg pointlessly.

Alago balls his hand into a fist and decks me in the face so hard I tumble out of the sky and black out. I come to a few moments later, and Alago has Swoop by the hair. He drags her face-first through the rubble that is New York.

Diana stands before him, opens her mouth, and starts to drain him of his powers. Alago drops Swoop's limp body on the ground and goes after Diana with full force. Although she has started to drain him, it isn't enough to make a major difference. The creature takes after her with vengeance. She takes off into the sky, desperate to outrun him. Alago effortlessly reaches out for her; I watch, horrified, as he makes contact with Diana. Dylan appears out of nowhere and grabs Diana from Alago's grasp.

Alago backslaps Dylan before he can disappear. Dylan falls to the ground like a bee after hitting an electric fence. Diana is able to fly down and get him before he hits the pavement. But she can't stop Alago from coming after them again. I take to the air and get into Alago's face, allowing the others a chance to flee and regroup.

There's a wall of white plasma surging in the sky; it belongs to the Kon. It's the first thing to actually slow down Alago. The beast blocks his face to protect him from the wrath of Bex's powers. I add my powers to the mix, and the Alago is now being attacked from two different sides. He reaches out for an electric pole and plunges it into Bex's chest. Bex cries out as the bolts of electricity surge through his body. I leap onto Alago's head and struggle to rip it off. He drops the pole, and Bex falls out of the sky. Diana goes to catch him, but she misses and he hits the ground hard. Dylan and Diana run to tend to him.

In the meantime, Swoop, East, and Aaden take to the air to help me. East wraps his lasso around Alago's feet and Aaden bends a streetlight around Alago's neck. Together, they work to bring the mammoth beast down. But he swings so violently, he is able to shake all of us off him and topple everything in his path. He stomps his foot into the earth and causes a ripple effect on the broken ground. He doubles the damage by pounding both fists into the earth; Alago is literally tearing New York City in two.

He turns his attention to the last remaining orb, where Malakaro struggles to break free. He tackles the orb and causes it to crack along the top. We quickly devise a plan. The team gathers in the air and looks at me to give them the signal. I give the go-ahead and hope we haven't miscalculated.

Bex summons up a massive Powerball, and East places his lasso inside of it. Arming the lasso with the energy of the Paras expands the hold and overall power. So this time when East sends the lasso around Alago's neck, he's unable to rip it off. Aaden, Diana, Swoop, and I help pull the lasso, dragging Alago away from Malakaro's orb. Diana and Dylan each jab metal rods into the center of Alago's chest and twist. It's working; we are slowly pulling him away from his partner.

Suddenly, just as things are turning in our favor, Alago rockets off the ground and into the air. Who the hell knew he could get airborne? Judging by the looks on my team's faces, they too had no idea. Alago latches himself onto the Statue of Liberty's head. He brings the giant sculpture down to the ground and uses the spikes of the crown to plow into Easton. East keels over to the ground, blood oozing from his side.

"East, hang on!" Diana cries out as she quickly rushes over to him.

Alago wastes no time; he runs across the field of scrap metal and bones, trying once again to free Malakaro. I take off after him and manage to get hold of the lasso hanging around his neck. I look for something to tie it to so that he can't move. Aaden signals towards the peak of the Chrysler building. He helps me drag Alago by the neck and loop the lasso. Alago struggles against the lasso and tries to break free. Each time he pulls on the electric rope, the building leans over.

"It's not gonna hold!" Aaden warns.

"We can't let him get to Malakaro. We have to kill him now!" Dylan shouts.

"He's gonna get free! We need to use the sword of light now!" Swoop yells.

"Pryor! Attack with me. We can end him now," Bex calls out to me.

"Pry, now is the best chance we have, use it! Use the sword!" Aaden says.

I pull out the coin-shaped metal from my pocket and it grows into the sword of Avery. I raise it high above my head and aim it at Alago. For once, he is bound and helpless. All that remains is for me to sink the blade inside Alago's chest. He will then die a painful death.

Randy will die a painful death...

As I bring the sword down on my target, the world seems to pause. I look around, and the scene is like something out of a movie, chaos and destruction all around us.

Humans running for their lives, the council on the brink of losing control over their orb prison, Alago inches away from connecting with his partner and bringing hell on Earth. The last movements of humanity's existence are playing out before me. Yet all the noise and clamor fade to the background. The only thing I see and hear in my mind's eye is Randy. My Randy. Suddenly flashes of our lives together play out before me in the sky.

I remember when Randy discovered that angels were real and that I had powers. We were in the warehouse after being attacked on the playground by demons. I had to call the team for the first time in years and ask for their help. The team came and saved our lives. We then took Randy to the warehouse and tried to explain everything to him.

"Randy, you weren't hallucinating. The guys back there had wings. They aren't the only ones; I have them too," I said.

My best friend then looked over at me and watched in amazement as my wings spread out behind me and flapped against the air. In the first few moments he was scared to death. I thought I had scared him for life. I feared he would never recover from the shock of knowing about our world. But in just a few moments, Randy went from fear to total elation. I hear his excited response as if he were right in front of me:

"YES! I KNEW IT! I FREAKING KNEW IT! YOU'RE A SUPERHERO! THIS IS SO FREAKING AWESOME! Can you bend metal like Magneto? Wait, I bet you can control the weather. Make it thunder, Pry!"

It didn't matter how much craziness was going on or how much danger we were in, Randy forced me to have a life outside the angel world. He helped me stay normal in a world where I was anything but normal. I recall him jumping on my bed a while back, gleeful and determined to cheer me up:

"C'mon, Pry, get up!" he yelled as he plopped down on the sofa next to me.

"Go away," I said, desperately wanting to go back to sleep.

"No, you have to get up so we can celebrate!"

"Celebrate what?" I asked.

"Hello? It's March first; it's your birthday! You're fifteen today."

"So?" I replied.

"So you are now officially a Taylor Swift song."

I sat up and grunted.

"So what do you want to do for your big day? I'm thinking we hit the movies. There's a slasher marathon in the Village. We'll stop off and get whatever angel power 'snack' you like, I'll gorge on popcorn, hot dogs, and Milk Duds, like a good American."

"Randy, I don't think—"

"Then we'll go bowling, where I will beat you. Then we'll fly to the other side of the world and see what breakfast looks like for the good folks in Papua New Guinea," he said with confidence.

"Why Papua New Guinea?" I asked.

"Cuz it's fun to say!" he replied with laughter.

It's not just his humor that I recall; it's his insane amount of courage. He went into a cave filled with the one thing that makes him wet his pants: spiders. He was terrified, but he did it anyway because we needed his help. He also braved demons right along with us even though he had no powers to retaliate when they attacked him.

But the bravest thing Randy ever did was standing up to Aaden for me back when the two of them first met. Aaden told me years later that Randy stood his ground and warned him about breaking my heart. According to my husband, he had walked into the kitchen that night and found Randy, the one-hundred-ten-pound human, had gone into full "badass" mode.

"Here's the deal, Silver, platinum, aluminum, or whatever your name is—Pryor is not just my friend. She's my best friend. Now she may have a thing for

'dark and handsome,' but I won't allow you to hurt her," Randy warned.

Aaden walked over and stood right in his face. Randy looked like a toy with Aaden looming above him. But although his voice was shaky and his eyes were wide with fear, Randy continued to stare Aaden down.

"If I hurt her, what the hell would you do about it?" Aaden said, just to see how far Randy would go.

"You hurt Pryor and I'll rip your damn face off," he said.

Aaden told me he liked Randy ever since that night because what he lacked in size, he made up for in sincerity.

The frantic cries of my team members pull me out of my daydream. Everyone around me is yelling and pleading for me to stab Alago in the chest. They shout over and over again that this is the moment we have been waiting for. Their voices rise like a massive choir in the middle of a soul-shaking chant.

Alago roars into the heavens, knowing he is about to be destroyed. He moves the very ground he stands on and summons a wave of wrath unlike anything we have ever seen. But my team is steadfast, strong and ready to die to save humanity. No matter what hell Alago raises, the team keeps him bound.

They have done everything they can; now it's up to me. I must be strong enough to kill Alago. I must be brave enough to take my best friend's life. I cry out as I raise the sword high above my head. The sword cuts through the air with the grace and brute strength of the Omari.

"AARRGH!" I yell as I put all my strength into lowering the sword into its target's chest.

Sorry, Randy. I have to do this. I have to kill Alago...wait! Shit! That's it! Kill Alago!

The sword comes down inches away from Alago's chest. Instead of striking him, I veer off to the side and hit only thin air at the last minute. The team looks at me in utter disbelief. I missed. I swung the sword, and I missed. They can see that I missed on purpose and it baffles them.

"I have an idea!" I call out to them.

Just as the words leave my mouth, Alago breaks free of the team's hold.

He howls with hatred and malice as he attacks at full speed. He plows right through the team, sending us all tumbling into the air. When we land, we are scattered among heaps of junk and debris.

We have been thrown too far to stop what's happening—Malakaro has finally broken out of his prison. He zooms up into the sky like a rocket, with Alago right on his heels. Together, they rise above us and link hands in the air.

The moment they touch, a series of blood-colored currents encircle them. They swell and emanate a blinding light that propels them further into the air and turns them in circles at inhuman speeds. The surge rips their skins away from them and grants them a new, thick, dark metallic, protective coating.

The spikes on Alago are now reinforced black steel. Malakaro's wings are nearly three times their normal size and coated in an impenetrable black liquid-like metal. The perfect partners of evil open their arms wide and, without saying a word, tear a hole the size of an ocean into the sky.

We watch as swirls of energy as large as cities form above our heads and start to inhale the world. A series of cracks spanning several miles appears, assuring that those who don't get swallowed by the sky will get eaten by the earth. All around us, angels, demons, Quo, humans, animals—anything that once showed signs of life—are being obliterated.

Malakaro simply looks in the direction of a forest and it gets wiped off the face of the earth. He turns his attention to the council, who are in the air, getting ready to attack. They never get the chance. Before they can strike, Alago nods his head and the sky turns against the council, casting them down to the ground like trash.

Malakaro laughs as he descends on the council. Fate is the first one to launch a wave of white energy at Malakaro. When the white light leaves Fate's hands, it's a raging sea of illumination, but once it makes contact with Malakaro, it becomes a mere speck of light he puts out with the tips of his fingers.

Malakaro looks over at Fate and lifts one hand in an upward motion, as if to say "Fate, stand up." But he's not talking to Fate, he is actually summoning a large army of dark entities with no faces to rise up from the ground and devour him. The disfigured shadowy figures do as their master says, and in one fell swoop, Fate is gone.

CHAPTER TWENTY
ONE OF US DIES

When Fate falls to his death, someone cries out, "Nooooo!" It's an outcry that can be heard around the world, a cry filled with anguish and sorrow. It's so gut-wrenching and primal, it sends chills down my body. I follow the sound to find out whom that much pain belongs to. On the ground, where Fate once stood, I spot an older woman kneeling down and weeping openly. Judging by the intensity of her moans, the Face has lost the love of her life. Suddenly, she gets up on her feet and charges towards Malakaro.

"Barbara, no!" my mother yells.

The Face doesn't heed the warning. She no longer cares about her own safety. All she wants is to avenge Fate, and she's willing to die to do it. She uses her powers to peel hundreds of metal strips from the scrap heaps that were once skyscrapers. She shapes the metal into makeshift arrows and launches them at Malakaro. They slice through the air with precision as they aim for his face. Alago catches them and throws them into his mouth; he then spits them out in rapid succession. The arrows land with brute force, impaling dozens of people.

Malakaro glares at the Face as he calmly waves his hand. He silently orders her to pick up one of the jagged rocks near her foot and slice herself open. The Face does exactly as he orders. She starts crying out as she watches herself carve into the side of her face. East barrels into her and wrestles to keep her from harming herself. The closest angels to her are Dylan and Swoop; they race to help East. They call out to Diana for backup, fearing the Face will skin herself to death.

Time harnesses all his powers and joins forces with my mother. The two of them attack together. They form a flood of brilliant light and send both Alago and his partner tumbling backwards in the sky. The team and I take to the air and add our powers to that of the remaining council. The blast of powers forms an all-consuming light that encapsulates the two evil entities.

Malakaro and Alago counter by ripping even further into the earth. The ground beneath us fractures and starts pulling apart. Thousands of shadow demons spring from the dark abyss below. They ravage everything they touch. They latch on to us like locusts and refuse to let go.

The all-powerful partners of evil laugh as they walk through the army effortlessly and command them to kill whatever is left standing. Time and Death are losing the battle due to the sheer number of shadow demons that have descended upon us.

"Why didn't you kill Randy?" Bex shouts as he tackles a shadow demon.

"I have a better idea. I'm not gonna use the ash-laced blade on Malakaro. I'm gonna use it on Alago. Once I take the power out of him, he's back to being Randy. He will be no use to Malakaro," I reason as I slice into a shadow demon.

"You're hoping that without Randy, Malakaro loses his enhanced powers?" Bex says.

"Yeah."

"What if you're wrong? What if he's just as strong?" Bex asks.

"Then we'll go to plan B."

"What's plan B?" Aaden asks as he pulls a shadow demon off Easton.

"I'll get back to you!" I reply as I dive down to earth, where Alago is about to trample on a group of angels he just plucked from the sky. I collide into him, forcing him to misstep and miss his target. Alago turns his rage on me by picking up a car and hurling it at me. I move out of the way but not quickly enough. My wings are pinned under the vehicle. Alago is headed straight for me.

Shitshitshit!

I blast him as hard as I can; it slows him down but doesn't stop him. He's still headed towards me. He looks venomous and eager to kill. There's glee in his eyes as he comes closer; he knows he has me beat.

C'mon, c'mon, c'mon...

No matter what I try, I can't pull my wings from the car. I reach over and grab an iron rod near me or at least I try. It's too far away. I try again and again. Finally, I'm able to reach it. I attempt to maneuver the car just enough to get free from its hold. But by then it's too late. Alago is now in striking distance.

I lift my hands up to attack, but Alago is quicker. He backhands me with a force that could rival Omnis's. The power of the blow shakes loose a few teeth in the back of my mouth and splits my cheek open. The pain is excruciating. Alago, enjoying the effects of his blow, slaps me again. I cry out as agony spreads through the other side of my face.

Alago yanks me from the car, causing a tear in the upper part of my wings. He throws me to the ground and kicks me like a football. I go flying backwards into a streetlamp. I bang my head on the base of it and the pain radiates all over my skull. Alago is nowhere near done. He bears down on me and stomps his foot on my chest. I manage to cover myself with part of my wings in order to soften the blow.

Alago is tired of playing around. He leaps into the air and goes to slam his body down on me. I see him descend, but the blow to the head slows down my reaction time. I can't get clear of him in time. I place my hands in front of my face and brace myself for what's to come. But I don't feel pressure from above like I thought I would. Instead I feel someone's arms around me as they tuck me into their chest and quickly roll me out of the way. The being hides us under a huge slab of concrete. I look up and find myself looking into Aaden's eyes.

"Hey," he says as if it were a casual day.

"Hi," I whisper.

"You good?" he asks.

"Yeah, just a little skull fracture," I reply as his face starts spinning in my head. I close my eyes, and Aaden goes into worry overdrive. I quickly open them back up so he knows that I am okay. I'm not, but this is no time to be technical.

We hear Swoop screaming for her life as six shadow demons literally try to tear her in two. We look around frantically and realize that everyone on the team is handling one awful situation after another.

"Go help Swoop! I got this," I assure him.

Aaden nods and takes off into the sky. I slide out from under the hideout. Alago turns just in time to spot me. The creature is delighted to find his toy again. He can't wait to break me into as many pieces as he can.

Alago bolts towards me. I hold the blade behind my back and get ready. He jumps into the air and comes down on me with the power of a mountain. My wings are still injured, but I'm able to move quickly thanks to the adrenaline pumping through me. I make it out of the way just in time. He comes after me again. He won't stop until I am dead.

Dead! I should be dead!

I pop the pill that I took from Dylan into my mouth. I hold my head in my hands as if the pain has finally gotten the best of me. I fall down seconds before Alago strikes again. He comes closer to see if the mouse he's been playing with finally died. I can hear him grunting as he stands over me. The pill is working. My wings are still and my body is unresponsive. Alago thinks I'm dead. If Randy is still in there, it will have some kind of effect on him.

I hear Alago coming closer to my body. I feel him stand over me. He rages to the heavens with a mix of anger and grief. Randy is still in him. And somewhere inside, Randy thinks I'm dead. That pain is causing Alago to feel confused. He wanted my death, but now that he has it, it feels...wrong. I can sense him leaning over me. He gets closer and closer. Knowing this is my only chance, I open my eyes and plunge the dagger into Alago's shoulder.

The blow doesn't affect Alago. He's pissed that I played him. He picks me up by my wings and flings me across the battlefield. I pay no attention to the pain and fly right back to him. The ash should work in a few moments. If it doesn't take Randy's powers away, I will have to kill him for real this time.

Please work. Please work.

Alago rips off a section of a fallen roof and brings it down on my head. I grab the remains of a telephone pole and strike him hard in his ankle. It causes him to stumble, but the slab of concrete is still in his hand.

C'mon, Randy. Come back to me. If I attack you as the Alago, you will be injured too. Come back to me before I have to kill you!

He raises the roof over his head again, this time determined to crush me under its weight. He comes down on me, and there is no way to avoid having to counterattack.

Sorry, Randy...

I hold out the coin in the palm of my hand and the sword of Avery quickly forms. As the slab of concrete comes crashing down on my head, I ram Alago in the knee and twist the sword as deeply as I can. Alago falls backwards on a heap of dead bodies. Although he's hurt, he's nowhere near powerless.

The ash should have taken effect by now. I don't know why it isn't working. But the fact is I can't afford to wait any longer for Randy's return. So I brace myself to take advantage of the only chance I will have to kill the Alago. I raise the sword above my head, this time certain that I will bring it down on Alago and end his life. Maybe I was fooling myself, maybe Randy was never really in there, just like Summit. Maybe it was all in my head.

Well, make-believe time is over...

I jump into the air, raise my sword above my head, and come down hard on Alago's chest. "Pry! Wait!" someone shouts. I look down and see my best friend's face looking up at me. Randy has transformed back into his human state. But by then it's too late. I can't stop the momentum. The sword is heading right into Randy's bony chest.

"NO!" Randy begs.

The sword touches his flesh, but it does not go all the way through and there is no blood. Stunned, I look closer at Randy's body and realize it's protected by a shield. East saw what was happening and moved like lightning to guard Randy against the attack.

Exhausted from the close call, I drop the sword and fall to my knees next to Randy. His shoulder is bleeding, his knee is seriously messed up, and he looks awful. But he's alive. He's back and he's alive.

"You're back, you're back." I weep with happiness.

"I knew you'd do it! I knew you'd save me," he says with tears in his eyes.

We hear someone wail in anger. Randy and I look towards the direction of the sound. Malakaro is in the air and sees that Alago has just been destroyed. There are no more vials, so he can't bring Alago back. No matter what happens from now on, he's on his own. His eyes glow with hate and madness. He's so incensed he's vibrating.

"East, get Randy to safety!" I yell.

As the battle rages on behind us, Malakaro and I lock eyes. I managed to get Randy back from his clutches. I took down half of the power team, and I can tell by his stare that he is going to try to make me pay for it. I don't care. Even if he ends up killing me, at least I got Randy away from him.

I brace myself for Malakaro's attack. But he doesn't come at me. He doesn't send sharp objects or command any demons to hurt me. Instead he stands very still for several moments, and then he smiles. Something about that smile sends a chill to my very core. He steps aside so he can reveal the reason behind his smile.

The moment he saw Alago was gone, Malakaro attacked. He didn't attack me, he went after the angel closest to him at the time: Swoop. Malakaro formed a long sharp sword made of red lightning and shadow. He sent it right into Swoop's face. Dylan, seeing what was about to happen, placed himself in front of the weapon to save his girl. But while his efforts were daring and brave, they were ultimately unsuccessful. The shadow sword stabbed Dylan in the back between his shoulder blades. It then continued its course right through Swoop's skull. The couple died facing each other.

Aaden and the others freak out all at once. They run towards the bodies and try in vain to revive them. I don't speak. I just look at Malakaro. He looks back at me. Both of us are so focused on each other, it's as if we were alone. The loss of Swoop is devastating and promises to bring about unspeakable grief. However, there is no room for that right now. Every inch of me is filled with concentrated, pure hate. Grief will wait.

I hear my team calling out to me, but their voices are just background. I take out the sword of Avery and slice into my arm. I use my dripping blood to form the start of a large circle. I am making a fight-or-flight line.

A fight-or-flight line is a barrier that's formed when two opposing sides mix their blood together on the ground. The two parties vow that once the barrier is formed, they will fight until one of them is killed. If Malakaro refuses to add his blood to the circle, then he must surrender and fly away. Once a fight-or-flight line has been drawn, no one other than the two fighters can enter the circle. And the only way out is when one of them dies.

"No! Pry, don't! Don't do this!" Diana begs.

I don't heed her warning. I want to take on that sick bastard by myself. I don't want help from the council, the team, or even my husband. Some dragons are meant to be slayed alone. I outline half the circle, knowing Malakaro will gladly finish the other half, thereby consenting to the arrangement.

I was right; Malakaro forms a small spark of lightning on the tip of his index finger and cuts into his hand. The team begs me not to go through with the fight-or-flight line. Everyone shouts at me for what I'm about to do, even the remaining council members. But one being doesn't speak. I turn to Aaden. His heartbreak over Swoop is etched in his face. I wait for him to tell me not to do what I'm about to do. But when he speaks, he says exactly the right thing.

"Kill him," Aaden says with cold certainty.

"I will," I vow.

Malakaro is finished drawing the other half of the circle with his blood. The fight-or-flight line has been drawn. My mother runs towards me, shouting in protest. I do not respond. I enter the circle. Malakaro enters the circle. Either Malakaro will make it out alive or I will. One thing is for sure—today one of us dies.

***

Everyone on the battlefield stops to focus on us. Both sides are too taken by the match to do anything else. My team watches while holding Swoop's lifeless body.

Malakaro looks at me from across the circle with malice and fury. I return his gaze, matching his ire. He begins to move around the circle slowly. I slowly start walking in the opposite direction, both of us sizing each other up. He studies me and addresses me in his usual calm voice.

"Are you sure you're ready for this, little sis?" he asks.

"Bring it."

"I wanted to kill your team first—all of them. But perhaps it's better to have them watch as you die. Yes, that might be even better," he says.

"You talk too much," I scold.

"You want to die quickly; I can make that happen," he says as he launches a flood of red plasma-like waves from his hands. I dive down to the ground; the attack misses me by a fraction of a second. From the ground, I send a torrent of black waves from my hands; he absorbs the energy with the palms of his hands as if it were nothing.

"You're going to have to do better than that," he warns me.

"Deal," I vow.

He blasts me again, and once again, I manage to avoid direct impact. He starts to laugh. It's a cruel, full laugh that seems to take up the whole world.

"Is that your plan, to keep running?" he asks.

"I'm not running—I'm not a coward like you."

"How ironic since I'm the one who broke the world and the one who broke your team. In fact, if memory serves, I remember breaking our dear father in half."

He's using my dad's death to distract me. I refuse to let him succeed. There's no way I'm losing focus. That's just what he wants.

"Did you know he begged for your life before you arrived? Yes, that's right, the great Marcus Cane begged me to spare you. Isn't that the sign of a weak angel?" he says, delighted.

"There was nothing weak about my father. If he had a failing, it was you. He should have put an end to your life years ago," I counter.

"Too bad he's not here to try."

"No, but I am," I reply as I take to the sky and tackle him. He throws me off him effortlessly and hurls a sea of lightning at my head. I move but not quickly enough; my midsection takes a hit that sends me to the ground.

"Too bad your father didn't know how to battle well enough to teach you anything worth a damn," he says.

"He taught me all I need, believe me." I gasp as I make myself get back up. He strikes me again, hitting my left leg. I feel the flesh on my leg ripping apart. He strikes again; this time the lightning hits my thigh. It cuts so deep I can see the bone. That shit hurts so badly all I want to do is cry out, but I won't give him the satisfaction.

I fire at him as he comes close to me. I finally make contact. It hurts him. I know because I can see him wince slightly. I strike again from the ground and make contact. Had he been an angel of normal power, he would have died on the spot. However, because of the magnitude of his power, my blow only causes a bloody gash across his face. He puts his hand up to his face, impressed. He didn't think I'd ever be good enough to strike him.

I fire again, but this time he blocks it by forming a small barrier in the air with his hand.

He grins as he strikes me. He sends out a constant flow of lightning. It feels like I'm being peeled, electrocuted, and stabbed all at once. I hear the team calling out and demanding that I get up. But the pain is so all consuming, it's hard to think of anything else.

"You're the one he should have given away! You're the one who didn't deserve him!" Malakaro says. The pain is so much now that I think I may actually be losing my mind. Why else would I start laughing?

"Why are you laughing? Why?" he shouts.

"I thought you were this big badass, but the truth is you are just a weak, needy little boy. Tell me what your daddy did to you. Did he forget to hang your picture on the refrigerator? Did he give me more hugs than he gave you? Awwww, come on, Jason, it's not your father's fault. He couldn't love you because, well—you're unlovable," I say as I continue to laugh.

"You really need to shut up," he shouts, losing his cool for the first time. He grabs me by my right wing, spins me around in the air, over his head, and flings me around the circle.

"ARRRRRRGH!" I cry in agony as I feel the bones in my wing break. Blood is oozing out from every opening in my face. I try to get up despite the pain. I make it halfway up, but Malakaro is right beside me. He kicks my right leg so hard the bone pops out. I hear Aaden's screams before I hear my own. I land back on the ground, now barely able to hobble.

"You have every right to be jealous of me. I had a home, a family, I was loved, and most of all, I was wanted. You didn't have any of that. And do you know why?" I mumble as I cough up blood. "C'mon, Jason, you're the smart one here. You put all this together. You must know the answer. Why didn't you have all the things I had? What kept you from being loved, you sick fuck?" I demand.

"YOU! HE PICKED YOU!" Malakaro rages as he rains down blow after blow on me. He kicks and bashes me in the face over and over. He caves in my nose with the toes of his boots. He pummels my eyes until they are all but swollen shut. He throws down a stream of red plasma at me. Once it makes contact, it shreds my skin and detaches the bones in my rib cage that were once connected. But no matter how close to death I am, I refuse to stop talking.

"No, I'm not the reason you weren't loved—you are," I reply as I spit out a tooth.

He picks me up, throws me over his shoulder, and sends me flying into the barrier around the circle. He takes my hand in his and starts to break my fingers one at a time.

"You will die here. The First Noru will find death right here on the ground, like a dog!" he vows as he snaps my ring finger off. There are no more words to explain the agony I am experiencing.

"Before you kill me, I…I want you…I…have…have to know something, Jason…" I slur as my vision gets blurry.

"What is it, Noru?" he says venomously.

"My father never stopped. Not even when you killed him."

"Never stopped what?" he rages.

"Love. He never stopped loving you. But you were too dense to see it."

"Bullshit! Marcus Cane never loved me! He never gave a damn about me!" Malakaro says as he pounds on me yet again. I am going to die at this rate. I can barely fly, my leg is broken, my wings are fractured, and I almost have no face left. But damned if I'm going to give up. His emotional outburst has distracted him. He's now walking in circles, furiously demanding that I stop lying.

"I'm not lying. He loved you. You had what I had. You just couldn't get past the hate. You just couldn't see it," I plead.

"MARCUS WAS A WORTHLESS PIECE OF SHIT WHO WALKED OUT ON ME!"

"That's not true. He looked after you; he was never too far. He gave up spending time with us to come see you."

"MARCUS CANE HATED ME!" Malakaro says, literally shaking with anger.

"He hated your jealousy, your darkness, and your need to destroy. But he loved you. He loved how brilliant you were and how resourceful you had become. But you wouldn't let go of the anger."

"He was my father; he should have taken me in. And now I will make him pay," he says.

"Then kill me; it won't take away what I had with him. He loved me; I will die peacefully because I was wanted. I was loved."

"Your mind may die in peace, but your body will feel pain like no other!"

"You can't kill me. There are always angels that will remember me. That will think of me when I'm gone. I'm gonna live forever. And you can't take that away," I swear.

"No one will remember your life. The only thing they will recall is the sad and merciless way you died."

"Fuck you!" I scream.

"Yes! That's it, Noru! Get angry. You will die in misery; that is the fate that awaits you!" he says as he prepares to strike one last time. I'm on the ground a few feet away from Aaden. We're divided by a shield, a shield I made by making the fight-or-flight line.

I'm going to die a few feet from Aaden, a few feet from paradise.

Aaden bangs his hands on the barrier and calls out to me. I can't reply. I can't move anymore. I want him to be happy when I'm gone. I want him to find love. But I can't tell him that; there's a tooth lodged down my throat. And I'm too weak to cough up any more blood.

I look next to Aaden and see my team. My team. I love them. I'm proud of them. I hope they know that. I hope they keep fighting no matter what happens to me. Standing next to the team is my mother, the woman who taught me about kindness, hope, and inner strength. I want her to close her eyes so she won't see this.

Mommy, close your eyes. Close your eyes.

Malakaro is preparing to attack for the last time when something above us catches his eye. I look up with what little vision I have left and spot something flying towards the barrier. I must be dreaming; nothing can get inside a fight-or-flight line once it is formed. But it's not just in my head because Malakaro is following it too. Something glides through the air gracefully and lands at my feet. The majestic silver bird comes close to my face and spreads out her wings.

Alexi.

Malakaro comes near the bird and picks it up in his hand. Alexis are generally impossible to kill, but Malakaro is far more powerful than anything we have seen. If anyone can kill Alexi, it would be Malakaro. I summon every ounce of strength I have, the last speck of hope I have left, and call out to him.

"Jason…please don't hurt Alexi," I whisper as tears run down my face. I forget about all the pain I'm in. Nothing matters right now but Alexi. Malakaro studies the animal as if it's the first time he ever saw one.

Aaden is banging his hands so hard against the barrier I feel it shaking. When it doesn't work, he creates a wall of blue fire against the barrier in hopes he can get in and save his daughter and me. Meanwhile, Malakaro holds the bird tenderly in the palms of his hands.

"Jason, I know you are hurt by what our dad did to you. I'm sorry he left you. I'm sorry it broke your heart, but that doesn't have to be the end of the story. We can make a new ending. The Alexi is your chance to start again. You have a son, Phoenix. And now he will have a cousin. Her name is Summit. You're her uncle. She will love you. Nix will love you. Please don't take away your only chance at love."

"You gave your Sib a name already?" he asks.

"Yes," I reply desperately.

"What does Summit mean?" he says.

I know I have to lie. If he knows the story behind Summit's name, it may send him off the deep end. He may be more resentful than ever that I got to be raised by my dad and he didn't. I proceed carefully.

"Summit means 'quiet strength,'" I reply.

"I suppose there's some poetry in that. Where did that name come from? Is it Greek, Latin…Dutch?"

"I can't remember," I lie.

"Let me help you out. I believe it's the name of a rather large waterfall in the Philippines…"

"Jason—"

"The waterfall where Marcus took you and told you how to be a leader! Did you think I would not know that? Do you have any idea how much I know about you? I spent my whole life studying you. You think you could trick me?"

"No! No! I don't think that. Jason, all of that was in the past. We can find a happy ending right now. Let us have a happy ending. Please don't kill my Alexi. Don't hurt my baby. Let the Alexi get her out of me, and then you can kill me. You can do whatever you want to me. Just please let her live."

Malakaro strokes Alexi's silver feathers gently. He then places the bird back down on the ground and lets it come over to me.

"Thank you. Thank you," I whisper, weak with relief.

"No, Pryor. Thank *you.* Now I know that when you die, you will do so without any peace at all."

Malakaro raises his hand towards the bird and summons a raging flood of crimson-colored lightning. The bird cries out as the surge of energy engulfs it. It convulses uncontrollably, then lies still on the ground. Alexi dies inches from my face.

BOOK III

AADEN "SILVER" CASE

It is better to conquer yourself than to win a thousand battles. Then the victory is yours. It cannot be taken from you, not by angels or by demons, heaven or hell.

-Buddha

CHAPTER TWENTY-ONE
BETTER THAN THAT

When Malakaro takes Alexi in his hand and listens as my wife pleads for the life of our child, for just one second, one brief moment, I think that bastard will listen to reason. But as he extends his hand and fires on the bird, I realize there is no reasoning with pure evil. I set the barrier on fire and try as hard as I can to break in, but it doesn't work. I double over in agony as my family gets taken from me.

"Silver, something's happening!" Bex yells as he forces me to lift my head up. I look inside the barrier. Pryor's eyes are healing themselves and soon go from pale purple to a plasma-like void of neon purple. In a matter of seconds, her whole body is healed and surrounded by energy. She has an expression on her face I've only seen one other time: the day her little brother died.

Pryor rises from the ground and floats in the air without needing to use her wings. Her entire body is a live wire of energy. She looks over at the dead bird, enraged; she opens her mouth.

"Everyone get down!" I shout at the team. They all take cover, but it's too late. There is no escaping the wrath of the First Noru. She lets out a sonic scream that shatters the barrier and causes it to explode into a million fragments. She opens her arms wide and pulls every single shadow demon from the sky. It's raining dead shadow demons for miles.

Malakaro looks on, shocked at the transformation. Soon he's back to his senses and retaliates by firing a sea of red lightning at Pryor. She counters with a flood of purple plasma. The two powerful energies converge in the middle. The struggle between the two of them sends sparks flying in the air.

Each side is determined to swallow the other. Malakaro tries hard to maintain his balance, but the power surge is hard for him to handle.

His hand shakes as he tries to combat the surge of energy coming from Pryor. However, his hate is no match for her appetite for revenge.

Pryor is just as livid, determined, and ruthless as her brother. Her surge of power overtakes Malakaro's. It hits him in the chest and tosses him to the ground. Pryor, using only one hand, grabs Malakaro by his neck and dangles him in the air.

Her eyes, mouth, and nose all work together to drain the life from his body. She no longer needs to extend her hands or use her palm. Pryor's entire body is a doorway to death. She's ripping life away from Malakaro, one layer at a time. Pryor *inhales* his life force in one big, long breath. He yells in agony as his flesh deteriorates, his eyes hollow out, and his skeletal frame withers in her hands. In a matter of minutes, the force that plagued our lives for years is gone. Pryor is back to her old self, and Malakaro, the most evil being in existence, is no more than a pile of dark dust.

"YES! THAT'S RIGHT, MOTHERFUCKER, DIE! DIE! DIE!" Randy shouts as he jumps up and down on Malakaro's remains. Bex is the first one to start laughing. Soon, it is contagious. We have lost so much, and we will definitely be grieving for Swoop, Dylan, and the thought of Summit. But right now it feels good to laugh. Randy is right, we did it! We. Did. It.

"Thank you for not giving up on me, on us," Randy says as he kisses Pryor on the forehead and goes back to dancing the worst dance I've ever seen.

"We have to get you lessons," Diana says as she watches Randy.

Pryor smiles as she stands over the ashes. She reaches out her hand. I come close to her, as does the rest of the team. She places her head on my shoulder as we gaze at the Alexi and what will never be. Although it hurts like hell to know we lost Summit, we take solace in knowing at least we killed Malakaro. We made it safe for other parents and their kids. And to make sure that that little fucker doesn't somehow find a way to come back to life, we stand there and wait, as a team, until a strong gust of wind carries his ashes away.

Peace, at last.

"He's dead. He's really dead," she says, beside herself with relief.

"Yes, babe, he's gone," I reply.

"I changed my mind. I don't think that Vampire Slayers chick has anything on you," Randy says to Pry as he hugs her again.

"He would have been so proud of you, Carrot," Death says as she steals a hug from her daughter.

"I didn't save the Alexi," she replies tearfully.

"I know, but you saved millions of lives," Death reminds her.

"But not Swoop, I couldn't save Swoop. And Dylan, he's gone and—"

"Hey, my wife just saved the world. Could you back off her, please?" I ask.

She laughs despite herself.

"Pry, they didn't die in vain. You have to know that," Diana says.

"That supernova thing, you have to teach me that," Bex says.

"All you have to do is be filled with hate," she says sadly.

"Duh, Pry, that's not it. You've hated Malakaro all this time, but that never happened. You went all badass because of love. You love Summit just that much. You love Swoop just that much…you tapped into the same force that Malakaro did. Except you used that to save lives, not take them away," Randy says.

"Yeah, I guess."

"Bottom line, you were fantastic," Diana replies.

"I think I can pull some strings and get you to be an Omari. If you ever need a job," Bex jokes.

"No, you are not working with your ex," Diana says.

"What makes you think you can tell me what to do?" Bex asks.

"Don't make me get my cuffs," Diana teases.

"You are so bad for my image; come here!" Bex says with a goofy smile as he pulls her close.

"Hey, you don't have a 'one hug' policy, do you? 'Cause I'd like another," Pryor whispers in my ear.

"I can do better than that," I reply as I take her into my arms and kiss her passionately.

"Hey, Pry, do dead Alexis move?" Randy asks as he looks across the battlefield.

"What are you talking about?" I ask.

Randy turns our attention to the Alexi on the ground. She is slowly starting to move her wings. Pryor and I exchange a look. Is it too much to hope for to both defeat Malakaro and save Summit?

"Alexi, come here, honey," Pryor says in a whisper, as if her voice could somehow scare it away. The Alexi takes flight away from us. Our hopes are dashed—until she dives back down and lands at Pryor's feet.

"Can this be?" Time asks Death as he comes closer.

"I don't know. I guess it can…" Death replies with hope.

"Aaden, she made it! She made it here to us!" Pryor shouts in a tearful cheer.

"But how did the Alexi come back to life. Death, did you or Time do that?" East asks the remaining council members.

"The Alexi came back to life for one reason—Summit ordered it to. Pryor, your daughter won't just be the First Toren; apparently she has the gift of resurrection. That is a gift only given to an Echo," Time says.

"A what?" East asks.

"An Echo, a being that's slated to replace another being who has great power," Pryor says.

"Yes, but…Echos are so very rare," Death replies in disbelief.

"If she has the power of resurrection, she must be here to replace Death," East says.

"Easton!" Diana says.

"It's okay. I am more than happy to move aside for my granddaughter," Death assures us.

"We won't know for sure until after Alexi takes in the Sib," Time replies.

Pryor then explains that the color the Alexi turns will tell us who on the council she is born to replace. Death is onyx, Time is ruby, and Fate is sapphire.

We help Pryor lie down on the battlefield, and I hold her hand as the Alexi gets on top of her chest. She looks over at me. I have never seen her so happy and so content in my life.

"This is really happening," she whispers, overjoyed.

"It's really happening," I reply.

"What if we suck as parents? We don't really know anything about kids," she says.

"We raised East. We know all there is to know," I remind her with a smile.

"Hey, I have matured greatly during these past few years," East says, offended.

"East, what did we have to do to you last month, in the middle of our meeting?" I ask.

"I was on a time-out," East says, avoiding eye contact.

"And why did you need a time-out?" Death asks.

"I was not making good choices," East says as he lowers his head.

"Like I said, we can handle anything," I assure Pryor. She and I share a laugh.

"I love you." She lays her head down on the ground.

"I love you too. Ready?" I ask.

"Hell yeah," she says.

The process doesn't take long at all. And if it hurts, Pryor does a good job of not letting us in on it. She lies there perfectly still and lets Alexi suck up the small Sib inside her.

We watch in awe as Alexi turns sparkling gold. Time and Death exchange a look. I can't read what they are feeling; is it alarm or amazement?

"The Alexi turned gold. What does that mean?" Pryor and I ask.

"Oh my…" Time whispers in wonder.

"Mom, what does the gold Alexi mean?" Pryor asks.

Death is too busy admiring the bird to reply. I take Death's hand and beg her for an answer.

"Emmy, tell us what you know. Summit is an Echo, meaning she is going to replace someone very powerful. But who? Who is Summit going to replace?"

"Omnis."

***

All our questions had to wait while we helped put the world back together. The aftermath of Malakaro's rampage was felt worldwide. It took almost a year, but the angel world was able to get everything back to the way it was. They rebuilt cities, revitalized nations, and held large parties where the humans unknowingly drank mixtures to wipe their memories.

We worked night and day along with the Quo to put things back together. The only time we took off was to have a passing, otherwise known as a funeral, for Swoop and Dylan. Losing Bird was harder than I can put into words. And Dylan was only a friend for a few hours, but he made a lasting impression. We were sorry we could not save him.

At first we were going to have the passing the way angels always did: with Paras on the mountaintop, singing a song of remembrance. However, East had another idea.

"Swoop would not want us standing on a stupid mountain, singing sad songs. She found a reason to dance and celebrate no matter what evil was after us. If we want to honor her, let's do it right. Let's throw a party!"

"You want to throw a big bash with drinking, dancing, and loud music?" Bex asked.

"Yeah, is that stupid?" East replied.

"No, Swoop would have wanted that kind of send-off," Randy said.

"And I know exactly where the party should take place," Bex said as he turned to his queen and smiled mischievously.

The party to celebrate Swoop's life took place in the Kon's newly formed castle. It lasted seven days. Some of Swoop's favorite bands played; they featured a pretty amazing laser light show, fireworks throughout the sky, and lots of drinking. I have never seen so much booze in my life. The party didn't just celebrate Swoop's life—it was for Marcus, Sam, Key, and all the other beings who gave their lives to stop evil from spreading. The party was just like Swoop: epic and over the top.

We also held a small ceremony so that Swoop's parents could say good-bye in their own way. We all joined together to help them as they mourned their daughters. The team bought the house next to the Guardian home so that Jay and Miku could literally live next door. Emmy and my father were also instrumental in helping Jay and Miku. They made it their mission to remind the parents that all was not lost.

In the end, what really helped the grieving parents was their grandson, RJ. He kept them on their toes every moment of the day. He had Jay's love of cars and Miku's love of destruction. He once flew in a car window and managed to start it. He lifted his hands in the air as the car took off. He beat down on the steering wheel as if it were his drum set. Miku and Jay had to zoom down the driveway to catch up with him. When they pulled him out of the car, the first thing he said to Miku was, "Again, Nana! Again!"

Although RJ is safe, there is an evil being chasing him; his name is East. And he insists on turning RJ into a miniature version of himself. He has bought that kid over fifty fedora hats. And every outfit East owns, he buys a replica for RJ.

"Would you leave RJ alone? Stop trying to make him your clone!" Mel said as she watched him place yet another hat on the toddler's head.

"Hey, I have to make sure that kid is dressed right. His mom is gone. It's up to me. If not me, who?" East said proudly.

"Are you sure you want to marry him?" Randy asked Mel.

"I was, but now I'm rethinking it…" Mel teased as she kissed East.

"Well, I'd love to help you rescue RJ from the cult that is 'Easton,' but I can't. I have a date," Randy said proudly.

"So things are really serious with you and Megan?" Pryor asked.

"I took her to a *Star Trek* convention. You can't get more serious than that," he informed us as he grinned and headed out the door.

Randy has changed since being the Alago. He's more confident than he was before. He's more certain about who he is and how much he matters in the world. He's still dealing with having killed his mom and the fact that we had to take out his father, but considering what he's been through, he's doing really well.

Pry and Randy went back to their friendship as if no time had passed. Randy comes over so often, she made sure that he had a room in our house just for him. It's easy to tell which guest bedroom is his. It has a sign on the door that reads:

"Keep calm and use the Force."

After Randy left, the Face joined us at Jay and Miku's house. She spotted the hat on RJ and came to the little boy's defense. "Leave that child alone. He should be influenced by sensible beings," the Face scolded East.

"It's okay, brilliance is never appreciated in its own time. You'll see, hundreds of years from now, my genius fashion sense will be celebrated," East vowed.

"I can see the future, Easton, and no, it won't be," the Face said with a smile.

"So now that you've been chosen to be Fate, does that mean no more teaching for you?" Mel asked.

"Certainly not. I intend to do just as Death does; I will have two jobs. I will be in school part time and on the council. There is no getting rid of me, Easton," she warned playfully.

"Great! I'm so happy to hear that," East said, clearly lying. We laughed at him and took the silly hat off RJ's head. He cried out in dismay; apparently he liked the hat. So we put it back on. RJ smiled and ran into the playroom, where his best friend, Nix, awaited him.

Over the past few months the two of them have been inseparable. Their friendship feels natural. After all, they will grow up to be on the same team. Bex and I were on the same team and things got complicated with us. I hope the future is better for RJ and Nix.

Amazingly enough, everyone's future seems to be moving towards a brighter path. My dad and Winter officially moved in with each other. She wanted to get married, but I just don't think my dad could ever do that with anyone who wasn't my mom. So Winter settled for living together. There are times I can see she's unhappy, but that's rare. For the most part, the two of them laugh a lot together.

Emmy suggested to my dad that it would be good to spend father-son time with Easton. So now the two of them go on demon-hunting trips once a month. East asked me to come along, but I declined. I think he needs to spend time alone with my dad. He needs to make up for all the times his adopted father, Frank, let him down.

Emmy hasn't fully recovered from losing Marcus; I don't think she ever will. However, knowing that she will soon be a grandmother has given her a lot of joy. She and Miku shop way too much for Summit. In fact, we would have to get another house in order to have enough space to put all the things they bought. Finally Jay and my dad had to sit the two of them down and beg them to stop buying clothes.

One of the most unexpected things to occur post Malakaro is the willingness of the Paras to accept their queen. They heard about how Diana fought for them and how she risked her life to save the Paras who came with us in the graveyard. They set aside their reluctance and welcomed her—for the most part.

There are still asshole Paras out there who hate her and would like nothing more than to kill her. But they'd have to get past the Kon. And the fact is, Bex is very much in love with Diana. He would never allow anything to happen to her. They may have started out as a "fake" couple, but now they are the real deal.

As for Pryor and me, things have been kind of…amazing. After helping put the world back in order, she gave the team some much-needed time off. We had plans to travel to these odd and interesting places around the world while we waited for Summit to be born. We talked for hours about the places we would go and what we would do there. However, we never left Roslyn. That's right, instead of traveling the world, we stayed in our new home on the mountain, doing two things: making love and preparing for Summit.

Over the next few months we found out more about what it meant that our child was an Echo. It turns out Omnis had given himself an end date. At that point he will cease to exist. No one knows what that date will be. However, he has chosen three beings that have the potential to grow powerful enough to replace him.

These three Echos are located throughout the world. For their safety, no one knows where. In fact, no one knows Echos exist. It's just a myth in some journal. That way, Summit and the other two Echos can lead normal lives until Omnis chooses which of them will take his place.

Summit's power as an Echo is resurrection. However, it's such a complex power, it will take her years to master. Her bringing Alexi back to life was just her way of fighting for survival. She won't be able to repeat that kind of power until she's older.

Until then, she has more than enough power from Pryor and me. Summit is the child of a Noru, which makes her a Toren. But because she is the only one with both a mother and a father who are Noru, her powers exceed the others'. She will be the First Toren. She has already started to show her Toren powers.

Pry and I were in her nursery one night, trying to decide on the color of the walls. We set out two cans of pink paint and placed them on the floor. Summit used her mom's body and sent a surge of purple lightning at the paint cans. They exploded on impact.

That was our daughter's subtle way of saying she's not into pink. We should have scolded her, but we were too busy laughing at the fact that Pry moved out of the way in time, but I was covered in pink paint. Pry sent a picture of me bathed in pink to everyone on the team. East now uses it as his Facebook photo and screensaver.

Pry told Summit she had to find a nicer way to communicate and tell us what she wanted. It took her a few days, but she finally figured out a way to talk to us. We were in the paint store when Summit used her powers to move a dozen blue paint cans across the store and place them at our feet.

"Wow, that is such a good choice. And you told us what you wanted without blowing anything up! Good job, Winnie," Pryor said.

Ever since Emmy came over and watched *Winnie the Pooh* with her on TV, it's all Summit wants playing in the house. When she's fussy and unhappy, she shows that by moving things around the house like a restless ghost. But then Pry will put on *Winnie the Pooh* and she'll settle down. Her favorite character is the big bear named Winnie on the show.

She loves when he says his popular phrase "oh bother" when he gets in trouble and can't access the honey he worked so hard to get. And when the bear laughs, Summit lights up. So we nicknamed her after the cartoon bear.

It's hard enough being the leader of a team, but being slated to be one of three that may replace Omnis...that's just too much to deal with. Pryor and

I have stayed up many nights, trying to figure out how we can protect her.

In the end, all we can do is train her and do whatever it takes to keep her status as an Echo a secret. It sounds crazy to say, but we hope she isn't chosen to be Omnis's replacement. We want her to live a normal, happy life. We want her to be as safe as possible. And we will do anything to ensure that.

***

"Silver, you are going to pace through the hardwood floors and fall right into the basement," Death scolds.

"I should have gone with her," I reply as I continue to pace.

"When babies come out of Noni, it's like coming out of the womb; they need to be greeted by a calm parent," Randy replies.

"I AM CALM!" I shout before I can catch myself. Everyone in the house laughs at me, even my dad. Today is the day I have been waiting nearly a year for: Summit is ready to come home. She's reached the maturation point where she is ready to come into the real world. In other words, my daughter will be born today.

My daughter…

I wanted to go with Pry to pick up Summit, but she said I needed to stay behind and get myself together. She may have a point. I have done nothing but pace and worry since she left. The Guardians and the Noru team have all come over to the house to keep an eye on me and to meet Summit. I told them that I was fine on my own, but they came anyway. In truth, I'm glad they are here.

"Damn it! I didn't baby proof the stairs!" I reply as I dash over to the staircase.

"Aaden, you already put a Trimeter up there. It will recognize that Summit is a toddler and the barrier will automatically appear if she gets to the edge of the staircase. And she has wings, remember?" Dad says.

"Oh, yeah. Yeah, you're right," I reply as I swallow hard.

"Silver, chill out. You're going to have a heart attack—and you don't even have one," Randy says.

"I'm fine—wait—did we baby proof the backyard?" I ask.

"YES!" everyone in the house says.

"What if something happened to them? What if some evil encountered them? What if they are lying in the street somewhere? What if—oh no! I need to go find them! How could I let them go alone? I have to go get them right now!" I shout frantically.

"Son, relax. There is no great evil anymore. Everything is fine. Carrot will be back with Winnie. And soon you will have your family," Dad promises.

"How do you know that? What if something goes wrong? Something always goes wrong! Damn it! They could be in trouble right now!" I counter.

"They aren't in trouble, Silver," Bex says.

"How the hell do you know that, Kon?" I blurt out.

"Because they're right behind you," he replies with a sincere smile.

I turn around and see Pryor standing a few feet away, holding a bundle in her arms. I can see Summit's gray wings peeking from the blanket. I should hurry to greet them, but I don't. I just stand there, too afraid to move. Pryor has never looked more beautiful than she does right now. And she's holding my daughter, my second chance. Yet I can't move.

Diana comes up to me. She takes my hand and whispers in my ear. "Silver, it's real. It won't move away if you get closer. The Center is gone. The great evil is gone. And over there is what you have wanted all your life—a family. I have mine; now you go get yours," she says as she gently nudges me to move.

I finally make my way towards them. I am inches away from everything I've ever wanted. Pryor smiles warmly and wipes tears away from my eyes, tears I didn't realize I had shed.

"Aaden, this is your daughter, Summit Avery Case," she says with a catch in her voice.

I look into the bundle and see my daughter for the first time. She has purple eyes and black hair with a few soft purple highlights. Her cheeks are full, and her rosy lips are open wide as she explores her surroundings.

Her beautiful eyes land on me for the first time. They glow with excitement. She looks at my wings and reaches for them. I bring them closer to her and she touches one with pure fascination. I laugh, and she recognizes the sound. She moves around excitedly as she reaches for me. I take her into my arms and cradle her. She's so light it's like holding on to air. She looks up at me, filled with wonder and enthusiasm. I lean in close to her and speak to her in a soft voice.

"Hi…I'm gonna teach you how to fly. I'm gonna show you how to get your mom to laugh when she's down. I'll show you how to protect yourself, and I'll tell you all about your sister, Sparks. I've waited so long to meet you, Winnie…I promise to protect and love you every day of my life…oh crap, I didn't introduce myself. My name is Aaden. I'm your dad."

EPILOGUE (AADEN SPEAKS)

Six years later...

I wake up in the house that has officially become our home: Roslyn. The three-story modern estate, perched on the hill, is filled with the voices of our family. Even in the master bedroom, Pryor and I can hear them downstairs running around.

"Don't you have to go downstairs and keep the peace?" I ask as I pull the comforter off her face.

"It's your turn." She groans as she goes back under the covers. I laugh at her and join her under there.

"Good morning," I say with a big smile.

"I know you're enjoying this. I'm exhausted. You should feel bad for me," she says, shaking her head, pretending to be disappointed in me.

"I would feel bad if you were tired from a battle or day-to-day life as the First Noru, but I can't feel bad for a woman who wakes up exhausted from girls' night," I tell her as I pull down the sheets. My wife is forced to face the sunlight.

"Argh! I knew I should have called it a night earlier," she scolds herself.

"Why didn't you?"

"It's Diana's fault. I'm telling you that girl can drink. I had everything under control until the strippers started to—"

"Strippers?" I ask.

"Did I say strippers? I'm so silly. I must still be half asleep," she says as she leaps off the bed and heads for the shower.

"No you don't, Mrs. Case! You left me here so you and the queen could go party!"

"Yes, but I was thinking about you the whole time," she teases.

"Really?" I reply suspiciously.

"Oh well, except that one time when the stripper let us touch his—"

I don't let her finish. I playfully tackle her back into bed. We end up wrestling and play fighting like we're kids. She climbs on top of me and raises both arms in victory.

"Ain't gonna be no rematch!" she says, doing an awful impression of the boxer in the movie *Rocky*. Her and Randy have moved on to classic movies, and so far that's her favorite.

I flip her over and I use my secret weapon—my lips. I glide them across her midsection, where I know she's ticklish. She squeals loudly and tries to defend herself. But she's too busy laughing to retaliate, so she wisely decides to surrender.

"Okay, okay! You win!" she says.

"Good, now where did you and Diana actually go?" I ask.

"Oh, honey, I wasn't kidding about the strip club. We actually did go, but it's your fault," she says.

"Oh, this ought to be good…" I reply, trying to suppress the laughter in me.

"Diana, Mel and I were having drinks and Bellamy had just finished her shift in the castle, so she joined us for girls' night."

"I'm waiting for the part where this is my fault," I reply, daring her.

"Well, imagine my surprise when I discover that I am having drinks with the woman who my husband lost his virginity to," she says, pretending to be hurt.

"She told you?" I ask.

"Yes, she did. Why didn't you tell me you and Bellamy hooked up years ago?" she asks.

"It wasn't my secret to tell. You know I'm not like that."

"Well, either way, I was the injured party. I was so devastated that I had to drink and drink…"

"And go to a strip club?"

"There's a lot of dancing at clubs like that and dancing is a form of exercise. It elevates your mood. And since I was so sad about everything, I was forced to go."

"You have no shame! Next month, when it's my turn to leave you with the kids…just know there will be payback," I joke.

"Bring it on," she says.

"Okay, seriously, you guys didn't harass her, did you? I know how you, Diana and Mel can be once you three get together."

"Are you kidding? Once Bellamy let it slip that she was the one who introduced you to the whole intimacy in bed thing…we brought her drinks—lots of drinks. We wanted to thank her."

"Oh really?"

"Hell yes! I would give my life for that woman. I thank Omins every day for the things she taught you. Although according to her, you came by your talents naturally."

"I need you to at least pretend to be ashamed." I laugh.

"We're all moms and we deserve to blow off some steam after missions and mom duty."

"The last time you three went out, we needed to wipe an entire town of their memories," I point out.

"Yeah, man, that was fun," she says.

"Get over here!" I tease as I pull her into me. She drapes her arms around my shoulders and looks deeply into my eyes and kisses me tenderly. But behind the playfulness, I can see sadness creeping in her eyes. She looks away.

"Hey, how are you feeling about today?" I ask.

"Good…"

"Pry, your dad is being honored today. He's having an entire school named after him—a school for angels, demons, Quo and a few select humans. That's huge. Nothing like this has ever been attempted before."

"I know. I think he would have been proud that his name is a part of a movement to better relations with other beings. It's just…it's still very hard to think about him. I miss him. I miss my dad so much. And my mom…I'm worried that today might make her more sad than anything else," she admits.

"Hey, my dad would never let her go through this day alone. He's coming and will be there the whole time. And you know the team will be there too. Then we're going to do that thing that your dad always insisted you make us do—get some downtime."

"You have something planned for after?" she asks.

"You know how we all keep saying we will get together and take the kids to the battle simulation town? Well, we've arranged it and we will head straight there when the ceremony is over."

"That's perfect! Thank you," she says. We hear a loud bang downstairs, so we head down to the living room, where mixtures have been shattered and thrown everywhere. Standing in the middle of the mess is my daughter Summit.

She's six years old, and while her gray wings are small, they are very strong for her age. She has purple eyes like her mother and grandmother. However, unlike the ones before her, Summit's hair has gorgeous dark purple highlights. We thought they would fade over time, but we were wrong. The humans think her hair is dyed and they glare at me when I'm with her. They wonder why a parent would dye their kid's hair at such a young age.

"Summit, what happened here?" Pryor asks.

"Um...there was an elephant with big wings...and, um...fire...and...a rock! And...um...I close my eyes and now I'm here," she says, stringing her best lies together.

Pryor and I exchange a knowing glance and turn to the other culprit, our youngest daughter, Dylann.

We were surprised when Alexi came to us again. In fact, we were in a state of shock. We were in a battle with a gang of Egans who had begun to terrorize a city. We just got back after winning the battle to find Alexi on the windowsill.

We named her after the smartest angel we knew: Dylan. Her middle name is Key. It's a tribute to our fallen team members. Dylann is three years old. She has gray wings, bright red curly hair and purple eyes like her mom. She has a habit of putting her finger up to her lips and asking that we be quiet while she thinks of what to say next. That usually means she's about to lie and is trying to think up a good one.

Although they are very close, my daughters are radically different. Summit is more reflective and likes to take things in before she does anything. Dylann, on the other hand, is the take-charge one. They both have big hearts and have cared about humans from the very start. It's not just humans, they both have affection for living things. Last month they both "staged" a project because they were unhappy with the way "Tim the Turtle" was being treated around the house.

"Mom, Tim should have his own island. So he can swim and stuff. This bowl is too small," Summit pleaded.

"Winnie, honey, I know you want Tim to be happy, but trust me, he is," Pryor replied.

"But look, he's green. That's not a happy color, Mommy!" Dylann said. We did our best to stop the revolt, but later that night the girls set Tim "free." By flushing him down the toilet. The funeral was the next day, and yes, the team came.

Dylann, like her sister, has powers. So far she is able to summon whatever she sees and make it come to her. We went on a tour of New York City so they could learn about the human city they live in; Dylann loved the Statue of Liberty. So she tried to bring it home with her.

In addition to training her, her mom does yoga with her so she can learn to stay calm and control her emotions. That's very important given her second ability—setting things on fire with just her mind. We've had to remodel the kitchen four times.

"Dylann, was there an elephant here? Is that who did this?" I ask.

"Shhhh, Daddy, I'm not ready to lie now. Hold on!" she says, thinking so hard she scrunches her forehead. At times like these my wife playfully reminds me how much I wanted kids.

***

The Marcus Cain Academy of Merit is a posh private school on the Upper East Side of New York City. It features a sprawling campus, a great hall, state-of-the-art library, and a training facility. Hundreds of angels and Quo come out to see Marcus being honored. The team is in the front row along with the Guardians. The security for this function is heavy. That happens when both the Kon and the queen are in attendance.

We are all seated in the front row, waiting for the ceremony to begin. Pryor points to Phoenix, who is walking towards us. He has dark hair, bright eyes and large wings. He is no doubt a handsome kid. He's smart and resourceful too.

"Nix! Come sit by me," Summit says.

"Me too!" Dylann declares. But Nix doesn't sit next to them; he doesn't even stop. That's strange since he and my girls are best friends. He walks past his mom, Diana, and his stepdad, Bex. Nix takes a seat in the back by himself.

"What's going on with him?" I whisper to Diana.

"Bex and I decided it was time he knew more about his father. We told him everything and he's not doing so well," she says sadly.

"Damn, you think he's gonna be okay?" I ask.

"I don't know, Silver. I'm trying to give him some space, but it's hard. I just want to make it better, but I don't know how," Diana admits.

"Don't worry, my Queen, I got this," RJ says with a cocky grin as he struts over to Nix. RJ has been living with Jay and it shows. He's a little older than the other kids, but they are all friends. RJ has Swoop's high energy and charm. He gets on our nerves, but it's hard to stay mad at him for too long.

"Don't worry, he just needs some time with this. You know our son, he needs to find his own way through," Bex says as he places a hand on his wife's knee.

"Dad, can we go now? You said we were going to practice how to disarm an aslant," Bex's son says.

"Lucas, we will, but we have to stay here until the end. Then all of us will go together," Bex says.

"Sweetheart, can you go cheer up your brother?" Diana says.

Lucas reluctantly agrees and goes over to Nix.

Lucas is Diana's second son. He's tall, has sandy blond hair, and already has girls in a daze. But what I like about him is that he is very much into the job of being the next king. He takes training seriously, even at his age. He's like his dad that way.

Diana makes it her mission to ensure that Lucas and Nix have a childhood and don't spend their whole lives training in a castle. That's why she makes sure to have the boys come over to the house and play when we are not on a mission.

And when we are away, oftentimes Mrs. Maybelle will gather all the kids and bring them down to her house. Mrs. Maybelle is the only one we trust enough to watch over our kids. In the angel world, the Toren are feared, much like the way we are. But we have a greater handle on how are kids are treated than our parents before us.

But no matter what we do, being the child of a Noru is never easy. No one knows that better than East and Mel's twins. They have similarities, but they are not identical. The girl's name is Parker, she gets her brains from her mom, but her humor comes from Easton. Parker's brother, Ryder, is skilled even for his age. Their powers are still developing, so we don't know yet what they can really do.

No matter how much power the twins will have one day, the one who is the most powerful is Summit. That also makes her the one in the most danger. And her being an Echo doesn't help ease our minds at all. Bex offered to give us round-the-clock security, but we declined because we don't want to draw any more attention than we already do.

No one is supposed to know she's an Echo, so we don't allow her to bring anything back to life. We only allow her to use her main power; the power she inherited from her great-grandfather "Trap." She can blink once and take away someone's ability to see, hear or even breathe.

The crowd starts to clap as Randy—the head of the Human Affairs Bureau—walks up to the podium. Randy is like another person. He has confidence with every step he takes. He's single, but it's by choice. It turns out helping to save the world gets you a lot of girls. In fact, I can't remember the last time Randy didn't have a date.

"And now let's have a hand for the amazing councilwoman herself, Death!" Randy says. Dad takes her hand and walks her over to the podium.

I look back at Winter and there is no jealousy in sight—mostly. She has had to accept that Emmy and Rage will be best friends for the rest of their lives. When Emmy speaks, her tone isn't aching or even sad.

"Thank you for honoring my husband like this. But the truth is this isn't just for him. Many lives have been lost in the past few years. Many sacrifices have been made. So this school, this monument to togetherness, is dedicated to Marcus and everyone who couldn't be with us today.

"To be honest, sometimes being a Guardian sucked. It felt like no matter what you did, happiness never found its way to us. And when we had the Noru children, they too felt the strain of leadership. They too felt loss. And now their children, the Toren, are in for their own adventures. And I want them to know the same thing I want my Marcus to know: There is happiness out there. And in the end you will find it. If you don't stop, if you fight with everything you have, you can find it.

"Marcus my love, you can rest now. Your daughter, your granddaughters and your wife, three generations of women, are strong, loved and, yes, happy."

***

After the ceremony, the Guardians take off to have their own celebration. We fly over to Glacier National Park in British Columbia. We land among the snowcapped mountains and frozen valleys. We enter the kids' favorite place, the City of None.

The city is like a real-life video game where the entire town is made up of human holograms. The point of this game is so that angels can practice fighting evil and rescuing humans. It's a great place to hone your skill and have some fun. The kids love it; it's the angel version of Disneyland for them. Before we enter the city, we make sure the setting on the device that runs the simulations is set to child friendly.

We expect the kids to start flying in every direction, playing around and competing with each other. But with Nix looking so sullen, word gets back to the kids, and soon, they all know something is up with Nix. The first being to go over to him is Summit. She feels it's her job to fix everything (like mother, like daughter).

"Where is Winnie going?" Dylann asks.

"Your sister is trying to make Nix feel better," I explain. My baby girl shakes her head as if to say "that's not what I would do." She then places her hands on her hips and addresses her mom and me.

"Okay, I gotta go!" she says, as if we would just let her cruise the frozen terrain by herself.

"Where are you going?" I ask.

"Dad, I'm the second Toren. They need me. What about mean icy men? What to do if they come? Winnie needs me. Bye," she says. Before her mother and I can really start to worry, East signals that he has an eye on her. I thank him and turn my attention to Pryor.

"Are you going to talk to him?" I ask.

"Yeah, I thought I'd let Summit try. It's her team, you know," she says.

"Yeah, I get it. Is Randy coming?" I ask.

"He has a lot of work, but he's gonna stop by this weekend," she says.

"I think it's time you talked to your nephew," I reply as I watch Summit walk away sadly, shrugging her shoulders in defeat. While I go to cheer her up, Pryor goes over to talk to Malakaro's son.

Nix is seated on a bridge that links two mountains together. Had he been a human, the height would have frightened him, but as an angel, a Toren no less, heights give him a sense of calm. I hear Pryor walking over to him; she sits in the middle of the bridge alongside him.

"There are some really nice peaks to jump off if you don't want to play rescue," she says.

"No, thanks," Nix replies.

"So you know all about your dad now. You wanna talk about it?" she asks.

Nix shrugs his shoulders and lowers his head, ashamed.

"You can ask me anything you want about your father," she offers.

"Did you kill him?" Nix asks.

"Yes. I had to."

"Why?"

"Your dad was sick—not like a virus or anything. It was a different kind of sick."

"What do you mean?"

"Your dad, Jason, was suffering from hatred. And sometimes when it's really strong, hatred can be just like a virus. It can get a hold of you and make you sick. It can change you. And that's what it did. It turned your dad from a smart little boy named Jason to a living nightmare called Malakaro. I had to end his life so he could stop hurting people and so he could stop hurting himself too."

"Why couldn't he get better? Why didn't he get medicine?"

"Nix, sometimes there is no cure. But he tried. I think he really tried to be…good. In his own way," Pryor says mostly to herself.

"They said he was the most evil being that ever lived. Is that true?"

"Very close to it. But that's who he became. That's not how he started."

"Aunt Pry, am I going to be sick like him one day?"

"No," she says with certainty.

"How do you know?" he asks.

"When he held you, I saw a light in his eyes, one I didn't think he was capable of having. When you were in his sight, he was…softer. I see that side of you every day."

"What if you're wrong? What if I am bad too?"

"Your dad told me something, something he wanted you to know."

"Malakaro left me a message?"

"No, Phoenix, Jason did."

"What did he say?"

"Tell my son my steps are not his steps. My pain is not his path. And tell him I left him with family, so I left him with…everything."

***

Once Phoenix starts to feel better, the rest of the kids drag him over to play. Soon they are jumping off mountains, saving hologram humans, and shoving loads of junk food in their mouths in between rescue games. Then they have the nerve to challenge all the Noru to a snowball fight.

"Alright! It's the battle of all battles! Noru versus Toren! Ready, set, go!" Easton shouts.

Snowballs are flying everywhere, angels diving off cliffs, children turning against their parents in an icy takeover. We have to cut the evening short because duty calls, but all in all, it was a lot of fun.

A few hours later, Pry and I pick up the kids from Mrs. Maybelle after defeating a horde of demons who had converged on a town in Italy. When we get home, we put the kids to bed and head back to the living room. We are not alone. We find Julian getting off his Port, in a hurry to talk to us.

"Grandpa, what's wrong?" Pryor asks.

"Listen, I've been keeping an eye on the other two Echos because I don't trust the angel world with my family, you know that. The power that makes someone an Echo gets left behind once an Echo is killed. If all three of them are dead, their powers can be harnessed to make a new Echo," Julian says.

"Someone wants to get their hands on all three Echos so they can use that power and replace Omins. Okay, we know Summit is protected. Who's looking out for the other two Echos?" Pryor asks.

"You're not hearing me. The other two Echos are dead! They were attacked in their homes. It was brutal and swift," Julian says.

"And now they're coming here. They're coming to take our little girl," Pryor says to herself.

"It's okay. We won't let that happen," I assure her.

"No, we won't. Who's coming? Who do I have to kill?" Pryor says venomously.

"Everyone who ever thought they could do a better job than Omins. So…everyone. Everyone is coming!" he says.

"Damn! How long do we have?" Pry asks.

"Pry…" I call out as I look out the panoramic window.

"Grandpa, talk to me. When will they be here?"

"Now…" I reply as I look up at the sky. We are completely surrounded by upper-level demons. Every inch of the house is covered by evil…

****

End of "NORU" series.

The author invites you to read the spin off series:
Book 1: The Toren (Release date to be determined)

CPSIA information can be obtained
at www.ICGtesting.com
Printed in the USA
LVOW07s0313270717
542820LV00002B/248/P

9 781540 835420